WITH SOUL SO DEAD

DI ROB MARSHALL
BOOK 5

ED JAMES

OTHER BOOKS BY ED JAMES

DI ROB MARSHALL SCOTTISH BORDERS MYSTERIES

Ed's first new police procedural series in six years, focusing on DI Rob Marshall, a criminal profiler turned detective. While he's London-based, an old case brings him back home to the Scottish Borders and the dark past he fled as a teenager.

1. THE TURNING OF OUR BONES
2. WHERE THE BODIES LIE
3. A LONELY PLACE OF DYING
4. A SHADOW ON THE DOOR
5. WITH SOUL SO DEAD

Also available is FALSE START, a prequel novella starring DS Rakesh Siyal, is available for **free** to subscribers of Ed's newsletter or on Amazon. Sign up at https://geni.us/EJLCFS

POLICE SCOTLAND

Precinct novels featuring detectives covering Edinburgh and its surrounding counties, and further across Scotland: Scott Cullen, a rookie eager to climb the career ladder; Craig Hunter, an ex-squaddie struggling with PTSD; Brian Bain, the centre of his own universe and bane of everyone else's.

1. DEAD IN THE WATER
2. GHOST IN THE MACHINE
3. DEVIL IN THE DETAIL
4. FIRE IN THE BLOOD
5. STAB IN THE DARK

6. COPS & ROBBERS
7. LIARS & THIEVES
8. COWBOYS & INDIANS
9. THE MISSING
10. THE HUNTED
11. HEROES & VILLAINS
12. THE BLACK ISLE
13. THE COLD TRUTH
14. THE DEAD END

Note: Books 2-8 & 11 previously published as SCOTT CULLEN MYSTERIES, books 9-10 & 12 as CRAIG HUNTER POLICE THRILLERS and books 1 & 13-14 as CULLEN & BAIN SERIES.

DS VICKY DODDS SERIES

Gritty crime novels set in Dundee and Tayside, featuring a DS juggling being a cop and a single mother.

1. BLOOD & GUTS
2. TOOTH & CLAW
3. FLESH & BLOOD
4. SKIN & BONE
5. GUILT TRIP

DI SIMON FENCHURCH SERIES

Set in East London; will Fenchurch ever find what happened to his daughter, missing for the last ten years?

1. THE HOPE THAT KILLS
2. WORTH KILLING FOR
3. WHAT DOESN'T KILL YOU
4. IN FOR THE KILL
5. KILL WITH KINDNESS

6. KILL THE MESSENGER
7. DEAD MAN'S SHOES
8. A HILL TO DIE ON
9. THE LAST THING TO DIE
10. HOPE TO DIE

Other Books

Other crime novels, with Lost Cause set in Scotland and Senseless set in southern England.

- LOST CAUSE
- SENSELESS

DAY 1

MONDAY

1

Holly Fenwick stood near the cliff edge, the wind whipping at her face, blasting her skin with salt. The ozone smell from the fresh rain lingered. She looked over to Eyemouth, with the large industrial units nearby. The tightly packed streets of houses seemed to shiver in the land between the sandy beach and the harbour running up the river on the far side. Further over, a path led across the rough grass towards other cliffs, more severe, more menacing.

Below, fierce waves broke against the rocks, spraying up a salty mist. Made everything inside her tighten.

She brushed her hair out of her face but it immediately returned.

'That's perfect.' Jamie's face was hidden behind his camera, but there was no mistaking his big body. A long torso and short legs. His fringe flapped in the breeze, snapping back into place with each gust. '*Perfect*, Hol. Just hold that. Wait for the next wave... And...'

Holly braced herself. Another spray lashed the air around her. April should be warm, but nobody ever told the North Sea that. Gooseflesh puckered her arms.

'Okay, that's good, that's good.' Jamie pulled his camera away from his mouth, revealing his ornate goatee beard. 'Over to you, big man.'

Despite those words, Toby Horsfall was about half of Jamie's size. He held his furry boom mic over his head, knuckles white like he was worried it might take off at any point. Another gust of wind hit them and Holly didn't blame him for that fear. Toby looked around like an owl perched on a stone wall scanning for prey. 'Alrighty...'

Holly walked over to Jamie and let his big arms wrap around her body. 'How was that?'

'Beautiful. Absolutely beautiful. Some awesome B-roll for Tobes to cut in between the edits on the interview. It'll work *super* well.'

'Good. I hope this is going to be worth all this.'

'Oh, I *know* it will be.'

'Alrighty, you lovebirds...' Toby checked his chunky watch. 'How about we do the bit now?'

The bit...

A nerve below Holly's left eye flickered. 'Now?'

'I mean, you don't *have* to...' Toby left the space, but it was the usual thing. Silent pressure.

Holly sucked in a deep breath. 'Okay.'

'Okay?' Jamie tilted his head to the side. 'You're sure you want to do this?'

Another wave sprayed up.

Holly stretched out her arms and spread her fingers, splaying them out wide. 'I'm positive. I've got to do this, haven't I? So why not now, eh?'

Jamie smiled at her. 'Okay.'

'Thanks.' Holly returned his grin, then ran a hand through her locks, slightly damp from the spray. 'How's my hair?'

'Looking good, despite the wind.'

'Alrighty...' Toby let his mic drop, then looked over towards the town, his lips twisting up at the corners. 'Nope...' Then out to sea. 'Nope...' Then at the caravan park just over the wall. 'Okay, so that's where it happened, right?'

'Aye, man.' The vein throbbed again. Holly's gut churned. Her mouth tasted of burnt toast. 'Sod it. Let's do it. Right here, right now.' She plastered on a smile. 'Where do you want me?'

Toby glanced over at Jamie, then he marched over to the wall. 'Okay... Jamie, you stay there.' He beckoned her over. 'Hol, let's get you here.'

She followed him over, each step heavy as if she was on the bottom of the ocean. 'Sure...'

'Alrighty...' Toby grabbed Holly's shoulders, his skeletal fingers digging into her flesh, then adjusted her as though she was a mannequin in a shop window. Then again. And again. Then a final squeeze. 'How's that looking, Jame?'

'Decent, man. Decent.'

'I want better than decent.'

'Little to the right.'

Toby nudged her over.

'Your right.'

Toby eased her back the way. 'There?'

'Smashing, mate.'

'Hold that pose, Holly.' Toby scurried over to look at Jamie's phone screen, showing his camera output. 'Okay, Hol. Just so you know, you're on the left of the frame and the caravans are on the right.'

'Sounds good.'

'Alrighty. Let's give it a try, then.' Toby hefted up his boom mic again and looked around the place. 'Ready when you are.'

Holly took a deep breath and scanned the area. A few nosy sods looked out from their caravans. Nobody she recognised – not that she should – but they surely couldn't recognise her, could they? Then again, someone talking to a camera with a fancy microphone looked famous. And people loved fame. 'Okay, let's go.'

'Alrighty. Remember, you just answer my questions and I'll edit it all together later to make it seem coherent. So don't sweat it if you lose track, just focus on it being real, yeah? And focus on me, not the camera.'

'Sure.'

'Ready when you are. Remember to clap so we can sync sound and video?'

'Cool.' Holly took a deep breath and shook out her hair. That fucking nerve was *throbbing* so hard she could practically see it in the corner of her vision. She looked at Jamie, spotted the red dot in the camera eye, then clapped her hands to signal the start of the take. She swallowed air deep into her lungs while she waited for the question, then locked eyes with Toby.

'Okay, Holly. Do you recognise this place?'

She broke off eye contact and scanned across the caravan park. Despite it being a random Monday in April, there were a ton of people there. Watching, going about their business, sitting on their arses. Maybe the fact the economy wasn't so much in the toilet as flushed, treated and halfway out to sea meant a few had sold their brick-and-mortar houses to live in a caravan here on the edge of the earth.

But she spotted it. The caravan, the same one. Still standing, after all these years.

She looked back at Toby. 'Aye, man. I see it. They've painted it. And it's got... what's that wooden mesh stuff you put roses and that on?'

'Trellising.'

'Right, aye. It's got trellising up. Actually looks quite pretty.' The nerve pumped away. 'Doesn't exactly look like the kind of place where someone would bring you to murder you.'

The waves splashed up another spray of salty water, but she was far enough away that it didn't touch her this time.

'And this was twelve years ago, right?'

'Right. Twelve years in March, just gone. When *he* abducted me from outside my home in Whitley Bay down in Newcastle...' Always give them a little bit of information. If it was redundant, Toby would cut. 'It's, like, seventy-five miles or something. He kidnapped me, then drove me here and shoved me in a caravan.' She pointed over at it. 'That one there.' She couldn't help but stare into the camera lens, tears tickling her cheeks. 'I narrowly escaped with my life. A serial killer was going to throw me off the cliffs here.' She waved a hand at the sea. 'From this very spot.'

'Who was it, Holly? Who did this?'

'His name was David Sylvester.' Saying the name after so long felt like a knife in the guts. 'Worst part is, I knew him. Trusted him. It's how it worked, wasn't it? Made me think he was a good guy. But no, he *took* us, like. Threatened me. Threatened my mam. Brought me here. Was going to hoy us into the fucking sea.' She frowned at Toby. 'Am I swearing too much?'

Toby sighed, then smiled. 'Don't worry about the swearing. I'll edit that out. Let's just focus on getting to the truth, okay? We can do another take if we need to.' He adjusted his mic. 'Why isn't he in prison?'

'He's not in prison because...' Holly looked away from him. 'Because the fucking police... The cops... They were either corrupt or incompetent. Maybe both. After I escaped, I went to them, but they didn't proceed with the case, did they? They just let him off with it. I mean, the case is shut and dry, or whatever the saying is.'

'Open and shut.'

'Right, sorry. I mean, the case is open and shut.' She looked right at the camera lens. 'David Sylvester tried to murder me.' She held it for a few seconds.

'Alllll-righty! That's a take!' Toby let his mic drop. 'Okay, let's take a few minutes and shoot that again.'

Holly felt herself go all floppy. The fizzing energy slipped away like she'd been drugged. Hard to relax when there's a sodding camera pointing right at you, then when it's over, everything slackens off. The tension just goes.

She shifted her gaze between Jamie and Toby. 'Was that okay?'

Jamie started fiddling with his camera, replacing the memory card. 'Looked great to me. Tobe?'

'Great, yeah.' Toby walked over to her. 'It was pretty good but, like I said, the swearing's going to need to come out. I'm not against it as I've told you many times. It's a natural expression of emotion, but if you avoid swearing when it's not necessary, then I won't have to cut it. Okay? Try to remember that when I edit it, I'm covering over your image with the B-roll of the sea or the caravan so the viewer doesn't see the jump in the audio. Bottom line, Hol, it'll just look better. And better will mean people pay attention to your story.'

'Right, sure.' Holly focused on the same couple on their chairs just inside the caravan, still looking at her. Talking about her. Cheeky sods. She gave them a wee wave.

Then her blood froze in her veins.

A man was walking towards the nearest caravan.

Blink and you'd miss him.

But she hadn't blinked and certainly hadn't missed him.

Before she could think, she was moving, running across the rough grass and vaulting the wall. Crunching over the gravel then bounding up the steps up to the caravan's front door. Twisting the handle and storming inside.

The living area was long, with a sofa and two armchairs. Empty. No sign of him.

Blood pumping. Heart racing. That sour taste in her mouth.

A pair of doors. She tore open the first one and stepped into a bathroom. Those fancy subway tiles. The shower was dry, the toilet bowl filled.

The other door was a bedroom, with a made bed. Stoor covered the bedside table.

Holly dropped down into a plank position to look under the bed. Nothing, just more stoor and dust.

She kicked back up to standing and opened the mirror-fronted wardrobes.

Nothing.

What the fuck?

He'd been here. She'd seen him.

So where the hell had he gone?

She raced back through the caravan, opening the doors again, checking in the kitchen cupboards.

'Babe?' Jamie was in the doorway, frowning at her. 'What's up?'

She slammed the bathroom door again. 'I saw him. Here!'

'Saw who?'

'Sylvester. David fucking Sylvester. He was *here*.' She barged past him and jumped down onto the gravel, then did a circuit of the caravan, her feet crunching the pebbles. No sign of him out here either. The only movement was the nosy couple watching her.

Where the fuck had he gone?

Had he even been here?

She went back inside the caravan.

'Uh, babe...' Jamie was standing by the sofa, his mouth hanging open.

The coffee table lay on its back. Two bookcases had fallen like broken timber, the novels scattered onto the floor in front.

In the middle of the carpet, a phone lay in a patch of wet blood.

2

From up here, the Innocent Railway looked like it descended from central Edinburgh into the bowels of hell.

DI Rob Marshall sucked in a bracing breath, then left the daylight and followed the lights into the steep tunnel, long since converted from rail tracks to the tarmac of a cycle path. The wind blew at his hair as he walked, hands deep in his pockets.

Halfway down, a uniformed crime scene manager guarded a sea of arc lights and white-suited figures.

Marshall stopped outside the perimeter and took the clipboard from him – even in this day and age, some things were still done on paper. No tablet computers or anything more sophisticated than a biro. Not even one of those NASA space pens. He signed in, gave a nod, then passed through into the huddle.

Edinburgh's chief pathologist was inside the inner locus, hunched over a body. An easy man to spot from a distance, a hard man to shake off from a trivial chat and a harder one to get to answer the phone. Not that Marshall had much cause to.

Forensics officers swarmed around him like wasps at a family barbecue. Photographing, dusting and cataloguing.

'Rob.' DI Callum Taylor shuffled over. Hair shaved close to the bone at the side, providing a grand foundation for a greying rockabilly quiff that should've been on a stage somewhere. At a rock concert or a travelling carnival, Marshall couldn't decide. Even taller than Marshall, his cleft chin looked deep enough to house a cycle path. Taylor thrust out his hand, with the long fingers of a concert pianist – or at least what Marshall imagined one would have. 'You took your time getting here.' His Glasgow accent was still as sharp as an ice pick.

'Left as soon as you called. Traffic on the M8 was murder.' Marshall shook the hand, giving it an extra tight squeeze for good measure. 'So, how's it looking?'

Taylor ran a hand through his hair, but didn't seem to shift a single follicle – God knows what he used to hold it all in place. 'Okay, so we've been at this a few hours. Or the local lot have, anyway. The powers that be wanted you and me to confirm this isn't related to our case over on the Best Coast.'

'What's your take?'

'I'm obviously keeping an open mind here, but...'

'You think we've got another?'

'Not my place to say.' Taylor grimaced. 'Thing is, Rob, I'm only here as a favour to my old DCI. She's having kittens about this, sure you can imagine. I haven't caught this case, thank the Lord.'

'Is that a "yet" I see before me?'

Taylor gave a flash of his eyebrows. 'Well, she's worrying this is the same killer as the one we found in Kelvingrove Tunnel in Glasgow last year.'

Marshall swallowed down something sour-tasting. 'You don't work there anymore?'

'Nope.' Taylor looked away from Marshall's gaze. 'I, eh...

relocated. But if this is the same killer, I might get called into this. Just when I thought I'd got away.'

'Let's have a look, then.' Marshall walked over so he could see the body.

A woman. Middle-aged. Lying on her back. Navy jeans and a rainbow jumper. Green woolly coat, probably ankle-length. Worn-down running shoes on her feet. Bright-red hair like a clown wig.

A world of difference from the Glasgow case.

Marshall didn't have to consult any notes to remember the detail – a naked man pinned against the wall of the tunnel, his throat not so much slashed as cut out, his chest a latticework of gouges.

Marshall let his breath go slowly. 'So Karen's worried this is the same killer because it's a body in an old railway tunnel?'

Taylor sighed. 'Didn't say it as directly as that, but aye.' He laughed. 'Suspect she's got someone scoping out every single disued tunnel in Scotland, looking for a serial killer.'

Marshall had seen more than his fair share of senior officers who hungered for a headline-grabbing case. 'I hadn't pegged her as one of those?'

'Oh, man.' Taylor laughed. 'Aye, she's as ambitious as a Tory MP. I mean, you could be generous and suggest she's doing it for some sense of civic duty, but...'

'You think she's a glory hunter?'

'I don't know. But she was at some stupid seminar in the summer and she's convinced herself there are hundreds of serial killers operating in the UK.'

'Well, I can't complain because that kind of thinking is keeping me in a job. But hundreds is stretching it. I'd put it at two or three, conservatively.'

Taylor smiled at him. 'Listen—' His phone rang. 'Just a sec, Rob. Hold that thought...' He walked away and answered it. 'Aye, Ryan. Just got here. What's up?'

'Guv!' DS Struan Liddell lumbered over, grinning wide. Shaved head, designer suit. He hugged Marshall and clapped his back. 'Good to see you, mate.' He held out a hand.

'Struan.' Marshall shook his hand, but had to check he came back with all four fingers and a thumb. 'Surprised to see you here.'

Struan shrugged, then adjusted his lapels. 'Supporting DI Taylor down in Gala, so he's asked me to shadow him up here.'

'Taylor's down in Gala?'

'Started two weeks ago, aye. He's the new you.'

Marshall would bet his sister's mortgage on Taylor only getting the gig because he was one of DCI Gashkori's old mates from the drug squad. 'I've been gone a year, though?'

'Acting DI didn't work out.'

'Was it you?'

'If it was, I would've worked out.'

Marshall flashed him a smile. 'I take it there's an Edinburgh DI here?'

'Aye, daft cowboy lad who's running around speaking to witnesses rather than doing things the right way.'

'Met a few of them in my time.' Marshall gave him a conspiratorial flash of his eyebrows, if for no reason other than Struan was a gossip hound. 'And what's your assessment, Sergeant?'

'They won't let me near the body.' Struan narrowed his eyes. 'You still working at Gartcosh, aye?'

Marshall stifled his sigh. The topic of the next dose of gossip would be his career. 'Been there over a year now, aye.'

'And how's it going?'

Marshall didn't want to admit to Struan of all people how much he missed being a cop, about how frustrated he was at his new boss insisting he was a profiler first and foremost, how he was just there to support DCIs, so he just smiled. 'Aye, it's good. Kind of like falling off a log, you know?'

'Don't knock doing something you're good at.' Struan laughed, like he was good at anything other than being a sleekit devil. 'So, what brings—'

'Sorry about that.' Taylor reappeared, frowning at his phone like he suspected he hadn't ended the call properly. 'Need to answer the boss's calls, you know?'

Marshall held out a hand. 'Congrats.'

Taylor shook it limply. 'What for?'

'DS Callum Taylor replacing me in the Borders MIT.'

'Right.' Taylor looked away. 'Doesn't mean we can't be mates, Rob.'

Not that Marshall considered him anything more than an acquaintance. 'Of course not.'

Taylor made eye contact again and held it. 'Anyway. That was the boss. He said She Who Cannot Be Named has been up his trouser leg, trying to get an answer on whether this is connected to the Kelvingrove one, so I'll go and wind this up now.'

Marshall stared hard at him. 'Not aware I've given you an answer?'

'Right.' Taylor shrugged. 'You're the expert. Come on.' He led them over, but stopped just shy of the crime scene tape rattling in the stiff breeze. He got a glare from the detective manning the inner locus, but raised his eyebrows in response. 'Okay, so what's your take?'

Marshall took another look at the body. No stab marks, just a nasty-looking wound on her temple. Not a knife wound, by the looks of it. Dried blood on her face.

Her handbag was still strapped to her, the mobile phone tipping out onto the tarmac.

Not a robbery, either.

He shifted his focus back to Taylor. 'My take is I've seen two crime scenes that only seem to be connected by the fact they're in railway tunnels in Central Scotland.'

'Okay, so you agree?'

Marshall felt that acid bubbling in his guts. 'Callum, this is nonsense. I can't confirm anything. That's not how this works. Sure, I can turn up and check it out, but I'm not clairvoyant. All you've got are two bodies in disused railway tunnels, found forty miles and the best part of a year apart. Now, that's a superficial take. We need to see if there are any deeper connections, but the bottom line with this is we can't rule anything out without further victims.'

Taylor shot Struan some side-eye. 'That's what I knew he'd say.' He shifted his focus back to Marshall. 'Okay, Rob, here's what we know.' He rubbed his hands together. 'Beverley Richardson. Female, early fifties. Lives in Niddrie, a few miles from here. Used to be a notorious shit hole, but it's been regenerated over the last twenty or so years, so bits of it are pretty nice. She lives in the gentrified bit.'

Marshall knew Edinburgh pretty well. 'This is on the way from the city centre, right?'

'Pretty much. She works in John Lewis in the St James's Centre doing back-office admin. Reported leaving work at seven o'clock last night. Walks this way most nights apparently. Takes her about an hour.'

'Who reported her missing?'

'Nobody. Beverley lives alone. Didn't turn up for her shift this morning. Boss put it down to her coming down with Covid. Waited for a text or phone call. Didn't know she'd been found by a cyclist at half four this morning until she called it in to us.'

'That's early.'

'Not a lot of people use this place after darkness. Beverley is one of them. That cyclist is another – works at the Tesco down off Broughton Street.'

'Okay, that's useful to know. Any idea when she was killed?'

'The good doctor reckons she died around about eleven

o'clock to midnight last night. Blood alcohol is pretty high, so
we think she had a few snifters on her way home.'

'Does he think it was murder?'

'Hard to say.'

'He must have an opinion, though?'

'It's why he's still here after an hour. It's ambiguous. Blunt
force trauma to the head. Trouble is, that's as easily caused by
her drunkenly falling into one of the lampposts as a nasty bad
man smacking her in the head.'

Marshall looked over again. The body was less than a metre
from the nearest lamppost. He could see it. Finishing a tough
shift, then going for her usual walk home. The quickest route
wouldn't take her past many pubs he could think of, but there
were a ton of them a street away. Just pop in for a glass of wine
or a gin or a pint. Get chatting to someone. A few too many was
easily done for some, then the Dutch courage meant her usual
walk didn't seem dangerously foolish at that time.

Maybe someone followed her.

But say those drinks were sunk at a decent rate, then the
booze wouldn't hit hardest until she was halfway home. Say it
was gin or vodka. They stung the stomach and only hit the
bloodstream after it eased off, when six or seven shots blasted
in at once.

Suddenly pissed, she staggered into a lamppost, clonked
her head and died.

Happened a lot more than people knew.

'Hopefully the good doctor will give a steer soon. And in
that direction.'

Marshall looked around at Taylor. 'What else do you know
about her?'

Taylor tilted his head to Struan. 'Sergeant?'

'Been speaking to some people who knew her at work.'
Struan puffed out his cheeks. 'Only dirt we've got on her is she
was caught embezzling funds from a cat-rescue charity.'

Marshall winced. 'That's pretty low.'

'Aye. She was on the committee. Bought a Berlingo with funds raised from charity events, then drove it herself. Someone grassed her up and our lot are investigating her. Or were.'

'Were?'

'Haven't followed up on it yet.'

'Okay.' Marshall scratched his chin. 'From my memory, the Glasgow victim was a DJ in his thirties who ran a nationwide indie disco chain. Guy had a podcast and did some music journalism, right?'

'Right.' Taylor was staring at the new victim. 'And we had him for dealing drugs at said disco. She Who Cannot Be Named has pinned it as a gangland murder.'

'So even she doesn't think it's a serial killing?'

'Ah, I didn't say that.' Taylor held a raised finger in the air. 'But that seems to be the conclusion we're officially drawing.'

Marshall stared over at the body. 'This isn't you trying to pass the buck, is it?'

'What, from the North Glasgow MIT to you? Rob, I'm down in the Borders. I don't care who claims it, but it certainly won't be me. I do want us to catch both killers. Or one killer, if this is an accident. Or one killer, if it is one of yours, Rob. Part of your new role is identifying hitherto unknown serial killers, right?'

'Right. And this doesn't feel like one.'

'Doesn't feel? Or isn't?'

'Well, the brutal truth is there's just not enough to go on. What you have is pretty scant. I'll tell the boss myself, but I'm not convinced there's a pattern between the victims as yet. Maybe when the full victimology is completed, but right now, I'm just reading tea leaves. And until we know if Beverley here was actually murdered, we're just buggering about, aren't we? As much as I like visiting Edinburgh, that hour's drive through shitty traffic's been a bit of a waste.'

Struan laughed. 'Someone crap in your cornflakes, gaffer?'

'No, I'm just saying. We've got two deaths, sure, but we need a bit more investigation. Sometimes there might be something connecting both lurking below the surface, but those occasions are vanishingly rare. And if there's a connection, we probably need a lot more data to identify it. And sadly, more data means more victims.' Marshall took one last look at the body. 'But I don't think these are connected. The Glasgow murder was a disused tunnel that's pretty hard to get into, whereas this is a cycle route. I think she's just had a drunken accident, sadly.'

'So you're saying they're not connected?'

'I'm saying—'

Marshall's phone rang.

Unknown caller...

Marshall scowled at it for a few seconds. 'Better take this, lads.' He strolled away from them and answered the call. 'Marshall.'

'Rob, it's...' A female voice. Soft Geordie accent. She was out of breath. Or maybe in tears. 'It's Holly Fenwick. I... Do you remember me?'

Holly Fenwick?

Who the hell was Holly Fenwick?

Then it hit him who she was.

Made his mouth go dry. 'Holly. It's been a while.'

'Aye, twelve fucking years.'

Charming. 'To what do I owe the pleasure?'

'I'm in Eyemouth, right?' She stopped. Wind rattled the microphone.

Took Marshall a few seconds to remember why that was pertinent. Eyemouth was where it happened, all those years ago. 'Must be pretty difficult for you being back there.'

'Harder than you think.' She paused again. 'Rob, I just saw David Sylvester. I think he's killed again.'

arshall followed the twisting road along the banks of the Eye Water, ancient woodland covering the river, sitting opposite a modern housing estate. He pulled up at the crossroads, his indicator flashing left. Dark clouds had rolled in, contrasting with the earlier sunshine in Edinburgh – that, or Eyemouth was always this grim.

Struan and Taylor were behind him, both bopping along to a solid beat Marshall could only feel rather than hear.

He put the car in first, then set off.

Stalled it.

Bloody hell.

This bastard of a car. Stupid four-by-four nonsense, bought for a snowy winter in the Borders, when he'd spend it in the dreich of Glasgow and Edinburgh. Two wheels that drove when you wanted would be infinitely preferable.

He took his time restarting it, putting it in neutral then twisting the key to off, waiting a few seconds, then shifting it back to on. It sparked and the engine thrummed.

Behind him, Struan and Taylor were laughing.

And Marshall was sweating. He gave them a wave as he drove off, heading the back way around the town.

Their car shot across the road, favouring going through Eyemouth.

Well, let's see who knows the town better...

Marshall powered along the road, determined to beat them to the caravan park. The thick trees on the left broke out into industrial units, then he took a right at the petrol station. Opposite the junction, someone had turned an old boat into a flowerbed, keeping alive the town's history as a fishing port.

Marshall realised he had no idea if it was still active – Eyemouth was about an hour from home and so close to Berwick and England it was like a foreign country itself.

He weaved through the industrial estate, past the fire station with its drill tower, then rolled up to another junction, where one shouldn't have been.

Bugger.

He was lost.

Bollocks. Bollocks. Bollocks.

Turned out Marshall didn't know Eyemouth as well as he thought. He took a quick glance at the map on the car's satnav, even though the target wasn't in there, and spotted his mistake. He took a left then a swift right, trundling through a housing estate at a solid twenty, then bingo – he was on the street he should've been. Past another petrol station and he saw where he needed to go – a single-track road climbing the hill away from the town. A steep bank, lined with post-war bungalows, which must have great views over the bay, then past the coastguard station.

The yellow-and-blue Battenberg livery of four squad cars surrounded the caravan park's reception building, with its shop and café.

Marshall pulled up behind a car he recognised from the

Gala station's pool. Looked like he'd won the race, though, despite driving this stupid tank.

This many cars seemed like overkill, considering he'd only called it in an hour ago, but Taylor must've escalated it to Gashkori, who must've crapped himself.

Or wanted to make Marshall look like a clown.

He'd thought he was away from such petty nonsense, but nope. His new role put him on the outside looking in. And cops just *loved* someone watching them. Even better, they loved it when they made suggestions.

Marshall got out and followed the path towards the fluorescent jackets. A pair of uniforms huddled by a tree. He checked his phone as he walked – still nothing more from Holly Fenwick.

His gut squirmed again. Such a strange thing to come out of the blue like that.

He approached the pair of uniforms with a smile and the warrant card showing the rank he'd retained with the new job.

And he saw Taylor and Struan, partially obscured by the tree.

Bloody hell – the bastards had beaten him.

Taylor was grinning at Marshall. 'Took you a while, Rob. Were you listening to 'Magical Mystery Tour' by the Beatles?'

'Nah, it was 'Can't Get You out of my Head' by Kylie.' Marshall arched his eyebrow. 'Callum, your love is all I think about.'

Taylor raised his own brows. 'Okay. Well. It's this way.' He thumbed over his shoulder then set off at superhuman pace. 'Last time I was at a caravan park like this was a place over by Jedburgh, in the back of beyond. Rough as a badger's arse, it was. A lot worse than here, actually.' He laughed. 'One of the caravans blew up after these two idiots got into a fight.' He frowned. 'Think that case might've been why they set up the

Borders MIT. Whole load of stuff went down. A cop died, I think.'

Struan laughed. 'Wasn't that when Shunty got his name?' He looked around at Marshall. 'Haven't seen or heard from him in a while.'

'I have.'

'Aye?'

'He's based in Gartcosh some of the time.'

'Batman and Robin solving crimes in Glasgow, eh?' Taylor bellowed out a laugh. 'The brave and the bold! Trouble is, Shunty's neither brave nor bold, is he?' He stopped at the corner and the smile slipped off his face.

A low wall surrounded about fifty static caravans, artistically placed rather than in a grid. Probably encouraged community or feng shui or something. Inside the wall, six uniformed officers had spread out and were interviewing residents. The white-suited forensics officers pinpointed the centre of the hubbub, guarded by a plainclothes officer.

A standard-looking caravan, painted a pretty blue. The mature shrubs around it implied it had been here a while. A white head popped up from between two giant hebes, adjusted their face mask, then disappeared again.

'Struan.' Taylor pointed over at some uniforms. 'How about you go and speak to the witnesses, aye?'

'Sure thing, gaffer.'

Marshall watched him go.

Taylor stepped in close. 'What did you mean about thinking about my love?'

Marshall held his gaze. 'You know, Callum.' He clocked Holly talking to two female uniforms, with a skinny wee guy lurking between them. 'Okay, how about we speak to her?'

Taylor blocked his path. 'One thing I've got to ask is why she still had your number?'

'Because she hadn't deleted it from however many phones she had in the last twelve years.'

'Ha, very good. You know what I mean.'

Marshall sighed. 'I was involved in that case. That's all.'

'Right. Sure.' Taylor stepped even closer, towering over Marshall. 'Remember the deal here. You're here because Holly contacted you, but this is my patch, okay? Gashkori's been very clear you remember that.'

'I'll be thinking of that, don't you worry.' Marshall walked over, his head throbbing with tension.

Holly looked him up and down, frowning. Then her forehead creased and un-creased. 'Rob?'

'Hiya. How are you doing?'

She wrapped him in a hug. 'I *saw* him, Rob. He was right here. But...' She broke away. 'These guys have been scouring the place but they said he's not here.'

'Hi there.' The wee guy held out a hand. 'Toby Horsfall.' Posh English accent that Marshall couldn't place, despite his years working in London. 'I'm the sound guy stroke producer stroke writer stroke teaboy on this joint.' His joke didn't land. 'Holly's a pal, so I'm trying to help her.'

Marshall shook his hand. 'Sure thing.'

'Alrighty...' Toby maintained his grip and kept his voice low. 'Can I ask you to speak through me? I want to guard her against the PTSD she suffered from her attack twelve years ago and from being re-victimised by the police.'

'Re-victimised?'

'Sure. She was almost murdered, but you made her feel like she was the killer. Or a liar. Or a timewaster.'

'Let me be clear. I wasn't a cop back then. But from what I saw, she was treated with respect and care.'

'If you say so. All I'm asking is you do the same now.'

Marshall let go of his hand and focused on Holly. 'Thank you for calling me. Surprised you still had my number.'

She shrugged. 'Surprised it still worked.'

'In my game, it pays to keep your number the same when you switch networks. Never know who might call you.' Marshall held her gaze. 'This is DI Callum Taylor. He's an experienced cop and he will be running the case to its conclusion.'

'Not you?'

'I'm not a mainstream detective.' Anymore, but Marshall didn't voice his own inner turmoil. She didn't need to hear that. 'So, you told me you saw Sylvester?'

'Right.' Holly swept her hand through her hair, eyeing Taylor with suspicion. 'We were... Eh...' She glanced at Toby, then at the ground.

'She was filming by the cliffs, Inspector.' Toby pointed at the blue one. 'And she saw Sylvester in this caravan.'

'Actually inside it?'

'No, walking towards it.'

'Holly, you told me Sylvester had killed again. How do you know that?'

'Sorry. She doesn't know. And she doesn't even know if it was him.'

'I saw him. I swear, but it...'

Marshall tilted his head to the side. 'Could it have been someone else?'

'Maybe. But there's blood in there.'

Taylor nodded slowly. 'The blood could be a pig's, for instance. Easy to acquire if you know the right people.' He smiled. 'Especially in the Borders.'

'Are you saying I'm lying?'

Taylor shook his head. 'No, and I don't want you to think I don't believe you. You can rest assured we'll get to the bottom of what's happened here.'

'Thank you. That's all I ask.'

Taylor gave a polite half-bow. 'Can I ask why you're in Eyemouth?'

She looked away again.

Toby cleared his throat. "We're recording a documentary about her ordeal. We've got Arts Council funding.'

Taylor glanced at Marshall. 'What ordeal's this?'

Toby snorted. 'Twelve years ago, Holly was abducted from near her home in Whitley Bay. Where she lived. Her abductor brought her here, where he was going to throw her off the cliffs. But she escaped and this documentary is part of her recovery. It's been over a decade. We're helping her document her ordeal to get justice.' He gave Marshall some serious side-eye. 'Justice the police wouldn't give her.'

Marshall held his stare. 'I wasn't a police officer back then.'

'But she didn't get justice, did she?'

'That's a long story.' Marshall focused on Holly. 'Have you named him in this documentary?'

'Course I have.'

'I'll warn you now. You could be defaming him, so be very careful. You don't want a lawsuit.'

'But he's a killer!'

'You're entitled to think that, but he wasn't convicted. Wasn't even charged.'

'Rob.' Taylor took a deep breath. 'Holly, a pal in Northumbria constabulary briefed me on your case as I drove down from Edinburgh. Seems a bit of a coincidence, how you just happened to see him here?'

'See? You lot still doubt me! I'm fucking sick of it.'

Toby got between them. 'Alrighty, guys, it's okay.' He glared at Taylor. 'If you ask me, it's like Sylvester knew she'd be there. Like he was baiting her.'

'Did you or the cameraman tell him?'

'No, of course not!' Toby's eyes popped out of his head. 'But... That's all I can think. Thing is, Eyemouth has particular significance to her. It's where she met Sylvester.'

Marshall frowned. 'This is news to me.'

'I told you, you just didn't listen. Nobody did. My family owned a caravan and we used to spend a few weekends here a year. A week with my grandparents. I was fifteen and met him one summer. He obviously kept tabs on me afterwards, then followed us back home. Knew when to strike, didn't he?' She was shaking her head. 'After what happened, Dad torched our caravan and sold the plot. He died eight years ago. Blamed himself for what happened. But I never did.'

'Okay, Holly.' Marshall gave her a kind smile. 'Look, I'll come back and speak to you, but DI Taylor and I need to get our arms around this case. So can I ask you talk to my colleagues here? Give them a detailed statement. Everything you can, please.'

She nodded. 'Will you catch him?'

'I don't want to promise anything, Holly, except that we'll do everything we can. I don't want anyone else to go through what you did all those years ago.'

'Thank you.'

'We'll be back.' Marshall marched off, followed by Taylor. 'Have we got uniform going around the caravans?'

'We have, aye, but—'

'What about seeing if anyone's got one of those doorbell cameras or a security system?'

'Not here. Just the basic stuff, mate.' Taylor blocked his path. 'Rob. Can I just remind you that you're here to support the Borders MIT, not lead an investigation. This is our patch and, despite your rank, you're not a detective anymore. Just because this is a serial killer from days gone by, it doesn't mean it's your case. Okay?'

Marshall wanted to fight back, to shout and scream, to win. But the trouble was, Taylor was right. Aside from keeping his rank, Marshall was just a brain in a vat, used by the cops to solve their cases. 'Fine, gaffer. You're in charge.'

'That's all I wanted you to—'

'Cal.' Trevor wandered over, his forensics suit flapping behind him like a mermaid's tail. His mullet hairdo was in danger of doing the same. 'Oh, Rob. Hiya. How are you doing?'

'I'm fine.'

'Aye, aye. Good to hear that.' Trevor patted the spikes on top of his head. 'Anyway, I know this isn't a murder case yet, but... Gashkori wants us to treat it like one.' He exhaled slowly. 'Truth is, we're a bit bored. Not a lot to do in the Borders, is there? So it's good to get out and about, do a little bit of work, you know?'

Taylor was going red. 'Are you getting anywhere?'

'Not really. We've scoured that caravan. Place has been upended and most of the furniture is broken. It's all IKEA and TK Maxx stuff. Decent quality, but cheap. A lot of holiday caravans have that.'

'Holly told me she found blood?'

'Yeah.' Trev nodded. 'Still wet too, so whatever happened in there happened this morning.' He swallowed, his Adam's apple bobbing up and down. 'And it's human blood.'

'Definitely?'

'Definitely. Pretty easy to test for it in the field these days. I'll head back to Gala to blood type it and run tests to see if it's Sylvester's or someone else's.' Trev winced. 'But if you want my expert opinion, I'd say someone took whoever lives there after an attack with a knife.'

Taylor folded his arms. 'I didn't ask you for it, but thank you anyway.'

Marshall got between them, focusing on Trev. 'What makes you think that?'

'The way the blood's sprayed is consistent with a knife attack. And I can't think of anything else it could be.'

'Please leave the thinking to those with a brain, son.' Taylor looked over to the caravan. 'Just focus on getting us the information and the data, then we'll do the rest.'

'Sure thing.' Trev wandered off, muttering 'wanker' under his breath.

'Heard that.' Taylor watched him go. 'You think I was too hard on him, Rob?'

'Not for me to say. I'm merely an observer.'

'Less of that.'

'I'm serious. You're the deputy SIO. I'm consulting. Your job is to decide if this is even a case, or just someone with PTSD imagining things.'

'What's your take on it?'

'Way too early to say.'

'Gaffer!' Struan walked over to them. 'This is Jamie. He's the cameraman.'

Jamie was a big guy, tall and broad. Ponytail and elaborate goatee beard. He wouldn't make eye contact. 'I've, eh, got footage from Holly's interview.'

Taylor raised his jaw, but he wasn't getting any taller. 'And?'

'You want to see this.' Jamie held up a high-end laptop with flashing lime-green lights. 'This is what we call B-roll. We shoot it to add colour or to cut between when we make edits. Usually it's silent, but Holly was speaking. We get much, much better sound from Toby's mic, but I like to record using the camera's internal one just to get them to synchronise better.' He thwacked the space bar. 'This is about fifteen minutes before she saw him.'

The screen filled with footage from the caravan park before the clouds had rolled in.

Holly was blurry in the foreground, then the camera focused on the caravan. Despite Toby's mic allegedly being better, her words were still pretty clear. 'There was this psychologist guy, Rob Marshall. Fancied himself, clearly. And he was obviously shagging the woman psychologist. Liana or something.'

Taylor stuck his tongue in his cheek, but didn't say anything.

'Heard Rob's now a cop. But if you ask me, he's the one who screwed up the prosecution. And he's been rewarded for it. I mean...'

Marshall sighed. 'Thank you for that.'

'Sorry, I didn't mean that bit.' Jamie hit the space bar again then pointed at the screen. 'You're not paying attention to the visual.'

Marshall screwed up his eyes to focus on the detail.

In the background of the shot, a man was caught in freeze frame walking between caravans.

David Sylvester.

4

DI Andrea Elliot drove along the main drag through Eyemouth, the old stone Victorian tenements glowing in a brief flash of sunshine. She glanced over at the passenger seat. 'Heard Marshall went the long way around.' She looked forward again and the light had dipped. 'Turned up two minutes after Taylor and Soppy.'

DCI Ryan Gashkori was clutching the oh-shit handle over the door. Suggesting her driving was bad in some way. Dark rings under his eyes and that fresh skinhead really didn't suit him, just revealed all the lumps and bumps on his scalp. 'Soppy?'

'Soppy Struan.'

'Right. Never heard that.'

Crap.

She'd just put her foot on a landmine.

And it wasn't that long since her last warning about nicknames...

'Know Eyemouth well.' Elliot took a right up the hill towards the caravan park. 'Folks used to have access to a caravan here. Spent a couple of weekends there when I was a teenager.'

'That with Gary Hislop?'

'No.' Elliot glared at him. 'With Davie.'

She didn't want to say any more. Couldn't – her throat was tightening to a clenched fist.

Wishing she could just take the turning into the harbour and get a delicious fish supper followed by some ice cream.

But that kind of lovely family outing was a distant memory and wouldn't return for a long time.

'Just remember, Andi – I don't want you getting too deep into this case, okay?' Gashkori looked over at her. 'What with you being in court the rest of the week.'

She still couldn't speak.

Jesus Christ, get a grip!

'You are in agreement, aye?'

She nodded as she climbed the single-track lane up the hill, then made a noise she hoped sounded like, 'Sure.'

Gashkori sighed. 'I'm more than a bit concerned we've caught a bastard of an abduction here.' Another sigh, deeper and more protracted. 'Or we're a small cog in the wheel of a serial murder case. Either way, I'm on the hook.'

Elliot managed to swallow. 'You're honestly worried about that?'

'When someone who's been through what this Holly Fenwick's been through calls us up, it's going to go one of two ways. Either she's lying or she's telling the truth.'

'What about if it's a mistake?'

'I'd put that under lying. Result's the same – Mr Serial Killer isn't here.' Gashkori rasped a hand across his scalp. 'Don't want that to sound flippant or profound either, but the possibility of a long-dormant serial killer we didn't bloody put away way back when returning gives me the willies, as my mum would say. Hope it's just her lying.'

'Careful what you wish for, Ryan. If this is a serial killer, you'll lose the case to a grown-up MIT, like Glasgow South or Edinburgh.'

'What's wrong with North?'

'You worked there.'

'Very funny. Listen, the whole reason I'm down here is to give that experience so we don't need those lot down here.'

Aye, sure you are...

Elliot pulled up, though it was hard to get a space in the car park. Car park in a caravan park. Hard to wrap her head around that one. She got out into thin rain and pulled her hood up over her hair. 'Given I'm clearing off, I'll let you lead.'

'Of course.' Gashkori scurried across the tarmac towards the huddle of officers, high-fiving Taylor and patting Struan's arm.

Soppy wasn't quite right. She'd come up with a better one. Sleekit or scoundrel, maybe.

Elliot caught up with them.

Gashkori reintroduced himself to Marshall with a fist bump. 'Good to see you again, Rob.' Big smile on his face, acting all friendly despite being the one who'd pushed Marshall out. 'Nice to have your expertise here.'

'Only reason I'm here is because a deeply traumatised woman who has been re-traumatised by seeing her attacker called me out of the blue.' Marshall grimaced. 'Me of all people.'

'I'll chat to you about that later.' Gashkori scratched at his thin beard, eyeing Elliot. 'Listen, I'll get up to speed, then catch up with you and we can shoot the shit. Agree an action plan. Whether you're needed here or can get on with some real work.'

Marshall narrowed his eyes at Gashkori. 'Sure thing, sir.'

'Good man.' Gashkori play-punched his arm, nodded at Taylor, then led him away, with Struan following them both like an over-eager puppy.

Marshall watched them trot off then let out a deep sigh. 'Doesn't get any better, does he?'

'Ryan? Oh, he gets worse.' Elliot smirked at him. 'In fact, he's actually *happy*. Must be getting some greasy ramrod action somewhere.'

Marshall screwed up his face. 'Jesus.'

'Sorry.' Elliot raised her hands. Hard to forget Marshall was as woke as a hippie at Glastonbury. 'How you doing, Rob? Looking like you've lost a wee bit of weight?'

'Have I?' Marshall finally looked at her, then smiled. 'Been a while since I've seen you. Thought we weren't going to be strangers?'

'So did I...' She ran a hand through her hair. 'Then again, you try going through what I've been in the last year...'

Marshall held her gaze. 'I know some of what you're feeling.'

She shut her eyes. 'Shite, aye. Sorry.'

'Hey, it's okay.' Marshall folded his arms and nodded at Gashkori. 'Tell me, how's he doing?'

'Ryan?' She shrugged. 'He's... Fine, I guess. Better than Pringle, but then again, who could be worse?'

Marshall grinned at her. 'Me?'

'Aye, I suppose.' She laughed. 'You'd be terrible. How's your new gig?'

'Aye, it's fine. Have to do the thinky for some DCIs who can't do it themselves.'

Typical Marshall, keeping those cards so close to his chest they were inside his heart and lungs.

'I mean, on the plus side, it means I've been working closely with DCS Mira—'

'Jesus! Don't say her name or she'll appear, shrouded in brimstone.'

Marshall rolled his eyes. 'Okay. In that case, I'm working

closely with She Who Cannot Be Named.' He frowned. 'Don't people like her?'

'No, most people do, it's just... Nobody wants her near a crime scene. Tends to take over and try to run things. And then bang on about her time shadowing the FBI. And that trans-Europe case. Yawn.'

'Well, I like working with her. She's supportive. And doing stuff with her can only be good for my career.'

'Glad you've still got one. Mine withered on the vine a few years back.'

'Don't you think that name's a bit daft?'

'She Who Cannot Be Named? Oh, aye. Not one of mine. The whole thing is just daft nonsense.'

'How's Taylor getting on?'

'Tell you something, him being at my rank is a total *joke*, Rob. Useless sod was a stretch at DS.'

'What happened to the Acting DI?'

'Soppy Struan?'

'Seriously?'

'Damn straight. Only good thing was it meant he wasn't reporting to me anymore. Had enough "sneaky" in my life with Davie. I don't trust Struan to tell me which day it is, let alone the truth.'

'He's that bad?'

'You've seen him. You've worked with him. He's a sleekit devil. I can't be having that, Robbie.' A gust of wind cut right through her, making her shiver. 'I've got Jolene instead.' She leaned in close. 'Between us chickens, I think Ryan has a bias against female officers. Every chance he gets, he brings in more of the boys' club. I'm leading the "broad squad" with Jolene and Ash Paton. Though anyone calling Ash a broad... Good luck to them.'

'Gashkori's actually used that phrase?'

'Not to my face.'

'But you've heard him say it?'

'A few times, aye. It's shite, Rob. It's really shite.'

'Rob?' Jolene rushed over and wrapped Marshall in a hug. 'It's great to see you!'

Elliot struggled to prevent herself raising an eyebrow. There was friendly, then there was... whatever that was.

'How are you doing, Rob?'

'I can't really complain.' Marshall shrugged. 'You?'

'Oh, when you work for DI Elliot, you pick up a good few tips on how to complain.'

Marshall laughed, then it settled into a harsh stare. 'Okay. Do we have any idea who the caravan belongs to?'

'Been working on that.' Jolene flicked through her notebook. 'It's owned by... let me check...' She looked up with a sly grin. 'The person who owns the caravan park.'

'Ha, ha.' Marshall rolled his eyes. 'Okay, so who's renting it?'

'Just spoke to the manager.' Jolene found her page. 'Registered to a Kayleigh Rothbury. Age nineteen.'

Elliot laughed. 'Anyone born after 1985 given that name is thanks to the joy of Marillion.'

Jolene scowled at her. 'The joy of *who*?'

'Marillion!'

Jolene shrugged. 'Never heard of him.'

'*Them*. They're a band! Fish was the singer.'

'*Fish*?'

'For God's sake, what do they teach you at school these days? They're Scottish, for crying out loud!' Elliot smirked at her. 'Still, it's pretty ironic.'

'What is?'

'Someone with your name not understanding *her* name.'

'Right.' Jolene plastered a fake smile on her face and went back to her notebook. 'Well, according to the manager, Kayleigh works at a surf school in Coldingham Bay. A few miles up the road.'

'Oh, that's interesting.' Elliot patted Jolene on the arm. 'Here's the deal. You and I will go up and track her down. Robbie, you brief Gashkori.' She set off before he could reply. 'And on the way, Jolene, I'll introduce you to the sheer majesty of Marillion.'

5

Marshall leaned back against his car and watched Elliot and Jolene driving off. He let out a breath he didn't know he was holding.

Weird how much things had changed in the year he'd been away from the team.

How Gashkori had reshaped everything from Pringle's chaotic old structure that just about worked into something different. A well-oiled machine, maybe, but what was it oiled with?

Marshall pushed away from his car and walked over to the picnic bench passing for a command centre. Gashkori and Taylor sat opposite each other, surrounded by a group of lads.

Elliot's point about the boys' club resonated. She seemed certain about the current staffing and division of labour being rooted in sexism, but Marshall needed to keep an open mind about it – Elliot was one for building things up more than they should be.

If there was no controversy, she'd create some.

But he didn't want anyone to endure that kind of thing, even her.

'Shame she called me in April, right?' Marshall swept his gaze around them, then settled on Gashkori. 'A month or so later and this spot would be the perfect place for you lot to sit out all day, slurping on ice lollies.'

'Wouldn't it just?' Gashkori looked up at Marshall. 'You still loitering with intent?'

A few stifled laughs.

Marshall felt his neck burn and not from the sun. He let it wash over him. Or at least he tried to. 'Afraid you'll need a bloke with holy water and garlic to get rid of me.'

'Ain't that the truth.' Gashkori rose to his feet, looking up at Marshall. 'Okay, brainbox, what's the thinking here?'

'I'll start with the basic stuff, Ryan. First, this isn't a murder case until we have a body. Have you got people scouring the cliffs?'

'Why would we do that? Looking for old pirate ships hidden in the caves up the coast?'

Marshall stifled his groan. 'Never know how much treasure you might find on an eighteenth-century galleon.' When the laughter didn't come, he stuffed his hands in his pockets. 'Given the MO Sylvester previously employed, we should be looking for bodies in similar places he used to dump them. Cliffs, train lines. I'm assuming you've been looking at deaths on the train line?'

Struan nodded, a bit too keen for Marshall's liking. 'Got a couple of officers going through them on the stretch between Newcastle and Edinburgh.'

'Well, that's good. But he much preferred to push them off cliffs, like these ones. Stands to reason if he's active again, he'll have done it here.'

Gashkori ran his tongue across his teeth. 'Struan, get some of the uniforms going around the place.'

'Sure thing, gaffer.'

Marshall focused on Struan, trying to impart some author-ity. 'Get around the caravans too. See if anyone else is missing.'

'Sounds good.' Gashkori tilted his head at Struan. 'Off you go, Sergeant.'

Struan raced away, like a rat scurrying into a drain.

Gashkori clicked his tongue a few times. 'I rifled through the old case summary on the drive over. The killer never killed in the same town twice, right?'

'Correct.'

'So why's he back here?'

'Because Holly didn't die? Because we missed other cases? Any number of possibilities.'

'Okay, Roberto, this isn't a murder case until we've got a body.' Gashkori walked away from Marshall, until he was surrounded by the lads in his team. 'And we presently don't have a body. Don't even have a missing person. The amount of blood found in the caravan isn't indicative of a presumptive homicide. All we've got is a report from a victim. I spoke to the lassie and she doesn't seem to be the full shilling, does she?'

'That's a bit crass, sir.'

'Aye, maybe, but you can't tell me she's all there, Rob. She's suffered a horrendous ordeal at the hands of a monster. Wouldn't be the first time someone with that amount of trauma imagined something and cried wolf.'

'Wouldn't be the first time someone with that amount of trauma had spoken up and wasn't believed, only for the wolf to bite her throat out.'

'Enlighten us, Roberto. What happened twelve years ago?'

Marshall shut his eyes and sucked in the deepest breath, right into his lungs. Someone was smoking upwind of him. 'Okay, this case happened when I worked in Durham as a forensic profiler. Jacob Goldberg was in charge of the depart-ment, which offered consultancy services.'

Gashkori smirked. 'Like a modern-day Sherlock Holmes?'

'Kind of. Liana Curtis was his Watson and now she's her own Holmes, I suppose. She's in charge of it now. Anyway, we were supporting multiple English police forces to catch a suspected serial killer. North Yorkshire, Humberside, Cumbria, Northumbria. Strategically, they decided to keep it out of the press, so Sylvester didn't earn himself a cute tabloid name like the Clifftop Mangler or the Geordie Holidaymaker or whatever.'

Taylor grunted a laugh. 'Eyemouth Ian.'

Marshall scowled at him. Didn't point out how shite his joke was – the lack of laughter from Taylor's mates did that work for him. 'David Sylvester was the only suspect the police presented us with. Goldberg agreed. He believed he was a sadist.'

Taylor grunted. 'Sexual?'

'Nope. The crimes were blitz-driven without a sexual component. In fact, given the age and gender of the victims, Goldberg suggested the suspect was impotent. Also, he judged that the killer had an inadequate personality with high introversion, perhaps with a speech impediment or was disfigured in some way.'

'A speech impediment?'

Marshall shrugged. 'I didn't necessarily agree with that assessment. Can happen in men, but it just felt a bit trite. But don't underestimate the power of childhood trauma and school bullying on someone's psyche.'

'Right. Guess so.' Taylor ran a hand down his face. 'You said Sylvester was the only suspect. How closely did he match the profile?'

'Very. He suffered from a brain injury that greatly impacted his memory and empathy, which made Goldberg believe he thought he was on some deluded mission of revenge.'

'What happened?'

'He was on holiday with his girlfriend in Greece. Got into an argument, she took his passport and left him stuck there. He got drunk, then got into a fight with some locals. The kicking he received was sufficient to also incur a severe brain injury. Bleeding. Fractured skull.'

Taylor shook his head. 'That's rough.'

'Thing is, because of the settlement from the assault, Sylvester's now independently wealthy. Doesn't need to work.'

Taylor laughed. 'Maybe I should get some numpties from Hawick to kick the shite out of me. Beats working, eh?'

'Nobody would notice if you suffered brain damage, Cal.' Gashkori held his gaze amidst the chorus of laughter, then he switched it to Marshall. 'Go on.'

'The way the case was put together, your colleagues in the north of England found that Sylvester lived his life by staying in B&Bs in coastal towns during the off-season. On-season, he'd get a six-month rental somewhere. Thing is, he didn't pre-select the victims. They were all crimes of opportunity. Lonely young women, all fifteen to eighteen. Mostly the daughters of the owners. Occasionally someone he'd bumped into in a café. Never another holidaymaker like himself – he needed to build up their picture over a period of time. Part of the fun was understanding someone's life before striking at the precise moment. Whitley Bay, Scarborough, Blackpool, Whitby, Seahouses, Blackpool, Morecambe, then Whitley Bay again.'

'That's a lot of victims, Roberto. And good memory.'

Marshall tapped at the side of his head. 'You'd be very surprised the things I've got stowed away up here.'

'Or horrified?' Gashkori laughed. 'Why wasn't he caught?'

'No audit trail, for starters. Sylvester paid in cash so he was never on a system or in the books. Then he'd check out and move to another place where he *was* on the system to give a veneer of an alibi. Only then would he strike, returning to kill his victims by pushing them off cliffs or in front of trains. The crimes were always opportunistic, but in a window where he knew he wouldn't be seen. No weapons, no dialogue, no pleading or negotiation, just pure action.'

'And Holly was the final victim?'

Marshall nodded. 'Taken from outside her home in Whitley Bay and driven up here to Eyemouth. She managed to escape and ran to the police.'

'That doesn't sound like the same MO to me.'

'It's not. Thing is, they'd met a few years earlier in Eyemouth. So it's either possible she was some ultimate target he was escalating towards, or... Some other reason. Maybe he was escalating towards abduction. Like I said, he was a sadist. But also, he didn't speak to us. Just denied it all.'

'But the first victim was from Whitley Bay too?'

'Right. First and last.'

'That doesn't strike you as weird, Rob?'

'Could be just the balance of probability. The other locations didn't have any other victims that we know of. Sometimes you expect duplicates. A return to a methodology that worked. Familiarity, comfort on his home turf, maybe?'

Gashkori stared off out to sea. 'But it's the only one. You don't think that's significant?'

'I'll run it through and see what I think.'

'Like Cal asked, why's Sylvester not rotting in prison?'

'Because there was no direct evidence of his involvement, just correlation. All of those stays were explainable by various reasons. And there was no DNA because these were sharp acts, with victims thrown into the sea or sliced into a million pieces by a train. No witnesses, either.'

'But you know his name. He was interviewed.'

'Because Holly pulled Sylvester from a VIPER line-up. He had a solid alibi for her assault and abduction. Less solid ones for the others. Crown prosecutor didn't see a case, so he never faced a trial.'

'Do you think he did it?'

Marshall sucked down a deep breath. 'Sylvester was never charged but everyone knew he did it.'

'Ah, guilty in the court of public opinion.'

'No, like I told you, we kept this quiet. I meant everyone involved in the case knew he'd done it. Either he's too smart for us, which is unlikely given his brain injury, or he was just lucky. Trouble is, luck runs out. The longer you get away with stuff, the higher the probability you'll leave behind some evidence.' Marshall nodded over to the caravan. 'The other side, though, is after Holly's ordeal, the bodies stopped appearing. We deemed he'd completed his mission. Maybe failing to kill Holly meant he'd somehow succeeded. Or he'd learnt a lesson. Or had a wake-up call.'

Gashkori looked around at Marshall. 'I don't hold much truck with that kind of thinking. Because from where I'm standing, it sure as hell looks like Sylvester's still hunting down young women. Assuming he ever stopped.' A wicked smile filled his lips. 'Thing I don't get is why she had your phone number?'

'Come again?'

'Well, you weren't a key player on the case. Not even Watson to this Goldstein's Holmes.'

'Goldberg.'

'Point still stands. Why'd she have your number?'

Marshall felt the sweat trickle down his back. 'She trusted me. I don't know why. But she latched on to me after the first time Jacob spoke to her. Insisted I sit in on all of her interviews. Not a cop, not Jacob or Liana. Me.'

'You didn't shag her, did you?'

'Ryan, of course I didn't. I was trying to help her. That's all.'

Gashkori looked him up and down. Eyes twisting and screwing. Then he gave a sharp nod, like he believed him. 'Have you found any potential victims in your new gig?'

Marshall shook his head. 'Not yet.'

Gashkori barked a laugh. 'Right.'

'What's that supposed to mean?'

'Well, when I moved you through to Gartcosh, I expected something good to come from that. But you're just sitting in an ivory tower, pondering the imponderable. Just a bunch of navel-gazing, right?'

'You know something, Ryan? The FBI reckon there are twenty serious unidentified serial killers active in the USA at any time. You know the country with the second most? The UK. Stands to reason. Now the good news is the difference between there and here is a factor of ten. But the bad news is, that means there are always at least two killers in this country.'

'O-kay...' Gashkori sat back down and took a slurp from a can of WakeyWakey energy drink, staring into space. 'I hear you, Roberto.' He focused on Marshall. 'Here's the deal. I'll give you Ash Paton. You go and track down Sylvester. Speak to him. Do some of this police work you reckon you're good at. Prove to me and She Who Cannot Be Named that you can still do it.'

6

'It's really good seeing Rob, isn't it?' Jolene got out of the car first. 'He did so much for my career.'

Aye, and thank you for not thanking me for all the work I did getting you there...

Tap-in merchant.

Elliot followed her out into the freezing air. 'You're talking like he's the second coming of Jesus Christ, rather than a numpty with a useless degree and erectile dysfunction.'

A frown danced across Jolene's forehead. 'Erectile dysfunction?'

'Just being daft.' Elliot plipped the pool car's locks, then walked along the lane. 'He is a numpty, though.'

Down the hill, the wide curve of Coldingham Bay looked out to the North Sea, all the way over to Norway. Or maybe Denmark. Elliot couldn't decide which. A steep path led up the bank to rough cliffs, but the south side was virtually impassable, blocking the long stretch to Eyemouth.

The only building was a giant Victorian hotel, just like you'd see in some Cornish historical shite on telly. A freshly painted sign read:

Big Sammy's Surf Shack

As they approached it, Elliot spotted a much humbler affair opposite, hiding behind some mature trees. A single-storey, flat-roof thing like you got everywhere across Scotland.

Matty's Bikes & Boards

Elliot blew air up her face. 'They didn't tell you which surf school it was?'

Jolene shrugged. 'There was only one last time I was here.'

Elliot frowned at her. '*You* surf?'

'Used to. And scuba diving.'

'Well I never.'

'Why's that so weird? I'm sure you've got hobbies. Or just your family life. We're not cops all the time.'

Speak for yourself...

Jolene stared down at the cove. 'Must be bloody cold out there today, mind. Still, it looks like great surf.'

'I'll trust the expert, then.' Elliot reached into her pocket for a 50p piece, then thumbed at the smaller of the two. 'Heads this one, tails Fawlty Towers over there.' She flipped it and caught it. 'Heads it is.' She walked into Matty's Bikes & Boards.

The room was like a hipsters' paradise, filled with the pungent fug of patchouli and incense. Surfboards stacked up along one wall, bikes along another. The middle was dominated by big tables stuffed with tat to sell to the mugs who came in there.

Elliot closed in on the desk and the smells mixed with the fug of ganja. 'Morning, sir.'

A big red-haired barrel of a man was propping up a counter by an old-fashioned till. 'G'day, ladies.' Australian words, Scottish accent. He could barely focus on them, like he hadn't put his glasses on that morning. 'Let me know if there's anything I can do to help.'

Elliot walked over. 'You the owner?'

'Aye.'

'Okay, Matty, my name—'

'Matthew. Not Matty.'

Elliot pointed behind her. 'But it says Matty on the sign outside?'

'Well, that's true...' Matthew sighed. 'But it's a joke.' He giggled hard. 'At my expense. My brother did the sign for me. And he did it wrong and refuses to fix it. How's that for fun?'

Elliot finally clocked it – the guy was absolutely baked. She looked into the ash tray by the side door – filled with butts from roll-ups. Spliffs. She wasn't going to attack him for it right now, but being stoned at work was something she'd keep in her back pocket. Instead, she pulled out her warrant card. 'DI Andrea Elliot. This is DS Jolene Archer.'

His eyes snapped into focus. 'Good morning, ladies. What seems to be the matter?'

'We're looking for Kayleigh Rothbury.'

Matthew smiled and nodded. 'It's in Northumbria. Just inland from Alnwick.'

Elliot frowned. 'Excuse me?'

'Rothbury. It's in Northumbria.'

Elliot took a deep breath. 'Sir, I asked to speak to Kayleigh Rothbury.'

'And I told you. It's down past Alnwick!'

'I know where Rothbury is. I'm trying to speak to someone with that surname.'

Matthew frowned. 'Oh, right. Sorry, I suffer from surfer's ear. Can't remember the name for it, but it's the deafness you get from surfing. Too much cold, salty water in my ears. Causes bone to grow inside them. Doc reckons I've got about twenty percent of my hearing now.'

'I'm sorry to hear that, sir.'

'Yeah, I can barely hear anything. But I live by a world-class surfing beach and I can't stay out of the water, so what can you do? This place is becoming a big tourist attraction.'

'Okay, but we need to speak to Kayleigh Rothbury. Does she work here? Kayleigh Rothbury.'

'Kayleigh Rothbury.' Matthew looked away, his face all screwed up. 'Kayleigh Rothbury... Kayleigh Rothbury... Kayleigh Rothbury.' He looked back at Elliot. 'Nope, she doesn't work here. What about over the road?'

Elliot gave him a smile. 'Okay, thanks for your time. I hope your condition clears up, sir.'

'No, it's perfect surfing weather.'

'Your condition.'

'Oh, right.' Matthew rubbed at his ear. 'No, it's pretty much incurable. Well, not without an operation, but I don't really trust Western medicine.'

'Stick to the herbal remedies, then.'

'Sure will.' Matthew shot them a wink. 'See you around, ladies.'

Elliot left the shop and crossed the road. 'Is it just me or was he absolutely wasted?'

'Toking and surfing go together.'

'You smoke?'

'I'm a cop, Andi. So, no.'

'You can tell me.'

'There's nothing *to* tell.' Jolene pushed into the front room of the surf school, shaking her head.

More like a wee tearoom in the Highlands. The kind that used to be a school and now sold pathetically weak cups of tea and local tat to tourists. Woolly jumpers, paintings of land-scapes and stags, board games, artworks that all said 'Live. Laugh. Love' just not necessarily in that order.

No sign of any surfboards, but a big man with red hair was

the only one in, sitting at a long table and tucking into a hearty breakfast. His nametag read 'Samuel'. He looked up at them, then took a glug of amber beer. At eleven in the morning.

O-kay...

Jolene sat opposite him. 'Hi, sir, we're looking for Kayleigh Rothbury.'

'Nope.' Another glug of beer and he went back to his fry-up.

'Gather she works here?'

Samuel speared the charred end of a sausage and stopped. 'No, she doesn't.'

'But you know her?'

'Aye. The Aussie lassie.' Samuel took a glug of beer then burped. 'I shagged her. About three months ago.'

'So you know her?'

'Aye, but she doesn't work here any longer. She quit and shifted over the road to work for Matthew.' Another sip of beer. 'My wee brother.'

'You're sure?'

'Of course.'

'We were just in there and your brother doesn't remember her.'

'Well, I do.' Samuel laughed. 'Remember every single notch on my bedpost.'

'Thank you.' Elliot nodded, then left him to his beer and food, holding the door for Jolene.

'Want me to lead with the brother this time, Andi?'

'Aye, why not. Maybe your screeching wail will cut through his buggered lugs.'

Jolene stopped outside the door to Matty's. 'My what?'

'You heard. It's called a joke.' Elliot ushered Jolene inside. 'Go on, then. Lead!'

'Fine...' Jolene pushed back inside the surf school. 'Hiya.'

'Back so soon?'

Elliot kept to the back of the room so she could better observe the place.

'So, we trudged over the road and spoke to your brother. Samuel? But he informed us Kayleigh works here.'

'Kayleigh? I told you, nobody of that name here.'

'You might know her as Kay?'

'Nope.'

'Your brother was adamant. Said he had a brief relationship with her.'

'He went on a ship with her?'

'A relationship.'

'Oh.' Matthew twisted his lips together. 'Look, I don't know a Kayleigh, but you're welcome to look over there.'

He was pointing right at Elliot.

The wall next to her was covered with photos of young people. Surfers, by the looks of it. Aussie backpackers, English yahs, the occasional local.

Didn't take long to spot Kayleigh.

The photo read:

Rainbow Sunshine. 2023-

Elliot let out a loud sigh. 'What the hell is this? Her name is Kayleigh.'

Matthew shrugged. 'Never to me. Some people prefer to have their own name.'

Elliot grabbed the photo off the wall. 'What can you—'

'Hey, hey, that's my property!'

'Sir. We're police. This is evidence. What can you tell us about her?'

'What's there to say? Rainbow was cool. Aussie girl. Eighteen, I think. Backpacking before she goes to uni back home. My idiot brother gave her a job for a few months in January. Sorted her with a berth in a caravan down the road, at least until peak season. Then she came in here, saying she'd quit and did I have anything going. Just so happened I did. She kept the caravan; I sorted that for her.'

'Why did she choose that name?'

'Who can say? Some people just like to reclaim their identities. She's a decent surfer. Trained as a lifeguard back home.'

'Where's home?'

'Eh, Australia?'

'I know that. Which bit?'

'Oh, Perth, I think? Talked a lot about Rottnest Island. Surfed there myself yonks ago.'

Jolene grunted a laugh. 'I've been there. Really cool place.'

'Lived in Sydney for a couple of years before that arsehole over there promised me the earth to set up his surfing school. Doesn't know his arse from his elbow, so here I am. In miserable Scotland, running a surf school, when I could be back in Oz.'

'When did you last see her?'

Matthew stared into space, then gripped his nose and pulled at something. 'Wait, has something happened to her?'

'We don't know.'

'Oh, well.'

'Is she working today?'

'I think.'

Elliot felt her shoulders slacken off. 'You think?'

Matthew scratched his head. 'Can't remember. Hang on.' He pulled out his phone and put it to his ear without pressing the button. 'Hey, Dom. Is Rainbow on today?' He nodded. 'Aye, cool.' He pocketed the phone. 'She's working, aye.'

Elliot scowled at him. 'You didn't call anyone there, did you?'

'No, I did. I was on with Dom. My business partner. We've got a constant call going with each other. Saves hassle on phoning each other. Or texting.'

Elliot didn't see the logic, but was prepared to give the mad stoner the benefit of the doubt, not that he'd really earned it. 'So she's here? Rainbow Sunshine?'

'Aye, she's teaching a class on the beach today. Eleven o'clock start.'

Elliot checked the clock. 'Which was five mins ago.' She nodded at him. 'Thank you for your time, sir.'

'Aye, sure.'

Elliot charged out of the shop then hurried down to the shore. 'This is such a bloody stupid case, Jolene. The lassie's not even missing, let alone dead. There's no murder. There's no nothing. If you ask me, that Holly lassie is pulling Dr Donkey's plonker.'

'Thought he had erectile dysfunction?'

'Aye, very funny.' Elliot stopped on the dunes and looked out into the foaming sea.

Ten people stood on the sand, shivering in their wetsuits, with another five splashing about in the water.

No sign of anyone teaching anything.

A man stormed out of the water and up to them. 'Excuse me, are you in charge of this outfit?' Posh Edinburgh accent.

'No, sir, we're police.'

'Good! I want to report a case of daylight bloody robbery. My son paid a lot of bloody money for this course, only for the instructor to not bloody show up!'

'That's far from ideal.' Elliot sighed. 'Leave it with us.' She raced off, retracing their steps, then pushed back into the surf shop.

Matthew was in a fit of giggles, staring at his phone. 'Aye, man. A monkey shop.'

'Here, you!'

Matthew looked over at Elliot. 'Sorry, Dom. Better go.' He pocketed his phone. 'G'day, ladies. Let me know if there's anything I can do to help.'

'We were just in here.'

Matthew squinted at them. 'Oh, yeah. You were. Sure.'

'Kayleigh didn't turn up to teach her class. Rainbow bloody Sunshine, I mean.' Elliot walked over and got in his face. 'Now, I've been very understanding and patient here, sir, but you seem to be doing a lot of forgetting here. Maybe better laying off the wacky baccy.'

Matthew burst out laughing. 'Wacky baccy?' A shrill giggle. 'Listen. What I smoke is medicinal. Helps with my ears. Thanks for the reminder.' He grabbed a pouch and a glass bong. 'Time for my next dose.'

'Not so bloody fast.' Elliot tugged at his sleeve. 'Did she turn up this morning or not?'

'I haven't seen her. Dom hasn't.'

'Okay, so it looks like we've got a missing person here, who has gone missing in very suspicious circumstances. Now, I need to find out if you're telling the truth. My colleague here is going to stay behind and you're going to tell her absolutely everything you can about Kayleigh Rothbury. Or Rainbeam Moonshadow or whatever she's called.'

7

D C Ash Paton drove like a robot, easing the pool car through a perfect arc on the road between Coldingham and St Abbs. She barely even blinked, then she looked around, her brown eyes glancing from behind her boyish fringe. 'You okay there, sir?'

'Just thinking.' Marshall sat back and looked out of the window at the rolling countryside. 'This case is bringing up a lot of things.'

'Sorry to hear that, sir.'

'What are you expecting to find in St Abbs?'

'A secret.' Paton tapped her nose then swept her fringe over to the side. 'How have you been since you left us?'

Marshall let out a slow breath, making it sound like a hiss. He'd barely interacted with Paton in the past, but here she was, treating him like an old friend.

Then again, he'd been the one to spot her being the recipient of some sexism. Whether that's what precipitated Gashkori's restructure, Marshall liked to think it made some kind of difference.

'To be honest with you, Ash, I've been treated like a mushroom. Kept in the dark and fed shite.'

She laughed like she'd never heard that before. Maybe she hadn't – she looked barely out of her teens and was already a detective. 'That can't be true, though?'

'Not far off it, to be honest. I'm supposed to be looking for undiscovered serial killers, which sounds very glamorous, but the reality is I'm stuck in a cupboard in Gartcosh, looking through unsolved murders from across Scotland, trying to connect them with England, Wales, Northern Ireland, Republic of Ireland, bits of Western Europe. Not to mention looking at hundreds of solved murders too, just in case. Occasionally, they'll be kind enough to let me out to speak to real people.'

'So you just speak to imaginary people?'

'Email them mostly.'

'And the real ones?'

'Occasionally I get to have a chat with someone on the phone, but they mostly feel like I'm auditing their work so they can be a bit truculent. Or very.'

'Sounds a bit shit, to be honest.'

'Never thought I'd say this, Ash, but I miss the Borders.' They passed the long row of old farm buildings which were all now craft studios. The coastal path to St Abb's Head started here, usually after a trip to the tearoom. 'Even though it was only a year I was based down here. Not even that, really. I miss the work. I miss the team. I miss the people.'

'Even DI Elliot?'

'Even her.'

Paton closed on the village, the spire-less church sitting proud on the hill. The sign read:

St Abbs
twinned with
New Asgard

She waved a hand at it. 'Have you seen those Avengers films, sir?'

'More a fan of black-and-white Swedish shite with subtitles that go on for hours and hours.'

She laughed. 'Seriously?'

'I mean, I like an Ingmar Bergman as much as the next man, but I have seen a Marvel film or twenty.'

'We could do with Iron Man and Thor to solve this, don't you think?'

'Solve what? We don't have a body. All DI Elliot's got is someone called Rainbow Sunshine failing to turn up for work. And besides, we don't need superheroes to solve cases. We just need people being honest with us. And a ton of shoe leather on the part of the police.'

'Easier said than done...' Paton followed the road into the village, then drove down to the harbour with mechanical precision. Nothing much there, save for a café and the independent lifeboat. Not even a fish and chip shop. 'Here we are, sir. This is the B&B Sylvester is staying in.'

'So this is your secret.' Marshall raised an eyebrow. 'How did you know?'

'Used to walk the beat around here. Or drive it, mostly.' She traced the line of the harbour wall and pulled into a rough parking bay outside a big white house sitting alone at an awkward angle to the water and the few other buildings nearby, like they were in the huff with each other. Net curtains obscured the windows except for the nearest one, which had a sign promising vacancies. 'I know people who know people. And they're always on the lookout for shady people. Just took me a few calls to track him down.'

'So they know David Sylvester?'

'They do... He's got a reputation.'

'What kind of reputation?'

'Just a bit eccentric. Very friendly with a particular age

range of women. People around here don't like unusual people. Sure you understand that.' Paton killed the engine and opened her door without waiting for a reply.

Marshall got out into the biting wind. Somehow it was ten times harsher just a few miles north of Eyemouth – nobody would be sitting outside in this, not even Gashkori and his cronies. He followed her over to the front door and stopped dead.

Sylvester was sitting in the breakfast room, staring into space.

Marshall hadn't seen him in twelve years, but he'd barely aged a day. He felt a fluttering in his stomach and noticed he'd clenched both fists.

He knocked on the door and waited. 'I'll lead here, okay?'

The door crept open and a stout man stood there, hands on hips, eyes dancing between them, his forehead creasing like he considered them to be a couple, but wasn't quite understanding something. The age difference, probably. 'How can I help you?' One of those local accents that pushed the Scottishness up to eleven. Berwick had a similar thing with its accent, but with a variant of Geordie. Almost like the proximity of the two towns pushed them to different polar extremes.

'DI Rob Marshall.' He flipped out his warrant card. 'I gather David Sylvester is staying here.'

'Oh, sure. Sure.' The owner nodded, like he finally understood their relationship. 'Name's Gavin, by the way. Gavin Bell. Mr Sylvester's...' A gruff sigh. 'He's through in the breakfast room.'

'Do you mind if we speak to him?'

'Of course not.' Gavin shook his head. 'Sorry if I'm a wee bit grumpy, but my daughter's off school the day. Wee madam's milking it. Of course, Kate works down in Berwick, so I'm in charge of her ladyship today, eh?' He scurried off into the depths of his home.

Marshall followed – Taylor Swift's vocals flowed down the stairs.

David Sylvester sat at a table in the window, but it didn't have much of a view, just the gable end of another building. The table had three pots of tea and a jigsaw on a tray. The box showed a religious tapestry. 5,000 pieces. And a pretty hard-core one at that – Marshall would be a month just sorting out the edges, let alone sifting through all the angel wings in the middle. Sylvester poured from one teapot into a tiny cup, both decorated with flowers, just not the same ones. His hands shook like he was totally wired. Sylvester stared at them, his forehead creasing, lips twitching. The scar on his head traced from his right eyebrow, up and over his shaved head.

Seeing it made Marshall shiver – the results of his brain injury, or the treatment for it.

Sylvester went back to his jigsaw. He'd managed to complete the edges, but was clearly toiling with the middle – nothing after three pieces in had been connected.

Being in the room with a serial killer was something Marshall could never get used to, even a suspected one like Sylvester.

But this was the part he liked the best about the job. Each encounter was like another year's worth of university. Protocol always meant guards in prisons, but Marshall preferred it one on one. You saw them behave naturally.

Sylvester was a big man. Tall. Broad. Strong. Marshall might struggle to contain him.

Marshall picked up a piece and slotted it in the top-left corner. 'You're making good progress there, David.'

Sylvester removed the piece and tossed it back into the box. 'I know you, don't I?'

Marshall nodded.

Sylvester sat back and sipped some tea. 'Robert Marshall. How are you?'

'I'm okay.' Marshall took the seat opposite and focused on the jigsaw, like they were just two old mates catching up. 'This looks even trickier up close, I have to say.'

'Do you?'

'What?'

'Have to say?'

Marshall smiled. 'It's a figure of speech.'

'Oh. Okay. It is a tough one. It keeps my mind sharp.' Sylvester slurped some tea. 'What do you want, Robert?'

'Just need to ask you a few questions. Like where you've been today.'

'Went for a walk. Along the coast.'

'North or south?'

Sylvester frowned. 'I don't remember.'

'You don't remember where you walked?'

'I'm not much of a cardinal directions man. My approach to walking is to just go outside and put one foot in front of the other, then see where I end up. Today I saw the sea. Just walked and walked. Then I turned around and came back to my jigsaw.'

'Was the sea on your left or right?'

'Well, both. But not all the time.'

'How long have you been staying here, David?'

'Since February.'

'Must be just about ready to move on, eh?'

Sylvester nodded. 'It might be.' He leaned in close and looked over at Gavin. 'Places like this get expensive in the summer. I know a few cheaper places that'll tide me over.' He tapped his nose.

'Are any of them caravan parks?'

'No.'

'Did you see a caravan park on your walk this morning?'

'I don't know. I don't think so. Why?'

'Have you seen Holly Fenwick recently?'

'That lying bitch!'

Marshall sat back and the chair creaked. 'Why do you call her that?'

'Because she lied about me! Said I killed those women. Said I tried to kill her. I didn't abduct her. I didn't try to kill her. She lied about it to the police.'

'You're still insisting on that?'

'Because it's the truth.' Sylvester picked a piece out of the box and slotted it into place, four in from the edge. It was Marshall's piece. 'I walked to St Abb's Head. Up to the lighthouse.'

'Anything you remember from there?'

'Why?'

'Well, if you were there, it'd help if we could corroborate that. Did anyone see you?'

'Two blue Range Rovers parked outside the holiday cottages at the lighthouse.'

Marshall smiled at him. 'Okay, that's handy.'

The music from upstairs got even louder.

Gavin tutted, then left the room. His footsteps cannoned up the stairs.

The music cut out.

Marshall leaned across the jigsaw. 'You mind giving me your phone number?'

'Why?'

'I like to keep in touch with people, David.'

'You think I've done something, don't you?'

'Not saying that. Just... I'm a police officer these days. We have ways of doing things. Procedures. If something happens, we need to speak to certain people in the immediate area. Sure you understand that.'

'Certain people. You mean me?'

'Because you're someone known to Holly.'

'Lying bitch.' Sylvester reached into his pocket and pulled out a business card. He put it on the table next to his jigsaw. 'Here you go.'

Marshall took it. Plain white card, with typewritten text:

David H. Sylvester

Man

And a mobile number beneath.

Marshall looked up with a smile. 'Ending 747, eh?'

Sylvester pushed his arms out wide, like he was a plane. 'Easy to remember, right?'

'Thanks, David.' Marshall pocketed the card and got to his feet. 'I'll be in touch if I need to be. Please answer. Okay?'

'Sure thing, Robert.'

Marshall gave him a nod then walked out of the B&B.

Gavin was thundering down the stairs. 'You're leaving already?'

'Aye, we got what we need.' Marshall stopped. 'Just one last thing, actually? Does he have a car parked here?'

'Sure.' Gavin walked over to a desk by the front door and picked up a hefty ledger. He flicked through it. 'A Volvo plug-in hybrid. Need the plates?'

'Thanks.' Paton got out her phone and snapped the ledger. 'Cheers for that.' She followed Marshall outside. 'Why are we not bringing him in for questioning?'

'Call your first witness.'

She stopped dead. 'Huh?'

Marshall turned to face her. 'Constable, we have no evidence and no witnesses. He's not done anything we know of.'

'Right, I see. But you do think he's still doing his thing of moving around places and staying for a few months, right?'

'Of course. It fits the pattern, but it's not a crime. It's not going to convict him, is it?'

'No, I guess not. Assuming there's actually a crime here.'

'Exactly. We need to disprove that alibi of going to St Abb's Head. Which is going to be your job.'

Paton's mouth hung open. 'Great...'

8

B ack down in Eyemouth, the sun was still out. In the
time Marshall had been away, Gashkori hadn't moved,
basking in the sun like a seal on an exposed
sandbank.

Gashkori opened his eyes, then blinked at Marshall, then
frowned. 'You're back already.'

Marshall sat opposite him. He hated picnic benches –
always felt he'd snap the wood or roll backwards or something.
'We've spoken to Sylvester.'

'Bloody hell, that was quick.' Gashkori cracked an elbow as
he leaned forward. 'What did he say?'

'He's got an alibi for the time of this attack and—'

'Assuming there's been one.'

'Right, sure. But I've asked DC Paton to validate his alibi.
We'll know where Sylvester's been and who with. If there's a
crime, we'll be able to exclude him.'

'Okay. Good stuff.' Gashkori puffed out across his lips. 'Do
you think he's done anything?'

All Marshall had done on the drive back from St Abbs was
run through all the avenues and possibilities. 'The way I see it,

David Sylvester's a difficult person to get inside the head of. He's an incredibly unusual man.'

'But you're an expert in profiling unusual men, aren't you?'

'And women too, but they don't tend to kill. Thing is, a lot of the stuff they teach us is about people with normal or abnormal brain patterns. Known conditions that are present in most people or there's a defined population we can easily identify, say psychopaths or narcissists.'

'But you're saying Sylvester isn't like that?'

'As far as we know, he's a unique case. He's a mentally normal man who suffered brain damage in a very specific way. I mean, there will be other cases like him worldwide, but they're vanishingly small. And there aren't any textbook examples I can draw on. Nothing really makes sense with him.'

'So glad we have your kind of expertise on staff. Where would we be without you?' Gashkori looked off out to sea. 'As far as I can see, Rob, all that's happened is someone's been seen outside a caravan. And between us, Holly's been as vague as hell.'

'Trauma will do that to you.' Marshall waited for a retort. 'You don't think she's telling the truth?'

'Didn't say that, Rob. It's just... We've got nothing here.' Gashkori blew air up his face. 'Uniform have spoken to the residents in the caravans adjacent to and opposite Kayleigh's. Nobody saw her leaving this morning, but her going away for days at a time without notice is nothing new, apparently. Quite often, she'd drive to Orkney or the islands to surf or walk.'

'And she didn't turn up at work? Does that make you think she's near here?'

'Her car's here, though.'

'Interesting...'

'She wanted everyone to call her Rainbow Sunshine, but most knew her as Kayleigh. It's a hippie thing.' Gashkori stared at Marshall for a few long seconds. 'Thanks for the help.'

'I haven't finished here.'

'No, Rob. You have. I don't need you. Never did, but you've been a great help. Thanks for dropping by. We can take it from here.'

Marshall held his gaze and tried to not smack his chops. Or scream at him. Or just walk away.

He froze everything, slowing all his instincts and tried to process his emotions.

Gashkori liked being the smartest in the room, but when Marshall was around he knew he wasn't. It wasn't arrogance, just what Marshall suspected – the brief interactions they'd had, Marshall had been the one to point to flaws in his logic.

He gripped the edge of the picnic table. 'You gave me DC Paton to work this case. I want to keep doing that, sir.'

'Doing what?'

'We need to get to the bottom of what's happened here.'

'We don't, actually. I get that this is unfinished business for you, but we don't have a crime. All I see is time being wasted.'

'Sir...' Marshall's mouth was dry. 'We've got someone missing who fits the pattern. We don't have a body, sure, but we have a credible report that matches the MO from that old case. No matter how you look at it, someone's killed all those women. A real-life serial killer. And that's literally my wheelhouse. Don't you want to be the one who prosecutes this?'

'Rob, don't play to my ego because I haven't got one. I hear you, but we haven't found a body. And that's why I don't need you. That case up in Edinburgh you were helping Cal with, that's your sort of jam. Academic, intellectual, passive. Focus on that. Because *that's* your wheelhouse, not this.'

Marshall wasn't going to win this by the direct route. 'Sir, I'm not just a profiler. I was a mainstream DI for eleven years. Let me show you what I can do.'

'You already have, Rob. We needed to know where Sylvester is, not that we ever really needed to speak to him. You've given that information to DC Paton.' Gashkori waved a hand to the side. 'I'll get Struan to pick up with her and take it from here. Cheers.'

Marshall knew he'd lost. 'Fine.' He got up and smiled at Gashkori. 'I don't know what I've done to annoy you, Ryan, but whatever it was, I'm sorry it's affected you this badly.'

'Annoy me?' Gashkori laughed. 'Rob, most weeks I don't even remember who you are. I'm glad I've left a big impression on you, though. You're just not that big a deal, to be honest. And why are you still here? Blethering on like what you do is work? Bugger off back to Gartcosh and bury your head in the sand.'

'I'll see you around.' Marshall walked off towards his car, pleased to score the moral victory of acting the big man. But maybe the smack in the chops would've been much more satisfying. He opened the door but didn't get in, weighing up the possibility of going back and fighting the good fight.

'Gaffer!' A cry from behind him.

Marshall swung around.

Struan was running towards Gashkori. 'Uniform have found a woman at the bottom of the cliff!'

9

'S hit!' Gashkori hauled himself up to standing. 'Is she dead?'

'Still sucking air, gaffer.' Struan thumbed behind him, towards the cliffs. 'Sounds like she's in rough shape.'

Gashkori bombed along the grassy path over to the cliff edge.

Marshall followed him, almost tumbling over, and stopped at the edge.

A boat skipped across the waves, heading towards the town.

'I'll see you down there.' Marshall ran over to his car and got in, then mouthed his secret incantation. The gods of the internal combustion engine were smiling at him – it started first go. He wheeled back in a smooth arc, then powered off back towards the town, down the lone single-track road, praying nobody approached. He lucked out and turned left onto the high street, driving into the town, passing a bakers and the old amusement arcade, somehow still trading in this day and age.

An ambulance was haring along ahead of him, so he tucked into its slipstream and followed it around the narrow road, then a sharp left. He had to brake when it pulled up outside the fancy-looking chip shop pub.

Marshall got out and raced over to harbourside. A jetty ran in parallel to the road, about ten feet below him. He couldn't jump down.

The coastguard boat ploughed in towards them, casting a wide wake.

The paramedics were over at the ramp up to the harbour. One ran down to the waterside.

The other glanced around and nodded his head. 'Marshall, right? Name's Todd.' Australian lad. 'Luckily for you, we were attending a call in Coldingham.'

Marshall recognised him from a case over by Melrose over a year ago. 'That's lucky.' He stopped next to them, sucking in the feral pong of a harbour. 'Is she still alive?'

'She *was*, mate, but whether she still is...?'

The boat pulled into a berth near them on the jetty. All that separated Marshall from toppling over was a pair of guy ropes running the length of the harbour.

Todd joined his colleague on the ramp, splitting the gurney between them.

Gashkori ran over, phone clamped to his head. 'Andi, we're at the harbour. Okay. See you soon.' He killed the call and pocketed his phone. 'Is it her?'

'Don't know.' Marshall placed himself between the ramp and Gashkori, trying to stop him interfering too much.

Todd helped a coastguard lift a trolley up from the boat onto the jetty, then with the other paramedic's help, he carefully lifted her onto the gurney and started wheeling up to street level.

Marshall joined them, but kept a respectful distance.

A young woman lay on her back, open cuts and bruises covering her face. Long hair in a tight ponytail, damp from the sea. Eyes closed and dressed for bed, like she'd fallen asleep on the sofa in front of the telly.

A giant gash cut out of her right arm, consistent with a knife wound.

Elliot barged between them, holding out a photo, her hand shaking. 'Aye, that matches Kayleigh Rothbury.'

Gashkori scowled at her. 'Where did you get that?'

'I stole it from her work.'

'Good effort.' Gashkori focused on the paramedics. 'Can you take her to Borders General?'

Todd finished resting her in the back of the ambulance, then scowled at Gashkori. 'Mate, that's like fifty minutes rather than twenty to Berwick? Hell, it's not much longer to ERI.'

'There's a big accident on the bypass this morning, so Edinburgh's out. Besides, the Borders has a much better trauma centre. By the time they piss around in Berwick and realise they're out of their depth, she could be getting life-saving treatment in Melrose. Her funeral will be your funeral, Todd.'

'Sure thing, mate.' Todd hopped in the back and slammed the door.

The ambulance drove off, blasting its siren to clear away the small crowd of nosy sods, then shot off along the line of the river towards the A1.

Marshall frowned at him. 'Since when does BGH have a better trauma centre than anywhere?'

'Rob, the Berwick place isn't fit for purpose.' Gashkori shook his head at Marshall. 'Besides, this is a disaster. You should've brought Sylvester in for a formal interview.'

'On what pretext, sir?'

Gashkori took a deep breath. 'It's not enough that you screwed up years ago, Rob, is it?' Another solid shake of the head. 'You just had to let him go *again*.'

'I'm not arresting someone when we haven't even got a crime.' Marshall held his steely gaze. 'Thing is, now we've got a victim, you need me. And a few heartbeats ago you were sending me back to Gartcosh because there was no crime.'

Gashkori looked away, shaking his head.

'But now you need me.' Marshall clapped a hand to his shoulder. 'And I get to annoy you some more.'

'Fine. Well, I want you to man-mark Sylvester. He doesn't leave your sight until we can clear him from this.'

Elliot pulled up outside Matthew's surf school in Coldingham and honked the horn.

The door shot open and Jolene jogged out, rounded the car, then got in the passenger side. 'Drive on to St Abbs.'

'Eh? Why?'

'I'll show you.'

'Fine, then, be enigmatic.' Elliot drove back up the country lane towards Coldingham village, bare fields on both sides, tapping her thumbs to the beat.

Jolene reached over and turned the stereo down from ear-splitting to barely audible. 'What the hell is this?'

'"Kayleigh" by Marillion.'

'Well, I can see why they don't teach it in schools.'

'Honestly, Jo, you've got no class.' Elliot was tempted to reach over and turn it back up, but she didn't. 'You get my voicemail?'

'I did, aye. So it's now an attempted murder, right?'

'Hopefully it'll just stay at that.' Elliot followed the road past yet another caravan park, back into the outskirts of Coldingham, slowing a little bit as she came to the T-junction, then took the right towards St Abbs. 'Gashkori's doing his nut in. Should've seen him. A serial killer's struck again and he's raging that Dr Donkey didn't bring him in. Letting all the psychobabble from the past colour his decisions in the here and now.'

Jolene scowled at her. 'I don't think that's fair.'

'Aye, I can see both sides of it. We'll see...' Elliot slowed as they approached St Abbs and its stupid Avengers sign. The kind of nonsense that had brought her here more than a few times since those films came out. The joys of having two young laddies who insisted on Captain America and Spider-Man pyjamas. 'Maybe I'm being a bit harsh. Marshall's less of an arse than Gashkori, but... that's like being nicer than Hitler. Still, us girls need to stick together.'

'Okay. Sure. Broad Squad, assemble.' Jolene pointed down to the harbour. 'I spoke to the staff at the surf school. Half of them are so stoned they don't remember much of today, let alone the last few months. Still, I got out of them that Kayleigh AKA Kay AKA Rainbow Sunshine was pretty popular with the staff. She kept herself to herself. Didn't socialise.'

'Is that after her and Samuel over the road made the beast with two backs?'

'Especially after that, I'd wager.'

'I get it. Once shagged, twice shy?' Elliot had to brake to let a Volvo climb the slope. 'Not that there are many boozers around here. Guess they'd be drinking in either of the surf schools?'

'Precisely. Probably cycle in. Though I'm not sure many of them actually drink. Okay, so the lead I got... After that incident, Kayleigh started going for her lunch at the café in St Abbs.'

Elliot pulled up outside it. 'This one?'

'There isn't another.'

'True.' Used to be an old school, by the looks of things.

Lights on, steam pouring out of the kitchen's extractor at the side. 'You lead here, then.'

'Fine by me.'

Elliot got out and followed her inside the café.

Pretty busy, considering it was a Monday in April. A waitress scratched 'scotch broth' in chalk under 'soup of the day'. Smelled delicious – meaty and slightly sour. Elliot was sorely tempted to get a takeaway cup or seven.

'DS Jolene Archer.' She held out her warrant card. 'This is DI Elliot. Wondering if we can speak to the owner.'

The waitress's name badge read 'Clarabelle'. 'That's me, aye.' Chewing gum snapped in her mouth. A streak of white through her hair made her look like a rabid badger. 'What's up?'

'We're looking to speak to you about a frequent customer who, eh, who...' Jolene patted her trousers. 'Sorry, I had it...'

Sod this...

Elliot held out the photo of Kayleigh. 'Do you recognise this woman?'

Clarabelle snatched it out of her hands. 'Oh, aye. This is Kay, isn't it? The wee Aussie lassie?'

'That's correct.'

'Sure, she used to come in for her lunch. We don't get a lot of customers, but if they're regular you get to know them. She'd have a plate of my soup, except mushroom. She hated mushroom. So I saved that for the weekends. All because of her. Tried to call herself Rainbow Sunshine but nobody could take that seriously.'

'She talk to you about herself much?'

'What kind of thing?'

'Did she mention any friends, acquaintances? Boyfriends? Girlfriends?'

'Well, she ate her lunch with a man a few times a week.'

Shite...

Elliot started rummaging around on her phone for the photo Marshall had sent her. 'Can you describe hi—?'

'David Sylvester.'

Jolene frowned at her. 'You know him?'

'Oh, everybody knows David.' Clarabelle folded her arms. 'Creep sits in there every other day. Monday, Wednesday and Friday one week, then Tuesday and Thursday the next. He'll have some porridge, then drink at least three pots of tea, then have some soup. Must be pissing for England, I tell you.'

11

Marshall left Coldingham and blasted towards St Abbs, trailing the squad cars tearing up the country lane ahead of them. 'What's your take on what Elliot told us?'

Struan was in the passenger seat. 'What, that the attempted murder victim was seen eating her lunch with a known serial killer?'

'That.'

Struan let out a breath slowly. 'What do you think I should think, gaffer? It's obvious, isn't it? Sylvester has struck again. Except he's missed again, because Kayleigh's still alive.'

Marshall couldn't have said it any better. Maybe less brutally. No, definitely so. He hit the button to redial and the phone hit voicemail again. 'Sylvester's turned off his mobile, hasn't he?'

'Two options, guv. One, he's not got reception. And we're out in the wilds here, so that's possible. But the other is that you and Ash-hole spooked him, didn't you?'

'Ash-hole? Really?'

Struan shrugged the shrug of a man who was protected from above.

Marshall pulled up at the B&B and got out.

Elliot was already there, briefing the squad of uniformed officers. 'I want two of you at the back door. Watch for him running, okay?' Then at the other pair. 'You two stay at the front, same deal just guarding a different direction.' She clocked Marshall's approach. 'Rob. You fancy chumming me inside?'

'Just a minute.' Marshall shuffled through the images on his phone until he found the image he'd taken of the Volvo earlier, then wheeled around the car park. 'Great, his car's gone too.'

'Bloody perfect... Let's go and see how long ago he left.'

'Could still be here.' Marshall pointed at Struan. 'You're in charge out here, okay?'

'Sure thing, guv.'

Marshall clocked Jolene and tilted his head towards her, like she had to keep an eye on the sleekit devil. He sighed and followed Elliot inside. 'He's a cheeky bastard.'

Elliot laughed. 'If Struan was just a cheeky bastard, it'd be a massive improvement.' She opened the inside door and stepped into the reception area.

Empty.

No Taylor Swift coming from upstairs, but voices from the corridor.

Marshall headed through to the breakfast room.

Gavin Bell was sitting at a table with a surly teenager, holding half a giant sandwich in front of his mouth. He craned his neck around then did a double take. 'Oh, hi there.' He rested his sandwich down then pushed his chair back and got up. 'What's up, guys?'

'Mr Bell, is David Sylvester still here?'

Gavin frowned. 'No, he finished his tea, did a bit more of his jigsaw then went out for a walk. Can be gone for hours at a time.'

Bloody hell...

'Which way did he go? Was he on foot?'

'Eh, not sure?'

'How long ago did he leave?'

'Not long after you went, truth be told.'

'Thanks.' Marshall ran back through the B&B until he was outside.

Elliot was already out, stabbing a finger at the uniforms. 'You, you, you and you. You are going to hunt for him, up and down the coast.' She pointed at Struan. 'You're going to take charge of that, okay?'

'Sure thing, gaffer.' Struan walked off, shooting a wink at Marshall. 'Good luck breaking the news to the DCI about how you let a serial killer go again...'

12

Gashkori was perched on top of the bench now, facing out. Right foot twitching, left knee jigging, thumbs tapping at his phone. He spotted Marshall's approach, put his phone away, then clapped his hands together and jumped down. 'Rob, I just want to be clear on one thing. I'm not angry with you. Mistakes happen and you couldn't have known. I'm just disappointed we don't have him.'

Marshall stopped a few metres away, wary he was going to get punched. 'Is that so...'

'Of course. I mean, it's totally understandable. You're a headshrinker and not a real cop. You didn't know to drill down into his statement earlier. Or leave someone watching him. I get it, Rob. Really I do. And like I said, I don't blame you.'

Marshall sucked in a deep breath and tried to stop himself from saying – or doing – something he'd regret.

Or later have to rely on in court.

Keep it factual.

Avoid any emotion.

He unclenched his fists, tried to will his heart back to under a hundred BPM. 'I've arranged a flag on Sylvester's plates and a trace on his phone. His car hasn't triggered a camera yet. His phone's off now, but if it gets turned back on again, we'll know where he is.'

Gashkori looked over at the cliffs. 'Assuming it's not in the North Sea.'

'I agree that's the most likely outcome, sir. I'm assuming it's a burner, so I'm not holding too much faith in it, but—'

'I'd say that's wise.'

'—*but* my experience as a police officer has shown me the value of doing the basics, no matter how futile they seem.'

'Right. Your experience.' Gashkori sat back on the bench like a normal person would, chuckling away, arms folded. Smug prick held up some paperwork. 'Rob, while you were away, I've been catching up on your old cases relating to Sylvester. Spoke to a few of the investigating officers, SIO to SIO. Two of them have retired and were a bit tricky to get hold of, but two are still serving and were very happy to talk to me. And by talk to me, I mean pass the buck on.'

'That's a good idea.'

'Just trying to get my arms around the story, Rob.' Gashkori narrowed his eyes. 'I'm trying to see how badly you screwed it up in the past. Neither had a kind word to say about you.'

'That figures.' Marshall had to stuff his hands in his pockets. 'Sir, with all due respect, I wasn't a cop back then and we were ordered to keep a distance from the police.'

'Actually, that's a good point. As a headshrinker you weren't much of a cop and as a cop, you're not much of a headshrinker. Jack of all trades, master of none. From what I gather, you were sufficiently involved for Holly Fenwick to have your phone number.'

'We've been over this, sir. She somehow fixated on me.' Marshall shrugged. 'Maybe she thought I was a weak link, I don't know. I sat in on some interviews with her. Police interviews are different to the broad-spectrum interviews we'd employ in the world of psychology.'

'Sounds like pretentious twaddle to me.'

'We take a scientific approach with ours, rather than relying on belittling someone.'

Gashkori laughed. 'Belittling someone. Right.'

'But I wasn't the lead consultant on the case. I advised on it, sure, sat in on those interviews with Holly, at her request. Spoke to her on the phone a few times. I even conducted a couple with her. But I didn't pull together most of the profile.'

'You worked on the profile?'

'Certain sections. A document like that isn't the work of one mind. We have strategies and techniques. Delegation. Cross-reference, peer review. We all look at each other's work to make sure the document as a whole is coherent and consistent.'

'But you were directly involved?'

'And I wish I was more involved in the case, because I would've made sure Sylvester was prosecuted for what he did. It was the cops who dropped the ball, not the profilers.'

'So you think he killed these women?'

'I do, but the age-old problem is the cops never felt they had enough evidence to that effect.'

'Evidence schmevidence.' Gashkori cracked his knuckles. 'While you were dithering, I got a call from Ash Paton. Bit crap that the resource you begged me for has to come directly to me, isn't it?'

Marshall didn't respond.

'Anyway. She's finished up at St Abb's Head. Managed to speak to the family staying in the holiday cottage, but nobody recognised Sylvester.'

Marshall instinctively looked north, like he could see the old lighthouse from here. 'You think the alibi is bollocks?'

'Not sure. Hard to say.' Gashkori ran a hand across the

stubble on his head. 'Just because they didn't see him, doesn't mean he wasn't there.'

'True.'

'Anyway.' Gashkori sucked air across his teeth. 'I asked DI Taylor to track down Kayleigh's family in Australia. Turns out Ash Paton was already on it.'

'Aye, I asked her to. Still waiting to hear back. Right?'

'Right. She's coming along as a cop.' Gashkori held Marshall's gaze, like he was expecting him to challenge him on that point.

'She'll go far, I suspect.' Marshall heard some rumbling from behind, so he turned around.

The knackered pool Audi was rolling towards them, with Ash Paton behind the wheel. She got out and didn't even kill the engine. 'Sir!' She was looking right at Marshall. 'Sylvester's Volvo has been clocked entering the A1 and heading towards Berwick.'

Gashkori barged Marshall out of the way. 'So why are you here and not in pursuit?'

'Because it disappeared, sir. Got on A1 at Eyemouth, heading south, but it didn't reach Berwick. Or still hasn't.'

'So it could be anywhere in the Borders?'

'Could be heading into England on the A68, sir. No ANPR cameras on that until Darlington. Could be heading up to Edinburgh, but there are cameras in Pathhead and Dalkeith. And there's nothing west along the A72.'

'And I take it he hasn't triggered them?'

'Correct.'

'Jesus suffering fuck.' Gashkori collapsed back against the bench. He jabbed a finger at her. 'Find it.'

'Uniform are scouring the shires for it, sir.' Paton held his gaze. 'But the reason I'm here and not over there is Trev sent me through Kayleigh's telephony. I had a quick glance through it.'

'Go on...'

'Kayleigh called a number last night at eight o'clock. A number that's flagged on the system.' She looked at Marshall. 'David Sylvester's.'

Another piece of the jigsaw puzzle slotted into place.

Marshall felt like he'd been kicked in the balls and punched in the guts. 'Shit.'

Gashkori scowled. 'So she called him?'

'This tracks with his old MO, sir.' Marshall's brain was going faster than his mouth could keep up with. Ideas firing off left, right and centre. 'DI Elliot's report of them being seen together in the café in St Abbs shows there's a relationship. But this shows it's even closer than that. But that's how he worked, sir. He befriended the women, then he left the town and struck, giving some cover. Sylvester knew all of the victims from daily interactions. Some even called him. He explained it's because they were friends, that the women always gave him their numbers because he wasn't a threatening man.'

'And you believed him?'

'Of course not. But we couldn't speak to the victims, could we? They were dead. Nobody else knew about the calls between them and Sylvester.'

'There was one victim you could speak to.' Gashkori glowered at Marshall. 'What did Holly say?'

'That's how she got my number. I persuaded her to pass it over in exchange for mine. Then we could drill into her telephony. Or rather, the Northumbria police forensics officers could.'

'This call last night, though...' Gashkori walked around the bench in a tight circle. 'We have no idea what was said, do we? They could've been discussing *EastEnders* or the football or anything.'

Marshall shrugged. 'But maybe it was an invite for him to come around in the morning. Maybe he even went there last night?'

'Nope.' Gashkori scowled. 'Uniform have no reports around that time or before Holly's arrival this morning.'

'Doesn't rule it out, though. Maybe he stayed overnight and something happened in the morning.'

Gashkori shook his head, hard and heavy. 'Truth is, we don't know. None of us do. Could be a lot of things. Maybe he turned her down and she threw herself off the cliff. Who knows, but it looks like you've got your wish, Inspector. We have a potential serial killer to investigate.'

'It's hardly my wish, sir. I'd rather—'

'Shhh, I'm not finished talking yet. I'll let Taylor know he's in charge of the crime scene while Elliot hunts for Sylvester.' Gashkori grabbed Marshall by the arm, bony fingers digging into his flesh. 'You and me, Robert, are going to speak to Kayleigh in hospital.'

13

When Marshall had been based down here in the Borders, it used to feel like he was in this place every single day, but it'd been the best part of a year since he'd last visited the Borders General Hospital.

All thanks to Gashkori pushing him out to pasture in a field just outside Glasgow.

Gashkori charged along the corridor, hands in pockets, head tilted forward. A man on a mission.

Marshall had to skip every couple of steps to keep up with him.

Gashkori stopped and Marshall almost collided with him.

Jen Marshall was standing outside A&E, hands on her hips, the navy uniform of a senior charge nurse smeared with something off-white. Hair scraped back, a real feral look in her eyes. She glanced at Gashkori, then directly at her twin brother. A slight reddening puffed up her cheeks. 'Hey, Rob.'

'Hey, you.' Marshall hugged her and she felt like a wood burner that'd been heating all day with a constant supply of logs. 'You're burning up. Have you got Covid or something?'

'I'm just a wee furnace, Rob. That's all. Always have run hot, eh? Unlike you, you cold tattie.'

Marshall broke off from her embrace.

Jen gave Gashkori a polite nod. 'Good to see you both.'

Aye, there was something going on between them.

Marshall smiled at his sister. 'Still wondering why Ryan wanted Kayleigh brought here.'

'It's pretty simple, Rob. I've had bad experiences in the Berwick hospital. Anything more than a scratched cheek and they bugger it up. And I've had great experience here. Quieter and the trauma unit sees a lot of action because of all the big roads nearby, with cars driven by idiots.' Gashkori checked his watch. 'Look, I'm bursting for the toilet, so give me a minute.'

Marshall watched him scuttle off, then smiled at his sister. 'What's going on between you?'

'Me and *Ryan*? Nothing.'

'Bullshit, Jen. He's staying in my old flat above your garage since I moved out and—'

'Do you still see Thea?'

Marshall frowned at the interruption. So that was how she was playing it... 'Hasn't she told you whether she has or hasn't seen me?'

'That's a low blow.' Jen stared at her fingernails, the colour almost matching her uniform. 'Little madam barely speaks to me.'

And Marshall knew all about it...

'Aye, I see Thea every week, if we're both free.' Marshall held her gaze. 'Come on, Jen, tell me the truth – are you seeing Ryan?'

'None of your business.' Jen gritted her teeth. 'Remember you're having dinner with me and our father on Wednesday night, right?'

Marshall felt something deep inside clench tight. 'I'd forgotten. Will Mum be there?'

'She's in Palma, remember?'

'Oh, right. Aye.'

'Don't you speak to her?'

'I'd love to be able to get a word in, Jen.'

'Aye, sure. Listen, this has been in the diary since February. If you're blowing us out, then just say.'

'It's totally fine. I'll be there with bells on.'

'Just your clothes. And Kirsten, that's all I ask.' She screwed up her eyes. 'We can do it in Edinburgh, if that's easier?'

'No, I suspect I'll be near the Borders anyway with this case, so let's do it in the Clovenfords Hotel.'

'See? You do remember...'

Gashkori walked back over, drying his hands on his trousers. 'Remember what?'

Jen glared at her brother. 'Nothing.'

Gashkori shifted his gaze between them, eyes narrowed. Had that *look* people often gave Jen and Marshall as twins. It freaked them out and they weren't even identical. 'Okay... So. Any dice with Kayleigh?'

'Nope, not even a coin toss.' Jen shook her head. 'Kayleigh suffered two serious injuries. First, the knife wound to her arm is easily treated. But she also received a significant head trauma, presumably from hitting the rocks. We've administered mannitol to help reduce the swelling to the brain and induced a coma to keep the strain to the least. The next forty-eight to seventy-two hours will decide if she awakens or...'

Gashkori grinned. 'Or if she's a turnip?'

'Crude, but correct. No sugar-coating this, Ryan. The internal bleeding is extensive, so it's possible she might die.'

Gashkori collapsed back against the wall. 'That's not ideal, is it?'

'Not ideal, no. Wish I could let you see her, Ryan, but there's nothing to see. She's...' Jen shook her head. 'A turnip, like you say. There's a body, but the lights aren't on. They might come back or they might switch off for good.' She shrugged. 'And that's where we are.'

'Okay, thanks.' Gashkori stared at Marshall. 'Rob, I had a think in the wee boys' room. Think I finally agree with you about something. The criminal profile is important.'

Marshall was suspicious of Damascene conversions, especially when they happened at a urinal. 'Why's that?'

'Investigative tunnel vision. Want to be absolutely sure this Sylvester lad is your killer.'

'He's not mine. He's yours if anything.'

'Sure.' Gashkori play-punched his shoulder. 'Can you bugger off back to the belfry and update the old one?'

14

S truan hated his life.

Being forced to babysit someone, when the real work was happening elsewhere. How was he supposed to be made a DI if he was just doing this shit work for a clown like Taylor? Should've been him here and Struan out doing the actual work.

Ach, he knew he needed to be patient. Like his old man said, what's for you won't go past you.

Sometimes felt like a sixteen-wheeler was what was heading his way. Broken brakes. Carrying tons of concrete.

Being Acting DI for the best part of a year had been magic, but being back to the stripes of a DS was a bit crappy in some ways. Having less pressure and a shitload less admin wasn't bad, mind.

Holly perched on the edge of the sofa, staring into space. Arms folded, legs crossed at the ankles.

Probably all an act. He'd seen this before. Someone milking the attention, like his mum would. Now his dad was doing the same, all just to get his attention. To get his food. To get his drink. To wipe his arse.

Ach, get over yourself, Struan Liddell. The lassie's been through hell and you're judging her? Everything she's said has come true, maybe time to turn on the charm...

Struan sat opposite her and waited for eye contact. Took a good while – the window looked out onto the high street in Reston. A train must've just come in because it looked like the M25 out there, full of slow-moving cars. Bingo, she looked over at him. 'Hiya, Holly.' He tried a sympathetic smile, but sometimes it looked like a sexy leer or so people said. Not that he was sure a leer could be sexy... 'I need to ask you a few questions, okay?'

She wouldn't look at him again.

Toby was sitting next to her on the sofa. One of those guys with a weak chin. Like his mouth just sort of blended into his wobbly neck. Not that he was fat, either, just... Ugly? Face like a slapped trout.

Toby made eyes at the door.

Struan didn't need to be told twice, so he walked out into the hallway.

Toby nudged the door shut. 'Alrighty...'

Struan kept his eyes on Holly through the glass. 'What's up?'

Toby smiled. 'So, uh, here's the thing? She gets like this. All catatonic like that. Jamie doesn't know how to handle her.'

'Her boyfriend?'

'*Correctamundo.*'

'But you do?'

'I do. It's all to do with her trauma, you know? I had a girlfriend who'd been through similar and it broke her. Very difficult to deal with, but I developed techniques.' Toby had a faraway look in his eyes. 'Right now, Holly's revisiting her experience. She's shut down.'

'That can't be nice for her.'

'No.' Toby looked over at Struan. 'What do you want to talk to her about?'

'It's good news, actually. Kayleigh survived.'

'Oh, shit. Seriously?'

'I mean, she's in a really bad way. Induced coma and all that jazz. But the water broke her fall. She's in hospital down by Melrose. They're hoping she might recover.'

'Shit. Okay.' Toby walked back through and sat next to Holly on the sofa. 'Alrighty...' He clasped her hand. 'Hol?'

She looked around at him, frowning.

'Got some good news. Kayleigh survived.'

'Kayleigh?'

'That's whose caravan you saw *him* in.'

'Oh.' She frowned. 'She's not dead?'

'Nope. DS Liddell here says she's in hospital.'

'Oh my.' She looked over at Struan. 'Thank you.'

'I haven't done anything. But I do have a few questions to ask you?'

And she went again, staring into space.

Aye, Struan hated his life.

15

'Okay, Struan, you do that.' Elliot ended the call and put up her umbrella. Had been so promising earlier but now it was chucking it down. Proper rain, long shards of hard water.

She looked over at the caravan, still being worked on by forensics techs trying to figure out if there were any angles they hadn't explored.

Harsh truth – it was now a crime scene, where someone had been brutally assaulted, spilling their blood and resulting in their attempted murder.

Kayleigh Rothbury.

AKA Rainbow bloody Sunshine.

An Australian lassie spending a gap year in a brutal Scottish winter.

Her birth name was local enough, in the hinterland between Edinburgh and Newcastle. Pretty sure electricity was invented near Rothbury or something. She hadn't paid attention on the school trip there, anyway.

And Kayleigh had done nothing to deserve what Sylvester did to her.

None of them had.

But Kayleigh was the one fighting for her life in the hospital.

Sounded as brutal as the weather just now, at least according to Gashkori's spin on things. Knife wound to the arm, which explained the blood in the caravan. Clonked head, which explained the induced coma.

And still she had no bloody idea where Sylvester was.

Jolene trudged over, looking like her football team had just been battered by local rivals. Glowering at the granite clouds over their heads. 'Ma'am.'

Elliot tilted her head to the side. 'You okay there, Jo?'

Jolene wouldn't make eye contact as she shuffled under the brolly. 'Just been speaking to Kayleigh's neighbours again, trying to pin down precisely what happened this morning. We've got a massive gap between Kayleigh waking up and her getting chucked off the cliff.'

'Hang on. Someone saw her wake up?'

'Saw the lights go on.' Jolene shook her head. 'But they saw nothing after that. Heard nothing, either.'

'Never ceases to amaze me how someone can get their arm opened up by a knife and nobody hears anything.'

Jolene gave a deep sigh. 'We've still got so many gaps and nothing to plug them with.'

'Look, Jo, this isn't going to be a quick and easy case, okay? Try to keep focused on moving everything forward and we'll get there. Alright?'

'Sure, I'll try, but...' Jolene flared her nostrils. 'How's Struan getting on finding Sylvester?'

'He's not.' Elliot broke off eye contact. 'He just called me, said he's been sitting with Holly at her place in Reston. Said she's still really cagey and saying nothing. Like she's the one in a coma, you know? But he's developed a good rapport with Toby, the sound guy who seems to do all the interviewing.

Sounds like he's getting her to talk, but it's like pulling teeth from a dragon's mouth. His words, not mine.'

'Do you need me to—'

'Sarge?' DC Jim McIntyre jumped down from a caravan. Elliot hadn't seen the big lump arrive. Now it was a murder – or an attempted one – the whole of Gashkori's team were out and about, even the troublesome ones like McIntyre. Or just the un-favoured ones. 'Just spoken to another neighbour.' He was twitching like a junkie itching for a fix. 'She wasn't in earlier, just got back. Said she's seen Kayleigh and Sylvester in a café.'

'Aye, we know.' Jolene rolled her eyes. 'The one in St Abbs.'

McIntyre shook his head violently. 'No, this is one in Eyemouth. Breda's Bakes.'

Elliot looked around at Jolene but she was already running towards the car. She tossed the umbrella to McIntyre. 'Take that.' Then raced after Jolene. 'You know it?'

Jolene stopped to open the pool car's door. 'Aye, just on the high street.'

Elliot got in the car and Jolene was driving off by the time she clicked her seatbelt in. 'This might be nothing, right?'

'Right. But we've got no choice but to hotfoot it down there.' Jolene sped off down the hill, her wipers going like the clappers. She flashed her lights at the cheeky sod who was trying to come towards them, forcing him to pull up onto the verge, in lieu of a parking bay. 'Wanker, you just stay there...'

'You okay there, Jo?'

'I'm fine.'

'It's just... You seem a bit distracted.'

'It's all good. It's just... I used to come here as a kid. Grandma had a caravan here, so we'd be here most summers. Weird how... ' She took the left turn onto the high street without slowing. Someone honked their horn at her. 'I'd no idea what happened to Holly happened *here*. Remember the story from the papers at the time. She's a similar age to me, Andi. It could've been me.'

'I know those thoughts, Jo. Male cops don't really get them. Sure, most crime happens to blokes, caused by blokes. But those are numpties, who are nothing like most cops. The crimes that happen to women could happen to *any* woman. And that's what melts your brain. But you can't beat yourself up about any of that. It's happened and there's nothing that'll change what did or didn't happen. Wasn't your time or place, no need for survivor's guilt here. The only thing you can control is doing your job and that means helping find this weirdo serial killer arsehole and bringing him to justice. Aye?'

'I hear you.'

But whether she listened...

Jolene pulled up outside Breda's Bakes, next door to the Rialto café and opposite the good chippy's smaller brother. The high street was so narrow it was like the buildings were huddling tight against the fierce wind. 'Never been to this place.'

'Me neither. Never even heard of it.' Elliot got out and raced through the rain.

Calm down...

It's not like he's been spotted...

She slowed as she followed Jolene inside.

The place was the polar opposite of the one in St Abbs. Urban chic with a high-end espresso machine hissing away below a wide chalkboard advertising hundreds of coffee variations and flavours, each with pairing options for the cakes and bakes. The joke was the owner was a coffee sommelier, but Elliot didn't think it was that far from the pretentious truth. Only two types of savoury food – sandwiches and stews, with today's a vegan chilli.

In Eyemouth...

Six customers, each at their own table. All working on laptops, with headphones on.

Elliot's phone rang.

Gashkori calling...

Great...

She hung back and let Jolene get on with it. 'Afternoon, sir?'

'Just at the hospital. Not getting to speak to the victim. Coma.'

'Right. Hear that.'

'Sure. Listen, Struan called me. Said you're not running the show?'

Sneaky bastard...

'I was. I am. I've been trying to get a hold of him but he's gone off—'

'He's at the caravan park just now and saw you rush off.'

The rain thundered against the window, the inside steamed up from the coffee maker. 'We're investigating a potential lead on his movements, sir.'

'Didn't think to tell me?'

Jolene stepped back and let a woman owner past. Her polo shirt read 'Keith's Bread', but her name badge read 'Breda'. Forties and small, but with an energy to her.

'I'll let you know how it pans out.' Elliot killed the call and walked over to Jolene and Breda. She didn't say anything, just observed their interaction.

Breda waved a hand at the table. 'Well, this is his stuff.'

The table had two teapots, a plate with brownie crumbs and a brand-new jigsaw still in shrink-wrap.

'I think he went to the toilet.' Breda pointed over past the espresso machine. 'No wonder, given how much tea he's drunk.'

'Thanks.' Jolene went over and tried the door. Didn't look at Elliot – they both felt the same. Hearts pounding, adrenaline spiking. 'Mr Sylvester? David? It's the police.' She pushed inside.

Elliot smiled at Breda. 'You see him in here often?'

'He's been in a few times with that lassie your colleague asked about. Once a week, maybe. Usually a Saturday. On his own every other day.'

So that explained what he was up to on the days he wasn't in the café in St Abbs...

Jolene came back, her face all red. 'Ma'am, he's climbed out of the window!'

'Shite!' Elliot shot out of the café and sprinted over to the side lane. A locked gate at the back, with a three-metre-high fence. 'This is the only way he could've come.'

She looked up and down the high street.

She'd been looking outside when she was on the phone to Gashkori and hadn't seen anything, so he must've headed towards the harbour. 'You go that way!' She pointed back towards the caravan park, then ran along the main street, her feet slapping off the slick pavement, heading towards the harbour – and the road out of the town.

The street rounded a corner and she caught sight of Sylvester's gangly form, walking ahead of her, hunched against the downpour. He turned around and his eyes bulged. Then he shot off into a straight-armed run.

Elliot gave chase, but each stride didn't get her any closer to catching up with him.

Sylvester bombed left at the church.

Crap, he was heading for the harbour.

Elliot sped up, passing the town's museums, but she just knew she wouldn't catch him by the end of the street. 'Police! Stop!'

Sylvester ran right over to the water's edge and turned to face her, the twin guy ropes behind him bouncing in the stiff breeze.

'Police!' Elliot ran towards him but stopped dead just short, like a dog chasing a deer and actually catching up with it – what the hell was she going to do now? She snapped out her baton and took a step closer to him, the rain slamming down, running down her nose, getting into her mouth. 'You're coming with me.'

Sylvester jerked forward and punched her shoulder.

Elliot's foot slipped and she went down hard on the pavement, dropping her baton onto the road.

Sylvester crashed a foot into her side as she tried to get up.

She slipped on the greasy surface and got tangled in the guy ropes. Her fingers gripped them, the rope burning against her skin. She caught sight of the narrow jetty below and the even narrower gap of ice-cold water between it and the harbour wall.

Sylvester stared at her like she was his lab experiment.

Another swift kick and Elliot tumbled backwards.

The filthy harbour water flew towards her.

Her shoulder smacked against the jetty.

The cold jolted through her as she went under the surface.

16

Marshall strolled across the car park through the driving rain towards the glittering building everyone called Gartcosh, or the Scottish Crime Campus as it was formally known. He waited for the three suited men to leave before entering.

The atrium was like a brand-new university building, shiny and gleaming, not yet soiled by slovenly cops, probably because they only occupied half of it – maybe a quarter when you excluded the Police Scotland forensics analysts. The usual filthy animals were on their best behaviour, keeping the other half clean for the NCA, the Procurator Fiscal's team and – for some reason – HMRC.

At least having the PF nearby saved a drive through shitty traffic on the abysmal road network around here – two-lane car parks.

Still absolutely baffled Marshall that Scotland's two major cities, both in the UK's top ten, were connected by a shoddy dual carriageway, when there were three lanes heading from Glasgow to Carlisle, and only one from Edinburgh to Newcastle.

Aye... Gashkori had got to him.

He thumbed the button for the lift, then remembered his sister's stern advice, so he took the stairs. One at a time, slowly does it, checking his phone as he climbed, trying not to break a sweat.

Just one message he needed to bother with, weirdly enough from Jen:

> Seriously, if you need to rearrange or meet in Edinburgh, I wish you'd just say, you dickhead.

Marshall stopped at the first-floor landing and tapped out a reply:

> Tuesday in Clovenfords is totally fine. Looking forward to it.

He set off towards the door to their office space, then it hit him. He stopped and tapped out another message:

> *Wednesday, not Tuesday!

> And I am a dickhead. Guilty as charged.

Aye, he'd be hearing about that for a wee while...

He swiped his card through the reader and walked through the door, shaking his head at the arrogance of the name:

Behavioural Sciences Unit

Imagine calling your unit of two and a half people after the famous FBI one from *The Silence of the Lambs*...

Wishful thinking – fake it until you make it.

Marshall stopped in the corridor. His office lights were on. Again. He nudged the door open, then stepped in.

DCI James Pringle was sitting at his desk, his erect posture like he still did a lot of rowing and yoga, rather than literally no exercise. His hair was lank and greying, wide curtains framing his face. Almost long enough to get chucked off the force. Almost. He looked up and frowned at Marshall. 'Afternoon, Rob. What's your favourite D:Ream song?'

'My *what*?'

'You remember that song from the New Labour campaigns. "Things Can Only Get Better"?'

Marshall slumped in the chair opposite. 'Not really.'

'They used it for the 1997 election. Tony Blair and Gordon Brown and John Prescott and the other one all danced to it at the conference before.'

'Still don't really remember it, sorry.'

'Come on! They won a landslide in 1997!'

'I was ten, sir. More interested in Pokémon and keeping my Tamagotchi alive.'

'*Ten*?'

'Election was in May, right? I was born in 1986. Birthday in October. You can do the sums, can't you?' Marshall grabbed the second-last apple from the bag in front of Pringle and crunched into it. So sour it felt like it was melting his tooth enamel. 'Why are you—'

'Which is your favourite, though? Is it that song? Or maybe "Shoot Me with Your Love"? Or "U R the Best Thing"?' Pringle cackled. 'I love it when bands do that. Letters instead of words. Usually happened before texting.' He rolled his eyes. 'You're probably too young for that. We used to have to type words using numbers.'

'I remember that, sir. Had a Nokia—'

'Prince did that all the time. "I Would Die 4 U" and – oh, of course – "Nothing Compares 2 U"! How could I forget? Shame the lassie died, eh?' Pringle clicked his fingers. 'What was her name?'

'Sinead O'Connor.' Marshall tried to lead him back to one

stray topic rather than let him branch further out on the tree of bollocks. 'I didn't know D:Ream had more than one song.'

'You know nothing!' Pringle took his last apple from the bag. 'You owe me one, Robert.' He sat back and nibbled at the skin, then took a big bite and let the juice run down his cheeks.

Put Marshall right off his own.

Pringle rubbed at his mouth. 'How was Edinburgh?'

'Not one of ours, Jim.'

'Sure?'

'Pretty sure.'

'You were away a while. Did you get lost?'

Marshall bit into his apple and sucked up the juice. 'Got a call and had to make a trip down to Eyemouth.'

'Oh, that's my old patch, you know?'

'I do, sir. I used to work for you down there.'

'Of course you did. Of course.'

'Our old chums have picked up the trail of a serial killer.'

'I'm very pleased for them.' But Pringle's focus was on the computer screen. 'I'm sure Ryan's up to his earballs.'

Marshall motioned at his keyboard, like he'd need to actually use it to do some work. 'Sir, I need my machine.'

'Sure.'

'I've got to update the profile we did a few years ago for this same killer.'

Pringle was still focusing on the screen, his lips twitching as he read something. 'Disaster, for Scotland.'

'Sir, it's real work on an active investigation. Doesn't that excite you?'

'Rob.' Pringle looked over at him with exhausted eyes, streaked with red. 'Nothing excites me these days. I'm dead from the waist up.'

'I'm sorry to hear that, sir.'

'Are you really?'

'Of course I am. You're a friend, Jim. I hate seeing you like this.'

Pringle looked away, swallowing hard. 'It's getting worse, Rob. Surely even you can see that?'

'Even me?'

'I don't mean anything by it.' Pringle drummed his fingers on the desk. 'I think I'd have to plump for "Things Can Only Get Better".'

Back to that again.

Marshall felt like he'd been making some progress, seeing down the deep core of the man, but nope. Back to the tree of bollocks.

Marshall dropped his apple into the bin. Thankfully it had a cover so it wouldn't stink out the room. 'Why are you asking about D:Ream?'

'You know.'

'Do I?'

'Of course.'

Marshall had no idea. 'And why are you in here and not your own office?'

'Now, now, Robert, *that* is something you do know.'

'Jim, we've been over this a few times. The computers are the same everywhere in this building. You don't log into that machine, but to a server somewhere. So they all gave out the same information.'

'Sure. Sure. That's what you think.' Pringle chucked his half-eaten apple in the bin. 'I'll go back to my own machine, then, and see what lies it spits out compared to yours.' He got up and walked off, without explaining anything.

Marshall took his own chair, now all warmed up. He had to log Pringle out of his account, then log in as himself.

Bloody hell, the dementia was getting worse.

And he had no idea what he was going to do about it. Or why it was up to him of all people.

A knock at the door.

Hardeep Singh stood there, laptop under his arm, scratching at his beard, his hair tucked inside a black turban. 'Hi, sir. Can I have a word?'

'Sure. Pull up a pew.'

Hardeep perched on the edge of the chair. 'It's two things, sir.'

'Please. I keep telling you to call me Rob.'

'Sure, sir. Of course. First, it's about my PhD...'

'Remember that I'm not allowed to help you on that, certainly not in office hours.'

'Oh, sorry. I'm dreadfully sorry.'

Marshall gave a smile. 'But if you were to, say, come back *after* office hours, I might be able to chat it through with you.'

Hardeep tapped his nose. 'Ah, I get it.'

'More than happy to help, Hardeep, but I've got a profile to rework. Kind of a breaking news thing.'

'Oh. That's the other thing. After you called me, I dug out the old files to start going through them. I've got them all on my laptop, ready to start decompiling for the revisions.'

'Good work.'

'But here's the issue, sir. Rob.' Hardeep looked as if he'd swallowed a cheese and liquorice sandwich. 'This case does relate to my PhD. Three of the victims feature.'

'Just three? I see, well. If you don't tell, I won't.'

'Tell what?' She Who Cannot Be Named was standing in the doorway, shifting her focus between them. Power suit and standing in a full power stance, her greying ponytail dangling over one shoulder. 'What's going on?'

Marshall smiled at her. 'Ma'am, I've been trying to get hold of you.'

'And I told you, Robert, the reason I bounced those calls is all work matters should go through DCI Pringle, as your direct superior.'

Marshall glanced at Hardeep. 'That's a matter we need to discuss.'

'I'd hoped we could delay that chat longer.' She sat down next to Hardeep. 'Okay, well. I got your message, so I will try to action it this evening. First, how did it go in Edinburgh?'

'Hard to say, ma'am. I don't think it's connected to the Glasgow case.'

'That's good news. But when you say, "I don't think", that makes me think you're covering your arse. How confident are you?'

'At least eighty percent. And I'm covering everyone's arse here. We deal in probabilities on this side of the fence. There's no black and white, just shades of grey. But that case looks like a tragic accident versus a definite murder. And there are no shared attributes you'd pair with a serial offender. Nothing appears to have been taken from the victim or left on them. But to smooth it all over, I'll look over the post-mortem and review the case with one of the Edinburgh detectives once they've had a chance to conclude their investigation.'

'Okay. That sounds good.' She Who Cannot Be Named jotted something down in her notebook. 'In the meantime, how about we take care of that other matter?' She closed her notebook and tossed it onto the desk. 'Let me get this straight, DCI Gashkori has asked you to dust off the old profile relating to Operation Tuesday Steeplejack with a view to updating it with what happened in Eyemouth today. Correct?'

'That's right.' Marshall had forgotten the codename for the cross-force investigation. Meaningless and bland like they should be. 'Are you happy for me to pick up that work?'

'Rob, that kind of thing is precisely why I pushed to set up the Behavioural Sciences Unit. Just wish I had more funding to allocate more than three resources to it.' She smiled at Hardeep. 'Well, two and a half.'

Pringle might've been one, but he barely did a tenth of the

actual work. And that usually subtracted time from Marshall's one.

Then she gave a real politician's grin. 'Now, do you need any help from me?'

'Not just now, but I'm warning you now that one of the things we'll be doing is searching for additional victims that aren't currently allocated to the case. Hidden ones.'

She scowled at Marshall. 'Why's that a problem?'

'Because it'll possibly mean pinning extra cases to DCI Gashkori's investigation. He's already got the twelve unsolved from Sylvester's previous spate.'

'That's all totally fine. As long as Ryan solves the case. And so long as you can help him solve this. Like Ryan said, this should be an open-and-shut case, right?'

'That's a bit of a stretch of the truth, but I'll certainly do all I can.'

'Good, good.' She Who Cannot Be Named stood up and slapped Hardeep on the arm. 'Sounds like you've got your work cut out for you, young man.'

Hardeep nodded. 'I'm on top of it, ma'am.'

'Good, good.' She returned the nod, then grimaced. 'All we need to do is track down David Sylvester, then bring him in for questioning.' She rapped her knuckles off the table. 'I'll get out of your way for now. Rob, can you and I reconvene before close of play today, vis à vis progress?'

17

Marshall kept glancing at the clock on the wall. There – it ticked over to seven o'clock. This job might've mostly been an empty and futile exercise, but it certainly filled out the days.

She Who Cannot Be Named sat behind her desk, tapping her pencil off her teeth. 'Okay, Rob, so this is a decent start. I'm impressed.'

'It's only a couple of hours of work, ma'am, and virtually all of it dates back to Operation Tuesday Steeplejack. All I've done is add some details pertaining to victimology from Kayleigh Rothbury and to remove some of the... more eccentric aspects.'

'Oh?'

'Jacob Goldberg had his own way of doing things, ma'am. Fairly unorthodox. I haven't really changed much of the content, but I've removed the cruft that was clogging it up. It's why you can read it in five minutes and get everything from it, rather than having to have it explained to you by a patronising berk like me.'

She smirked at him. 'I thought it was because I was so talented.'

'Well, most officers would take twenty minutes to read the first page.'

'That's good to hear. Flatterer.'

Marshall pushed his chair back. 'Okay, I'm going to get some food, then I'll do some more work later.'

'Sounds good.' She Who Cannot Be Named tossed the document over, covered in more scribbles than anyone should've been able to produce in such a short space of time. And legible too. 'There you go. My notes might prove helpful.'

'Thanks.'

'I appreciate your patience, Rob. You've been here a year now, but this is the first time you've had to do something in anger that isn't just rocking up at a crime scene and persuading an SIO with stars in his eyes that he's not looking at the next Dennis Nilsen or Fred West. It's testament to your persistence that you haven't resigned.'

He'd come close... More than once...

'Thanks.' Marshall gathered up the documents and got to his feet. 'I'll see you tomorrow.'

'Eight o'clock, sharp.'

Marshall winced. 'Right. That doesn't give me much time to make many changes.'

'I know, but this isn't just reviewing a stack of old documents relating to cold cases. This is a live investigation. So let's use it as a training exercise, a chance to get to know each other a lot better and to formulate some processes around things. Besides, Ryan's briefing is at seven, which I've agreed you'll attend by video feed.'

Fantastic...

Having his moon face on an iPad screen in front of a room of his old colleagues was just going to be great...

'I'd rather it was audio, then I could work away...' Marshall got to his feet. 'I'll see you tomorrow.'

'Oh, one last thing.' She nodded at the chair.

Marshall took the hint and sat back down. 'What's up?'

'You'll notice I haven't invited Jim to sit in on this.'

'This is what I wanted to discuss. I'm worried about his mental state.'

'Me too. I had a chat with him earlier and... I'm sorry. It must be really hard for you, working under the direct supervision of someone who's lost his marbles.'

Marshall didn't say anything. Didn't even look at her.

'I'm being brutally honest here, Jim was being kept on in a purely admin capacity, but even counting paperclips is beyond him, isn't it?'

'Agreed.'

'I'm wondering if maybe it's time we put Jim in a home.'

Marshall sat back and tried not to think of D:Ream again. Or any number of weird obsessions he'd had. Way more than in his previous post. 'I hear you, ma'am, but I don't think so. At least, not yet.'

'Look, we've both tried to make this work. Jim sold his homes in the Borders to buy a house in Milngavie. You stay with him a couple of nights a week. You look after him, Rob. You are his guardian, after all. But that's incredibly unfair on you. And is that enough for a man with his condition?'

'Sounds like you're saying he shouldn't be working?'

'We might be past that point, yes. I've realised I thought Jim was living the life of that guy in that *Slow Horses* TV show you recommended to me.'

'Go on?'

'You know. Gary Oldman's character. Jackson Lamb. He's a disgraced spy, but they can't get rid of him because of what he knows, so they've shoved him into a back-office job with all the other rejects.'

'Are you saying I'm a reject too?'

'No, of course not. You're a strategic asset. But Jim has been side-lined, it's fair to say. Put in a position of minimal impact. I think it's been wise to keep him close. Keep his brain working. He won't be spilling anything, because his brain is that badly rotten. But maybe it's time to reconsider that. Him still working in the police service isn't what's best for him.'

Marshall sucked in a deep breath. 'Okay, you think about whether he should be working and I'll consider what the consequences of that will be.'

'Me? You're his guardian.'

'I never asked for that.'

'Rob. I recommend we move him on.'

'Okay. Listen, I really need to leave. But I'll have a think about it and we can discuss in the morning.'

'That's all I ask.' She winked at him. 'Have a fun evening. Whatever you're doing.'

18

Elliot stomped back into the kitchen and dumped her bag on the counter. Her shoulder throbbed like it'd been pulled out of the socket, or the socket had crashed into a jetty. Either way, she'd need more physio on the bugger.

And despite the shower at the station, she still had the bubbly ache of water in her ear. Filthy harbour water.

'Mummy!' Her two lads buried her in a lovely cuddle.

She crouched down to embrace it. Embrace them. Shutting her eyes, trying to hide the tears from them.

Harry reeked of deodorant and puberty, but Charlie still had *that* smell to him, the one she missed from all three when they were babies.

Certainly beat the salty stink of the Eye Water meeting the North Sea, despite having changed clothes.

She snuggled in tighter and stayed like that for a few seconds longer than was strictly necessary, but this was the highlight of her day. She eased herself back up to standing, getting another throb in the shoulder for her trouble, and brushed the dampness from around her eyes. 'How's your homework going?'

'Great!' Charlie raced back over to the kitchen table in the corner.

Harry had the slouch of a teenager as he followed.

'There you are.' Mum stood by the sink, drying a glass with a filthy tea towel.

No matter how many times Elliot told her to use the dishwasher as the Good Lord intended...

'Hi, Mum.' Elliot wrapped her in a hug. 'How've they been?'

'Quiet. Diligent.'

'Not usually words I associate with them.' Elliot smiled at her sons. 'What have they been up to?'

'Nothing. They've been good lads for their granny. Doing their homework like I asked them.'

'Thanks, Mum. I appreciate it.' Elliot felt a lump in her throat. Mum wasn't getting any younger and Elliot's need for help was only going to get worse over the next few years. And hopefully the demands would remain one-way until she could get it all back under control. 'Where's Sam?'

'Upstairs in her room.'

'Right. That's good.'

'She said she's heading out, though.' Mum tilted her head to the side. 'Said she's staying the night with her boyfriend?'

'Bloody hell.' Elliot sighed. 'Is she now...?'

'It's not my place to say, but...' *Here we go...* 'If you ask me, Andrea, the wee madam's taking advantage of your situation. Given what's happening, young Samantha is being ... opportunistic.'

'You mean what's happening with Davie?'

'What else?' Mum's voice was a harsh whisper. 'Without her father around, she's running free. Mind what it was like when your father was working up in Aberdeen for a year? And I was at home full-time. Andrea, you're so busy, you just haven't got the time to provide a firm hand.'

Way to make a girl feel great...

'Mum, I hear you. I'm doing the best I can.'

'I know, it's just... I know. Sorry. I shouldn't have said anything.'

'No, you should've done.' Elliot smiled at her mum, despite the burning feeling in her guts and in her nostrils. 'I apprec—'

Sam swept into the room in a whirlwind of perfume and designer clothes, grabbing an apple from the fruit bowl, then swept back out.

'Sam!' Elliot stormed after her. 'Sam!'

She was kicking her shoes on by the door, the laces dangling free. 'What?'

'It's nice to see you too.'

'Cool.' She reached up for her jacket. 'Bye.'

'Not so fast.' Elliot blocked the door. 'Where are you off to?'

'Seeing Tam.'

'But I've bought you a cake?'

'Don't want it.'

'Sam. What's going on?'

'What? What do you mean?'

'You're acting like—'

'—like someone whose dad's in jail? For being corrupt?' Sam shook her head. 'And you *knew*.'

'I didn't know, Sam. Of course I didn't.'

'Bullshit.'

'I had no idea what he was up to.'

'Sure.' Sam rolled her eyes, then glared at Elliot's hands against the door. 'You mind?'

A year ago, Elliot would've run after her, would've visited all of her friends in pursuit of her.

But now...

Now she was so broken down and battered, she didn't have the energy.

She let go of the door handle and stepped aside. 'I want you home by nine, okay?'

'Sure.' Sam walked off without looking back, jumping down all four steps in one go. 'Night.'

Elliot tracked her progression down the drive, then out onto the street, all the way typing on her phone. Then she was gone, lost to the thick hedge blocking the curve around to the main road.

She shut the door and turned around.

Mum was in the hallway, already in her jacket, watching her own daughter. 'You okay there?'

'I'm fine.' Elliot smiled away, despite the churning in her guts. 'Off you go, Mum. Dad will be wanting his tea.'

'Aye, sure. Of course he will.' But she wasn't moving. 'Are you sure you're okay?'

My husband's corruption trial starts tomorrow, what do you think?

But Elliot gave Mum another of those smiles. 'It's all good. Sam's just acting out.'

Mum sighed. 'You were twice as bad at her age.'

'Was I?'

A laugh. 'Oh, aye. Ask your father.'

Like Dad hasn't told me at every available opportunity...

Elliot pecked her on the cheek. 'Love you, Mum. See you tomorrow.'

'You'll be okay getting them to school what with—'

'Aye, I've got a plan.' Elliot opened the door and held it for the second-most important female in her life. 'I'll let you know how it goes.'

Mum brushed her on the arm. 'Good luck.' She grabbed the door handle and eased herself down onto the top step, then took her time getting down the rest of them.

When did you go from jumping down all of the steps to needing to carefully plan your progression?

Mum walked more easily over towards her car, then gave a wee wave before she got in.

Elliot nudged the door shut and let her breath out in a slow hiss. She took a few seconds to process everything, to blot out all the dark thoughts, to put her game face back on. Then she walked back through to the kitchen. 'Ready for your tea, boys?'

'Starving!'

'Can we have pizza?'

'No, you can't.' But Elliot had no idea what to actually give them. Never enough time to cook properly, was there? Except for batch cooking at the weekends, but her cousins and their joint birthday parties got in the way of that on Saturday...

And Sunday was a hungover write-off.

She had a root through all the shite in the freezer, then found a pack of three turkey escalopes that looked okay. A start. Just need some—

Aha, those potatoes Davie cooked the Christmas before last. *Christ.*

Elliot got them out, then shoved the potatoes in the microwave and started heating the oven. She'd get on with chopping some veg to steam in a minute.

She brushed more tears out of her eyes.

Christ... What's happening to me?

She got a glass out of the cupboard and poured herself some of the hair-of-the-dog Rioja she'd opened last night.

It was only Monday, but the week felt like it'd already lasted a few years. And it was only going to get worse.

'Be back in a second, boys.' Elliot grabbed her phone and her glass then stepped outside into the darkness. Not exactly warm, but her body was burning after her dook in the harbour.

She stared at her phone. Amazing she could go from hundreds of messages a week to literally none.

Not that people were judging her for standing by Davie…

She sifted through her contacts, then hit dial. She sat on the bench, which was almost dry enough.

'Andrea?' Marshall's dull voice came out of her speaker into her lughole. 'You okay?'

'Hi, Rob. Take it you heard?'

Sounded like he was driving. 'About what?'

Elliot took a nibble of the wine and savoured the taste for a few seconds. 'I almost caught Sylvester, but he got away when he kicked me into the harbour.'

'Oh, shite. Are you okay?'

'Probably get hepatitis from drinking the water, but I'll survive.' As if on cue, her shoulder gave a dull throb of pain. 'Feel like such an idiot, Rob.'

'I get it. Thing is, Sylvester's in good shape and he's pretty strong. Not the first time he's escaped capture.' Marshall left a pause and the driving sound swelled up. 'Hopefully the last, though.'

'Can't believe he got away.'

'Andrea, there's no crime in running from the police if you've done nothing wrong.'

'Aye, running's fine but assaulting an officer isn't.'

'Sure, but staying and co-operating didn't pay well for him in the past.'

'Robbie, are you *defending* him?'

'No, just trying to get inside his head. That's all.'

'Right. You weirdo. That's not a great place to be.'

'No. No, it's not, but somebody has to.'

She took another glorious drink of the wine and felt a different kind of burning rage through her system. 'Listen, Rob, I've tried calling Pringle, but I'm getting no response from him.'

'Right. What do you want from him?'

'Just a chat. Been a while and this is… Well, it's a total bastard of a week already.'

'I get it.' Marshall sighed. 'Sorry, I don't mean to mother him, it's just... I've had a few interesting interactions today. He's been listening to that D:Ream song from the nineties on a loop, like he's some New Labour super-fan.'

'*D:Ream?*'

'Aye.'

'Christ.' Elliot almost laughed, but the decline in her old boss's mental state had been brutal to witness from a distance – she'd no idea how hard it must've been for Marshall. 'Is he okay?'

'I'm just focusing on looking into stuff for this case, but She Who Cannot Be Named says she's got a decision to make that'll force my hand with Jim.'

Elliot didn't want to question him too hard on that decision. Not her business. And she'd learnt to keep away from things that weren't. 'Have you thought about respite care?'

'I've talked to the place where my granddad's staying. They offer it, but... It feels like there's no coming back from that.'

'Could be just what you need. Both of you.'

'Aye. Could be.'

'Listen, Robbie... About the case. You know I won't be working it tomorrow, right?'

'Because it's Davie's day in court, right?'

'Right.' She finished the glass. 'I'm worried about it, Rob. He's fucking guilty. So fucking guilty. And it's just... Having three kids on my own wasn't something I planned. Mum and Dad are helping... Davie's parents try too, but they're a bit ashamed of what he did... And I feel like I'm losing.'

'CHARLIE!!!'

The scream from inside snapped her to attention. And Christ, she'd been talking way too openly. 'Listen, I'd better get on to their tea.'

'Sure, I've got an appointment.'

Elliot laughed. 'Oh, aye. Dinner with some young lady?'

'Something like that. Catch you later, Andrea.' And he was gone.

Elliot stood up and sucked in a deep breath. She went back inside and had no idea why she'd called him. Or why he'd been so cold and useless.

She wanted to talk to Pringle, but their last chat had been a confused mess.

Despite the shout, both boys were heads down at their homework.

The microwave pinged and she gave the dish a wee shoogle, then stuck it back in. She got the bag of mixed veg out of the freezer, then poured another glass of wine, desperate for that numb feeling.

19

Marshall had managed fifteen years without visiting Glasgow and now it felt like he was there all the time. A constant stream of meetings and appointments, all of them in the city's thin rain.

Rodrigo's Tapas was lit up in the gloomy West End back street, the window blinds half shut. Marshall pushed in through the stiff door. Not many diners inside, but he recognised the shape by the window.

She looked up at him, hair cut short to an elfin bob. A bull's nose ring. Left arm dotted with Celtic tattoos. The difference the best part of a year as a student made... 'Uncle Rob.' Thea stood and wrapped him in a tight hug. 'Thought you wouldn't show?'

Marshall tried to let go of her but she was clinging tight. 'I said I'd see you every week, if you wanted. So here I am.'

She finally let go. 'Thank you, anyway.' She sat down again, the table already covered in small plates. 'Sorry, I ordered. Hope you don't mind. I was starving.'

'Of course I don't mind.' Marshall tipped some patatas bravas onto his plate. 'This looks good.' He took the last of presumably four meatballs. 'You know, most kids became vegans at university, not the other way round.'

'I'm not proud of it.' Thea sipped at her water. 'But it's helped my allergies. Hopefully I can go back at some point.' She ate a slight mouthful of potato. 'How are you doing?'

'Busy day.' Marshall finished chewing the meatball – he could easily go another four, but there was a ton of food here.

A waiter appeared. 'Evening, sir, can I get you a drink?'

'Just a tonic water, please.'

'Ice, lemon?'

'Thanks.' Marshall waited for him to leave then looked at Thea, just as she smeared her chin with tomato sauce. 'Saw your mum today.'

'Right. Great.' Thea wiped at her chin. 'How was she?'

'You know your mum...'

'I do.' Thea skewered half a Spanish omelette with her fork. 'Take it she still doesn't want me to come home?'

'I'm not sure it's that simple.'

'No, but it's not that complicated, is it? Soon as I'm out the door, she's shagging every Tom, Dick and Harry. Last thing she wants is me back home interrupting one of her bunga bunga parties...'

'Come on, I don't think—'

'No, but not being welcome in your own home sucks balls. "Oh, Thea, I don't want anything to upset your education." How about me being able to see my pals from school when we're all home?'

'You know, when I left home and went to Durham uni, I didn't come home for the whole year.'

'Aye, but you're a weirdo. And Granny...'

Marshall laughed. 'True.' He sat back to let the waiter deposit the most elaborate soft drink on the table in front of him. Looked like a fancy cocktail in its spiralling glass. 'Cheers.'

Thea refilled her water from the jug. 'Trouble is, I *want* to come home *some* weekends, but Mum really doesn't want me to. It's hard to take... I mean, I get it. She likes her independence, but... She doesn't care about me.'

'Thea, she shouldn't be making you feel like that.'

'No. Fucking hell, I've stayed at *Dad's* more than hers. And he's a useless twat. I mean... Sure, he's paying my accommodation and living costs, so I'm eternally grateful, but...' She looked deep into Marshall's drink. 'I think the real reason is Mum has a new boyfriend...'

'Oh?'

'You and I didn't meet last weekend, so I'm telling you this now. I was home two weeks ago, staying at Dad's in Cardrona and I got the bus over to see Mum. She's putting away a *lot* of booze. I'm kind of grateful the council don't collect glass in the weekly recycling, so I could see how bad it was. Her cupboard was filled with empty bottles of wine and gin. She said she had to take a call, but she sneaked over to the bottle bank behind the Clovenfords Hotel to get rid of it. I mean... I'm sick fed up of parenting my mother.'

Marshall knew that feeling. Had worn those shoes. Had bought all of the T-shirts and limited edition pink vinyl. 'She's got a busy job, Thea. Try to see things from her point of view.'

'And be less harsh on her? Sure. Right. She's been seeing someone. I think that's why she doesn't want me home.'

Aye, and Marshall had a good idea who.

'Maybe it's safer to just stay here in Glasgow. She's been a mum more than a person and needs to find herself. It's just... It hurts.'

'I get it. But that's not on you. She shouldn't be making you feel like that.'

'No... But... Thing is...' She snorted. 'No, I shouldn't say.'

'Shouldn't say what?'

'Promise not to tell her?'

'I don't know what it is, so I can't promise anything.'

'Right, right.' Thea sipped some water. 'I think Mum's doing coke.'

Marshall dropped his fork and it clattered off the plate, then bounced onto the floor via his trouser leg. 'Cocaine?'

'When she was dumping those bottles, I found some residue in the kitchen behind the toaster.'

'Residue? Sure it wasn't flour or sugar?'

'Neither. I tasted it.'

'Thea, what the hell were you thinking?'

She shrugged. 'It was, like, really bitter and my tongue was numb for a few minutes after.'

Certainly sounded like cocaine to Marshall. 'You shouldn't have done that.' He exhaled slowly. 'Thea...'

'She went mental when she came back in, insisting on cleaning up the whole place.'

Shite.

Trouble with a problem shared was who you shared it with.

Marshall accepted a replacement fork from the waiter. 'Look, I'll have a word with your mother.'

'Not about the coke!'

'No, just a general chat. I'm seeing her this week, so I can—'

'That's not what I wanted.' She crunched back in her chair and looked up at the ceiling. 'I shouldn't have mentioned it to a *cop*. Not everything needs to be fixed; I just needed to say it out loud to another person.'

'Thea, I'm listening as your uncle, not as a police officer. Okay?' Marshall held her gaze until she nodded. 'Do you need any money?'

'I'm good.' Thea rested her fork down on the plate. 'I just needed to talk about this.' She leaned over and pecked him on the cheek. 'Listen, I'm meeting some pals tonight. We're going to see a band in the Merchant City, so I better bugger off.'

'Okay, well. It's been good seeing you.'

'Thank you.' She got up and put on her jacket. 'Oh, did Hardeep speak to you?'

'No, why?'

'Nothing. Just wondered if he might. Him being my tutor and your assistant is a bit weird for both of us.'

'Doesn't have to be.' Aye, Marshall would have to see what that was all about from Hardeep's perspective. 'Who's the band?'

'They're called West End Girls. They totally *slay*.'

'Right. Slay. Are they a Pet Shop Boys tribute?'

'Who?'

Marshall raised his eyebrows. 'You've never heard of—'

She laughed. 'Of course I've heard of them. No, they're a bunch of art-school wanks. But my pal's in them. They don't *actually* slay, but they're okay.'

'Cool. Well, I hope you have fun. See you next week?'

'Sure thing.'

Marshall watched her go. He used to wish he'd been more present in her life, but he was glad he was still in it now.

Unlike her bloody mother.

And he had a ton of meaty tapas dishes left to eat on his own...

20

Marshall pulled into the drive behind Pringle's car and killed the engine. He sat there, his guts churning. He'd overeaten, definitely – those four extra meatballs were a mistake and kept repeating on him like they wanted him to know how bad a mistake.

He checked his phone for messages. Nothing.

He called Jen again, but she didn't answer *again*.

Aye... He needed to sort that out, but it'd have to be later rather than now.

He got out into the thin rain and walked towards the new-build McMansion that had way too many features for the size. One of the neighbours was playing music really loudly nearby. The closer he got, the more he realised the din was coming from inside the house.

'—*they can only get, they can only get better!*'

D:Ream again...

Marshall got out his keys then noticed the door wasn't so much unlocked as hanging open. 'Jim?'

'—*can only get better!*'

Marshall raced over to the hallway Sonos speaker and

jabbed the play/pause button. The music died and he could feel the pain inside his ears recede.

Then the heat and smoke alarms drilled into his eardrums.

Smoke was pumping out of the oven.

Marshall grabbed an oven glove and opened the door. A charcoal disk in the middle that had once been a pizza.

He grabbed a fish slice and weeched it out, then dumped it in the sink with a hiss of water.

He left the oven door hanging like that then opened the window to clear the smoke. 'Jim?'

No sign of Pringle in the kitchen, dining room, conservatory or the lounge.

Way too big a house for one man. Or even one man and someone staying here two or three times a week.

Marshall climbed the stairs. On the landing, the iron spat away. A pile of clothes on the ironing board was dangerously close.

A second fire hazard in two minutes.

Marshall switched it off. Jesus, this was becoming a nightly occurrence.

The music started again, picking up where it had left off. Attacking his ears like someone was driving knitting needles in.

He ran into the nearest room – his own bedroom – and stopped dead.

Not content with using his office at work, Pringle was now using his bedroom here, sitting at the desk in the corner.

Marshall pressed this speaker's play button and killed the music again.

'Bloody thing.' Pringle picked up his phone and stabbed a finger at the screen.

The music started up again.

Marshall killed it again.

'Jim!'

Pringle jerked backwards, dropping his phone on the carpet and grabbing at his chest. 'Get out of my house!'

'Jim, it's Rob!'

'Rob?' Pringle looked at him with milky eyes. Then they snapped into focus. 'Rob. Of course. I was just listening to some music.'

'I know. So does half of Greater Glasgow.' Marshall hammered the volume button several times, then hit play and the music came out at a sane volume. 'You've left the iron on again. And burnt a pizza.'

'Whoopsie pumps!' His breath stank of sour milk. He went back to the laptop.

'Jim, why are you using my computer?'

Pringle looked at Marshall, shaking his head as though the reason was completely obvious. 'More data!'

'More data? But your phone plan is—'

'Not *that* kind of data. Not my sodding data allowance. No, I wanted to cross-check for more data about D:Ream.'

Marshall felt like someone was grabbing at his heart and squeezing it. 'Jim, what's the obsession with them?'

'According to Wikipedia on *five machines now*, the singer is alive.'

'Okay. Why's that a problem?'

'Because he died in 2004. Peter Cunnah. A drug overdose in Ibiza.' Pringle jabbed a finger in the direction of Marshall's laptop. 'But it says he's still alive! There are even YouTube videos of him from last month! I swear, Rob, he died!'

Marshall barely remembered the song, let alone the singer. But he was very familiar with how broken Pringle's brain was now. 'Okay, are you saying they've faked the videos?'

'Of course not. I'm not paranoid, if that's what you think.'

'Why is this important?'

'Don't you see? It's happening again!'

'What is?'

'The Mandela Effect.'

Marshall sat on his bed and shut his eyes. She Who Cannot Be Named was right – this was getting worse. Much, much worse. 'The what now?'

'I would've thought you'd know all about it, Rob? Nelson Mandela died in prison in the eighties, but according to Wikipedia, he actually died in 2013 having been South African president for years. Same with *Sex in the City* – apparently it's called "Sex *and* the City", which is a stupid name.' Pringle snapped Marshall's laptop lid shut, way harder than was necessary. 'I remember different facts, Rob. Like Mandela dying in prison. *Sex in the City*. And now Peter Cunnah dying. But they don't match up with what's allegedly happened.'

Allegedly...

Marshall swallowed hard. 'Jim, I studied False Memory Syndrome at university. In most cases, it's just people making an honest mistake. Convincing themselves something happened that didn't.'

'Most cases. What about the others?'

'Those are related to your condition.'

'This is *nothing* to do with my condition, Rob.'

'So what is it? People are lying to you?'

'No!' Pringle shook his head. 'Don't you see? This is evidence of me travelling between two parallel universes.'

Right then, Marshall saw precisely how badly cracked Pringle's brain was.

'And I'm the nexus point between the two realities.'

She Who Cannot Be Named was definitely right.

'Jim, it's time to consider moving you into a home.'

'Fuck off.'

'I'm serious.'

'No fucking way. I'm still working, despite travelling between universes eating away at my brain. And I'm still delivering – I'm working up a new strategy for your Behavioural

Sciences Unit that'll expand the unit to cover rapes and other serious crimes. So of course I'm functioning.' Pringle got up and walked over to the door. 'So don't fucking give me that bullshit about moving me into a home again. Okay?'

Marshall watched the door shut and listened to D:Ream lying about things getting better.

DAY 2

TUESDAY

21

Elliot hated this place.

Not just the whole city of Edinburgh, which was shite, but this court...

Man, the number of times she'd been here over the years, only to be verbally belittled by some arsehole in a wig and stupid coat...

All the modern blonde wood where you'd expect dark oak panelling made the High Court feel like a university lecture theatre. And there wasn't a whiteboard to be seen, but it still stank of marker pens for some reason she couldn't fathom. Marker pens and chicken soup. And not particularly nice stuff either – not the kind your granny would make, but the crap you got out of the vending machine that made everything else taste of chicken soup.

Elliot checked her phone.

No messages.

No notifications other than shite on Schoolbook, Instagram and loads of stupid shopping emails.

Real stuff. Family stuff, but stuff she couldn't face just now.

So she waited...

The cheap seat numbed her arse. Aye, it was just like a university. The kind of anonymous place she'd be having to take Sam soon enough.

Christ, when did that happen?

She'd been a baby just five minutes ago, wrapped in her arms, and now she was doing her Highers...

The door to the main entrance hall opened and a lawyer walked through, clutching his bulging briefcase. Gave her a curt smile, then buggered off along the corridor. As the door eased shut, she clocked two people deep in conversation.

DS Rakesh 'Shunty' Siyal and Detective Superintendent Bob Cook.

The men who'd put Davie in here.

She tried to think of two people she couldn't face speaking to any less than them, but really struggled.

Who was she kidding? *Davie* was the man who put himself here.

The consultation room door opened and a red-faced man peered out, his left cheek marbled with scars like a ribeye steak. 'Inspector?' He disappeared before she could acknowledge him.

Elliot got up and crossed the corridor. She stared hard at the door and tried to take as deep a breath as she could manage. Everyone was far too shallow.

Sod it.

She opened the door and pushed inside.

A tiny wee room with more of that horrible, cheap wood. Everywhere – surely paint would be cheaper on the walls? Another door at the back leading to God knows where.

Actually, Elliot knew precisely where – into the custody suite.

Davie sat on the chair facing the door, arms folded tight across his chest. Dressed in the sharp black suit he'd bought for his uncle's funeral, but with a navy tie rather than black. Clean-shaven, but his cheeks had a couple of nicks and his throat was a bloodbath. Despite his defensive body language, he grinned at her. 'Couldn't stand close enough to the razor, eh?'

The red-faced guard stood beside her door, facing Davie.

Elliot smiled at him, her heart pounding, then sat opposite her husband. 'How are you bearing up?'

'Shite.' Davie ran a hand across his smooth cheeks, dislodging some of the dried blood. 'Thank you for coming.'

'It's okay. We're married, aren't we?'

He looked back at her. 'Are we?'

Elliot held up her left hand. 'Still wear your ring, you daft sod.'

'Right. Right.' Another brush of his cheeks. Like he was just a daft sod who'd got caught doing something daft. And not aided a monstrous criminal empire who killed people. 'You asked me how I am... Truth is, Andi, I'm upset my parents aren't coming. Didn't even speak to me, just passed on an email to my brief. How they're down at their caravan in Berwick, holidaying while I fight for my future. For *our* future.'

'Davie. You can't request anything from anyone.'

Davie looked away, then shut his eyes.

Despite him being a selfish prick, she couldn't handle seeing him looking so broken.

He looked back at her. 'Covid's totally fucked the justice system, you know? I've been on remand for a year over something I haven't even done.'

'Davie...'

'I'm sticking to the not guilty plea, Andi.'

'Why?'

Davie looked past her at the guard. 'Because I've done fuck all.'

Blood thumped at her throat. 'You were caught red-handed. Tried to implicate me! Even signed a fucking deal!'

'Not saying I'm totally innocent, just not pleading guilty.'

'Jesus Christ, Davie. You're going to prison. Your pension's already gone.'

'Come on, Andi, it's—'

'Attempted murder? Breach of trust?'

'Going to make the bastards prove it. Make me look bad and I'll take a few of them with me. I have a war chest of dirt I can bring out.'

'Davie... Why did you negotiate a deal?'

'I... I know the lay of the land, Andi. I could help the case and make up for... for what happened.'

'For what you did.'

'I did what I needed to do.'

'Davie, you signed a deal. You gave up that arsehole to trim time off your sentence. As it stands, you'll be inside for about three years. Probably less.'

'Aye, but that's if I change my plea to guilty.'

'Jesus Christ, so you're actually going to face trial?'

'I'm entitled to my day in court, am I not?'

'Davie! You could go away for ten years! The kids will all be in their twenties!'

'Andi, I can't...' Davie brushed tears from his eyes. 'I can't stand up there and admit to everything as if I made a conscious choice. There were extenuating circumstances.'

'Davie, you took money from Gary Hislop.'

'Prove it.'

'Come on. He paid you in cash.' Elliot held his gaze until he looked away, then held out her hands. 'All I'm missing is precisely how much you sold us out for.'

Davie took her hands in his. 'Andi, I can't...'

She pulled her hands away. Took a couple of goes. 'Come on... Don't give me that...'

Davie leaned across the table and spoke in a whisper: 'I don't want to give it up. That money is there to take care of the boys and the other one.'

'The other one...' Elliot sighed. 'Davie. Please, just plead guilty. Take the deal. Go for the sure thing. You could be away *forever*.'

Davie looked past her at the guard. 'I've thought it all through. And it won't be that bad.'

'I said I'm going to stick by you, but it's going to be really difficult if you're away for ten years. Or fifteen.'

'I won't be.'

'Prison's a nightmare, Davie. Especially for someone who worked for the police. They'll treat you like an ex-cop.'

'I know. Don't you think I know? And that's just remand! Don't you see how they want me to suffer? I've had to do time in prison because I'm still a danger to the victim?'

'Bullshit. Gary Hislop refuted the threat you posed under interview, but *you* declined bail. Preferred time in prison to being a free man and having to discuss your actions with our children.'

Davie's head slumped forward. 'You're being selfish here, Andi.'

'Right. Of course I am. Selfish. Davie, I'm the one who has to get through *your* sentence alone. I'm the one who has to raise our three kids alone. Sam, Harry, Charlie. Mum and Dad are helping me, but who knows how long they'll both be able to do that for. I don't want Sam to have to do more than be a teenager, no matter how annoying she is. And I want her to be her. Same for Harry and Charlie.'

'You don't have to...' He trailed off, swallowing something down.

'Davie. Stop this insanity. If you plead guilty, you'll get three years. I can handle three years. The kids can handle it too. Obviously they'll be scarred by this. And when you get out, Sam will be at uni. Or doing whatever she wants. Harry will be doing his Highers and his UCAS stuff. But you'll be back out and we can get back to normal.'

'No.' He shook his head. 'My plan is better.'

'Davie, there's more than enough evidence to put you away for over a decade. Think about it!'

'No! The case is weak and you know it. It's all being held together by the tiniest of threads and if I can just tug at a few of them, it'll all fall apart.'

'No it's not.'

'Look, I was charged with accessing the information, sure. There's evidence there, maybe. But the case is short of a trace or corroboration that it was Hislop. Or that he paid me.'

'Davie, this is bollocks. Please. Don't kid yourself. You'll be found guilty. You'll do at least ten years.'

'My only chance here is if a jury acquits me.'

'Davie, no. Just do the three years. They'll take a year off from the time you've served on remand.'

'I won't.'

'You're making a mistake. A huge mistake. Grass on Hislop.'

'I can't. Andi... This is my only hope.'

'What?'

'Come on. I can't do that time. I need to get off.'

'You can turn in Hislop. He sought out a police official and paid for information that led to people dying – that's conspiracy to commit murder. He'll be the one inside. Add a few items to your deal.'

'Andi, if I turn on Hislop...' He leaned in even closer. 'If I do, I'll be a marked man. I'll die in prison. And the threats will get ten times worse.'

'What threats?'

'I get threatened every day. My family. You, the kids, my folks. I thought going down without squealing is the only way to stop that. It's the bloody code and you know it. But if I can get off...'

'Davie... I'm begging you.'

'The only way I could prove I was on the take from Hislop

would be to surrender the money.' He leaned in really close. 'Andi, I've got over two hundred grand. I want to keep it...'

'Hoy, what's going on?'

Davie sat back, arms raised. 'Sorry, just wanted to whisper sweet nothings to my wife.'

'Keep it civil. I've just had my breakfast.'

Elliot kept her voice low. 'Davie, give them the money.'

'There was no money and I won't testify against Hislop. That way, the threats will go away. The men in prison will stop talking to me about slitting your throat and raping Sam.'

'Turn it over.'

'There is no—'

'I can persuade the PF to ensure no prison time. We can all relocate, be a family again.'

'No!'

'Davie, *please.*'

'Not happening, just stop.'

'So you're putting that money ahead of my needs. Of Sam's? Of Harry's? Or Charlie's?'

'I'm denying it even exists because it doesn't.' Davie sat back. 'They asked me about you getting the wine, but I backed up your story. And I told them I just received threats. Which is the truth.'

'One last chance, Davie.' Elliot stared hard at him for a few seconds. 'Please. I'm asking you. Give up that cash. Come home to us.'

'I can't.' Davie got up and walked over to the door behind him. 'I just can't.'

The guard opened the door and he slipped through.

Elliot just wanted to sit there and cry. But this was the last place you could show emotion.

22

She Who Cannot Be Named sat back and tossed the document onto the table, then folded her arms and stared hard at Marshall, her pupils scanning his face like some high-tech airport security device. 'So, can you give me a confidence scale on this?'

Marshall was aware his leg was dancing a jig. Absolutely bursting – trouble with hard work like this was he leaned on coffee to get him through it. And coffee made him pee buckets. He sat back and cast his gaze across the conference room table, at the scattered paperwork, all scribbled with a million notes he needed to consolidate and update and think through.

Over and over again.

And that took time, but everyone wanted results yesterday.

Marshall looked up and locked eyes with her. 'I'd say ninety percent.'

'And that other ten percent, how hard is that going to be to flush out?'

'Hard to say.' Marshall ran a hand down his face. His leg was jigging again. 'The devil is in the details. I don't know if it's actually ten percent. Could be zero, could actually be ninety.'

'But you must have ballpark?'

'I reckon I'll need two days to get an idea.'

'Two days...' She Who Cannot Be Named looked over at Hardeep, sitting stock still like he was meditating. 'Is that one of those woman day things?'

Hardeep frowned. 'Woman day?'

'By that, I mean if a woman was pregnant, is it just going to take one person nine months to have the baby? Can you take the two days and divide that by two people?'

'Bit of both, ma'am.' Marshall tried for a smile, but it wasn't coming today. 'Some of the work could be sped up, but Hardeep's already doing the bulk of that. And the rest is me sitting in a darkened room, thinking about stuff and tapping away. That part can't be sped up.'

'Okay, I get it now.' She pulled her papers together and stacked them up. 'Fine. Groovy.' She held them out for him. 'This is good work, Rob. A serious upgrade from yesterday's.'

'Thanks.' Marshall took her papers, then stacked them with his. 'I'll set up some time tomorrow to review progress.' He grabbed his paperwork and his laptop, then got up.

Hardeep was standing over him. 'Sir?'

'What's up?'

'We need to have that chat about Thea...'

'What's she done?'

'Oh, nothing.'

'What have *you* done?'

'Nothing! It's just I don't think it's appropriate for me to be her tutor.'

'Are you in a relationship with her?'

'No!'

'So what does the guidebook say about professional conflicts like this?'

'Well, there's nothing.'

'Exactly. Because there's nothing. Have you spoken to your boss at the university?'

'She thinks it's fine.'

'Then there's no issue. Okay?' Marshall left the room, heading right for the toilet across the corridor.

There was being a stickler for the rules, then there was trying to conjure up new ones...

'Rob?'

He swung around.

Liana Curtis stood there, wearing an emerald trouser suit that matched her eyes. Her hair was now its natural brown. And her tummy bulge made her look about six months pregnant. Not that Marshall would say.

'Oh, hi.' Marshall smiled at her. 'What are you doing here?'

'Working.'

Marshall couldn't help but glance down.

She scowled at him. 'What are you looking at?'

'I just... Nothing.'

'What's up?' She ran a hand across her tummy. 'Oh, this little thing?' She looked away with a shrug. 'Bit of a whirlwind romance, to be honest. Accidentally fell in love, didn't I?'

Marshall felt the blush throb on his face. 'I'm really happy for you.'

'Well, let's just see how I feel when Tigger's ruining my life in a few months.' She ran a hand over her swollen belly, then grimaced. 'Thinking of calling him Jacob.'

'Right.' Marshall swallowed hard. 'You blanked me at his funeral.'

'It wasn't just you, Rob. Sorry, I was going through some difficult stuff.' A wince flashed across her face. 'Can't believe how long he was there before they found his body.'

Marshall looked away. 'I was a bit thrown by it myself. Jacob lived locally, but I didn't go and see him. Maybe I could've done something. Maybe, I—'

'Oh, shit. There's that famous messiah complex!'

'That's a bit harsh.'

'Is it?'

Marshall put his hand on the bathroom door. 'Anyway, who are you working with?'

'The Behavioural Sciences Unit.'

'That's my team. I say team, but it's pretty much just me and my assistant.'

She rolled her eyes. 'Wherever did you get the name from?'

'Not my doing. Who brought you in?'

'Me.' Gashkori appeared from behind her. 'I put in a request for her to consult on my case. She accepted. Your boss is paying for it.'

Marshall felt an ice blade slice through his heart. 'Could've sworn that was my role.'

Gashkori shrugged. 'It's not like too many cooks will spoil the broth with a criminal profile. In my experience, your egos cancel out.'

'Our *egos*?' Marshall took a deep breath. Of course it'd ruin the broth. 'Ryan, I'm worried having two profilers will—'

'It'll be fine.' Liana smiled at Gashkori. 'DI Marshall acts professionally, so it won't be an issue. We've worked together before. Many, many times.'

Gashkori winked at her. 'Better speak to She— the super.' He barged past into the conference room.

Marshall watched him go in and speak to She Who Cannot Be Named. 'You're working the David Sylvester case too?'

'So I gather.' Liana dropped her rucksack at her feet. 'I've been through the information on the drive up.'

'How did you—'

'I've got this app that dictates the paperwork to me over my headphones. You know how I work, Rob, just bask in all the police work and see what strikes me. Interviews, statements, notes. You name it, I've been through it.'

'Wow.' Marshall hated that idea – he'd drown in that lake of information. 'And what's your take on the new victim?'

'It fits. Superficially, at least. Same MO. The same crime, right? Befriending victims in a seaside town. Only differences I can see are one—' She raised her thumb. '—it's in Scotland, but barely, and two—' She raised her forefinger. '—Holly just happening to spot Sylvester is the only reason we're aware of the crime.'

'Why's that a problem?'

'Well, it *was*. Holly was always an outlier, because she survived. But now Kayleigh has survived too. Once we can speak to her, it might open up alternative avenues.'

Marshall put his hand back on the bathroom door. 'I wouldn't hold much hope on that.'

'She's dead?'

'No. She hasn't succumbed to her injuries yet, but she's still in a coma. I'd say it's touch and go whether she'll pull through, but that's generous.'

'I see.' Liana winced. 'From what I've reviewed, I'd say all the hallmarks are there to put it with him.'

'No.'

She frowned. 'Excuse me?'

'There are gaps, Liana. Starting with the fact Sylvester hasn't moved on to a new location before striking.'

'That we know of.' Liana winked, picked up her rucksack, then entered the conference room.

Marshall shot into the bathroom and raced over to the urinal furthest from the door. As he peed, document and laptop under his arm, his thoughts raced.

Bloody hell – they were going to be talking about him in the conference room. Gashkori really had it in for him.

He finished peeing, then washed his hands and followed Liana in.

Gashkori was sitting opposite She Who Cannot Be Named.

He looked around at Marshall, shot him a glower, then turned back around. 'Thing is, ma'am, this is all theoretical bullshit.' He dropped a document onto the table. 'There's *nothing* in this that's going to help our number one priority, which remains finding Sylvester. He has all the answers, not this document.'

Marshall sat in the chair to the side of She Who Cannot Be Named. 'How's that going?'

Gashkori didn't look at him. 'Got fifty skulls on it, but most of them are from Edinburgh, so they don't really know the area. And Sylvester's the master of buggering off, isn't he?' He gave Marshall a sideways glance. 'No idea where he could be, to be honest. Or if we're even looking in the right place.'

'I get it.' She Who Cannot Be Named pinched her nose. 'DI Marshall has been busy updating the profile from the old case.'

Gashkori arched his eyebrow, but didn't look at Marshall. 'I'm sure there's a lot of work gone into that, but like I—'

'Not as much as you'd think.' Marshall gestured at She Who Cannot Be Named. 'Like I was telling the super here, I've got to add in the data points we've gleaned from speaking to Holly and now from what happened to Kayleigh. The big work ahead of us is in assessing whether any of what's happened to her matches with the previous cases. And whether we can ask Holly any additional questions to learn anything useful for your team.'

'That all sounds positive.' She Who Cannot Be Named focused on Gashkori. 'Ryan, you know this case is the highest profile we've got on the books just now, okay? Even with that incident up in the Highlands still taking up our time. So we need a result.'

'I get it.' Gashkori sat back and let out a deep breath. 'Trouble is, I've got all those skulls, but I'm lacking leaders.'

'You've got two DIs, right?'

'Right. But DI Elliot's in court this week, so I'm one down...'

'Okay, well that's far from ideal.' She Who Cannot Be

Named smiled at Marshall. 'Rob can chum you down to Eyemouth and help.'

Gashkori shook his head. 'I'm not sure he—'

'Liana gives him backstop on the profiling work. She's just as familiar with the case and more up to date with latest methods and techniques. Rob is a DI, need I remind you?'

'Sure thing, ma'am.'

She Who Cannot Be Named pointed at Liana. 'Professor Curtis will stay here and go through the statements you've gathered, then update the profile accordingly.'

Marshall stood up but didn't leave them. 'One thing I was going to do was to get Hardeep looking for any other cases.'

'*Others?*'

Marshall shrugged. 'Well, my logic is we've got two populations of cases. First, from over twelve years ago. And now a second one, which just has Kayleigh in it. So far. What I'd like to know is what Sylvester was up to between those dates. We assumed he'd stopped, but maybe not. And if it's not Sylvester, what was our killer up to?'

'Okay, good idea. Liana, can you take that up?'

'Sure, but I'll need some help with field work.'

Marshall raised his hand. 'I can help with that.'

Gashkori coughed a laugh.

'Excellent.' She Who Cannot Be Named got to her feet and clapped her hands. 'Time for a coffee. Ryan?'

'Sure. I need a comfort break first.' Gashkori glared at Marshall, then set off for the toilet.

'See you later, Rob.' Liana followed him out.

Marshall got to the door before She Who Cannot Be Named. 'Ma'am, I need a word.'

'Because of Ryan bringing in your ex-girlfriend?'

'She's not my ex.' Marshall gave an embarrassed laugh. 'But it's something else. I think I agree with your assessment about Jim.'

'Oh. Pringle.'

'I don't think he can work anymore. We've tried to hide him here for a year, but it's becoming untenable. I don't think he's mentally well enough to continue working. It's not my place to—'

'Okay, well, I don't think we can move him on from here. I don't think he can work here at Gartcosh, but there's nowhere else for him to go.'

'I know. And I don't think he's even safe enough to be at home on his own. He left an iron burning away last night. And a pizza in the oven.'

'So, you're putting him into a home?'

'I've got the offer of respite care. It's a tough decision but I'm the one who's got to make it for him, right?'

'That's true.' She gave a kind smile. 'We'll both look after him, Rob. It's not just on you. And as for my part, I've got the paperwork ready to make sure he's medically retired. I've been given approval to offer a full pension, even though he's a few years shy. That should at least make it easier to explain to him.'

'Thank you.' Marshall let out a deep breath. 'I'll speak to him about the home...'

23

The wiper hammered at the windscreen, scraping hard as it tugged rain from glass only to have it all immediately replaced by thick splotches.

Marshall kept the gear low as he navigated the road under the Leaderfoot Viaduct. For years he'd avoided the whole of the Borders, but now he tried to come this way once a month. Not so much lancing a boil as trying to heal a burn wound with ice-cold water.

That bridge was the reason he was back in the Borders. The reason he was still a cop.

The reason for so many things in his life.

'I mean, it was such an epic tune.' Pringle was in the passenger seat, looking around and scanning the damp scenery like a kid on a school trip. Despite the fact he'd grown up in the area and worked here for over two decades, it still seemed to offer novelty to his broken mind. 'It was everywhere. Everywhere. It was a hit single when it came out. Me and my pals from school went to Ayia Napa that summer and you couldn't escape it. Must be 1993? 1994? Can't remember. Then the Labour

Party co-opted it in 1997 and you couldn't escape it *again*. It's why his death was such big news, Rob. Are you sure you don't remember it?'

'Sure.' Marshall slowed as he drove into Gattonside, hitting the Borders-wide 20 limit. Spending time in Glasgow, it felt like his heart rate had slowed to Olympic diver levels of fitness. 'Still too young to remember any of it, really.'

'Come on, it was a massive single. That science guy off the telly, he played keyboards in D:Ream!'

'Which one?'

'Brian Cox.' Pringle laughed. 'Not the actor!'

'Well, I never.' Marshall took the left past the fancy restaurant that looked like an American diner, then pulled into the car park and let the engine idle. 'I really don't like doing this, Jim.'

Pringle frowned at him. 'Doing what?'

'Come on. You know what I'm talking about.'

'Right.' Pringle sat back and kneaded his forehead. 'I...' Something must've clicked inside that skull. 'Sometimes I get flickers of what it must be like for you. I mean... I don't know if any of this is real. Any of it. At all. Keep asking myself if I'm a brain in a vat, like in *The Matrix*, if someone's just dreaming this all up.'

Here we go again...

Marshall braced himself again for another round of it. 'Jim, we discussed this and—'

'I get it, Rob. That incident with the oven and the iron tipped you over, didn't it?'

Of course it did.

'Jim, come on, that's—'

'You were my biggest supporter. When I insisted I stay in the job, you had my back. But I get it. That was a year ago and you've decided I can't even look after myself.' Pringle waved a hand out of the car. 'That's why I belong in there with all the loonies.'

Marshall shifted his focus towards the low-slung sheltered housing, a seventies renovation of some pre-existing outbuildings, a mishmash of stone and stucco, not to mention the slapdash slate roof that was probably leaking badly today. 'You say that like—'

'I know I'm a looney, Rob. Whatever's happening to me, it's...' Pringle gasped. 'I just hate that you've changed your mind about looking after me.'

'Come on...' Marshall gripped the wheel tight in his hands. 'Remember that I never signed up for that. You just put my name down on a form and—'

'We talked about it!'

'No, we didn't. You thought we did. We hadn't discussed it. I've really tried to help, Jim, but I can't look after you, not with a full-time job and... my other commitments.'

Pringle shook his head. 'So, what's this all about? You're just dropping me off here?'

'We discussed this, Jim. You're only here for a few nights to see if you get on. It's respite care.'

'For you or me?'

'Bit of both.'

'Right. I get it.'

'Listen, this is a good place. My grandfather's lived here for like fifteen years.'

'It's a *care home*.'

'It's sheltered housing, Jim. They let you maintain some independence, but they can keep an eye on you. I don't think you'll be allowed to drive, but you can come and go as you like. Melrose is just over the river. You love Melrose.'

'Aye, but Melrose hates me.' Pringle laughed. 'Why do you think I based myself down in Hawick? I mean, nobody wants to be based there, but I was so I didn't have to spend time in fucking Melrose!'

'Why?'

'Why do you think?'

Marshall had no idea and didn't have the energy to get into this – the clock was ticking and he needed to be over in Eyemouth. 'Jim, the last time I came here to see Grumpy, I—'

'Who the hell is Grumpy?'

'My granddad. When I came here a few weeks ago, I spoke to the warden about your condition. You won't be the only... person in your situation.'

'Right. So there's another looney?'

'Three or four other people with early-onset dementia. I spoke to her and she's earmarked a flat for you. If you like it, you can move in straight away.'

'What, so someone's died?'

'What do you mean?'

'That's how it works, isn't it? Dead man's shoes.'

'Nobody's died. The resident moved into a care home. Look, you go in there and speak to the warden. See how you feel. Spend the day in that room. Go for a walk around here.'

Pringle sat there, muttering to himself. 'Just remember to take my phone this time...'

'Right, aye. And if you do like it, we can bring the rest of your stuff down at the weekend.'

Pringle clapped his hands together. 'Cool, let's do this.'

Marshall sat back. 'Eh?'

'I want to move in.' Pringle got out and charged over to the front door. He looked around, eyes narrow, pleading for Marshall to hurry.

Marshall got out and followed him over. 'You want to move in?'

'I love the idea...' Pringle tapped his nose and leaned in

close. 'I get the ruse now, but you really just could have said so. I'm working undercover here, right?'

'That's not what—'

'It'll be great getting away from Gartcosh. Problem with that place is everyone there is crazy. Can I keep my laptop? Will they bring me snacks and drinks?'

24

If anything, the rain was even worse over by Eyemouth than at Gartcosh. So bad, in fact, that Marshall almost missed the police station in the greasy haze.

Unlike the sixties concrete vulgarity of the other nicks in the Borders, Eyemouth had the look of a post-war house. Its pitched roof seemed to be at too sharp an angle. And despite the supposed manhunt Gashkori's lot were currently undertaking, all of the parking bays were occupied by squad cars. As was most of the street outside.

Marshall bumped up onto the kerb and let the car's engine fizzle and die. He let a sigh escape his lips, then set off across the road. The rain hammered down on his shoulders, blurring his phone screen as he sifted through his many messages. Mercifully, nothing yet from the warden in Gattonside – maybe Pringle's invented cover story would make him settle in there quickly. Knowing Marshall's luck, it'd come to bite him on the arse later.

Still, going an hour without any fresh hassle rearing its ugly head felt almost like winning the league.

Another sigh escaped his lips as he entered the station.

A bored-looking civilian was behind the desk – one of the few stations in rural Scotland that was still staffed. His head was wider than it was tall and his cheeks wobbled with the massive wad of gum he was chewing. 'Can I help you, pal?'

'Looking for DCI Gashkori.' Marshall gave a flash of his warrant card. 'Gather this is the makeshift command unit, right?'

'Makeshift's right, aye.' A derisory laugh, then a slurp from his gum. 'Call it what you want, it's still just a kettle and a petrol station beer fridge.' He thumbed behind him. 'End of the hallway.'

'Cheers, mate.' Marshall smiled, then passed through the door into a long hallway that still bore the marks of a home rather than a police station. He waited outside the door, with its scarred wood and that ancient poster with the jacket sleeve reaching into another's pocket.

The door at the back led into some open-plan office space.

Nobody there, save for Paton.

Marshall walked up to her. 'Ash, how are you doing?'

'Getting there.'

'Looking for Ryan. You seen him?'

She pointed back the way. 'In the kitchen. Second on the left.'

'Thanks.' Marshall retraced his steps and stopped outside the door, listening to the voices chattering away.

'Couldn't get Munich, but got Cologne and Stuttgart.' Sounded like Struan.

'Lucky, lucky bastard.' Taylor's Glaswegian twang, definitely. 'Couldn't get anything.'

A laugh. 'Should see my credit card bill, gaffer.'

Marshall knocked and the voices stopped.

'Come in.'

Marshall opened the door and peeked inside.

Taylor was sitting at a table, while Struan manned the

kettle, rumbling away. The place had the acidic stink of instant coffee and sour UHT milk.

Gashkori was by the narrow window, tapping away at his phone. He looked up and nodded, then went back to whatever he was up to. 'Struan, get DI Marshall a coffee, would you?'

'Sure thing, gaffer.' Struan got another chipped mug out of a cupboard and stared at the kettle like he could get it to boil quicker by giving it that level of attention.

'I'm fine.' Marshall leaned against the door jamb. 'Had a coffee in Melrose.'

'Of course you did.' Struan put the mug away. 'Nice seeing you again.'

'You too, Struan.' Marshall looked around the small room like he was searching for something. 'Take it you've found Sylvester, then?'

Gashkori smiled. 'No, Inspector. *Uniform* are still hunting for him. Led by Jolene Archer and her team. I believe she's competent enough to manage such a task, judging by your performance review and pushing her through her sergeant's exams.' He shifted his finger between Struan and Taylor. 'Meanwhile, we're working on the wider strategy. Seeing as how you let him slip from our grasp.'

Marshall countered the passive-aggressive barb with a grin. 'Sounded more like you were strategizing your accommodation for the Euros in Germany.'

'Sorted all that out when the draw was made.' Gashkori waited as the kettle rumbled to the boil, then watched Struan fussing with their drinks in a rattle of clattering and clanking. 'You mind giving us a minute, lads?'

'Sure.' Taylor got to his feet and took his mug from Struan, sipping at the liquid like it hadn't just boiled. 'I'll get an update from Paton.'

Struan handed Gashkori a mug, then scuttled off out of the room.

Gashkori watched the door shut and set his mug down on the melamine worktop. 'Paton's a cracking wee officer, isn't she? Tracked down Kayleigh's folks in Brisbane. Poor sods are getting a flight today, stopover in Doha. Imagine that, flying all that way just to see your poor lassie in a fucking coma."

'Definitely got potential.'

'Agreed. Just a bit... baffling.'

'Baffling, how?'

Gashkori blew on his coffee. 'What I'm baffled about is how quickly she managed to find them. That's astonishing work.' He sipped at his coffee and gasped. 'I'll need to keep an eye on her, mind. She'll be after my job before long. Someone with those pronouns will trump a brown brother like me in the woke stakes, eh?'

'I don't think that's how things work.'

'Sure. A white guy would think that.' Gashkori laughed. 'Are you pinning this case on me as petty revenge?'

'If I was, would I tell you?'

'Aye, well played.'

'What would the revenge be for, sir?'

'Because I moved you to Gartcosh.'

'I like it there.' Marshall ignored that particular trap. 'Ryan, I know you don't like me but I'm here to work for you, as per the boss's orders.'

'It's not that I don't like you, Rob. I think you're a good laugh. Decent copper too. It's just I think your skills are better used elsewhere, strategically. I mean, a criminal profiler working in the Scottish Borders? That's... insane. Who'd think that's a good idea?' He laughed. 'Right, Jim Pringle. And he was batshit mental.'

'That's a bit crass.'

'But it's not untrue.'

'Sir, I'm a DI first and foremost. I stopped being a criminal profiler eleven years ago when I joined the Met. And now, with Liana here...'

'Sure, of course. But thing is, Jim Pringle had you as a civilian profiler for budgetary reasons.'

'I didn't know that.'

'I mean, he pulled a few tricks to get that, but you were never actually on the payroll as a cop...'

Marshall took Taylor's seat and didn't know what to think about that. 'What do you want me to do, sir?'

'After our pointless little meeting in sunny Gartcosh, I had a chunk of time to think about Sylvester on the drive down here.' Another bracing sip. 'A few things don't quite stack up. One thing I can't fathom is why Sylvester returned to the caravan.'

Marshall had similar reservations and was a bit surprised to hear them voiced by Gashkori. 'What do you mean, sir?'

'Well, the blood was still damp, but it had started congealing.' Gashkori picked up a document and passed it over. 'This is the draft crime scene report. According to our friends in forensics, that points to an attack between seven forty-five to eight-fifteen, give or take ten minutes. Thing is, Holly was there about quarter to nine.'

'Your point is why did he return to the caravan after the attack?'

'Right, exactly.' Gashkori set his cup down on the counter. 'He attacked Kayleigh, spilt some blood like Struan pouring milk... Then chucked her off the side of the cliff.' He scratched at the stubble over his ear. 'Actually, there's a flaw in that. Cal was assuming he'd already left, but he had to have, right?'

'Right. Holly told us she saw him arriving. But you're asking why he went back if he'd already been there to kill Kayleigh?'

'Indeed.'

'It's a good point.' Marshall sat back. 'Sylvester usually shoved victims over and ran. No witnesses. Isolated locations. Limited contact before the assault. But this attack was risky. A

home invasion, followed by transporting her a few hundred
metres to push her off the edge of the cliff. And he failed to kill
her. Doesn't fit the MO, but suppose he was desperate? Suppose
Kayleigh knew something? Maybe even threatened him.'

'That phone call?'

'Right. Have we proved it was him?'

'Paton's been working with the forensics team, but you and I
both know you can't get anything from it unless you have a time
machine.'

'But forensics must have an idea?'

'Fast-tracked a DNA profile and Sylvester left traces. He was
inside that caravan at some point since its last deep cleaning.'

Marshall felt a held breath escape his lips. That was a big
thing. Knowing he was actually in there meant it wasn't some
figment of Holly's imagination, where some deep-rooted
element of her trauma projected her attacker onto the present.
'Could he have left something behind?'

Gashkori shrugged. 'Given the victim lived alone and she's
still in a coma, it's hard to tell if anything's missing or there that
shouldn't be. Forensics are cataloguing everything, but maybe
you're right and he left something, then went back and got it.
They're tossing the room in the B&B up the road, but it's
spartan as fuck. Owner reckons Sylvester's just left a toothbrush and three boxed jigsaws. Maybe he's got a wee hidey-hole
somewhere, but... It's pretty slim pickings, I have to say.'

Marshall played it all through, but there was enough that
didn't sit right with him. 'Do you mind if I speak to Holly?'

'Why?'

'Just a few follow-up questions for the profile.'

'Well, I'm not sure she's comfortable with you, Marshall,
given your history. So you'll need someone else to sit in on it.'

25

Marshall gripped the oh-shit handle on the door in a desperate attempt to keep himself inside the car. Struan was behind the wheel and proving himself to be an absolute idiot of a driver, weaving in and out of cars on the stretch of single-carriageway A1, no matter how many were approaching. He zipped out to pass a slow-moving bread van, then glanced over at Marshall just as he pulled in. 'You're quiet there, gaffer.'

The countryside on both sides was like paddy fields, deluged by the recent rain. 'I'm known as the strong and silent type, Struan.'

'Right, aye. Sure.' Another quick move to overtake a grey Tiguan. 'Listen, why didn't you want my coffee?'

Marshall eyeballed the driver as they passed, a big man singing along to something, then over to Struan. 'Because I'd just had one in Melrose.'

'Sure, but if there was something wrong with the way I make coffee, you'd say, right?'

'Struan, there's nothing wrong with your coffee-making

skills. But making coffee doesn't make someone a decent officer.'

'I'm not saying it does. Just...' Struan ran a hand through his hair. 'The old man ran a café in Kelso. Always said good coffee made meetings go well.'

'That's certainly true.' But Marshall didn't point out that a dusty old tin of out-of-date clumped-together instant was nobody's idea of good coffee, even those who actually liked the stuff. And he assumed there were some.

'Speaking of which, gaffer, if you don't mind me asking, how's DCI Pringle doing?'

'He's fine.' But Marshall couldn't make eye contact with him and didn't want to tell Struan Liddell of all people that he'd just put him into a home...

'Sure. Well, I feel for him. He's, what, fifty? And he's like my old man. Tell you the truth, gaffer, he's... he's getting worse, to be honest with you. And I'm the one who has to deal with it, day in, day out. All the anger and rage and...'

Struan battered towards a section of dual carriageway section that would allow him to overtake without risking life and limb, but he took the left turning just before the second lane spread out. 'Sod's Law, eh?' He whipped off the road, heading inland towards Reston, lurking down in the valley. 'If you don't mind me saying, it's kind of weird you being back.'

'In what way?'

'Well, you and DI Taylor basically swapped over, right?'

'I guess.' The fields were drier here, as if all of the rain had drained down to the sea. 'But I'm based in Gartcosh in the forensics area, whereas he is Glasgow South MIT. Or was.'

'Aye, you can say it out loud, though, if you want. Taylor's a *basic* detective.' Struan laughed.

Marshall didn't join in.

Struan cleared his throat. 'Which is what the big gaffer wants, of course, rather than a headshrinker like yourself.'

Marshall smirked at Struan's brutal honesty. 'I've been a detective for eleven years.'

'Aye, but you were a direct entry into the Met at DI, weren't you? And you used to be a criminal profiler? Not saying there's anything wrong with either, but that's like the polar opposite of being a *basic* detective. Like DI Taylor or myself.'

The constant stressing of basic...

He was trying to goad Marshall into saying something he'd regret. Something that'd fly around the force. That'd get him into trouble.

'I suppose my skills and background are different to most other detectives, Struan, but there's room for everyone. There's all kinds of criminals out here so it takes all kinds of cops to catch them. And it's not like I haven't done my share of police work.'

'Here we go.' Struan pulled up outside a semi-detached cottage with a 'for sale' sign outside, opposite the village's train station. 'This is her.' He got out and knocked on the door.

Bloody hell – trouble with these *basic* cops was they just rushed ahead and did stuff without a strategy.

Trouble with people like Marshall was he'd let him drive the chat rather than focusing on devising a strategy.

Marshall followed him over, just in time for the door to open.

That big lad stood there, stroking his goatee. Jamie. The cameraman from the previous day in Eyemouth. He smiled at Struan, then looked Marshall up and down. 'Take it you're here to see Hol?'

'That's right.' Struan returned the smile. 'She in?'

'Aye.' Jamie pulled the door to. 'Listen, she's totally all over the place so if you can make this quick and easy...?'

Struan winked. 'Quick and easy are my middle names, pal.'

Jamie laughed. 'Right you are. In you come.' He stepped aside and let them past.

Marshall nodded as he followed Struan into a functional living room. Barely any furniture, just a big sofa and a TV resting on a unit.

Holly was watching some shrill reality TV where a woman in an overly tight dress was shouting at a man in an overly tight suit. She switched it off and shifted her focus to them. 'Hey, have you caught him?'

Struan walked over to the window and shook his head. 'Sorry. Not yet.'

'Oh. Okay.' Holly sniffed. 'Listen, do you mind taking your shoes off? It's just, we're staying here while Jamie's pal sells it. I've got a place in Berwick, down by the harbour. I'm getting an extension built and it's totally impossible to live there. Hopefully it'll be done by the time we have to move out of here.' She checked her watch. 'Got a viewing in half an hour, so...'

'We'll be long gone, Holly.' Struan nodded. 'You used to live in Whitley Bay, right?'

'Aye.'

'Why did you leave?'

'It's just... Why do you think? I couldn't face living there after what happened. My gran died and I inherited a load of money, so I moved up here. Thought I'd be getting away from my past. But God didn't have that in His plan for me, did He?'

Marshall stood there, astonished that Struan's clumsy question had got her to open up like that.

'The first victim was there, wasn't she?'

'Exactly. It's like a circle. All those women, stuck between me and the first one.' She smiled at the cameraman. 'It's why I want to make this film. To get our story out there.'

'Who are you making it for?'

'Me?'

'I meant Netflix, BBC, anyone like that?'

'Oh, it's us. I started dating Jamie a few years ago... Met at a pal's thirtieth. Then his mate Toby started speaking to me at *my* birthday. He was interested in my story, wanted to make a documentary about what I've been through. A few months later, he told us he'd got funding... And that's when I knew I just had to embrace what I'd been through. Maybe even make some money from my suffering in the process. Maybe forge a new career. And it's why we're doing this fucking thing to... to give me closure on it... And it's why we saw that fucking... That fucking...'

Marshall could see the way their setup worked.

Toby was the mouth, the guy who got her talking about what she went through.

And now he wasn't here, it was going to be even harder.

Marshall stayed standing, hands in pockets. 'Listen, our number-one priority is trying to find Mr Sylvester.'

Jamie thumbed at Struan. 'DS Liddell here told us he's killed again?'

'We don't know if he has.'

'But you think so.'

'We believe he's attempted to kill someone, but she's still clinging on.' Marshall focused on Holly. 'Listen, I wanted to ask you a few questions about when you saw him yesterday morning, if that's okay?'

'Like what?'

'The thing I'm struggling to understand is why he'd return.'

'Saying you don't believe me?'

'I do, Holly.' Marshall raised his hands. 'I saw the video. It's irrefutable proof that he was there. It's just... We've... Did he just turn up?'

She frowned. 'I mean... I can't say if he was there before, but he was heading *towards* the caravan. That's why we went inside it.'

'You're sure of that? You didn't see him leaving?'

'No. I don't think so.'

Struan shook his head. '*Think* isn't good enough, Holly.'

She shot to her feet and prodded a finger into his sternum. 'So you *don't* believe me?'

'Of course we believe you, Holly. Okay, let's go back to when he took you.'

'What? But that's ancient history.'

'I know. Did he say or do anything before you were abducted?'

'I didn't see him.' She waved a hand at Marshall. 'Told him so many times back then... The only time I saw him was when I came to. He was sitting there on a chair. Then I managed to escape.'

'How?'

'I think he fell asleep. Passed out drunk, you know?'

Exactly how she'd described it back in time. 'It's just we need to be absolutely certain. I'm building up a profile of your attacker, so—'

'It's David Sylvester.'

'I know. But we need to build up a profile, just in case it's someone else.'

'You're saying he wasn't a serial killer?'

'No. But we want to catch him. So anything you can think of will be absolutely crucial.'

'This is what happened last time, you fucking prick. They put too much pressure on me! I'm the fucking victim here! And you lot let him go! Why isn't he in jail?'

'Holly, we will protect you from—'

'Aye, bullshit. Fuck off.' She pointed to the door. 'The pair of you. Fuck right off!'

'Come on, Holly, that's—'

'FUCK OFF!'

'Guys.' Jamie pointed at the door. 'I'm asking you to leave. Please.'

Marshall saw they wouldn't get any further. 'Sure. Sorry for upsetting you and thank you for your time.' He led Struan outside and walked over to the car.

'Listen...' Jamie was resting against the front door. 'Listen, boys. Holly's... She's broken by this... By whatever this is, by it happening again. Completely broken by it. Didn't sleep a wink last night. It's brought up a lot of things.'

'I understand. It's a lot for her to process.'

'It is. Thing is... Her investigation... this bloody documentary it's... it's unearthed some other potential murders.'

'Other murders? You mean the ones from twelve years ago?'

'No. Since. See, she's kind of gone a bit crazy over this. Become ridiculously obsessed. She's found another, like, ten lassies she thinks were killed by Sylvester. Me and Toby were a bit... thrown by it. We've no idea what to do with it.'

'Right. Has she shared—'

'Hasn't shared anything with us. She definitely doesn't want to go to the police because of how that went the last time.'

'But here you are...'

'Right.'

'Listen, if she's got a list of other potential murders, something in that could help us find Sylvester. Can you speak to her and see if she'll share them? Please?'

Jamie nodded slowly, then let out a deep breath. 'Okay, let me have a word with her.'

26

E lliot hated being on this side of the court. In the public area, watching the action happen.

The lead prosecutor in his wig and tails half facing the witness stand, half facing the jury. That curious dance lawyers had to do, shifting their focus between three people, always wary of the judge's intervention.

Behind, the judge sat in the middle of the bench, his heavy-lidded eyes looking as though he was asleep. Elliot had come up in front of him a few times and his mental sharpness was as renowned as his handsiness.

Gary Hislop stood in the witness stand, head bowed, clutching his cane. Even now, a year after his accident, he looked like a broken man. Scars lined his face and he grimaced every time he moved. And when he didn't. Even though he was probably exaggerating it for effect, he still looked... buggered.

Someone shuffled into the seat next to Elliot. An elbow dug into her arm and a foot crushed her shoe. 'Sorry, boss.'

She looked around.

DS Rakesh 'Shunty' Siyal, smiling. He'd got a suit that fitted his gangly frame now. And had grown a beard that didn't suit his face.

Elliot got up and moved to the only other free seat, right up at the back, her view obscured by both a tall man and a pillar. She couldn't see Davie from up here without getting onto the lap of the woman next to her.

Shunty looked around at her, frowning, his face as sour as week-old milk.

Elliot ignored him and focused on the actual court case.

What did the daft sod expect? He was the one who'd arrested Davie. Who'd pulled together all the evidence against him.

And that new suit wasn't fooling anyone – he was still functionally useless as a cop.

So much for ignoring him...

She turned away from him and tried to focus on the case.

'No, no, no.' Hislop was resting on his cane and shaking his head. 'I'd like to assure the court that I have never paid David Elliot a single pound.'

The prosecutor raised his eyebrows. 'But we have an understanding of money received by the accused from yourself for services rendered.' His Midlands accent betrayed why Elliot hadn't come across him before – he was new. The intricacies of Scots law would no doubt trip up the arrogant sod at some point.

Hislop snapped back with a glare. 'What services are you talking here?'

'We, uh, understand for intelligence pertaining to active police investigations.'

'Right.' Hislop stood up tall and, even from up in the gods, Elliot heard a crunch of bone. 'He might've told you and the police that, but I can assure you there are no traces of money leaving my account—' He flicked a hand in Davie's direction.

'—or of Mr Elliot here obtaining it from me. Because it did not happen.'

'And yet we have this backed up by statements from other people.'

'Are they here in court?'

'We have been unable to contact them for one reason or another.'

'Aye, well, that's not on me, is it?'

'So you deny paying Mr Elliot?'

'It. Did. Not. Happen.'

The prosecutor was looking flustered. Normally they'd rehearse the hell out of this charade and present a coherent story, but then again, Hislop wasn't on the stand as a defendant but as a witness.

Still, this pathetic showing was undermining the case. Maybe Davie's gamble would pay off and muggins down there would be shipped off back to Wolverhampton or Walsall.

'Mr Hislop, you have already attested to the veracity of certain articles of photographic evidence, namely—'

'I know which ones, so you don't have to list them again.'

'—wherein you were seen with Mr Elliot.'

'Aye. Don't deny that.'

'But you do deny dispensing money to him?'

'Course I do.'

'So how do you explain the photographs, then?'

Hislop winced as he leaned forward on his cane. 'Have you heard of rugby?'

'The sport?'

'Aye, the sport.'

'This wasn't at the rugby.'

'Right. You didn't ask me, so I'm telling you now.' Hislop flashed a serpentine grin. 'I'm a patron of Melrose RFC. If you look behind both goal posts, you'll see an advert for my businesses in nearby Galashiels and Kelso. Sadly, finding suitable premises in Melrose has eluded me.'

'This isn't answering the question. You don't deny being with Mr Elliot?'

'Of course I don't. If I was seen at the rugby with Davie over there, it's because I go to every match. It's as much business as pleasure for me. Every person there is either a friend, a customer or a potential customer, so I have to speak to them. A few are financiers who are interested in investing in a growing business. I'm an innocent businessman whose good name has been hauled through the muck by the police.' Another flick of the wrist. 'This is after David Elliot over there drove *a car* into me and severely injured me. I'm lucky to walk. I'm lucky to still be alive. And the worst part is I still don't understand why he did it. Maybe I sold him a hammer he didn't know how to use. Maybe I cut him up at a roundabout once. Maybe he thought I was sleeping with his wife again.'

Jesus Christ...

Elliot sat back, her teeth chewing into the flesh inside both cheeks.

The prosecutor held Hislop's gaze for a few long seconds, then grabbed his stuff and turned away. 'No further questions, your honour.'

The judge nodded at Hislop. 'You are free to leave, Mr Hislop.'

'Cheers.' Hislop looked around the court, locking eyes with Elliot. He gave a subtle wink, then took his time descending the steps, his knee clicking as much as his cane.

The couple next to Elliot got up and left, allowing her to stretch out her legs a bit.

'Who is your next witness, Mr Byatt?'

'We call PC Liam Warner to the stand, your honour.'

Nobody moved. Silence.

The judge cleared his throat.

The clerk of court turned around. 'PC Warner is running late, your honour.'

'Mr Byatt, this isn't the first time in this court, is it?'

'No, your honour. We, ah, we will— Ah, there he is.'

Warner bounced up the steps towards the witness stand, then stood there, grinning at the jury as if they were the audience in a stand-up gig and he was about to ask them what they did for a living and if they'd travelled far.

Something clicked to Elliot's right.

'Fuck me.' Hislop stepped towards her, leaning heavy on his cane. Up close, he looked pallid and ashen, but he still smelled like fresh morning surf off the coast of Alaska. He sat next to her and moaned. 'Andi.'

'Gary.'

'You've no idea how much pain I'm in.'

'I can see it.' She flashed up her eyebrows. 'Unless that's all an act.'

'Oh, it's genuine. Believe you me.'

'You managed to get up here very quickly.'

'It's going down that's the bugger.' Hislop pointed his stick towards Davie at the opposite side of the court. 'Your husband is a stupid prick and he's completely fucked.'

'I wouldn't go so far. You just blew apart the prosecution's case there.'

'Nah, I just told them the truth. If they're relying on me, then they're fucked.'

'Maybe they are.'

In the witness stand, Warner was frowning as he dug a nail into his teeth. 'Sorry, can you repeat the question?'

Elliot sighed and turned away from him. 'You still think he drove a car into you, right?'

'Because he did.'

'You said it was someone else.'

'Remind me to ask you what you see the next time someone runs you over.'

Elliot shook her head. 'Gary, answer me this straight. How much did you pay him?'

'Nothing.'

'Come on, that's bullshit.'

Hislop nodded towards the witness stand. 'Like I said up there, I never paid him a penny. Or a pound.'

'Aye, sure.'

'I'm serious, Andi. From one lover to another, a-ha.' Hislop cackled at his joke.

'I believe you. Thousands wouldn't. Two hundred thousand wouldn't.'

'Listen, I don't know who he's been doing all that shite for, but it sure as hell wasn't me.'

'And I'll just believe you.'

'If I lied up there, you could do me with perjury.'

'We'd have to prove that. Trouble with proving things is you need people who know stuff about you, and those people have a habit of going missing and dying.'

'That's nonsense and you know it. Besides, Davie's the reason I can't walk properly and won't play rugby ever again.'

'Just tell me how much you paid him. That's it.'

'Andi, there's no money from me. Davie's a paranoid mess and is making this shit up. Maybe he's in league with Balfour Rattray, maybe they're attempting to discredit me. After all, Balf's a guy with money to burn.'

'Rattray wouldn't pay anyone.'

'Wouldn't he? Cops were swarming all over his farm a while back.'

'Aye, wonder who put the drugs squad up to that...'

Hislop winked. 'Anyway, I better go. This weekend marks the grand opening of Northgate Hardware in Peebles and there's a lot still to be done.' He pushed up to standing and winced. 'I hate breaking from the Something Street Hardware pattern, but needs must, eh?'

'You're still doing it, then?'

'Selling screws and drills and bits of wood, aye. It's an honest job, Andi.' Hislop leaned in close. 'And you'll never get at me.'

27

Despite the breakneck speed up to Reston, Struan's pace driving back to Eyemouth was less boy racer and more old boy out on a Sunday drive to the supermarket.

Marshall killed the call when it hit voicemail yet again. 'You okay there?'

'Me?' Struan looked over, frowning. 'Why wouldn't I be?'

'You're driving like my niece before she passed her test.'

'Oh, right.' Struan kicked down and overtook another bread lorry, then started indicating for the Eyemouth turning a good distance early. 'Different to after she passed it?'

'She failed it three times.' Marshall's phone exploded in his hands.

Liana Curtis calling...

He put it to his ear as Struan waited in the lane to turn towards Eyemouth. 'Finally got a hold of you, Liana.'

'Eh?'

'I've been calling. Left a voicemail.'

'Sorry, I haven't seen anything. Then again, the Wi-Fi in Gartcosh is a bit crap. And there's no mobile reception either. Oh, and I might've turned my phone off to do some deep work.'

Deep work...

Marshall hadn't heard that kind of pretentious terminology in a long time. Almost a refreshing change from the grunts and swearing of most coppers. 'That explains it, then. You get anything from that work?'

She sighed down the line. 'Sadly not.'

'Well, at least I can rest easy, knowing I haven't missed anything blindingly obvious.'

'Don't flatter yourself, Rob. This isn't *your* work. You might've topped and tailed it for your boss, but it's Jacob's document, even with our minor input way back when.'

'Fair point.' Marshall gritted his teeth and had to brace himself as Struan took a corner too fast. 'Listen, the reason I'm calling you is I need to ask you and Hardeep to dig into some additional cases Holly Fenwick has unearthed.'

'Wait, what?'

'She's found some additional murders she believes were committed by Sylvester in the gap between her ordeal and Kayleigh.'

Her exhalation was harsh and shrill. 'Shit.'

'I've no idea if there's anything in them, but I've emailed the names and locations through to Hardeep. I don't have your current email address. I'd normally pair him up with a cop, but it's his half-day for his coursework, so—'

'So you're asking me to do your donkey work?'

'I'd do it myself, Liana, but Gashkori—' Marshall caught himself before he put his foot in it in front of Struan. '—has got me chasing down leads like a basic cop.'

She laughed. 'You're anything but basic, Rob.'

'Sure I am.'

The car pulled in outside the Eyemouth station. Struan got

out then walked into the station without looking back until he opened the door.

Marshall gave him a wave, but stayed seated in the pool car. 'Anyway, I had a quick look through the list. They're all locations in southern Scotland, plus one in Cumbria.'

'Okay, so he's shifted over the border... I'll dig into them.'

'Sorry if you feel like I'm treating you like you're my skivvy. I'll get some cops to help out.'

'It's fine, Rob. I've got a system that'll automate a lot of the work. Besides, most police officers are as much use as a canoe in a volcano when it comes to this work.'

'Right, aye.' Marshall almost bit his tongue. 'There was one in North Berwick the Edinburgh MIT worked. I can get you someone to help with that. A DC Simon Bu—'

'Isn't North Berwick in England?'

'You're thinking Berwick-upon-Tweed.'

'No, isn't North Berwick part of it?'

'They're about forty miles apart.'

'Okay, Rob. I'll focus on the others first. Catch you later.' And she was gone.

Marshall unbuckled himself and got out into the Baltic air. At least it wasn't raining anymore. He crossed the road and entered the station, then got a wink-click from the civilian manning the desk, so he headed through to the office space at the back.

No sign of Struan – he hadn't been *that* far ahead of Marshall, had he?

Jolene was working away at one of the four desks, the others unoccupied. She looked over, her desk phone cradled in her ear, then waved at Marshall and covered the receiver with her hand. 'You okay, Rob?'

'Just looking for DCI Gashkori.'

'He's off for lunch with his clan.' She checked her watch.

'Said they'll be back around one.' She frowned, staring into space. 'Go on?'

Marshall perched on the desk next to her and waited, arms folded.

'Okay, I'll see what I can do.' Jolene slammed the receiver into the phone. 'You put *her* onto me?'

'Put who?'

'Liana Curtis.'

'Bloody hell, she's quick. I only just passed those leads on to her.'

'What leads?'

'Wait. What's she been hassling you about?'

'She's been on my case all morning, asking these stupid questions about the case. I mean, I'm trying to collate the statements myself, but she's asking a gazillion pedantic little pieces of nonsense about each one and not letting me do my job.'

'Those pedantic little pieces of nonsense can be how we catch the bad guys.'

'Sure, I get that, but...' Jolene picked up her mobile, checked the screen and swore under her breath. 'She's your ex, right?'

'Liana? No.' But Marshall was blushing. Christ, he really needed to get better at handling these difficult questions. 'Did Gashkori say where he was going?'

Jolene tapped away at her keyboard. 'Fish suppers, I think.'

'So, one of the two places in town.' Marshall couldn't be arsed to check them. 'He'll keep. How's it going with the statements, then?'

A final flourish on the mouse, then Jolene sat back. 'Well, I just sent them off to your not-ex, not that I believe you. So that work is her fault now, not mine.' She laughed. 'You fancy a coffee?'

'Not here. But I'll get you one if you know of anywhere decent in town?'

'There's a great one in Reston. Ash says there's a couple of decent cafés on the high street.'

'Just been there. I'll head somewhere in a minute or two. Has anyone got Sylvester's bank records?'

'Yup. That's one of the gazillion tasks I've been trying to get through while she's been hammering my phone. She's after ancient history. Trying to pin down his movements over the last twelve years. Hard to get anything past seven, obviously. And she wants telephony too. That's a massive undertaking. But I had a brief lull of about half an hour when she wasn't calling me and managed to check through the recent stuff to see if we can track him down.'

'What have you found?'

'Looks like he gets paid from a trust every month.'

'Because of that accident?'

'Probably, but I can't say so either way just now. It's a lot of money, though. He's not poor, put it that way. And the balance just keeps going up every month.'

'Any transactions since he ran off?'

'Nope. Last transaction was—' She looked over at her screen again. '—withdrawing money from a cashpoint in Jedburgh.'

Marshall frowned. 'Jedburgh?'

'Aye, why?'

'That's pretty far from Eyemouth.'

'I thought that too...'

Marshall walked over to a giant map on the wall and stuck a pin in Eyemouth on the coast, just north of Berwick and the border's curious northwards kink through north Northumbria. Then west and south to Jedburgh on the A68, the long road running between Edinburgh and Newcastle. 'Not the obvious place to go. Just an hour away. No easy roads between the two towns, no obvious connects between them. But no ANPR cameras, either.'

Jolene scowled. 'Maybe he's on his way over to the west coast? Or down to Cumbria?'

'For either of those, you'd go up via Edinburgh or down via Newcastle, wouldn't you?' Marshall felt a stabbing in his temple. 'Unless you don't want to be spotted. It's a series of slow roads, but you'll get over or down easily enough. And like you say, no cameras.' He focused on Jolene. 'Have you got an update on his plates?'

She looked around the empty office space. 'DC Paton was doing that.' She leaned forward, tapped her phone screen a few times and put it to her ear. 'Hey, Ash.' She rolled her eyes. 'I said I wanted a sandwich.' A shake of the head. 'Peppered ham is fine. Okay, doesn't matter. I'll get something myself.' A sigh. 'Look, have you finished with the plates? Number plates!' She leaned even further forward, frowning. 'Okay, cheers.' She stabbed the screen and dropped her phone onto the desk. 'Okay, she's run the car from outside the B&B in St Abbs. Was that Sylvester's?'

'We believe so. Why?'

'Well, she found it on CCTV in Jedburgh.'

28

Marshall hadn't been this far south in a while – every time he'd been back in the Borders in the last year, he'd stuck to the two main roads down from Edinburgh, depending on whether he was seeing his sister or his mother. That horizontal-ish line between Clovenfords, Galashiels, Tweedbank and Melrose – if it wasn't for the massive hills, it'd all be one big city, not several towns and villages.

The A68 towards Newcastle was a bugger of a road, though, and this stretch proved it was based on an old Roman road through the borderlands – it bumped up and over the hills rather than evening them out.

Jolene was a better driver than Struan, not that that was saying much. Too cautious if anything – giving a bit too much respect to the old boy in front, who seemed to think thirty was the speed limit. '*Hate* overtaking on this road...'

'I know that feeling well.'

'That bloody Audi's right up my tail too.'

Marshall craned his neck around to look at the sweaty big guy in a suit. Red-faced and glaring at them.

'Think it's here.' She pulled in opposite the Edinburgh Woollen Mill, next to the Jedburgh Woollen Mill, which were seemingly in a war over competitively priced leisurewear and low-cost cups of tea.

Marshall spotted the ANPR camera. 'Ash said there weren't any until Darlington?'

'That was true, but this was installed a couple of months ago.'

'So, let me get this straight. On Friday, Sylvester left the B&B in St Abbs, then drove across country on one of those back roads between Gala and Berwick, then he came down this way?'

'Looks like it.'

'And it was triggered again today?'

'Correct.'

But there was no sign of Sylvester or his car. He could be halfway to Newcastle by now.

Marshall's phone rang. He fished it out of his pocket. Didn't recognise the number, but answered it anyway. 'Hello?'

'Is that Rob Marshall?' Irish accent. One of the two Dublin ones, north or south, but Marshall could never get them right.

'Speaking?'

'Sir, it's PC Liam Warner. We've worked a few cases over the year, you know?'

'Oh, I remember.'

'Grand. Anyway, I can't get hold of DS Archer. Someone said you'd be able to—'

'Jolene's with me right now. She's been driving. What is it?'

'Right. Okay. Just, you know this car you're looking for?'

'What about it?'

'I'm standing beside it.'

'Where are you?'

'I'm in Jedburgh, sir.'

'Which street?'

'Ehhhh. Hard to say, you know?'

'Can you describe it?'

'The main one?'

'What can you see?'

'A shop. Clothes shop. A bookshop. I think?'

'Stay right there.' Marshall clicked his fingers and pointed at the car. 'Sylvester's here!' Then back with Warner. 'Can you see David Sylvester?'

'Not unless he's hiding in the boot.'

Marshall tried to cross the road, but the traffic was thick and heavy. 'Listen to me. Sylvester usually stays in accommodation in coastal towns, so—'

'Sir, Jedburgh's pretty far from the sea.'

'I know that.'

'You think he's dumped his car and switched it?'

'No, I think he's staying there.'

'So you're looking for a hotel, right?'

'Or a B&B or a guesthouse.'

'Okay, well. There's a business card on the passenger seat. Teapot Cottage. Wee place up a lane here.'

'Okay, we're five minutes away. Can you call your mates and get them to help? Sylvester is dangerous.'

'Sure thing, sir...' And he was gone.

Marshall raced over the road and got in the car. 'That was PC Warner. He's on the main street here. Outside a bookshop. Sylvester's car's there.'

'On it.' Jolene got in and drove off, waiting to join another long queue of traffic heading south. 'Wasn't Warner due in court today?'

'No idea.'

'Pretty sure he was.' Jolene joined the queue and followed the road south, over the Jed Water, then it veered east, around the ancient town huddling on the hill.

Marshall couldn't sit still. Sylvester was here. And the bloody traffic was in the way.

Jolene got into the right-turn lane. A tractor trundled towards them, dragging a column of irate drivers behind it. She took her chance, though, and blasted across, then up the long bank into the town. Townhouses on both sides, with shops in the ground floor.

Marshall spotted a police car parked opposite the bookshop, Heron & Willow.

A Volvo was next to it, but no sign of Warner.

Marshall got out first, racing over to the car, a plug-in hybrid Marshall had considered buying before settling on his current mistake.

Same plate as the one outside the B&B in St Abbs.

He twisted around, taking in the surrounding area – they were on the literal outskirts of the town, just an industrial unit and a rugby pitch that way. 'So where the hell is Warner?' He got out his phone and hit dial, but it just rang and rang. He peered into the car and saw the card. 'Teapot Cottage. Any idea where that is?'

'Think so.' Jolene pointed to a lane running up the hill. 'Come on.'

Marshall followed her up, calling Control.

'Yep?'

'This is DI Rob Marshall, checking on a back-up request from PC Liam Warner.'

'Not got anything on the system.'

'Might be under William?'

'No, I know Liam. Calls in most days. He's not done so today. Yet.'

Great.

'Okay, cheers.'

Jolene stopped by a gate.

Two old mill workers' cottages had been wedged together and, despite the hard grey stone, someone had put up a sign reading:

Teapot Cottage
Bed, Breakfast & More!

Jolene frowned. 'Wonder what the "more" means...' The gate squealed like a pig and she stomped up the path, then rapped on the door. 'You want me to lead here?'

'Sure.'

The door opened and a bearded face beamed out. 'Hello, there!' Hands on his hips. His Killers T-shirt was stretched out by the distended belly hanging over trousers dusted with flour. 'Oh, even more police! What have I done now!' A loud laugh.

'DI Rob Marshall.' He held out his warrant card.

'Simon Rutherford.' He thrust a hand into Marshall's. 'Pleasure to meet you!'

Marshall took his hand back. 'Has a colleague showed up?'

'Yes, he's just speaking with Thomas.'

'Thomas?'

'Thomas Rutherford.'

An assumed name. Interesting...

'Are you related?'

'No, just a mere coincidence. Curious man. Just settling into his third pot of tea. That's a man who likes a cuppa! Been here a couple of weeks now. Of course he hasn't been here all that time, but you know tourists... Like to take a trip up to the Highlands or over to Skye or somewhere even further afield. Have to say I like it down here myself. Best place in the world.'

'Can you show us through?'

'By all means.' Rutherford led them through the quaint old building.

Marshall followed. He heard Jolene snap out her baton behind him.

Rutherford opened a door to a large conservatory. 'Thomas? I've got the police for you.'

Warner lay crumpled against the sofa, blood pouring down his face.

29

S hunty was a curious bugger. In one-on-one discussions, he could hide away as if you were talking to yourself. But in the full focus of the jury and the public gallery he seemed to grow in confidence and stature. Like he was a performing killer whale or something. Or a trained and experienced lawyer.

Elliot looked around the court. At least Hislop wasn't watching anymore, but no doubt he had at least one person observing for him.

She caught Davie looking up at her again. Kept doing that.

His strategy was brazen and relied on his defence lawyer not being shite. And Anthony Burgess-Strang KC was anything but shite. Unfit, maybe, with thick beads of sweat running down his forehead, despite the room being cold. His wobbly jowls gave him the look of a fat walrus. 'For the benefit of the court, I am requesting you divulge the information in full.'

'Okay.' Shunty got out his notebook and flicked through the pages. 'This is what I captured at the time and have subsequently validated. Mr Elliot was accessing information he shouldn't have been. A full trace was executed which showed that, although different people had logged in to access the salient information, the MAC address was always his terminal.'

'And can you elucidate on what MAC stands for?'

'Sorry, I don't know the exact terminology.'

'And you expect us to believe you?'

Shunty blinked. 'I don't need to. Much like you don't need to know what a calliper in your car does to drive it.'

'So what is it, then?'

'The MAC address is the unique identifier the network records for the machine in question.'

'I can barely get my phone to connect to my network half the time. Can you explain that in layman's terms?'

'I'm talking about the network in the police station, not a mobile phone network. Each machine connected to has a fixed hardware code which is given a network address at the point of setup. The closest analogy would be the VIN for a vehicle, which is installed at the end of manufacture. You might change the licence plate, but the VIN is fixed. It's part of how you can identify which user is requesting what information. So if I were to go in and check the PNC for Anthony Burgess-Strang, I can get your home address, car licence plate, any dealings with the police, outstanding warrants.'

'Of which there will be none.'

'Correct, but it's all logged to my account and to my machine. The wizards in IT can tell you who's looked at your record.'

'Okay.'

'Similarly, if I'm accessing information I'm not supposed to, such as your daughter's drink-driving conviction.'

'Excuse me?'

'I tried to access it, but I can't for some reason. That's because my user credentials don't match the security level required.'

'But that's nothing to do with the MAC address?'

'Correct. Suppose I was a superintendent, say, with the required security level to access your daughter's drink-driving conviction, then I could only do that from a machine on Police Scotland premises. Such sensitive information would be blocked from me accessing the information remotely from, say, my home office or a mobile phone.'

'Why would that be?'

'Because the necessary security protocols couldn't be proven to be enforced to protect your daughter's privacy.'

'Mr *Siyal*.' Good old Shunty had got Burgess-Strang on the ropes. 'Are you saying that it was Mr Elliot's machine that made most of the requests?'

'That's my understanding, yes.'

'But I understand the terminal of DI Andrea Elliot was also used.'

Shite...

Despite the freezing court, Elliot started to sweat here. She'd known she'd be dragged into this eventually, but not like this... And being this side of a court case was a nightmare. All the focus was on her and she couldn't say anything about it.

Shunty nodded. 'That's my understanding too.'

Over in the dock, Davie looked as if he tried to cover his wince.

'And yet you confidently say it was Mr Elliot who accessed the information?'

Shunty looked over at her. 'Because DI Elliot was in a police interview room when the information was accessed.'

'And why was that, mmm?'

'Because she was under suspicion and answering questions about previous leaks.'

'Because they had traced back to her machine?'

'No, to her account.'

Burgess-Strang let out a theatrical sigh. 'Sergeant, how are we supposed to believe the evidence we are being presented with? It seems like you're as confused as anyone about machines and accounts!'

'I'm perfectly sanguine about accounts and machines. For those instances where DI Elliot's account was used to access the data, I have validated and verified alibis. For instance, she was standing in this court being cross-examined by yourself for one of them.'

Burgess-Strang flashed his eyebrows. As close to a touché as anyone would get, at least in here. 'Why should we believe that it was the defendant accessing the information and not some third party? Such as yourself? Or a cleaner? Or anyone in the police station?'

Shunty sucked in a deep breath. Never a good look to be a smartarse anywhere, but in court... Well, that's the one place it was okay. And he was a royal smartarse. 'My understanding is, due to its nature, Police Scotland's security system is more stringent than, say, your Pornhub account, Anthony.'

Elliot enjoyed his glare. 'Excuse me?'

'I was using that service in contrast with your Google or Apple accounts, which have advanced security.' Shunty smiled. 'To stop this kind of thing happening, there are rules over the password, which has to be quite complex. And the distinct user identification isn't obvious either.'

'Can you elaborate?'

'Well, it's not Andrea dot Elliot as the login. It's her warrant card number, paired with some random digits. And for the password, you can't just put in "Password123" or your mum's sister's goldfish's best friend's date of birth. You've got to put so many upper-case letters and symbols and numbers. Words and common phrases are monitored too. Upshot is your password is pretty much impossible to guess – we're talking the opposite of those scenes in a film where someone looks around an office to see pictures of the computer's mum's sister's goldfish's best friend and susses it's their date of birth that's the password.'

'Don't get smart with me, Sergeant.'

'You asked me a question. I answered. We also have to change our passwords every three months.'

'None of which provides a suitable explanation for why, say, you weren't the one accessing the information the defendant is accused of?'

'Because I was in the interview with DI Elliot.'

'Okay. But, say, a colleague. Or, like I said, a cleaner.'

'Under interview, DI Elliot stated she shared her login credentials with Davie.'

'Despite all that rigmarole you just told us?'

'Because of it. Having to change your password quarterly means it's even harder to remember it. She thought it was okay to share with Mr Elliot. He was her husband, after all. Still is, despite what he's being accused of.'

'So it could've been her?'

'No. Like I told you, she was in court or being interviewed for them.'

Elliot wanted to punch Shunty. He had the defence lawyer on the ropes, ruining Davie's chances of getting out of this...

'Right, yes, of course.' Burgess-Strang cleared his throat and took a few seconds to check over his notes again. 'But did DI Elliot share user credentials with her husband?'

'According to DI Elliot, she recorded her passwords in a small notebook she kept in her purse.'

'That doesn't sound very secure.'

'That purse never leaves her side.' Shunty looked over at her and she held it up.

'Why did she have this unorthodox system?'

'Because she kept forgetting her passwords. Like I said, she had to change them so often. This book has the ones for her banking and Netflix and Amazon. You name it. You may have similar for your Pornhub account.'

'And DI Elliot thought this was okay?'

'It was approved by the security officer at Melrose station then Galashiels.'

'Who is the accused, yes?'

'Her husband, yes. The number of password resets DI Elliot got through in a week all came through him for approval. He approved the system.'

'Just like that?'

'No. His boss had to agree to it and hers too, DCI James Pringle. It's not unique, sir.'

'So they shared their passwords, then.' Burgess-Strang shook his head, then gave that lawyer look, the sheer disdain, like you were a piece of shite they'd just stood in. 'She isn't much of an officer, is she? Forgetful, dim-witted.' He licked his lips. 'Or maybe that's a ruse and she's the mastermind. Isn't it true, Sergeant, that DI Elliot and Gary Hislop were in a relationship?'

That was supposed to be a secret.

Elliot glared at Davie – the sneaky wee shite had passed that on, just to get him off. So much for nobly seeing trial, he was dropping her right in it.

Burgess-Strang couldn't interview her on the stand, but he could train all those questions at bloody Shunty.

'That was in high school, I believe.'

'But you do acknowledge the fact—'

Davie got to his feet. 'Tony!'

Burgess-Strang turned around to scowl at his client.

'Come. Here.' Davie beckoned him over.

The judge seemed to wake up, frowning at the unorthodox antics. But he let them persist.

Elliot sat back, clutching her purse like an unused prop in a shitty small-town amateur dramatics play.

Shunty was looking at her, frowning like he was unsure what he'd done.

Burgess-Strang stepped away, shaking his head and giving

Davie *that* look again. He turned to the judge and sighed. 'Your honour, I request to approach the bench.'

'Up you come.'

Elliot sat forward now, watching Davie. Head bowed, scratching at his hair. Chancing a glance at the judge in conversation with his lawyer. Then over at her, with a coy wink.

The prosecutor joined them and the conversation seemed to get even more heated. Until they stopped and returned to their posts.

The judge banged his gavel. 'Mr Elliot, please rise.'

Davie got to his feet, almost filling the dock with his bulky frame.

'Mr Elliot, I understand you wish to change your plea to guilty?'

Davie nodded. 'That's correct, sir.'

'Then, in that case, the trial ends. Mr Robertson, please can you send these good people home and I'll hear submissions as to the penalty in due course. Court is in recess.' The judge got to his feet and hurried towards the exit.

Davie was still smiling at Elliot.

She'd been wrong – he hadn't tried to deflect the blame onto her.

Instead, the stupid sod had called off his own lawyer in a last act of chivalry, hadn't he?

30

W arner's face looked like an extinction-level comet had collided with it. His nose had exploded, leaving a trail of blood. 'Have to keep touching my dose to check I still have one.' Just a little tap and he squealed. 'Feels like I've been stabbed by an ice pick.' He inspected his finger and it was smeared with blood again. 'C'mere, how bad is it?'

Jolene was squatting in front of him. 'Better than it looks.'

Marshall checked his phone, but still nothing from Gashkori. No bollocking. Yet. It was coming. Oh boy, was it coming.

Jolene clenched her hand over Warner's. 'Told you! Keep the pressure on that.'

'But it *hurts*.'

'Yeah, no getting away from that. That's the price of letting someone head-butt you.'

'It's not stopping bleeding, though.'

'No.' Jolene let out a sharp sigh. 'Back before this when I was a paramedic, we used to get you to tip your head back, but now we pack the nose like this. Huh. Okay, tip your head back.

That's it. Now hold that and let's see if we can get it to congeal a bit further up, aye?'

Warner did as he was told and looked up at the slate-grey sky. Blood still dribbled down his lip, into his mouth.

Marshall wasn't one of those all-action cops who got into scrapes and relished nothing more than a roll around with an idiot on a Saturday night pavement.

But Warner was supposed to be.

Christ, it must've been fifteen minutes now...

And Sylvester had got away.

'You want to tell me what happened in there?'

Warner shrugged, keeping his nose in the air. 'I lost a fight.'

'I told you to call in for backup.'

'I did.'

'I called Control. There was no record.'

'Stish was on his lunch.'

'Stish?'

'You know, PC Steven Taylor.'

'I know who he is, but you don't phone your mate! You call Control and they allocated the nearest resources!'

'Sir, that's not what you said. Call my mates. I only have the one, right, and Stish was on his lunch.'

'So you just went in there on your own?'

'You said you were five minutes away. Made me think I should get stuck in.'

Marshall took a deep breath. This was getting nobody anywhere. 'Constable, was your body-worn video recording at the time?'

Warner sucked in a bloody gulp of air. 'Right. I think so.'

'Can I have your data card, please?'

'Sure.' He unclipped his recorder and passed it to Marshall, keeping his nose raised. 'You know, you lot treat me like I'm a right eejit at times.'

'Wonder why...' Marshall popped the SD card out and

handed the rig back to him. 'Give me a sec.' He walked over to the squad car and waved at Jolene. 'Sergeant, need a hand.' He held out the SD card. 'Can you pull up the body-worn video from that?'

'Can't you?'

'Lost my operational credentials when I moved to Gartcosh.'

'Okay.' She got behind the wheel of the car and slotted the card into the laptop mounted on the dashboard. Took a few seconds, then the screen flashed up. She logged in and opened an app.

The screen filled with blurry video of Rutherford walking along a hallway. 'He loves a cup of tea!' He opened a door to a large conservatory. 'Thomas? I've got the police for you.'

David Sylvester was sitting at a table in the middle of the room, brazen as hell. He looked up from his jigsaw. 'Hello.' Then back down.

Warner beckoned for Rutherford to leave them, then walked over. 'That's a mighty tricky jigsaw there, David.'

'I'm doing nothing wrong.'

'Okay, sure. But you run away every time we try to speak to you.'

'I've not done anything!'

'Attempting to murder someone and assaulting an officer is something.'

'*Attempting*?'

'Kayleigh Rothbury.'

Sylvester held a piece over the board, looking for where to slot it in.

'You assaulted her in her home, then carried her to the cliff edge where you threw her off. That's not cool.'

'I didn't do it. I haven't done anything. Ever. But that hasn't stopped the police from hounding me for the last twelve years, has it?'

'Then you disappeared from your lodgings, didn't you? And you ran from my colleagues.'

'That's... That's... She was hassling me! How was I to know that old bag was a cop?' Sylvester slotted the piece in. 'I've done nothing wrong!'

'If that's the case, why do the police want you for murder?'

Sylvester shot him a furious glare. 'I have never even so much as *touched* a woman in anger before, let alone attempted to kill someone.'

'Sure. I believe you. Come on, David. We know you did this. Come with me and we'll straighten this whole thing out.'

Sylvester picked up another jigsaw piece. 'I have done *nothing.*'

'See, this is why we need to get you into the police station and get this whole thing on the record. Mr Sylvester, you assaulted a police officer. DI Andrea Elliot. As such, I am arresting you for—'

'NO!' Sylvester shot to his feet and cracked Warner in the face with a giant fist.

He stumbled backwards but didn't go down. The video was shaky, then it resolved on Sylvester grabbing his shoulders and pushing him against the wall. 'Leave me alone!' He crashed his forehead into Warner's face, just above the camera.

Warner went down, covering his face with both hands.

Sylvester stood over him. 'I've done nothing and yet you still think I did that to those women!' He kicked Warner a few times in the stomach, hard enough to make Marshall feel like he was going to be sick – and it wasn't happening to him.

Then all the video caught was footsteps running away and Sylvester leaving by the conservatory door.

Jolene sighed as she got the machine to back up the video to the remote server. She looked over at Marshall. 'We need to get uniform going door-to-door on neighbouring properties.'

'I'll sort that when Ryan bothers to show up.'

Jolene looked back at him and her eyes went wide.

Marshall looked behind him and saw Gashkori staring at the screen, rubbing at his nose. 'Second time we've let him go in twenty-four hours.'

Marshall got out of the car. 'I'm sorry, sir.'

'This is on you, Rob.' A hand on his back. Tight, not reassuring. He led him away from the car, past the bookshop and the clothes shop. 'Marshall, I'm going to tell you it straight. You're an arrogant arsehole. You thought Sylvester's MO is of taking young women by surprise, so you assumed he was weak. Assumed DI Elliot was either unlucky or overpowered yesterday.'

'Sounds a bit sexist.'

'I'm not being that in the slightest. What were you thinking letting him tackle Sylves—?'

'*Sir*. PC Warner didn't listen to my instruction correctly. I told him to wait and get backup. He phoned one guy, who was on lunch, then went in there and got the shit kicked out of him. That's all on him.' Marshall gestured at Warner beside their pool car. A trickle of wet blood burst out and slid down his top lip. 'We just watched the body-worn video. He tried arresting Sylvester for assaulting DI Elliot.'

'And then he battered him? Magic.' Gashkori looked over at him. 'Warner's as useful as a paper ashtray. We need to get shot of that clown.' He switched his glare to Marshall. 'Rob, I'm not saying you're not up to being a police officer, but that's the impression you're giving here.'

'Excuse me?'

'You're an inspector, for crying out loud. I wouldn't expect that kind of rubbish from a dead-end sergeant like Struan. Look, I get it. It's not your fault you were a direct entry and you didn't learn how to hold your own on the street, so—'

'Sir, that's *bull*shit. I've held my own with people *much* worse than David Sylvester. I've broken apart fights on Saturday nights in parts of London you've never even heard of. Believe me, I might've got in straight as a DI, but I was made to learn on the job. Hard and fast. This isn't on me. This is a useless officer not under my direct command ignoring an order.'

'Rob.' Gashkori sighed. 'We'll deal with this later. Our focus right now is on tracking down a serial killer who is *still* at large but is now *very* much aware of there being a manhunt for him. And I'm out of ideas over how to track him down.' He looked at Warner dabbing at his nose. Blood covered his fingers. Wet, thin, streaming down.

Gashkori put a hand on his shoulder. 'Rob, I'm worried about the state of him. '

'I'm fine, sir.'

'If you're fine, Constable, why won't your nose stop bleeding? Are you on anticoagulants or something?'

'What are they?'

'That shouldn't be happening.' Gashkori pointed at Marshall. 'Get him to A&E. Now.'

31

Marshall would've thought Warner being a cop would get them preferential treatment. That or him being the twin brother of the senior charge nurse, but nope. They had to wait in the Borders General A&E just like everyone else. Rows of seats filled with the walking wounded. And one guy in a mobility scooter who had a gouge taken out of his cheek. All dried, though.

And Warner's blood kept dripping onto the floor.

Despite Jolene's expertise. Despite the wads of toilet tissue he'd stuffed in there.

Aye, David Sylvester had done a number on him.

Marshall got up and went into the bathroom, tore off another length of tissue then walked back over. 'Here.'

'Cheers.' Warner replaced the soaked tissue with a fresh one, stuffing some paper into his nose to fill it out and soak up the drips.

Marshall crouched and started clearing the tiles of spilled blood.

And his phone rang.

Great.

He stood and checked his display:

Liana Curtis calling...

He answered the call. 'Hey.'

'You okay?'

'Why wouldn't I be?'

'Sound a bit weird, that's all.'

'I'm in A&E.'

'Jesus, Rob. What happened?'

'Tell me you didn't listen to that voicemail I left without telling me you didn't listen to that voicemail I left...'

Liana sighed. 'Are you okay?'

'I'm fine. PC Warner got head-butted and has a nosebleed that won't stop.'

Blood splashed onto the floor in rapid-fire pattern.

Marshall tore out more paper and Warner replaced it, packing it even more roughly than before. He used his shoe to guide the wad of paper over the latest spillage. 'Anyway. What's up?'

'What's up?'

'Well, why did you call? You making any progress?'

'Ish. But I was processing what you told me in your voicemail.'

'So you did listen to it?'

'I did, but sorry. I zoned out about the blood bit. I get squeamish about live people.'

Marshall had seen that a few times in action – she could be in a room with a rap battle or poetry slam in full flow and not be aware of her surroundings. That ability to disassociate was pretty impressive. 'Which bit were you focusing on, then?'

'How Sylvester told Warner he denied everything. Our

profile had him proud of his crimes. Goldberg's theory was that the killer is a narcissist who demanded attention from his victims. When it was withdrawn, that was when he struck. Jacob said that when we caught him, he'd be happy to take full credit for them. But when Warner went to arrest him, instead of taking credit, he attacked him. Remember that other case where the guy just came in and talked to us? But to violently attack a police officer...'

'I was never a hundred percent on that part. I've left it in the profile document for now, but I told She Who— the boss... I told her it should be thought through.'

'Did she agree?'

'Didn't disagree.'

'Okay... It's just...' Liana clicked her tongue a few times. 'It kind of goes against the whole thrust of the profile, doesn't it?'

'Does it?'

'Rob. You've only just updated it and you can't remember?'

'No. It's not that. It's just... I think that part is a little chocolate star on top or a dusting of icing sugar. It's not the cake.'

'Well.' She paused. 'Thing I keep coming back to is Holly was the only victim we spoke to when we were creating that profile. The others all died. We've no idea if her experience was typical or an outlier.'

Warner dabbed at his nose. And it started gushing again.

'I see your point, Liana, but I still think the profile fits the evidence pretty well.' Marshall passed Warner another wad of toilet paper. 'But you're wrong.'

'How?'

'Goldberg spoke to Sylvester's ex-girlfriend. Remember?'

'Vaguely. But she wasn't a victim.'

'No, but she knew Sylvester. Said the reason she left him boiled down to his narcissism.'

'You want to assume she was a victim on his escalation path and include her in the victimology?'

Marshall shrugged, even though she couldn't see him. 'Maybe we should try and track her down again.'

'Us and whose army? Hardeep's off tomorrow as well, apparently.'

Marshall had forgotten that. 'Someone in Jolene's team can help.'

'A cop. I'm not sure what they can add.'

The door opened and Jen appeared, resting her hands on her hips. 'Warner?' She spotted Marshall, rolled her eyes, and walked off.

'Sorry, I need to go get his nose fixed. I'll call you later.' Marshall pocketed his phone, but his pockets were full of Warner's bloody tissues. He caught up with Jen again and Warner's nose was in full flow again, dripping on the floor as they walked. 'Thanks for seeing him.'

'Didn't know it was him.' She was shaking her head. 'What happened?'

'Got the shite kicked out of me, what's it look like.'

'So you want me to stuff the shite back in for you?'

'Ha bloody ha. No, I got head-butted. Won't stop bleeding.'

'In here.' She took Warner into a treatment room at the side, then sat him down and started prodding around. 'Well, your perfect nose is still intact.'

'Seriously?'

'It's hardly perfect, is it? But it's not broken.' She gripped the sides of his nostril and splayed them wide.

Warner yelped.

'Easy.' She pulled out the toilet tissue. 'If it was broken, you'd be squealing at me breathing on it, not making that sound at me doing this.' She grabbed both nostrils in her gloved fingers and held his nose closed. 'I'll stop the bleeding. Now lean back.'

'Won't stop. That's weird, isn't it?'

She frowned at him. 'You're not on any anticoagulants, are you?'

'No. Your man here had to explain what they were.'

Marshall stared at her. God knows what she was doing, but Warner's legs were dancing like it hurt. 'How's Kayleigh?'

'Kayleigh? She's still in intensive therapy, Rob. Not my circus, not my clown.'

'Gashkori got the paramedics to bring her here rather than to Berwick. Is that because they're clowns too?'

'No, it's six and two threes between there and here. Besides, Ryan knows us. Both places are absolute chaos just now. And it's people like me who bear the brunt.'

Marshall sat back. 'The patients are suffering too...'

She pulled out a giant homunculus of congealed blood from Warner's nose, then dropped it into a dish. 'That's the problem. It's congealing but not blocking the damage. I'll get you right in a jiffy.' She sprayed something up there.

Warner squealed. 'What the hell is *that*?'

'Lidocaine spray. Constricts all the blood vessels long enough so the blood can coagulate in the vein. You're lucky; we used to use cocaine.' She pulled her gloves off and dumped them in the bin. 'Right, that should be you.'

'That's it?'

'Aye. Now clear off.'

'Right. Thank you.' Warner touched his nose and it was encrusted with blood, but dried this time rather than the constant dribble of fresh stuff. 'Just need to go to the bog, so I'll see you outside, yeah?'

Marshall leaned in close to his sister. 'Listen, Jen, I wanted to talk to you about Thea.'

She shot him a hard stare. 'That's none of your business.'

'Except that Thea's making it mine.'

She looked away. 'It's not easy, you know?'

'Not saying it is. But she told me you're seeing someone. Is it Ryan?'

'Ryan?'

'DCI Gashkori to me.'

She looked away and exhaled. 'When you moved out after your transfer, I was toiling financially. Big time. Ryan moving into the flat over the garage was a godsend. So thank you for that.'

'I'm not a god, but I'll take that.'

'Ha, ha.'

'But something happened?'

She let out a deeper sigh. 'A couple of drinks in the pub one night, then one thing led to another. So aye, we're sleeping together.'

'I'm pleased for you, Jen.'

'Really?'

'Sure. Even though Gashkori's a wanker...'

She punched his shoulder. Hard. 'I'm so lonely with Thea away at uni now.' She jabbed a finger at him. 'Now get out of here before I break *your* nose.'

'Later, then.' Marshall left her and walked back to the corridor.

Warner was adjusting his flies for longer than seemed necessary. 'Ah, there you are.' He patted his nose. 'That feels a lot better.'

'Let's get you back to the station so you can change your clothes.'

'Sure.' Warner was shaking his head, gurning away. 'C'mere, sir. You've been in court, right?'

Marshall didn't have time for this kind of digression. 'Many times, why?'

'Well, I was today and the judge... He was a right arsehole to me. I was only fifteen minutes late, but you try getting parked in Edinburgh.'

'Next time, I suggest you get there an hour early.'

'An *hour*?'

'Then if you're late, you're still early.'

'So, what, I just sit around for an hour?'

Marshall shrugged. 'That's kind of the idea, yeah.'

Warner blew air up his face. 'Starting to think I'm not well suited to this gig.'

Marshall had reached that conclusion a long time ago.

32

'Stupid. Stupid. Bastard.' Elliot couldn't find an angle where she could focus on Davie without either wanting to be sick or to smash his face off the desk. 'Why the hell did you do that?'

Back in the consultation room. Davie's head rested on the table. He sat up. Eyes closed, mouth stretching to a rictus. All the physical attributes of a smile, but none of the joy, happiness or even smug sarcasm. No, all it showed was pain. He opened his eyes again. 'Andi, truth is I... I don't... I...'

'Did you get your deal?'

'I don't know.'

'Davie!'

He scratched at his neck. 'I think I still do.'

'You *think*? But you don't know?'

'No. It's... I've got a meeting with someone about that.'

'Jesus, Davie.' Elliot wanted to shake him hard. Throw him against the magnolia walls. 'Why the hell did you do that without agreeing it first?'

'Look, my lawyer spoke to the prosecutor. I've got *a* deal, which they are honouring.'

Something unclenched inside her. Some deep relief. 'But it's not the same one, is it?'

'No, it's... Complicated. Basically, I'm being placed in prison.' He raised a finger to stop her. 'Ahead of sentencing. Anonymously.'

'Anonymously?'

'I don't know which one I'm going to. I'll be under an assumed name, so nobody can pick it up from the jungle drums. You know as well as anyone, Andi, my only chance of serving my sentence is if nobody knows where I am... And where I actually go, it's better if nobody knows *who* I am.'

'This was the old deal?'

'Part of it.' He reached across the table for her hands. 'Andi, even you won't be told where I've gone.'

She pulled her hands away before he could touch her skin. 'And you're okay with that?'

Davie shrugged. 'I'm okay with living.' He sat back and started rolling up his shirt sleeves. She hadn't seen him like this in ages. He seemed... rattled. Shaken. Usually, everything with him was so relaxed it was horizontal, but now he was edgy, like he couldn't settle. 'Andi, it's all cool. I'm totally at peace with what's happened. I've made a big mistake and now it's time to pay for it.'

'A big mistake... Give me strength. It's not just you who's paying for it, though, is it?'

'I get that, but... Do you have any idea how bad it is having the threat from an animal like...' He craned his neck around and scanned the walls. 'Like *him* hanging over you?'

'Hislop isn't that stupid.'

'No, but his men are. Aren't they? Worse thing is, the threats aren't aimed at me. A lot of it's at you and the kids.'

Exactly as she'd feared. They must teach that on the first day of hoodlum school – go after the family. Second day, go after the friends.

'If that's the case, Davie, why did you change your plea?'

'Because I thought I had the choice to protect you from him, but...' His tongue swept across his lips. 'Seeing Hislop on the stand made me think it all through. I knew he'd come after my family because he told me he would. He sent you that wine, remember? And he had those photos of us. I thought if I went down for it, they'd just take it as that. But the way I see it, he'll have another cop on the payroll by now. Maybe he always has. If I take the rap for what's happened, they'll cover it over. But...'

'Is that why you changed your mind?'

'No. My lawyer told me he was going to use Plan B, which was attacking Shunty.'

'What was Plan A?'

'Get the judge to throw it out. That didn't work, so his intention was to really tear him a new one. Totally discredit him on the stand. Make him look like an arse. I did the sums and, truth be told, I didn't much like Shunty. So I was okay with it. But what I didn't know was my lawyer had a Plan C if Shunty survived. And that was casting doubt on you, Andi. Since you can't take the stand because we're married, the jury would never hear from you on the matter. So there'd be reasonable doubt about you. The boys and Sam, well they need one functioning employed parent, don't they? So I want to keep you out of jail. Trouble is, they wouldn't settle for me, would they? So they were going to come after you as well.'

'Davie. I can handle Hislop.'

He sat back, shaking his head. 'Not him. The police.'

'What?'

'I didn't know he was going to... My lawyer knew about you and Hislop, from way back when. I hadn't told him. But he was going to use that to try to get me off. If the legal system didn't have me, then they'd need someone. And I didn't want it to be you.'

'Davie, I haven't done anything.'

'No, but he was using that ancient history to put you in the frame.'

'I haven't *done* anything. There's no chance of my being prosecuted.'

'No, but *I* have and it's his job to get me off.' He held her gaze, gripping it tight. 'Please, Andi. Take the money.'

'What?'

'All the cash he gave me, take—'

'No. I don't want that *blood money*.'

'It's not—'

'Of course it is!'

'But I haven't killed anyone!'

'No, but people have died because of that information.'

He was frowning. 'Like who?'

'Why do you think he kept asking you for stuff? Our investigation was getting close to people in his world... He jokingly called them "friends from the rugby club" and the weird thing was they were. Used to meet in there, get sloshed and sort stuff out. Illegal stuff. Very careful, of course, but they did. Trouble is, the more we found about the business, the tighter the security around it got. And the witnesses we'd spoken to started dying. I didn't know it was because you'd been leaking information to him!'

He couldn't look at her. Wouldn't.

'Want me to give you their names, Davie?'

'No.'

'Because what you did is just as responsible for their deaths as the animal who abducted and killed them. So don't talk to me about not taking blood money. Okay?'

'Please. I want the kids to—'

'The kids will be fine.'

'Andi, I'll tell you where it is and—'

'The second I know where it is, it's all getting turned over as evidence.'

That shut him down. 'What? Why?'

'We can prove Hislop gave you the money. You can use that to your advantage speaking to this person about your deal. You'll be going in there with a nuke instead of a butter knife.'

'I'll bide my time, then.'

'Davie, I just want my life back. Please.'

'That's not coming back. Not until I'm out.'

'No, it's not. I want *a* life. Looks like I'll have to shape it without you or your blood money.'

'I just want to look after my kids.'

'Should've thought about that, shouldn't you? Best way to look after your kids would be to, you know, actually be their dad!'

He jolted back in his seat, wrapping his arms around himself. Then clawed at his hair, the brown now streaked through with silver. He stared up at the ceiling and swallowed hard, then focused on her. 'In the months I've been under lock and key, I've had a lot of time to myself. A lot of time to think. I've thought a lot about what Sam's been through. I don't want the boys to get the same way.'

'The *same way*?'

'You know what I mean. All that gender-bender stuff, it's—'

'Davie, that's Sam discovering who she is. As much as you painting those Warhammer miniatures when you were a kid or playing golf or wanking with your mates from school in the woods that one time.'

He was blushing now. '*Told* you never to mention that.'

'So masturbating in the woods with your pals when you were fifteen is somehow worse than handing the names of leakers to a known killer?'

That shut him up.

'Sam's our kid, Davie. Both of ours. When I gave birth to her, I didn't have a choice but to be there for her at any time in

her life. Whatever she did. Whoever she was. She's our kid.'
She clenched her jaw. 'Well. She's *my* kid.'

'Please.' He looked at her through damp eyes. 'Just take the
money. *Please.*'

'No.' Elliot scraped her chair back and got up. 'I hope you'll
be safe inside, Davie.' She walked over to the door without
looking back.

Not even when he shouted at her.

Not even when he ran over and grabbed her arm.

Not even when the security guard opened the door and clattered him on the head.

Only when she stepped out into the corridor did she finally
look back at her husband, father of her children.

'Please, Andi!'

The pathetic scumbag who'd lied to her and cost people
their lives.

33

Marshall stepped up to the entrance to Galashiels nick. First time he'd been in here since he'd cleared out his office and moved over to Gartcosh. Felt like no time and yet felt like forever. He fished out his warrant card with one hand and noticed his fingers were all covered in blood. Warner's blood.

Jen was someone who just *knew* they were right, even when they weren't. *Especially* when she wasn't, which was fairly often.

He smiled at the new security guy, then swiped through the door into the office space. Just like he used to.

It was Davie Elliot the last time he'd been here. Hard to process what he'd done. It took a lot for someone in his position to leak like that. To betray everyone he worked with and those they'd sworn to protect. Not to mention what his wife was going through...

Hardly anyone about, which was a good sign – nobody should be in the station during a manhunt like this. He could only see Gashkori's PA and the red-faced admin officer, phone to his ear as he struggled to update the whiteboard. Probably on with Gashkori himself, and Marshall figured he was more likely to be the recipient of the information than the provider.

The door on the far side opened and Ash Paton walked through, matching the slow pace of a middle-aged man. Heavy jacket, heavier expression, but his giant belly almost made the purple Maroon 5 T-shirt read more like Macaroon 555.

Marshall clocked him – Simon Rutherford, the owner of the B&B in Jedburgh.

Rutherford stopped dead. 'Okay, so how do we go after the unsub?'

Paton's shoulders slumping.

Marshall clocked it – someone who'd watched too many TV dramas and read too many novels. Just wanted to get involved.

'Sir, you're here to provide information, which you kindly have.' Paton pointed towards the door and saw Marshall. 'You're now free to go.'

'But I want to help. Like, I could wear a wire? Speak to him? Get him to confess? What are the laws on that here? Is this a one-party or two-party consent country?'

Paton just smiled. 'Don't you want to get back to your child?'

'Sometimes you need to make sacrifices, right? Help the greater good.'

'That's right.' Paton looked across the room and spotted Marshall. 'Just a second, sir. Before I can progress your request for a wire, I need to seek approval from a superior officer.'

'Got your back, ma'am.' Rutherford stared at Marshall. 'Oh, how is your colleague's nose?'

'It's healing, thank you.' Marshall stepped to the side to speak to Paton. 'You get anything?'

'Nothing, sorry.' She glanced back the way. 'He's a *nightmare*.' She shook her head. 'Anyway, the bottom line is he said Sylvester's been staying there for two weeks.' She raised a finger. 'Sorry. He's been *checked in* for that time, but he hasn't slept there much. Just last night and... Sorry, I need to check my notes, but the night when he took out the cash.'

Marshall still felt the whole thing was shady as all hell. 'That didn't strike him as weird?'

'Happens a lot with longer-term leases. Booked through to the end of June. Cash in hand, all paid up front. Three grand.'

'Nice work if you can get it...' Marshall frowned. 'He's staying there, what, ninety days? So, that's...' He felt like a giant cog was grinding away inside his head. 'What, thirty quid a night?'

'Give or take, aye. It's a decent chunk of cash, like you say, but it's for the worst room he's got in the place. So he sees it as free cash. Oh, he explained why Sylvester has two places at a time. He worries he'll be made homeless.'

'Seriously?'

'What he said.' She shrugged. 'Man, the room is *grotty*.'

'You've been inside?

Paton nodded. 'Didn't get anything, though. Not even a bag or rucksack. Just a toothbrush and a phone charger. Oh, and a wrapper from his bloody jigsaw.'

'Got it. So his bag's somewhere else?'

'We're trying to get into the car.'

'You mean they haven't already?'

She shrugged. 'Forensics are being dicks about it.'

'You want me to speak to someone over there?'

'Not sure, sir. Best take that up with DI Taylor.'

'I might just do that.'

The door buzzed and PC Steven Taylor strolled through, chatting with a teenage girl. Fifteen, maybe. Dressed in a uniform with a red tie, marking one of the houses from Jedburgh Grammar.

Rutherford raced over to her. 'Myleene!'

Marshall followed him and let them get their hug out of the way. 'Sir, is this your daughter?'

'Correct.'

And it hit Marshall – Myleene ticked all the boxes in Sylvester's MO. A potential future victim. 'Listen, do you mind if I have a word with her?'

Rutherford frowned for a few seconds. 'By all means.' Then he stepped back. 'Just don't take too long, okay?'

'Sure. Sure.' Marshall smiled at him, then led Myleene into his old office.

Callum Taylor had made himself at home in here, turning it into a shrine to Glasgow Rangers, with a signed Graeme Souness shirt on the wall flanked by a few half-and-half scarves split with European teams. Not only a supporter but an active fan. Interesting.

He sat behind his old desk, but Taylor had messed about with the settings for the chair and something cracked and rattled beneath him. He smiled at Myleene, gesturing for her to sit opposite. 'I'm DI Rob Marshall and I want to ask you a few questions, which might help us greatly. You okay with that?'

She nodded. 'Sure thing, sir.'

Marshall held out his phone, showing a photo of David Sylvester. One of many. 'Do you recognise this man?'

She didn't take long to nod. 'That's Mr Rutherford, right?'

'That's right.' Marshall put his phone away. 'You know him well?'

'He's not related to us.' She smiled, using her dad's same joke. 'I'm glad, though, because he was, like, *super* creepy last year.'

'Last year?'

She nodded. 'He's stayed with us for like the last three years.'

Marshall looked out of the door and locked eyes with her father, waiting just outside. 'Back in a moment.' He got up and joined him out in the office space. 'Mr Rutherford, your daughter said this isn't the first time the... other Mr Rutherford has stayed with you?'

'Correct. Last four years, I think.' Rutherford laughed. 'He came in at the tail end of the first lockdown. I was on my knees, mate. I gave him a cheap rate for the whole summer in this room. It's...' He shook his head. 'Between you and me, mate, it's rubbish, quite frankly, but he doesn't seem to mind. The cash kept the wolf from the door for a few months at the hardest time of my life. Let me paint some of the other rooms, put in some new furniture. All basically for the price of several pots of tea a day and the room I use to store stuff in.'

'Why was he in that room? Did he ask for it?'

'He asked to see them all. The others were too pricey for him, or so he said, then he asked to see the other one.'

'And I'm guessing he paid cash?'

Rutherford coughed. 'Now I didn't quite say that, did I?'

'Come on, don't be evasive now.'

But he was looking away from Marshall. One thing about tax avoiders is they knew when to shut the hell up – or when they'd talked too much.

Time to give him it with both barrels...

'Thomas Rutherford is better known as David Sylvester. It's an assumed name, sir. We're currently executing a sizeable manhunt to track him down.'

Rutherford put a hand to his mouth. 'What the hell has he done?'

'At least one murder, possibly several.'

'Shit.'

Marshall nodded at Myleene in his office, messing about on her phone. 'It's not uncommon for him to target the children of the owners of the premises he's staying in.'

'Oh my God.'

'Did he ask to pay cash?'

'He did. I didn't mind. Keeping it on the QT was good for

me, because my ex-wife was chasing me through the courts at the time. I mean, I'm the one saddled with a child to support while she... While she... I'm so sorry. I feel like I've failed Myleene. My God...' Rutherford raced into the office and wrapped his daughter up in a cuddle she looked like she didn't want. 'I let him give you a lift to school today!'

Her face went white, despite the heavy makeup.

Marshall couldn't decide if it was shock or the embarrassment from a public display of affection. 'We don't believe he's an active pursuer. He tends to strike in secrecy, after he's left the location.' Didn't seem to soothe either of them, though. Proximity to a murderer put everything on edge. 'Myleene, can you tell us what happened this morning?'

'What's there to say? Went in his car, drove me to school and I walked in. It's not *far*, but I have to help Dad with the breakfasts and I've never got enough time.'

Poor kid...

'You know something?' Myleene shot him with an angry look. 'He was *extremely* inappropriate to me. Are you saying he *is* a pervert?'

'Myleene. What did he say to you?'

'Nothing.'

'So how was he extremely inappropriate then?'

'He was just... weird. Always staring at me. Like when I glanced at him, he was already looking at me. Made me feel as though he was undressing me with his eyes.'

'Myleene, do you know who he was going to see afterwards?'

34

All Myleene had said was 'the garage', but it'd taken Paton less than three calls to track down which one. Marshall was getting a bit spooked by her knack of guessing correctly, but then again lightning had a habit of striking twice and he didn't want to mess with it.

Luckily, the garage in question wasn't far from the station, just up a back street near the Aldi in Galashiels. The late sun caught the trees on the hill above them as traffic swelled on the main east-west road through the town.

A long single-storey building in black and neon yellow. Three wide doors, all down. Clanking and hammering sounds. The sign read:

Max Power

'I've been here before.' Marshall got out and couldn't figure out where he knew the place from. Then it hit him – the case that had brought him back home from London. Another serial killer. Felt like another lifetime.

He looked over at Paton as they walked over to the building. 'How did you narrow it down so quickly?'

'Well, it's like playing Wordle.'

'Wordle?'

She grinned at him. 'Tell me you've heard of Wordle, sir.'

'Of course I've heard of it. I tried it, but I didn't get on with it.'

'Well, that's your loss. Great way to start your day.' She tried the door but it didn't budge, so she pressed the buzzer. 'My point is it's as much about the possibilities you exclude. Sylvester drives a brand-new Volvo, right? So I called them first, the one over by Langlee. Nope. Then I tried the main garage in Jedburgh and they hadn't heard of him either. Then it struck me. One thing you've been clear on is he doesn't shit where he eats, does he?'

'You mean, the way he moves on before he strikes again?'

'Exactly that.' She pressed the buzzer again. 'This is the one place in the Borders that lets anyone walk up...'

Marshall nodded slowly. 'But if it wasn't here?'

'There's a guy who does MOTs in pub car parks.'

Marshall laughed.

The door opened but there was nobody there.

Marshall followed her into the garage's reception area. Rather than Korean chart pop, the speakers belted out "I Was Dancing in a Lesbian Bar" by Jonathan Richman, like some hipster coffee shop in London.

The owner was behind the desk, glaring at them as he tapped away at a grimy old keyboard, singing along to the track. He coughed, rattling like a bag of bones, then muttered under his breath. Marshall knew him – Max Power, the name behind the sign. He turned to look at them, then sucked down a deep glug of tea. 'Uh oh, it's the filth.' He got up and shook their hands. 'DI Marshall, right?'

Marshall was impressed by that. Must be almost two years ago now and he still didn't just recognise him but knew his name and rank too.

Max smiled at Paton. 'Take it this isn't about your Clio, sweetheart?'

She was blushing slightly. 'Not today, but the clutch is giving me some aggro, so I'll pop it in soon.'

'Told you a V6 engine was daft in a motor that size.'

'Need it on these roads.'

'Aye, maybe.' Max's gaze shifted between them with a slight hint of nervousness. 'So. What brings you here, doll?'

Paton showed him a photo. 'Recognise this man?'

Max licked his lips. 'Should I?'

'Gather he was visiting here today.'

'Wouldn't be the first time some lowlife pretended to know me.'

'Wouldn't be the first time you knew some lowlife, though.'

'Aye, fair enough.' Max sat back in his chair. 'David Sylvester, aye?'

'That's right.'

'Weird bastard. Boot was full of jigsaws from charity shops.' Max rolled his eyes. 'What's he done?'

'He *was* here, then?'

'Aye. Came in about nine. His MOT was overdue, so he was desperate. Paid double. Had our work cut out for us – that car's a rust bucket.'

Paton frowned. 'Hang on a sec. He drives an electric Volvo. Brand new.'

'Nope.' Max folded his arms across his chest. 'An old Astra. '03 plates. Popped in with it last week, asked for the full service. That's when I pointed out the MOT was overdue.'

She was nodding along. 'So when's he due to pick up?'

'Already done.'

'You're serious?'

'Might be a rust bucket, darling, but the engine's still sound.' He shifted his ratty eyes between them. 'You mind telling us what he's done?'

Marshall smiled at him. 'You mind giving us his plates?'

35

Elliot swiped her card through the reader and got a red light and an unsubtle honk. She tried it again. Same. 'For fuck's *sake*.' She looked over at the security desk, but Davie's replacement was already on his way over. 'Steven, this is the fourth time in the last month.'

'Aye, sure.' Steven swiped her card slowly, but got the same result, so he tried again. 'And you're about to say this wouldn't have happened under Davie's watch...' He sighed, then walked over to his desk and fiddled around with the card. 'I won't get into how I don't leak information to gangsters or how—'

'Gary Hislop's hardly a gangster.'

'Pedants often miss the point of the message.'

'In case you hadn't noticed, I'm not in the mood for this bullshit.'

'Oh, I'd noticed alright.' Steven handed back her card. 'I advise you to keep it away from your phone.'

'Aye, aye.' Elliot swiped through the door, then stuffed it back into her phone case.

Stupid prick.

She stormed through the quiet area towards her office and stopped dead. Then did a double take.

Marshall and Struan were in Taylor's office, deep in conversation.

Dr Donkey looked over at her and frowned. 'Andrea. You okay?'

'Just fine and dandy, Rob. What are you pair up to?'

Struan wouldn't look at her. 'Nothing.'

She caught a frown on Marshall's face, then he smiled at her. 'We've caught a fresh lead on Sylvester. Just making sure DS Liddell's team are fully focused on that.'

Struan nodded. 'And we are.'

'Aye, that sounds like total bullshit.' Elliot laughed. 'You pair know full well not to lie to me.' She shifted her gaze between the pair of arseholes. 'So? What's the gossip?'

Marshall gestured for Struan to go first.

Struan cleared his throat. 'Just been to BGH to check up on the lassie. Kayleigh, you know? And I got chatting to one of the nurses there who... I'm pals with. And she heard that someone killed Dr Owusu.'

'What?'

'Back in South Africa.' He pointed a finger pistol at his head and fired two bullets. 'Carjacking.'

'Is that true?'

'No reason to doubt it. Just passing it on to DI Marshall seeing as how, well, he's looking after DCI Pringle.' Struan shrugged. 'Thought he'd like to know.'

Marshall was looking away. 'I don't *like* to know but it's useful to.' He got his phone out of his pocket and stared at the display. 'Sorry, I'd better take this.' He left the room. 'Hi, it's Rob.'

Saved by the phone, like he was so many times.

'Don't think I don't know what you're up to, you wee dick.' Elliot rounded on Struan. 'Stirring the pot, eh?'

'You can't talk to me like that!'

'Oh, I can. I can and I will. Even when I can't, I will.' She stepped close enough to smell his Old Spice. 'And I do. You're always sneaking around, you wee fud. Getting these little secrets, then taking great glee in passing them on to the person who'll be most upset by them. How do you manage that? Eh?'

'I thought he'd want to know!'

'Sure. Sure.' She wanted to smash his face against the wall.

Marshall walked back in. 'Hey, hey.' He pulled her away from Struan. 'Sergeant, give us a minute.'

'I'll give you an hour.' Struan stared at her. He wasn't backing off any. Got to hand it to him, he was a brave man. And showed no signs of leaving them anytime soon.

Marshall was pointing at the door. 'Can you please get us an update from DC Paton?'

'Sure thing, sir.' Struan took a look at Elliot, then stormed out of the office.

Elliot wanted to follow and trip up the gaping arsehole, then smash his head off the floor. 'See that snidey wee c—'

'Andrea, whatever you're thinking of doing or saying, I'd say from bitter personal experience – don't give Gashkori any ammunition.'

'Eh?'

'Just don't. I thought you knew when to keep your powder dry?'

'I've kept it so dry, Rob. That prick... He just stirs and stirs and stirs.'

'What's happened?'

'Eh?'

'Your face is tripping you. Did you go to court?'

Aye, he knew her pretty well, didn't he? What looked like the A-story of her rage frequently turned out to be the B-story. She looked around at him. 'Davie changed his plea to guilty.'

'Good.' Marshall stepped away. 'That was what you hoped for wasn't it? Shave time off his sentence?'

'Yes and no. The stupid prick turned down a deal to fight his case, but now he's done that anyway without a deal. He would've got three years, Robbie, but he's looking at... God knows. Ten?'

'Andi, his plea should still mitigate that down to five at the most. But there has to be some increase from the three offered because the victim testified.'

'The victim?'

'Hislop.'

'Okay, but that's time *served*.'

'That sucks.' Marshall focused his eyes on her. God, he had such an intense stare – she couldn't handle it for longer than a few seconds. 'There's nothing you can do here, Andrea. I suggest you go home and spend time with your kids. Maybe go to the cinema.'

The cinema?

The fucking *cinema*?

But Sam had been on about seeing that film about that trans seahorse kid. Charlie or something like that. Though she didn't want her own Charlie getting any ideas...

Maybe she should just take them out of school for the day and make an afternoon of it. Go into Edinburgh and do something touristy there. Go into the wilds of the Borders forests and get completely lost.

She smiled at him. 'You know something? For a total dickhead, you can be okay at times.'

'That's almost a compliment.' Marshall smiled at her. 'Now, I've got to sort this out. And that means dealing with Struan...'

'You really think Owusu is dead?'

'Who knows. South Africa's still a pretty violent country.'

'I really hope she's okay, Rob. She's a good person.'

36

Marshall watched Elliot get in the car then slump back in her seat. The grimy office windows obscured her, but she looked completely broken.

He hated to think what she'd be going through. She'd been working on the basis that Davie would be away for a few short years, which would be almost tolerable. Now it was likely to be more than five...

How could anyone put up with that?

Well, Marshall had. Much longer.

Different circumstances, sure, but pretty similar outcome. A long time alone.

Marshall didn't have kids, but raising three on your own... That was going to be brutal.

'Here we go, gaffer.' Struan was waving at Marshall. 'Just finished running the plates. No ANPR hits on that motor.'

'But that's to be expected around here. Right?'

'Right, aye. I mean, I could tell you about six different routes between Jed and Gala that don't go on the A68 or A7, just off the top of my head. And I could also mention that there's huge stretches of those roads which don't have cameras.'

Marshall was used to working in London where the Met had the luxury of every square inch being under constant surveillance. Or at least it certainly felt that way. Up here... Talk about being in the middle of nowhere. 'Have you set up a flag?'

'Sure. Soon as that motor shows up, you and I get notified. DC Paton too.'

'Excellent. Got the owner?'

'Thomas Rutherford.'

'His assumed name?'

'Right. We're trying to track it down, but it looks like he's got some pretty good fake ID from somewhere. Must be because the cops were searching for him.'

Marshall took the seat next to him and leaned in close. 'What you were saying earlier about Dr Owusu... How sure are you?'

'Pretty sure, gaffer.' Struan sat back and stretched out. 'Thing is, word on the street is someone in Hislop's orbit put a hit out on her in South Africa.'

Marshall narrowed his eyes at him. 'Thought it was a nurse who told you?'

'Always double-source your gossip, Rob...' Struan tapped his nose. 'The nurse was one person, but I've got a few other people to talk to about stuff.'

Marshall stared into space. He knew Owusu a bit from work over the time he'd been based here, but more from her relationship with Pringle. The last year had meant a few messages and calls – Durban was thousands of miles south but only two hours ahead.

And she'd pushed back so many times and so hard.

Was she really dead? Was that why she hadn't been answering his calls over the last few days?

Sod it.

'Keep me updated.' Marshall got to his feet and walked

away, calling Owusu again. He headed into the corridor under the stairs, the best spot for discreet calls.

Expecting the local police to answer.

Maybe a neighbour or their daughter...

But nope. It just went to voicemail.

Great.

Marshall didn't regret putting Pringle into a home, just... He hated it all landing on his shoulders. He'd never asked for this and he knew he'd have more than enough of that malarkey when his own parents got to a certain age. And they were blood relatives, rather than someone he'd worked with for a year. He pocketed his phone and walked back through to the office. 'Struan, who's—'

His phone exploded again. He checked the display:

Liana calling...

'Hold that thought.' He stepped away again and answered the call. 'Hiya, what's up?'

'How are you doing?'

'I've had better days, put it that way. You?'

'Well, I managed to get someone in Northumbria police to track down Sylvester's ex-girlfriend. She lives in Hull now. Problem is, she wants nothing to do with us.'

'As in the police?'

'As in anyone.'

'Should I try contacting her?'

'Doubt it'd get us anywhere, Rob.' Her sigh erupted down the line. 'I'm not a cop and when I called her, she told me where to go.'

'She explain why?'

'Just some psychobabble mumbo jumbo about how she's establishing clear boundaries and not even thinking about Sylvester, let alone speaking to anyone about him. Between us,

Rob, I think being in a relationship with a serial killer broke her.'

'Not surprising, is it?' Marshall didn't mention his own mum, but it'd had the same effect on her.

'But it's got me thinking... I want to speak to Holly again.'

'Why?'

'Well, because the big difference from the other cases lies with Kayleigh and Holly. He took Holly from Whitley Bay, rather than just killing her. He abducted Kayleigh from her caravan and dragged her a few hundred metres to throw her off the cliff. As far as I'm aware, we haven't managed to dig into Sylvester's actions when she was captive.'

'Listen, we tried speaking to her last night, but we got told where to go.'

'Really? Well, I just called her and she's happy to speak to me.'

'What?'

'She told me she's been filming down in Whitley Bay today, but she's happy to speak to me at her home. You're welcome to tag along.'

37

M arshall pulled up outside Holly's home in Reston. At this hour, the village was quiet, surrounded by inky darkness with just a few dots of light.

Liana was standing by her car, tapping away on her phone. She looked up at him, waved, but went back to whatever was diverting her.

Marshall got out into the cold night and walked over. 'You okay?'

'Just making some notes. Long drive here from Gartcosh, so that gave me a lot of time to think.'

'Aye, try coming here from Galashiels. Got stuck behind two tractors at separate points.' He smiled at her. 'Were your insights insightful?'

'Not sure. Just thinking about the ex-girlfriend, really. Whether she survived a similar ordeal to Holly and Kayleigh.'

'Why do you think that?'

'We just don't know what happened in Greece. Leaving someone on a holiday like that is pretty extreme. So it's either come from a place of extreme behaviours or driven by an extreme event.'

'And what do you think?'

'It's something I'll mull over, maybe make contact with her again.'

Marshall's phone blasted out again. 'I swear, I know how Commissioner Gordon feels when the Batphone rings.'

Ash Paton calling...

'Better take this.' He answered the call. 'What's up, Ash?'

'Sir, do you remember the flag you requested about that burner?'

'Sylvester's phone, right?'

'Right. I've just been alerted. It was turned on an hour ago. A phone called it.'

'Can you—'

'Another mobile. But Sylvester's location was in Duns.'

'*Duns?*' Marshall tried to process the map of the Borders. Jedburgh was pretty far south, almost at the border before it swept up to enclose a lot of coastal land, whereas Duns wasn't far inland from its northern equivalent by Berwick-upon-Tweed. Or from here in Reston. 'That's pretty far from Jedburgh.'

'Twenty-nine miles, sir.'

'Have we got anything on him in Duns?'

'No, but we've had nothing on him in Eyemouth or Jedburgh. He could have another wee hideout there.' She cleared her throat. 'It's turned off again, though, but I'll dig into this other phone and see if I can get something.'

'Thank you. Have you told DS Liddell?'

'I have. He's briefing DCI Gashkori just now, sir.'

'Excellent. Keep me updated.' Marshall ended the call and pocketed his phone.

Liana was frowning at him. 'You okay there?'

'A bit spooked, to be honest. Sylvester had a burner phone.

And I expected that burner to be burnt by now, but no – seems like he's still using it.'

'Or someone found it?'

'Possible. Most likely is it wasn't a burner.' Marshall rubbed at his temples. 'Anyway. That's Gashkori's problem, not mine.' He gestured at the house. 'After you.'

Liana opened the gate then started up the path, passing Holly's Toyota. 'You two don't get on, do you?'

'Who?'

'You and Ryan.'

'Is it that obvious?'

'It always is with you, Rob.' Liana knocked on the door and waited. 'How was Holly when you were here earlier?'

'She... wasn't exactly helpful.'

'Are they ever?'

'True.' Marshall scanned the house. No sign of anyone inside. No music, no lights, no cooking smells. 'She's not bloody in, is she?'

Liana tried the door knocker again. 'She said she'd be back by the time I got here.'

'Can you call her, please?'

'On it.' She put her phone to her ear and looked around.

Marshall set off through the garden and did a tour of the property, stepping over the low wall. The kitchen at the back was dark and empty. Not even a boiling kettle or a cooling coffee mug or teacup. Or a pizza being calcified in the oven.

The dining room on the side was the same – two Bose speakers in there, but not playing. Not even a candle burning in the middle of the table.

He stopped by the living-room window and looked over at Liana. 'Any joy?'

'Still no answer.'

Marshall wanted to chuck a rock through the window. 'Where is she?' He stepped up to the window and listened hard.

'Heellllpp!'

A low voice, sounding desperate and pretty broken.

Shit!

Marshall walked over to the front door and tried the handle. Nothing. 'Step out of the way.'

'Are you breaking in?'

'Heard a noise inside. A man screaming.' Marshall stepped back and took a deep breath. Counted to three. Then launched his foot at the door.

The chunk of wood around the latch broke off and crashed into the hallway, bouncing off the floor as the door swung open.

Marshall raced inside.

A man lay in the middle of the living room.

Jamie, Holly's cameraman boyfriend.

Marshall looked back at Liana. 'Call an ambulance! Now!' He raced over to Jamie.

A knife was plunged into his gut.

First rule of knife wounds – don't touch it. If they aren't dead with it in, they probably will be with it out.

Marshall crouched in front of him. 'Hey there, how are you?'

'Fucking... fucked...' Jamie pointed at the door. 'Holly.'

'Where is she?'

'Holly!'

'I'll find her! Wait here!' Marshall raced up the stairs and did a quick scan of both bedrooms. Then the bathroom between them.

No sign of her.

38

Liana was shivering so hard Marshall could hear her teeth rattle, even above the drone of the car engine.

'Seriously, get off back to your hotel.' Marshall turned the heater up another notch of power – it couldn't go any hotter. 'Get in the shower or the bath and warm yourself up.'

'Not going.'

Marshall shook his head. 'Will you please just take my jacket, at least?'

She looked over at him, frowning, then held out her hand. 'Fine.'

Marshall shrugged it off and handed it over. 'Zip it right up, okay?'

'Sure.'

Truth was, Marshall was absolutely baking in the car. That jacket was thick enough to cope with a hike in the Borders in sub-zero temperatures. Not that he'd had many chances to try that.

No sign of the forensics lot outside in the darkness, or even any detectives, but the local uniform were doing their jobs – the house was now a crime scene, marked off with tape.

Headlights glared so hard Marshall had to look away. A car sped past them, then slid back into a parallel park in the space in front of them.

Through the windscreen, Gashkori stared at them with the intensity of his headlights. He got out, then got in the back seat of Marshall's car. 'Evening, guys. How are you doing?'

Liana hunkered deeper into the jacket, but at least she wasn't shivering anymore.

Marshall swivelled around. 'It was a bloodbath in there.'

'A bloodbath, eh?' Gashkori was trying to keep his cool, but the stress emanated off him in waves. The pressures of being a DCI and an SIO made him twitch like someone had shoved an electric cable up his arse. 'Another murder on this case.'

'No, sir.'

He scowled at Marshall. 'Eh?'

'Jamie survived. The ambulance is on its way to ERI.'

Gashkori's eyebrows shot up. 'Why Edinburgh?'

'Because it's about thirty minutes on a dual carriageway if you drive an ambulance with the siren blaring and lights flashing. He needs a thoracic surgeon and one is standing by waiting there. Did you honestly expect us to send him to BGH?'

'No, but...' Gashkori puffed out his cheeks then let out a slow breath. 'Okay, what do you both think?'

'About what, specifically?'

'This cameraman. Jamie. What happened?'

'All we saw was the aftermath. He'd been left to die, basically. Pointed at the door and said Holly, twice.'

'Why was he talking about her?'

Liana hugged Marshall's jacket even tighter around her. 'Safe to assume whoever attacked him also abducted Holly.'

'Right.' Gashkori nodded along with that. 'My thinking too.'

Marshall frowned. 'I had to break down the door, sir.'

'Well done, Rambo.' Gashkori gave him a withering look. 'Do you want an MBE for that?'

'No, sir. I'm pointing out the fact it was locked. Why would you abduct someone, then lock the door behind you? Doesn't make sense.'

Gashkori drummed his fingers on his thighs. 'Don't know, maybe to give him a better head-start? You're the headshrinker, Rob, so you tell me why people do what they do.'

'Right. Okay, so Sylvester's struck again. The same way as with Kayleigh and with Holly.' Marshall let out a sigh. 'And we still aren't any closer to finding him.'

Gashkori sat back. 'And now Sylvester's got the one who got away.'

Marshall stared out of the window and watched the forensics van arrive. Six bodies jumped out onto the tarmac, then set off towards the house, all lugging boxes of equipment. He followed their progress up the path – stopped by a uniformed sergeant and made to sign in. 'Something doesn't stack up about this.'

'Time for more psychobabble...'

Marshall waved a hand at the house. 'This is an abduction and attempted murder, right? With the earlier cases, Sylvester would gain intel on the victims over a month or more, then he'd leave and return to strike. But abduction was only part of his MO for Holly's attack. Now she's been taken a second time. And Kayleigh was taken too. It... Something doesn't feel right about this.'

'I disagree.' Liana sat forward, rubbing her hands together. 'This isn't that far outside his usual patterns of behaviour. It's not like *all* the rules are different here. Besides, we've got more data points, so we can see there are two distinct sets of victims. The first were all standard cases where he struck quickly, like you say. But with Holly, he broke that pattern. And Kayleigh was the same. And now Holly for the second time. Abduct, then strike. Why? Could be something as simple as him realising he could abduct as well. Gaining the confidence in his actions. He's evolving.'

'I love listening to you two discussing all this stuff. It's mind-blowing. Like watching foreign language films with the subtitles off.' Gashkori chuckled. 'Why would he change, though?'

'If he can take his victims off the streets or out of their homes easily, then he's entirely in control of the situation. All of the dimensions you can consider, they're under his control. Previously, he'd be looking at the where and when aspects, hoping he hadn't missed some dog walker or something. This way, he can be fully in control. When he has them under his control, there are far more possibilities. And the when isn't just a short period of time, it can be days, weeks, months, even. And when he does finally kill them, he can take his time. It's not a simple push.'

'It was with Kayleigh. We don't know what he intended to do with Holly the first time because she got away.'

'This is all fascinating, but it doesn't help me any.' Gashkori ran a hand across the stubble on the top of his head. 'Rob, do you agree with this evolution thing?'

'I know killers evolve their methods, but there's no literature on brain-damaged killers evolving or not. Like you said, Holly was the one who got away. Maybe he didn't want to repeat the riskiness of that, so he decided to change his plans.'

'Where's he taken her?'

'We don't know. He had a sneaky B&B in Jed we lucked out in finding. He's not short of cash, so it could be he's got a few places he could take her.'

Gashkori nodded along slowly. 'Okay, that doesn't help me any.'

Liana eased off the zip. 'Ryan, we've had Sylvester pegged as a narcissist in the profile. A large part of that is devoted to getting the attention and fear from the victims. Previously, he could only get that by killing them. Now he knows he can get it by abducting them first. But with Kayleigh, we don't think it was long between the abduction and the attempt.'

'Unless he was there overnight with her.' Marshall sat back in his chair. 'Isn't that what you wanted to ask Holly?'

'Right. When he abducted her in Whitley Bay, I wanted to know precisely what he said and did to her. How long he had her for. Because it's not recorded in the file – she didn't remember, but a detailed interview with her might help.'

Gashkori frowned. 'I don't see how.'

'Come on, Ryan.' Liana had her hands on her hips. 'Think about how much experience I've gained in the twelve years since we published that document. Questions we'd never thought to ask before. Not to mention been allowed to by Jacob.'

Marshall let out a sigh. 'Trouble is, I asked her about that. She still doesn't remember much. Kind of lost her shit about it. But Liana's right. She's been doing this job full time whereas I've dabbled at being a cop. So she maybe could've got more out of it.'

'You've more than dabbled. Don't sell yourself short.' She laughed. 'But you're right. I have different ways of eliciting information than Rob. Sometimes it's just as simple as needing a woman's gentle touch.'

'Guess we'll never know, eh?' Marshall thumbed behind him. 'Like Ryan said, Holly's the one who got away. The one who almost got him convicted.' He looked over at Liana. 'Could be she's the ultimate target.'

'Right.' Liana clicked her tongue a few times. 'And that'd explain the abduction. And the return to her as a target. His failure has been festering away at him for twelve years.'

Gashkori coughed. 'So why kill Kayleigh?'

'I don't have any answers, other than the obvious – he could fail once, but he can't fail again. He needed to make sure it worked this time.'

'So she's a practice run?'

'Exactly. We've focused on the way he threw Kayleigh from the cliff, but what if the important bit is how he controlled her in a confined situation?'

Marshall nodded. 'I could buy that.'

'Could we have less of the theoretical and instead give me some concrete directions here?' Gashkori popped his head between them. 'From a layman's perspective, the part I'm trying to get my head around is why there are no links between Kayleigh and Holly. With the others, the victims just happened to visit a café he frequented or be the kid of the B&B owner.'

'Kayleigh fits that too. Met in a café.' Marshall craned his neck around to look at Gashkori. 'According to Warner, Sylvester admitted to having contact with her. So we know that's his phone.'

'Right, right. But Holly?' Gashkori waved at the house. 'How did he know where she lived? This isn't even her place. A mate's place, right? Someone who's been through what Holly has is going to be *very* cagey about revealing where they live. I mean, look at it. We're in the middle of nowhere here.'

'Are you trying to say something, Ryan?'

'Not really. Just... Right, well, thank you for listening to my inane ramblings and for letting me watch your mental gymnastics.' Gashkori clapped his hands together. 'I'm going to get my arms around this case here, get the real cops to take charge. You two, get your arses back to Gartcosh. I want my brains trust digging deep on this. After all, I'm paying you both a small fortune.'

39

Marshall slid his key into the lock and twisted it. Gorgie Road milled around him, that part of Edinburgh he didn't really know but was now grudgingly getting acquainted with. People moaned about gentrification, but when you could pick up a freshly baked loaf of rye sourdough at nine o'clock in the evening, Marshall wasn't going to be one of those complaining.

He stepped inside and scurried up the stairs, almost getting to the top before he lost his breath.

The flat door was already open. Kirsten stood in the doorway, grinning away. 'Evening.'

'Evening.' Marshall wrapped her in a deep embrace and kissed her even more deeply, then let her lead him into the flat. 'What's that smirk for?'

'Nothing.'

'Come on...'

'Oh, it's just... I saw someone's shite car break down and block traffic. Then I spotted it was you.'

Marshall dropped his bread on the counter. He was tempted to get stuck into it, but he needed some affection, so he sat next to her on the brown leather sofa. 'I'm still trying to sell it.'

She rested her head on his shoulder. 'And the market for clapped-out bangers has dried up, eh?'

'It's not *that* bad.'

'No. But when a group of blokes have to help you kick-start it again...'

'There is that, I suppose. Also, I don't really need it, given I don't actually live in the Borders anymore. Staying with you here in Edinburgh... and with Pringle near Glasgow... it's pretty redundant.'

She looked over at him. 'Jesus, Rob! You've got blood on your collar!'

'It's not mine.'

'Whose is it?'

'Warner got into a bit of a fight with a suspect.'

'Are they in custody?'

He shook his head.

'Christ, Rob. Glad it wasn't you, I need you in one piece.'

'Very funny.'

'Hey, sorry I didn't call you back earlier. It's been a day from hell.'

'Same for me.' Marshall exhaled slowly. 'Did your lot get called out to Reston?'

'We did. Luckily, Anderson took it, otherwise I'd still be down there.' She snarled. 'Wasted a few hours in court today, by the way. Davie Elliot's case was called off just before I was due to take the stand. You know why?'

'Changed his plea to guilty.'

'Yeah, I know that. I mean, he was as guilty as a puppy in a puddle, but do you know why he chose then to do it?'

'I saw Andrea and she didn't let on.'

'Poor woman. How is she?'

'Like you care?'

'I mean, I actively dislike her, but it doesn't mean I want her to suffer like that. I wouldn't want to go through what she is. And I wouldn't even want her to.'

'I can reassure you I won't be selling off any police evidence to dodgy gangsters.'

'That's good. I've been worried about that.'

Marshall kissed her on the forehead. 'I'm starving.' He walked over to the kitchen area and got some cheese and butter out of the fridge. Some tomatoes and the wee jar of chutney his mum made. 'You want anything?'

'Had something when I got in.'

'Okay. I'll sort myself out then.'

She flicked the telly on and some inane property crap turned on. 'How was Pringle last night?'

Marshall cut deeply into the loaf. 'He's getting worse.' Then another slice. 'I've put him in a care facility overnight.'

'Shit, seriously?'

'The same one as Grumpy. I'm familiar with it, at least. Makes it easy enough to look in on them both, plus it's a nice place, good staff, not overly expensive. But...' Marshall started buttering the bread. 'I tried calling Belu Owusu to speak to her about it... No answer.' He eased the cheese out of the packet. 'I heard she died.'

Kirsten looked round. 'Shit, seriously?'

'Word is. Though the source is Struan Liddell.'

'Wouldn't trust him.' She shook her head. 'So you've got to look after his giant house?'

'Right. I mean, I'll probably have to sell it to pay for his accommodation, but... It'll be a weight off my shoulders, you know? The whole thing will.' He cut into the block of cheddar. 'I don't want to sound selfish, but Jim's a danger to himself.'

'Can't help but think the stress of looking after him is partly to blame.'

'For what?'

'Rob. It's been a year and I haven't got pregnant.'

'Thank you for saying "we" haven't got pregnant.'

'Well, it's supposed to be a fifty-fifty operation.'

'Okay, so fate hasn't intervened, but we've still got plenty of time.'

'Do we? We've gone from waiting to see if I get pregnant to actively trying and now to wondering why the hell nothing's happened. And I'm wondering if it's all this stress you're under.'

'I mean, it could be.' Marshall's turn to shrug. 'I haven't exactly been happy with my work. There's only so many hours a day you can shuffle paperclips around a desk. Not to mention the fact my old man's suddenly not dead.'

'You never thought he was.'

'No, but I'd hoped.'

'Rob!'

'I'm serious. At least that way I wouldn't have to deal with him.'

'It's not like he's hassling or harrying you, is it?'

'No, but... Just the knowledge of where he is... It's not easy to deal with.'

'I get that.'

'And there's aggro about whether I'm living in Glasgow or Edinburgh.'

'Why's that a problem?'

'I haven't had a home since I moved up here from London. Staying in a hotel, then Jen's granny flat, then shuttling between here and Pringle's...'

'Your stuff's all here.'

'I know and I appreciate that, but... Jen's looking after Zlatan for me and...' Marshall sliced his sandwich diagonally, but the shape of the bread made that pretty tricky. 'And there's two possibilities to it, right? There's because of me and there's because of you. I can get an appointment at a fertility clinic and see if my swimmers are swimming.'

She shifted over to let him sit down. 'I've got an appointment on Thursday.'

'You didn't tell me.'

'Don't know why I didn't...'

Marshall bit into his sandwich and chewed. 'Look, the thing is, I've been thinking.' He looked over at her. 'We should get married.'

'No.'

'Come on. I know we've talked about—'

'*No.*'

'Look, it's important we both know where this is going.'

'It's going the same way as if we'd got married. It doesn't mean anything, Rob. And that was never the deal. Family, yes. Stupid piece of paper, no.'

'I still wish you'd think about it.'

'And I still wish you'd listen to me about it.' She glared at him. 'This sudden rush into marriage isn't because Liana's back on the scene?'

'So you did read that text.' Marshall rested his sandwich on the plate. 'No. Not at all. In the slightest. Weirdest thing having her there again. Weirder still, she's pregnant.'

'You're kidding me?'

'Nope. All shacked up with some fella. I'm pleased for her, it's just... I want that for us.'

'I know.' She shifted over and gave him a hug. 'Look, there's no drama. Okay? That's the thing. Never any drama. Now, you have your sandwich and see if we can have another go, eh?'

DAY 3

WEDNESDAY

40

'We saw *Charlie the effing Seahorse: The effing Movie*.' Elliot leaned back against the car and stared across the car park to the new train station in Reston. Hadn't been open that long and the locals weren't too impressed with the service. Going to be a glorious morning, the dim light already golden. 'Not my choice, but it shut the kids up for a few hours. And it stopped me thinking for that time, so maybe it wasn't a bad thing.'

Jolene tore the lid off her coffee and took a sip. 'Still think you're brave coming in to work after what happened yesterday.'

'Ach, it's all priced in, Jo. That shite all happened a year ago, didn't it? I'm just feeling the effects of it now. And to be honest with you, I feel a weight off my shoulders about Davie. Always had that doubt about whether he was being stitched up, but now I know the truth? Well. I *know*. And knowing *why* he did it helps me get some closure.' She laughed. 'It's not coke and hookers, but him trying to be a bloody superhero for our kids.' She hadn't thought too much about his experience in prison and why should she? 'Now I can start to think about getting closure. And it might not be *that* bad. Say he's in prison for five years? I can plan around that.'

Jolene's mouth hung open. 'Seriously?'

'What? You thought I'd ditch him?'

'Uh, yeah?'

'Thing is, Jo, I'm nothing if I'm not loyal. And I still love him.'

'A five-year prison sentence takes a *lot* of love. A lot more than he deserves, if you ask me.'

'Thing is, Davie did it for the right reasons. He wanted to look after his family. We were skint. So fucking skint. A DI's salary and a security officer. He's a civilian, so he's not even got the advantages I have with Police Federation mortgages and what have you. And ours is pretty massive. And now it's just me paying it...'

'Will you be able to afford it?'

'Just about. Ten-year fixed. Got in just before everything started going up.'

'That's lucky.'

'One way of looking at it. Hopefully by the time it's up, he'll be out and working again. And maybe things will be a bit more sane again on the old interest rates front.'

Someone tramped out of the front door and tore off his crime scene mask. Gashkori. 'Ladies, there you are.'

'Sir.' Elliot cradled her coffee in her hands. 'Just waiting for instructions here.'

Gashkori eyed their cups. 'Where did you get that?'

Jolene waved down the long high street. 'There's a decent coffee shop in the village.'

'Nice one.' He smiled at her. 'Did you get one for me?'

'Sorry, just me and Andi.'

'Okay, well. Can you go and get me a flat white?'

Jolene scowled at him. 'Sir, I'm not driving there for one coffee.'

'Well, that's not very collegiate of you. First, you should've asked who wanted one before you went for those. Second, make it two flat whites, two Americanos and two teas, milk and two, then I'll consider the matter settled.'

Jolene looked at Elliot, but there was no way she was wading into this nonsense. 'Fine, then.' She held out her hand, rubbing her fingers together.

'Seriously? You want me to give you some cash?'

'DCI pays a hell of a lot more than DS, sir.'

He handed her a crisp twenty. 'And with that attitude, you'll never make it to my rank.'

'Thank you, sir.' She got in her car and sped off through the village.

Elliot watched her go. 'Walked right into that one, Ry. And it's a bit cheeky getting her to do it. What about Struan?'

'Do you trust him enough to drink a coffee he'd made or bought?'

'Fair point.'

Gashkori clapped her on the shoulder. 'Andi, you shouldn't be on duty, should you?'

'I'm fine, sir. Totally fine.'

'You can take as much time as you need.'

'Thanks, but I am taking as much as I need. Which is zero. My mum's taking the kids to school today, while I earn enough corn to pay for their school clothes and the roof over their heads. But I appreciate the concern.'

'Okay. Well, the offer's there. Sometimes things hit us hardest when we least expect it. If it bites, you get yourself off home. Okay? No messing around, just go.'

'I'll bear that in mind.' Elliot finished her coffee but didn't have anywhere to put the empty cup. 'Take it we're not having a briefing today?'

'Nope. And I've got three strands to run here. First, DI Marshall is working up that criminal profile, which will be about as useful as a wax tea cosy, but I'll get pelters from She Who Cannot Be Named if I don't let them play their daft wee game. Second, DI Taylor is in charge of tracking down the Scarlet Pimpernel, AKA David Sylvester. Which is going pretty badly, I have to say. But you, my dear, are going to get to the bottom of what's happened here.' He pointed at the house.

Elliot looked across the road. A light flashed inside the cottage. 'You want me to supervise the forensics of an attack?'

'Oh, no. It's more than that. Just heard from the ERI. Jamie died of his injuries about an hour ago. Need you to break the news to his parents.'

41

Marshall knew he'd be cutting things tight, but an early drive down to Gattonside before a long journey over to Gartcosh was the only way he could look at himself in the mirror.

Juggling so many balls at the moment, but hey ho.

And of course, he was sitting in the TV room on his own. Not even someone of his grandfather's vintage to give him company as he watched the inane drivel on the screen. He checked his watch.

Pringle bounced into the room, with all the energy of a man who'd slept for the first time in months. Grinning wide, his eyes shooting around the room. Grey chinos and a dress shirt, like he was going on a date. He walked over and grabbed Marshall in a bear hug, smelling of fancy aftershave. He hadn't seen him pack that the previous day, but it was better than the sour smell of spilled milk. 'Rob, it's great to see you.'

'And you.' Marshall stayed sitting as a way of deflecting some of the fizzing energy. 'You seem well, Jim.'

'That's because I *am* well.' Pringle clicked both fingers and gave him pistols. He took a seat on the sofa and focused on the breakfast TV playing. Then looked over at Marshall with a raised eyebrow, and tapped his nose. 'Got a few suspects.' A crafty wink, then back to watching the screen. 'It's great how they let me keep my laptop. I can continue my research and, trust me, the data here is far better than in your office, even. This Mandela Effect is more widespread than I thought, Rob. I think it's *definitely* why my brain is Swiss cheese nowadays. Flipping between these parallel universes has melted it like a cheese toastie.'

Up close, Marshall could see that he actually didn't look like he'd slept at all. Red eyes, underlined by black bags. But the energy must've come from somewhere. 'Did you get much sleep?'

'Sleep? Rob, who needs sleep when you've got very strong coffee?'

'You know how your condition is affected by—'

'Rob, aren't you listening to me? This isn't some disease, caused by some genetic bullshit. This is because I've been slipping between parallel universes.'

The mad stare was like facing a car with headlights on full beam.

'What about the other guy?'

'Eh?'

'If you're slipping between a universe where Nelson Mandela died in the eighties and this universe, where he didn't, what happens to the Jim Pringle who grew up here in this world?'

'Well, what do you think? Right now, he's being forced into a home and wondering why nobody believes him that Mandela was president of South Africa. I'm not saying either is wrong, by the way. This isn't a race thing, it's just...' He trailed off and was focused on the screen's visual noise again.

Marshall wasn't going to win by reasoning with him, but something sprang to his mind. 'You say it's not a race thi—'

'It's not.'

'—but you keep coming back to him. Is it because Nelson Mandela was president of South Africa?'

'Not in my home timeline.'

'Okay, but the fact you keep fixating on him of all people. Is it because he's South African?'

'I've told you. This isn't a conspiracy theory.'

'Jim, your ex-wife is South African.'

'Belu and I were never married. But that's by the by. What's your point, Rob?'

'Just feels like your brain's connecting two things there and fixating on—'

'*Rob!* It's totally obvious what's happening here!'

Marshall stared hard at him. 'Jim, when did you last hear from her?'

'Ages ago. Months. Years. I mean, I don't really know what year it is. 2021, maybe? Besides, Belu hasn't wanted to see me in years. In *that* way. Just to speak to me about Sarah. I wanted to talk, of course I did, but she was having none of it.'

'Have you spoken to her since she left Scotland?'

'That's right.' Pringle inched forward on his seat, eyes narrowed. 'Have you?'

'A few times.'

'Of the world!'

Marshall frowned. 'Excuse me?'

'Of the world.' Pringle pointed at the TV screen, showing The Darkness playing a gig somewhere. 'Really like that band. Saw them loads of times. Found out recently how their current drummer is the son of the boy from Queen. Someone Taylor.'

'Roger?'

'No, Rufus, I think.'

Right, the son was called Rufus.

At least in this universe...

'Anyway. One of these so-called Mandela effects was how

"We Are The Champions" by Queen ends with "... of the world!" But it doesn't.'

'Sure about that?'

'Sure.' Pringle walked over to a hi-fi and put a CD in, then fiddled with the controls. The song started playing, but he fast-forwarded to the end and the last few bars played, but he was right. 'See?'

'It's in the song, though? Isn't it?'

'Aye, but a lot of people remember it being the last line of the song. See it at a sporting event and they'll sing it.'

Marshall sat there and didn't know what to do. How to win this battle. Maybe he just needed to let Pringle live in his fantasy world where Queen songs ended a different way and South African presidents died in prison.

A mobility scooter rattled into the room. 'Freddy, Freddy, Freddy. Some boy, him!'

Marshall got up and smiled at Grumpy. He didn't get too close in case he passed anything on – unlike Pringle and his mental issues, Grumpy was here because his body wasn't working the way it used to. 'How are you doing there, old timer?'

'Up with the lark because my prostate's like a bloody grape-fruit again.'

'Is that a bad thing?'

'Supposed to be the size of a walnut, son. Off to the doctors again so he can shove his finger up my hole.' Grumpy cackled. 'Studs up!'

Marshall didn't know what to think, other than to be a bit worried. He was ninety now. There weren't too many more birthdays.

'I saw Queen, you know?' Grumpy pointed at the screen. 'Up at the Playhouse in Edinburgh in 1976. Braw band.' He whizzed his scooter over to Marshall. 'Had this exact same chat with him last night, Rob. He doesn't believe me that song ends like that and it's just numpties misremembering things.'

Marshall nodded along with him. 'It's a battle you can't win.'

'I mean, if the kid wants to believe he's in a parallel universe, who am I to disabuse him of that notion?' Grumpy watched Pringle like he was examining something in the lab. 'Will he be here long?'

'It's just respite care for now.'

'Respite for him or you?'

'Him. So he doesn't burn the house down.'

'Great, so he'll burn this place down. Cheers, son!'

'Why are you asking?'

'Why? Because he's nucking futs, is why. He spent a ton of time last night with Dalrymple Rattray, who's also more idiot than not and he didn't seem to notice the laddie's got half his brain missing. Pair of them are away with the fairies.'

Marshall smiled at him as he got up to leave. 'Just keep an eye on him for me, would you?'

'Aye, if you increase my pocket money.'

42

The Alexanders' living room overlooked Dunbar, the old harbour town sprawling out way below. Elliot could just about make out the giant green behemoth that was the Asda, down by the roundabout.

Elliot took a cup of tea from Jolene, even though the super strong coffee was still whizzing around her system. 'Thanks.' She looked across the living room towards the couple.

Early sixties, just retired, but clearly didn't expect their dearly beloved to leave the planet before them.

'Can't believe it.' Alison Alexander held a teacup, her shaking hands spilling some of the dark liquid into the saucer. Staring into space. 'Just back from a week in Madeira. Got a phone call from my sister as we landed. Can't... Heard he'd been attacked. We were going to head down there now. Can't believe it. Gordon's struggling to drive at night, so we needed the light to get around there. But...' She grabbed her husband's hand. 'We should've gone straight there, Gordon. Got the taxi to drop us at the hospital. Would've seen him... Would've...'

'You can't beat yourself up over these things, Mrs Alexander. Your son never woke up after the incident.'

Alison locked eyes with Elliot, tears starting to fill them. 'How is he dead? I just don't understand it.'

Her husband slurped his own tea, then gasped. 'An absolute tragedy is what it is.'

'How close were you to your son?'

'Very. Jamie was a homebody. Still stayed nearby. He's got a flat down in the town.' She meant Dunbar. 'Always liked to come home after being away somewhere. He worked in Glasgow a lot, you know. Edinburgh too. But he travelled around a lot too. Down to England every so often, but mostly to the Highlands and islands.'

'He was a proud Scot.' Gordon was nodding along. 'We raised a laddie who understood what it meant to be Scottish.'

'Aye...' Alison rubbed at her eyes with a tartan hankie. 'Will you catch who's done this?'

'We're doing everything in our power to catch his attacker.'

'You think this is related to...' Gordon set his teacup down on a side table. 'To all that stuff with his lassie?'

'We're investigating that as a possibility, yes. But if there were any other options... Anyone he'd fallen out with. Owed money to. Had some disagreement with. Anything.'

'Can't think of anything.' Alison looked at her husband. 'He never talked to me about any bother. You?'

Gordon shook his head. 'No. And we used to meet up for a round of golf every week or so.' He shook his head. 'Over the eighteen holes, he'd usually tell us a few things. Sounded like his life was going well. Lots of work. And he had a lassie he liked.'

'Holly?'

'Right, aye.'

'How well did you know her?'

Elliot clocked *that* look passing between them, the one that said 'it wasn't their place to say anything' about how much they disliked her.

'She's nice enough.'

'Aye, what Alison says. Nice enough lassie.'

'Sure?' Elliot left a pause. 'It sounds like there's a "but" in there.'

Gordon wrapped his hairy hand around his wife's. 'Truth is, Inspector, we never liked Holly. It's nothing personal. Nice enough lassie, like I say, but... She seemed deeply traumatised and I don't want to hold what happened to the lassie against her...'

'But?'

'But she just seemed entirely focused on herself, you know? Like she was incapable of love. And Jamie... This film they were making with that other laddie. I just... It didn't feel right.'

'In what way?'

'Jamie was such a good laddie, you know? Always took on these hard-luck stories. Never time to focus on what he wanted or what was good for him. He always thought he could fix people. And it got him into a lot of trouble over the years.'

'What kind of trouble are we talking here?'

43

'Sorry I'm late.' Marshall raced into the meeting room and put the tray of coffees in the middle of the conference table. 'I brought these.' They'd be lukewarm at best, but it'd appear he'd made the effort. He handed a hazelnut latte to She Who Cannot Be Named.

'Thank you, Rob.'

Then a chai latte for Liana. 'I thought I heard you say you were off coffee, so...'

'Oh, you didn't have to...'

'No, I did.' Marshall smiled at Hardeep. 'Sorry, mate, I thought you weren't in today.'

'My tutorial got cancelled. And I'd much rather be here for this.'

'Thanks.' Marshall took his seat at the head of the table and opened the lid of his coffee. Somehow it was still insanely hot. He took a few seconds to centre himself, shutting his eyes, but all he saw was the motorway between Edinburgh and Glasgow. 'Thanks for waiting.'

'We didn't.' She Who Cannot Be Named sipped at her coffee. 'I was just saying how Liana's time is being given free of charge by her university, counter to what DCI Gashkori said about her being expensive last night. I'll be having words with him regarding that matter...' She smiled. 'Anyway, that's all by the by. How are we doing on the profile?'

Marshall beckoned for Liana to go first, not least because he'd done the square root of bugger all on it since clocking off last night. 'You were taking the lead on it, right?'

'Sure.' Liana cleared her throat. 'Apologies as I've barely slept. Junior was as restless as I was.'

She Who Cannot Be Named gave a sympathetic frown. 'Sorry to hear that. I'd love to say it gets much easier once they're born, but I'd be as bad a liar as the average DCI.'

Liana smiled at that. 'Anyway, I worked most of the night and revised the profile. It's not in a fit state to share, really, yet, but—'

'DI Marshall shared his updates with me?'

'Yes. And that's fine. But the rest of it's a bit sketchy. Needs shoring up.'

'Okay. Can you give me the edited highlights?'

'I'm thinking it's still a solid match to Sylvester.' Liana sipped some of her drink but the sour look implied it'd be the last one. 'Even with the work Hardeep has done in unearthing a few connections we weren't aware of.'

Marshall looked over at him. 'Such as?'

'Sylvester grew up in Whitley Bay.'

Marshall sat back. How the hell had he missed that? 'I thought he was from central Newcastle?'

'That's where he spent his time at high school, sure, but he spent his primary school years in Whitley Bay. It's not exactly far, but it's tying in with a few details Jacob Goldberg had inferred. That Holly might offer a geographical hook into his killing MO. We never knew this.'

'And the first victim was from there, so he struck close to home first. Then Holly later.'

She Who Cannot Be Named gave her a narrow-eyed frown. 'Okay, well, we—'

'Actually.' Marshall sat forward. 'It might explain why Holly was treated differently. He wanted to kill her, sure, but he didn't want to do it on his doorstep. He'd already killed there, so he took her north...' He tapped his coffee lid. 'Holly said she knew him from the caravan there, didn't she?'

Hardeep nodded. 'I've got that logged from the police side. A Struan Liddell? She said she met him when she was fifteen.'

'And seems to have been some contact subsequent to that.' Liana pulled out a document. 'Sylvester's maternal grandparents lived in Whitley Bay, but the other end of the town from where Holly's parents were. Turbulent upbringing, as you know, and his mother moved in with them a few times.'

'That'll maybe explain why we didn't know about that. No permanent address in Whitley Bay.'

She Who Cannot Be Named shifted her gaze between them until she was sure they were done. 'Okay, if you're quite finished? Our priority just now is in finding him, which DI Taylor is leading on. But understanding his psychology could be the way to succeeding where his team's more orthodox tactics might be failing. So I suggest we take this from first principles. Sylvester was thirty when you caught him twelve years ago, so he's forty-two now. Correct?'

'Correct.' Marshall might not have spent the night working away, but he did know some of the detail off by heart. 'He suffered his accident when he was twenty-five, I think, and he started killing five months later.'

'Of course, not all people who suffer that kind of injury go on to murder.'

'No, but people who murder tend to have some kind of trigger that causes them to escalate.' Marshall took a glug of coffee that was very definitely now lukewarm. 'He was killing for four and a half years before Holly, with increasing frequency, but he could've been operating beforehand. Liana, we had a list of possible assaults back in the day, didn't we?'

'Correct, but he had alibis for most of them.'

'Most.' She Who Cannot Be Named tapped her pen off her notebook a few times, then dropped it onto the table. 'Can the remainder be pinned to him?'

'They were all in the Newcastle area, I think. So the MO of him being in holiday towns hadn't kicked in.' Liana gestured at Marshall. 'And he pretty much started killing as soon as he recovered. But like Rob says, he needed a trigger. It's just possible the incident in Greece tipped him over, in more ways than one.'

She Who Cannot Be Named didn't look convinced. 'Okay, so that's one side of the equation. The other is Holly. Understanding her might help. She was twenty-five when he took her and is thirty-seven now.'

Marshall felt something tugging at his brain. 'Hang on.' He rifled through his paperwork and found the list of victims, including their ages, then started going through it. 'When she was attacked, Holly was seven years older than the maximum age of the other victims.'

'I noticed that.' Liana patted her sleeping laptop. 'It's in my working draft of the profile.'

'And what do you make of it?'

'Well, there are a couple of possible outcomes. First, it just is what it is. Sylvester saw her, maybe thought she was eighteen and decided to kill her without knowing her age. In that case, biological age is irrelevant and unimportant. Second, she could remind him of his ex-girlfriend. She was the same age.'

She Who Cannot Be Named frowned. 'So that adds weight to your theory that she's the objective of his mission?'

'I think it...' Liana's lips twisted up. 'I'm not sure, to be honest. It could add credence to it, or it could not. I need to think it through.'

An impatient sigh escaped the lips of She Who Cannot Be Named. 'You just said she'd known him since she was fifteen? He would've been twenty-seven, correct?'

'That's right.'

'Okay, so the number one question, other than how to find Holly and Sylvester, is why did Sylvester kill Kayleigh after all that time?'

'Rob and I discussed that. We think Kayleigh might be a practice run before he went after Holly again.'

She Who Cannot Be Named took a long drink. 'Do you think he's been quiet in all that time?'

Marshall frowned. 'Holly has a list of people she thinks might've been killed by him in that period. We've not confirmed any of them, have we?'

Hardeep raised a hand. 'Prof Curtis just passed this work-load on to me this morning, Rob. I'm sorry I haven't got around to it yet.'

'You weren't even supposed to be here, so don't sweat it.' Marshall looked at Liana. 'Did you manage to get anywhere with them?'

'I had a look. Lots of late teens and early twenties women falling off cliffs and in front of trains. But the thing is, you could just as easily pick them out of the newspapers. There's nothing in any of them to explicitly connect them to Sylvester. Both death methods are also very common forms of suicide too, so they may not be murders at all.'

'Knowing his movements over that period would be a good thing.' Marshall sat back and stared up at the ceiling. 'Say he was in Thailand for that time, then—'

'Thailand?' She Who Cannot Be Named frowned. 'You think Sylvester was in Thailand?'

'No, I don't. We don't really know where he was. But say he was somewhere, and we can prove he was, then these cases weren't done by him.'

'Right, I see your logic.' She Who Cannot Be Named finished her coffee. 'And the converse is true – if we can pin down his movements for this period, we might be able to capture an additional set of murders?'

'I think so. And that'll boost the profile.'

'Okay, in that case... You need to do more groundwork.'

Liana cleared her throat. 'I might have something.'

'Go on?'

'Sylvester's brother refused to talk to us way back when, but my pals in Northumbria constabulary tracked him down.'

44

A round them, it seemed like Clovenfords still slept. Elliot pressed the doorbell again, then looked along the road towards Peebles. 'Doesn't Dr Donkey live here?'

'You mean Rob?' Jolene folded her arms. 'He used to. In his sister's granny flat. He's splitting his time between Glasgow and Edinburgh now.'

'Well, I never.' As much as Elliot wanted to delve deep into that, she wanted to find this sound guy more. 'This Toby lad said he was going to be here?'

'Said he was, aye. Popping out for some breakfast first.' Jolene checked her watch. 'Should be back by now.'

'When did going out for breakfast become a thing?' Elliot looked over the road at the Clovenfords Hotel, a big old coaching inn fronted by a statue of Sir Walter Scott. 'Not exactly a million places around here. Shall we see if he's in there?'

Jolene was already crossing the road, so Elliot jogged to catch up. The houses on this side were older and grander than the modern estate Toby Horsfall lived in. Even at this early hour, the car park was pretty busy.

Elliot held the door and let Jolene go inside first. Been a few years since she'd visited. The ancient layout was tempered by a modern paint job, but the place had a cosiness to it, both figuratively and from the massive fires burning at either end.

The car park users filled a big table by the pool table, a group of ramblers getting their breakfasts in before walking the Clovenfords-Torwoodlee circle or even maybe a hike up Meigle Hill.

Aye, Elliot remembered a time when she could fill a weekend how she wanted, rather than being lucky to carve out ten minutes to neck some wine.

She spotted Toby, working at his laptop in the window seat. Headphones on, nodding to a beat. A massive cooked breakfast sat in front of him, half gone, and a large coffee mug still steaming. He took a sip, then eyed up the taps on the bar. At nine o'clock...

Aye, he was a pisshead.

Jolene perched on the stool opposite him. 'Mr Horsfall?'

He frowned at her. 'Can I help?'

'We spoke over at Eyemouth yesterday? After Holly's sighting?'

'Alrighty...' Toby watched Elliot sit on the smaller stool. 'You're cops, yeah?'

'That's right. I take it you heard your friend Jamie was attacked—'

'I heard.' Toby picked up a pink sausage with his fingers and chewed it. 'That why you're here?'

'Partly. He died first thing this—'

'Shit.' Toby dropped the sausage. 'What happened?'

'The injuries he sustained were serious. Took a while for paramedics to arrive. Touch and go in hospital, but he succumbed to his injuries first thing this morning.'

'That's... That's awful.'

'We believe that whoever attacked Jamie also abducted Holly.'

'Oh, shit. Have you found her?'

'Afraid not. When did you last hear from her?'

'Yesterday afternoon. We were filming down in Whitley Bay. Finished up about three and I came back here. They were heading up the A1, whereas I cut up the A68.'

'How long have you been working together for?'

'Known Jamie from working on various documentaries and series over the years. A few things on Netflix and the BBC. Once you get your foot in the door, it's amazing what you can pick up.'

'And Holly?'

'Just on her documentary. So about three months. Known her a bit longer, obviously, but that was through Jamie. She told me her story at a party and I saw a solid idea there. A fantastic one. The pitch pretty much wrote itself. Got funding with minimal hassle, which never happens. We were able to just make the film without too much trouble. Up to the money guys to sell it. That was the plan, anyway.'

'Sounds like you're more than a sound guy.'

'Who told you that I was just a sound guy?'

'Jamie's parents.'

'I'll put that down to grief or ignorance. I don't just *record the sound*, I'm the production researcher, the interviewer, the screenwriter, the confidante, plus I do all of the editing. And there's a *lot*.' Toby gestured at his laptop. 'It's what I'm working on just now. This laptop is as good as any editing rig, so I can work wherever I like. And quite often I have to. Like in the Outer Hebrides last year, on a super-tight deadline for that Netflix show. Or when I got stuck on the Isles of Scilly for a fortnight. Most of the time it's just slicing and dicing the raw footage. Seeing what I've got to play with, you know? For the big editing work, I've got six 4K screens in the house, all powered by this bad boy.' He nervously looked around the pub. 'Just don't mention that to anyone, would you?'

'Secret's safe with me.' Jolene winked, then put her finger to her lips. 'Now, when we spoke to Jamie's parents, they mentioned some trouble he was in. Have you any idea what that might be about?'

'Sorry. None at all.'

'Are you sure?'

'Whatever Jamie's been up to, it's news to me. Sorry.' But Toby wouldn't look at them.

Sod was lying.

'See, the whole reason we've driven down here from Dunbar is to pick your brains on the matter.'

'I'm sorry, but it's been a waste of time.'

Elliot sat back. Time for a different tack. 'What are you working on?'

'Me? Oh, I've just been going through yesterday's stuff from Whitley Bay.'

'Including the video?'

'Jamie sent it across before... Not sure how useable it is, but we'll see. Of course... The whole thing is unfinished. I doubt I'll be able to use any of this, but you never know.'

'It's part of a murder investigation. That might be evidence.'

'Evidence?' His face went white. 'You mean I'll lose the footage?'

'You won't *lose* anything, but it will have to be reviewed to make sure there's nothing pertinent to the investigation in amongst it all.'

'Of course. Of course.' Toby pushed his laptop away from him, like he'd already lost the work. 'I'm guessing the sooner I help you, the sooner I get it back?'

'That's not how it works. We'll send someone from our digital evidence team out to clone the drive.'

'Clone? As in copy the whole drive?'

'That's right. We'll only have cause to look at the recent video.'

'Alrighty...'

'My colleague will be out soon. Suggest you just wait here.' She pulled the laptop away and closed the lid. 'Just leave it like that.'

'Sure. Cool.' He sat back and blew air up his face. 'Sure.'

'Did you get much in Whitley Bay?'

'Nothing much, to be honest with you. I had been picking at some holes in Holly's story, which are going to be hard to fill now Jamie's popped his clogs. Shiiit. And she's gone too... Fuck.' Toby ran a hand across his face. 'I mean, Jamie had such a unique style. Not so much unique as... Expensive. To get someone else in is going to break this...'

'What kind of holes are we talking?'

'Nothing major, just... the trouble with editing is it pulls out problems. It's all about narrative logic, making sure A goes to B goes to C, etc. Like I said, I do it all myself and I try to build the assembly as we're shooting. That's basically sticking the film together as per the script. But it made me ask some questions at some points, you know? And sometimes, those questions mean you need to reshoot or just add some new material. We can't anymore, so this documentary is fucked. Wasted a year of my life on this!' He smashed a fist down on the table, making his breakfast jump.

'Listen to me.' Elliot grabbed his hand. 'One of your colleagues is dead while the other's been abducted, but you're worrying about this *documentary*?'

'Of course I want you to find her and catch the killer, but... I'm skint. Absolutely brassic. I've sunk so much time into this film. Re-mortgaged my house! This was supposed to be a massive payoff. I'm going to lose my home. And all of this AI shite is going to make my job redundant.'

Elliot sat back. 'Did Holly mention anything about why David Sylvester might've taken her?'

'What, back in the day?'

Toby nodded. 'Not to me. But...' He looked away again. 'Sorry. I've no idea.'

Elliot had enough. 'Okay, sunshine. You're lying about something. Time for you to spill. Otherwise, we could take you into the station and have a wee word about obstructing a murder investigation.'

'Come on! I've said I'll give you the files!'

'Sure. But there's something you know. And I reckon it's about Jamie.'

'I told you, I don't know anything.'

Elliot stood up. A few heads at the walkers' table looked over at her. 'Come on, then.'

'Look, it's probably nothing, so I didn't want to waste your time...'

'Go on?'

'Jamie met Holly when he was filming her being interviewed for a true crime podcast. One of those podcasts that's actually a YouTube channel. You know, videos. When we were down in Whitley Bay yesterday, I was asking a few questions and Holly couldn't answer them, so she called up this guy who hosted the podcast. Afterwards, she was a bit spooked. She said he seemed to know a lot about Sylvester. More than he should.'

'And how does this fit with Jamie?'

'Because he said he thought he'd sorted him out.'

'Like, violence?'

'I don't want to speak ill of the dead, but Jamie had a temper. Took him ages to get to boiling point, but you didn't want him angry. He was a big guy. Powerful too. And he owned a fucking massive knife. I'm guessing the trouble he got into involved one or both of them.'

45

'Brian Sylvester?'

'Depends on who's asking?' Thick Geordie accent. He shielded his eyes and looked at them. Athletic to the point of a mental health problem – one of those guys who'd cycle to London from Peebles for a cheeky weekend bit of exercise. He stood up from fixing a muddy mountain bike and held out an oily hand. 'You two look like cops.'

'I'm not, but he is.' Liana shook his hand. 'Professor Liana Curtis.'

'DI Rob Marshall.' He smiled at him, but didn't shake that paw. 'Mind if we ask you a few questions?'

'Sure.' Brian stood there, hands on hips. 'Fire away.'

Marshall looked around the area. Glentress was a world-class mountain biking centre not far from Peebles and, for a Wednesday in April, it was absolutely rammed. Not exactly the kind of place you could have a subtle chat about your brother the serial killer. 'Somewhere a bit more private would be ideal.'

'One of those chats. Got it.' Brian pointed inside the giant wooden building. 'Come in. I've got some space in here.' He led them into an open-plan office, all subdivided into various sections. No windows, but the doors were open wide enough. A meeting was going on with twenty or so people, while a few others were dotted around at desks. Not exactly private, but better than outside.

'I'm project managing the extension work to the course here. Trouble is, the new orange trail is proving to be a bit of a nightmare. A load of trees came down in those winds at the weekend, so I was going to ride out and check on progress. There's guys sorting out the problem by chainsawing some logs, but I need to see if it's impacted the difficulty of the run.' He grabbed a rag and wiped off the oil. 'Hence me fixing up my bike.'

Marshall leaned against the wall. 'Used to be an orange route here, right?'

'Still is. I mean, technically, but that's just a mile of free riding to let people develop their technical skills. The black route's been a huge success, but we're putting in a branch off it that'll be a thirty-mile extreme-level course. It'll slay you, man.' Brian laughed. 'You ride yourself?'

'Not for a long time. I've done the blue and red routes here. Just about had a heart attack last time.'

'Should get back on the bike, man. Delay that heart attack.' Brian grinned wide. 'Anyway, I'm going to guess and say you cops are here because of my brother?'

'Right. Are you clairvoyant?'

'No, but you lot have been hounding him for years.'

'Sorry, but that's not exactly what—'

'Relax.' Brian smirked. 'I'm winding you up.' He looked away across the workshop. 'I'm not close to David. Haven't been since all that stuff with the cops. How long ago was that?'

'Twelve years.'

'Right. I'm not a cop or a judge or whatever, so it's not really my place to... But do I think he could've killed those women? Sure. That whole thing in Greece messed him up. All that stuff with the ex-girlfriend... David was in a coma in Greece for three weeks. Metal plate in his head. Never the same after it. Massive insurance payout, which he's lived off ever since. I mean, he was already damaged goods. Our childhood wasn't the best. Chaotic. I had therapy, but David...'

'Why haven't you been in touch?'

'Why would I? I told him to confess, but he didn't listen to me. Worse, he denied it all. Said it wasn't him. But you could catch him stealing chocolate from your advent calendar and he'd deny doing it.'

'Sounds like that happened to you.'

'More than once.'

'We're looking for him. We need to speak to him in connection with some cases.'

'*Some* cases?' Brian sighed. 'You think he's killed more people? Or is this the old stuff?'

'We never exonerated him for those. A witness withdrew her statement and we couldn't proceed with prosecution.'

'Right, well. I'm sorry. In the incredibly unlikely event he gets in touch, I'll call you. I promise.'

Marshall could tell they'd get nothing more out of him. He might live not too far from his brother, but... their relationship was fractured. 'Okay. Here's my card.' He handed one over. 'Have a good day, sir. I hope the tree damage isn't a problem.'

'Oh, it's a problem, just depends on how much of one.' Brian sighed. 'I'm serious. If David's done what you think he's done, he's no brother of mine.'

But Liana wasn't finished. 'I wanted to ask you about your parents.'

'What about them? Both died years ago. Mum had breast cancer. Heart attack got him, thank God.'

'You didn't get on?'

'Hell no. He was a menace. Made Mum's life hell.'

'I gather you lived with your grandparents a lot?'

'Right. Exactly. Made of solid gold, them two. Made me and David feel like normal kids.'

'And you lived with them in Whitley Bay?'

'For a few years, on and off. Aye.'

'Okay. Thank you.' Liana walked out of the bike workshop.

'Thanks for your time.' Marshall nodded at him then followed Liana through the crowd towards his car. 'Well, that was a disappointment.'

'Don't know.' Liana rubbed at her belly. 'When I drop this one, I'll be straight up here to ride that orange route.'

'You're a mountain biker?'

'Big time. Not a lot of great courses down my way, but decent enough. Much better up here.' She ran a hand down his arm. 'And don't be too harsh, we might've got something useful out of that.'

Marshall was a bit thrown by the stroke. 'Go on?'

'Well, I'm starting to think the abduction angle is valid. The part about him taking her from Whitley Bay to Eyemouth.'

'I didn't think we ever doubted it, did we?'

'No, we always accepted it, but just noted how it broke the pattern. Thinking about it now... it's bloody obvious, Rob. It's another evolution. David Sylvester was in a coma for three weeks. Locked up, locked down.'

'And you're saying that's like abducting someone?'

'Don't you think?'

'Maybe. Feels a bit tenuous.' Marshall unlocked the car, but didn't get in. He watched a group of old guys in Lycra teeter off up the hill. 'Do you think he blames Holly for what happened? She wasn't in Greece, was she? It was locals who kicked the shit out of him.'

'That's true. But... God, I wish we could speak to his ex-girlfriend.'

'Okay. We're getting nowhere with this.'

'This was a long shot. Why did you ask about his parents?'

'It's part of the profile. Jacob said the killer came from a stable home, but theirs was anything but that. The narcissism formed from too much parental praise at a young age. Not entirely current thinking, but still has its fans.'

'I didn't know what to do with that bit, have to say.'

'Well, we just have to fill it in. Profiles are never perfect, but as long as we can help find them, it's all good, right?' She brushed his arm again. 'Probably better to head back to base, right?'

Marshall looked around at the cyclists and... sighed. 'I don't see a better option. Getting a bit peckish.'

'Try being pregnant. I'm constantly hungry.'

46

You could practically see Peebles from Traquair, give or take a few hills. Felt to Elliot like she'd travelled back in time a hundred years, though – around here, nothing had changed since the merger of the crowns. Fields, farms, hills and miles and miles of bugger all.

Jolene drove through Traquair village, a real blink-and-you'll-miss-it affair, just some cottages and a tiny church. The only real thing there was the right turn for the stately home, a place Elliot had taken the kids a few times for Halloween and Easter stuff. Maybe she should do that kind of thing again – she'd have so much time to fill over the next few years.

Elliot's phone rang.

Shunty calling...

She bounced it and looked up.

They were powering on along the main road, then Jolene took a left onto a farm track tracing a river up a valley. Probably an ancient drovers' road to Carlisle.

Aye, maybe the Borders trade was a bit more two-way than the popular folkloric myths had it.

'How are you feeling about Davie?'

Elliot looked over at Jolene. 'Nothing. Absolutely nothing.' She laughed. 'Thinking about how they used to take cattle to Carlisle down these roads.'

'Really?'

'Aye. Until the First World War, I think.'

'No, I meant... I thought you'd be preoccupied with Davie?'

'Oh, I've made my peace with him...'

'Really?'

'Don't feel like I've got any option but to stand by him, do I?'

'That's... Wow.'

A big man with two greyhounds gathered them in close to let them past, so Elliot gave him a wave he didn't seem to notice.

The hills to the south were covered in trees, but harvesting them didn't seem to be on anyone's radar. Just acres of tranquil nothingness.

Jolene pulled up outside a tiny cottage just off the track. 'Talk about a hermitage.'

'This is real off-grid living.' Elliot got out. The wind whipped down the valley, making her shiver – not only did it feel ancient, but this place was about ten degrees colder than the towns she was used to.

Jolene thumped the door and stamped her feet. 'Sure it's April? Because it feels like January.'

The door opened to a crack and an eye peered out. 'Aye?'

'Douglas Fairbairn?'

The eye shot between them. 'Depends on who's asking.'

'DI Andrea Elliot.' She unfolded her warrant card. 'This is DS Jolene Archer. Looking to speak to you about a murder case.'

'A murder?' The door opened and Fairbairn stood there,

wild with excitement. Wild hair like he was wearing a clown wig, two diagonal cones of brown and silver. Purple-and-lime tartan dungarees, belonging to no clan Elliot recognised, over bare skin. Silvery hair. Barely a gram of fat. 'Which murder?' He frowned, then stopped dead. 'Stop it, Dougie. Don't let them tempt you like that.'

Elliot frowned at him. 'Is there someone here with you?'

He chuckled. 'Sorry. When you live alone like I do, you tend to talk to yourself. Don't even know I'm doing it half the time.'

Elliot had seen that a few times. Even did it herself a bit now Davie was gone. 'Mind if we come in, sir?'

'No. You can't.'

'Okay. That's fine. We'll do it out here.' Jolene rubbed her gloves together. 'Sir, we wanted to ask about Holly Fenwick.'

Douglas stared at her. No emotion, no movement.

'She's been abducted.'

'What?'

'Taken from her home last night.'

'My God.'

'Know anything about it?'

'What? No! Of course not! I... I spoke to her yesterday.'

'We know. We wanted to ask you a few questions about it.'

'I haven't done anything.'

'Gather you had a bit of a beef with Jamie.'

'You think I killed them because of that?'

'Wouldn't be the first time.'

'Listen, the beef was over me accidentally paying him twice. I'm not good with technology, so I made a mistake. He refused to return the money. He, uh, threatened me with a knife. A massive thing, hunting. Kind you'd get in jungles or on the streets of London. We came to an arrangement, though. Got some free work from him. And he didn't stab me.'

'You've got evidence of this?'

'I do.' Douglas slipped inside his home, without giving them an invitation to enter.

Elliot didn't need one, so she followed him in.

His house was an absolute mess. Stacks of newspapers filled one room, wall to wall, floor to ceiling. Douglas was in another, sitting on a bed covered with rumpled sheets, emptily staring at the piles of books on the floor. 'It's here somewhere. The proof. The receipts. But...' He looked up at them. 'Has David Sylvester taken her?'

'Why do you ask that?'

'She was... Well, he took her before. Tried to kill her. Makes sense to me that he'd try to repeat it.'

Elliot clocked some of the spines on the books. As many cheesy true crime things as there were academic tomes. Maybe this guy knew his stuff, so she decided to play his game. 'We are investigating Mr Sylvester as a potential suspect, yes. We understand you've had some dealings with Holly over the years?'

'You might see me as a crackpot hermit living off the grid and going slightly mad. The truth is I'm deeply knowledgeable about the darker side of humanity. I choose this lifestyle to avoid people and devote myself to my work of documenting and solving cases. And Holly... Yes, Holly's been a guest on my podcast.'

'What's this podcast about?'

'True crime... I try to avoid it being cheesy, you know? Factual. Informative. Educational. Making people aware of the monsters lurking next door. Aiding them if the worst were to happen. I did a PhD in Criminology, so I do know my stuff.' He cast his hand across the floor. 'I read obsessively, as you can see here. Keeps me updated on the latest thinking and I try to bring that out in my work.'

One of those guys who gave his CV every time he met a new person.

'You record that podcast here?'

'God, no. I don't go out.'

'So you don't record it here and you don't go out. Does it exist?'

'Except when I have to record new episodes. I'm technically inept, so I have to brave the train into the big, bad city. I pay people to record me in a studio. I pay someone else to interview the guests. Then I assemble it all and write scripts to read out, talking like I'm the one doing it. But all of the work is mine. I try to record a few in one go, so the sessions can go on and on for hours and hours. It takes a lot out of me, you know. I've got an electrical allergy, you see, so I have to wear a special costume to go into places with Wi-Fi.' He pointed to an antique wardrobe.

A Jack the Ripper-style cape hung from a corner, the inside not lined with red velvet but silver foil.

Elliot gave him an empathetic smile. 'I'm sorry to hear that.'

'Should've called it die-fi. People don't understand what they're exposing themselves to.'

'So you'd meet Holly in Edinburgh?'

'No.' Douglas walked over and put the cape on over his bare shoulders. 'Can feel the rays coming off their phones...' Some tension seemed to slacken off. 'I did that interview at a studio in Newcastle. A friend of mine, Alex Vickers, was getting into YouTube videos and his setup down there... It's quite incredible. So I did the interview with her live. Just the two of us across a table.'

'How was it?'

'The whole thing was a disaster. I was suffering like crazy with all the electricity in the room and the cape wasn't cutting it. And Holly... I took it out on her, I'm afraid.'

'In what way?'

'Well. She didn't seem to understand her own story. I kept having to point out corrections. It's fairly common with victims like her, but still. I'd done so much reading and research...

Survivor's guilt makes them focus on incorrect elements in their story and blow them up. It deforms the storage of memories. Or at least the recall of them. The technical term is source misattribution, where they've relearned a version of their story incorrectly but they've forgotten where the edits came from. But I just drove a lorry right through it all and, after all that, we couldn't broadcast it. Apparently, me going apeshit at a survivor didn't look good. I pulled some elements out for a series of my podcast, but it was a painful exercise. Luckily, Holly was willing to record some new material. But she made some fundamental errors.'

'What kind of things?'

'David Sylvester. I mean, she knew far too much about him.'

'Wait a sec. She said *you* knew too much.'

'I mean, I know enough, but Holly took it too far. It can be common for a survivor to obsess about the man they believe attempted to kill them, but Holly knew far too much. To help her, I saw it needed to be done in the right way. Not some trivial live interview. So we did a full series. We needed to catalogue the crimes, assemble the evidence, lay out the story. All of it. Done right.'

'When was this?'

'About three years ago.'

'When did you last hear from her?'

'Last interview was six months ago. We had a follow-up episode to discuss the film she planned to make.'

'And she stayed in touch after all that?'

'Of course.'

'Why?'

'Why?' Douglas seemed baffled. 'Well. Because I wanted to help her get closure on her experience. I haven't stopped pressing on with her case. And I could offer some help with her own research. I let her use me as a resource for this documentary she was making. Paid, of course. I need to put food on the table, after all.'

Though Elliot couldn't see who exactly the food would be for. Not even a dog to chat to or take for walks in the hills.

'I mean, it's incredibly brave of Holly to make a documentary about her ordeal. When she told me initially, though, I was outraged. She was stepping onto my turf. I mean, I covered that case over six episodes, but we didn't reach a verdict.'

'A verdict?'

'Part of the conceit of my podcast is to present the information like it's a trial. We request the listeners to vote guilty or innocent.' Douglas wagged a finger. 'None of that not-proven nonsense in my court!'

'How often did you speak to Holly recently?'

'Sporadically. I started to feel like she was only speaking to me to get what I knew. To milk me, as it were. But she was an incredibly warm woman. While I was being milked, she settled each invoice very promptly.'

'You were being milked?'

'Well, even dairy cattle need to be fed grass once in a while.' Douglas picked up a book and tossed it onto another pile. 'Do you honestly think David Sylvester has returned to finish the job?'

'No comment on that score, sunshine.'

'Sunshine? P-lease.' Douglas rolled his eyes. 'But it's why you're here, isn't it?'

'Do you think he's capable of that?'

'If you want my professional opinion... David Sylvester is a narcissistic psychopath. While his initial crimes all pertain to seemingly opportunistic murders, there was a high degree of preparation to them. With Holly, though, I'd surmise he felt like he could abduct her without fear of jeopardising his goal – to murder her.' Douglas's eyes glowed with mischief. 'But the one time he deviated from his standard operating procedure, he failed. Holly was the one time he didn't manage to secure the kill.'

'It's not the only time.'

'Oh?'

'There's another attempted murder victim who has, touch wood, survived.'

'Interesting.' Douglas picked up another book and started leafing through it like they weren't there. 'Holly was obsessed with the idea that he'd been attacking and killing women in the intervening period.' He snapped the book shut. 'But I tried to press home to her that he'd changed his MO with her. Once someone escalates, it's vanishingly rare for them to revert back to prior methodologies.' He stormed through the house towards the other room and its collection of newspapers. 'If what you're saying is true, then the cases I found are null and void.'

'What cases?'

'I picked up some reports of abductions in several of the newspapers I follow. I, uh, shared them with her.'

'You didn't think to share this with the police?'

'With all due respect, the police are amateurs. To solve a case like this, you need a professional like myself.'

Elliot bit her tongue, hard enough to taste the blood.

'The police let David Sylvester go, whereas I have assembled a set of cases I believe he's committed in that intervening period.'

'Which you've just said he probably didn't do because of de-escalation.'

Douglas scratched at his clown hair. 'I need to assess the evidence again.'

Elliot stepped close to him. 'Holly called you yesterday, didn't she?'

He wouldn't look at her.

'Apparently what you told her upset her.'

'That isn't true. You've got it the wrong way round. I didn't upset Holly. *She* upset *me*.'

'Right, sure. Of course she did.'

'Despite my severely strong recommendation not to have any engagement with him, Holly told me David Sylvester called her on Sunday...'

47

M arshall held the door for Liana.

The traffic along Innerleithen high street was slowed by a long row of cyclists riding two abreast, which seemed to inflame the fury of at least two Audi drivers.

Marshall followed her inside.

'I've got to pee.' Liana ran off towards the café's toilet. And she'd only just been.

Marshall spotted Elliot at a long table by the window, big enough for eight – just her sitting on her own looked sarcastic. But Elliot always looked sarcastic.

Jolene was over at the counter, ordering for them. She clocked Marshall and nodded – she knew his standing order. She'd have to wait for Liana. Or Liana would have to wait.

'You're lucky.' Marshall sat diagonally opposite Elliot. 'We were just on our way back to Gartcosh when you called. Got as far as Eddleston before we turned back.'

'Sounds like I'm not the lucky one.' Elliot grinned. 'Being back on your old stomping ground must be weird, right?'

'Weird, but not bad. Comfortable, maybe?' Marshall sat back in his chair. This was going to be one of those chats with her, where she'd try to draw everything out. 'Being out and about here certainly beats the alternative, which is being stuck back at Gartcosh. Liana wants us to go through old case files to build up the old profile into something that might help find Holly. No pressure, eh?'

'And no point?'

'Not sure about that, but...' Marshall let out a deep sigh. 'It's not real policing work, is it?'

'Sounds like you're fed up, Robbie.'

'I am. The worst bit is I haven't really got anything new on Sylvester to show for our work.'

'Feeling that pressure like the rest of us humans, eh?'

'Something like that. All we've got are lots of tiny little nuggets that don't add up to anything. It's incredibly frustrating, Andrea, to be brutally honest. Sylvester eludes capture and the next thing we know, he's killing Jamie Alexander and abducting Holly.'

'That's on all of us, Robbie. He gave me a dook in the Eye Water for my troubles. What a pair we make. No wonder Gashkori wants rid of us.'

'He's said he wants rid of you?'

'I don't know that he does, but—'

Her phone rang again. She checked the display, glared and bounced it.

'You not going to answer that?'

'It's Shunty.' She stuffed her phone back in her bag. 'Arsehole.'

'Come on, Andrea, Rakesh is a good guy.'

'That's a bit of a stretch, Robbie. The wee prick was trying to chat to me in court yesterday. Then his testimony absolutely annihilated me. Made me look like a fucking idiot. Worse than Pringle.'

'Wow.'

She sighed as her phone started ringing again. 'What kind of arsehole doesn't take the hint over someone bouncing *six* calls?'

'What kind of arsehole bounces a call six times? Maybe you should answer it next time and see what he wants?'

'He's hardly going to have the solution to this case, is he?'

'You'll never know until you find out.'

Liana sat down opposite Marshall. 'My bladder's the size of a walnut, I swear.'

Marshall smiled at her. 'Learned this morning that a walnut is about the right size for a male prostate.'

'Take your word for it.'

Elliot sat forward. 'Okay, reason I've got you two here is we spoke to this true crime banana. Real nut job who lives off-grid. Name of Douglas Fairbairn.'

Liana grinned. 'Douglas?'

'You know him?'

'He was in my year at Durham.'

'Really? He looks about three times your age, hen.'

'He was a mature student, I think. Started the course at twenty-five.' She looked at Marshall. 'You remember him?'

'Must've been after my time.'

'You're not that much older than me. Do you remember the undergraduate student who started taking tutorials?'

'*Him*?'

'Yeah, him.' She looked at Elliot. 'He suffered mental health problems, I think.'

'You think? The lad's lucky he's not in a padded room with one of those comfy jackets that wrap up at the back.'

'That's a bit cruel.'

'I mean, his cottage is a fucking midden. Books and newspapers everywhere. And he had the cheek to say we were amateurs.'

'You and DS Archer?'

'No, the police!'

Liana sat back and ran a hand through her hair. 'From his perspective, though, you are. Rob is the only one who could be classed as a professional in that sphere.'

'Aye, he's a crap cop.'

'I do have feelings, you know.'

'I'm joking.' Elliot winked at Marshall. 'But also I'm not. See, arrogant tosspots like him who think they can conjure up solutions without having to do anything practical. I mean, he told us he doesn't even do his own interviews. Isn't that, like, half of what you do, princess?'

'Princess?' Liana rolled her eyes. 'Tell me the point of Rob and me being here?'

'Okay. Right. Douglas told us he's helping Holly with her documentary. Paid work. Admitted he's been in touch with her. And she told him Holly spoke to Sylvester on Sunday.'

'Did this come up in the telephony?'

'Not that I'm aware of. Robbie, have you?'

'I know DC Paton found a call between Kayleigh and a number we believe belongs to Sylvester, but I'm not aware of anything further.'

'Might be worth speaking to Ash, then, eh?'

Marshall got out his notebook and added it to the groaning list of items he had to do. 'What was the chat about?'

'This info came from that wee English lad. Toby. So I'm confident it happened. All Fairbairn got out of Holly was that she had spoken to Sylvester. Didn't say what about, but they got into an argument about the ethics of doing that. He was very much against it.'

Liana narrowed her eyes. 'This isn't helpful.'

'Eh?' Elliot sat back and folded her arms. 'Your whole shtick is getting so old, missy. You just sit there while we do our work and you conjecture some shite like "the killer was a human being" or "the killer was a fucked-up psychopath". How does that help anyone?'

'If you were capable of doing your job, you wouldn't need my help, would you? You wouldn't have let him go.'

Elliot laughed. 'That's priceless, coming from a wee princess who sits in her ivory tower.'

'Here.' Jolene put the tray down between Liana and Elliot. 'Is she being an arse to you?'

Elliot nodded. 'You heard that?'

Jolene took the seat next to Elliot. 'I was talking about *you* being an arse, Andrea.'

Liana laughed, then took her smoothie. 'Thank you. You say that like she's nice to anyone.'

'Oh, I'm nice to lots of people. Just not arseholes.'

Jolene distributed the coffees. Four plates; brownie, blondie, rocky road, millionaire's shortbread. 'Have a cake and improve your blood-sugar levels.'

Liana gritted her teeth and sliced into the blondie, then took a quarter.

Elliot sipped at her coffee and glowered at the cakes. Or maybe at Liana. 'All I'm asking of you two brainboxes is why Holly would be in touch with the man who attacked her.'

Liana finished chewing, then set about dividing up the brownie. 'Happens more often than you'd think.'

Elliot took the whole slice of millionaire's shortbread. 'Don't you think it's a bit weird, though?'

Liana frowned at the empty plate. 'What part of being abducted and almost murdered by someone you trusted wouldn't make someone "a bit weird"? That kind of ordeal can warp your brain in ways you can't imagine.'

'Take your word for it.' Elliot slurped at her coffee. 'So what are you two up to down here?'

'We spoke to Sylvester's brother.'

'Didn't know he had one. He know where he is?'

'No, but he pointed out that Sylvester was in a coma for three weeks. My theory is he abducted Holly as an inverse of his coma. Keeping her in a—'

'Blah, blah, fucking blah.' Elliot laughed. 'What the hell does that even mean?'

Marshall took his coffee and tipped in the pot of oat milk. 'Enough of this, please. You're acting like kids.'

'She started it...' Elliot finished chewing then let out a deep sigh. 'Thing you don't get is he's probably killing her right now!'

Liana slurped smoothie through the straw. 'Okay, so if he contacted her, it's likely he did it to torment her. It's very common in crimes like this.'

'It's also a Wednesday, so is that relevant?'

'I'm being serious here. A narcissistic psychopath like David Sylvester takes great pleasure from watching the suffering of others. And from them pleading with him. Hearing it directly would be even better for him.'

'Bugger this.' Elliot necked her coffee and pinched a quarter of the blondie. 'We need to explore this. We've got the telephony on the burner that didn't burn. We can find out the facts from these calls. Get actual hard facts. Start building a case.'

Liana rolled her shoulders. 'Fill your boots.'

Elliot's phone rang again. She looked at the display. 'Bloody Shunty.' She bounced it one more time. 'Don't tell me to fill my boots, Toots. Okay?'

'Don't call me Toots.'

Jolene mouthed the word *meow* to nobody in particular, then took a quarter of brownie.

The rocky road was calling Marshall's name.

Elliot's phone rang again. She looked over at him. 'He's as persistent as you, Robbie.' She stood up and stepped away.

'Rakesh, my old friend. Are you ringing to offer an apology?'
She swung around to face Marshall. Her mouth hung open.
'Shit.'

Marshall frowned at her. 'What's happened?'

48

Marshall stormed into Gala nick without looking behind him. Jolene and Liana were following, but he just needed to get inside. Wonder of wonders – his card actually worked for once and he swiped through without requiring adult supervision. He paced across the soiled carpet tiles to Gashkori's office and, bloody typical, he wasn't in.

Sodding hell.

Marshall put his phone to his ear and it just rang and rang – the sound of someone saying you're not important.

'We're sorry but the caller is unavail—'

He didn't leave a third voicemail, instead killing the call and pocketing his phone. Then he looked around the office.

Jolene and Liana still hadn't appeared yet.

But something caught his eye – over in the corner, Struan was standing over Ash Paton, making her cower like she felt she was going to get hit.

Workplace bullying...

Marshall raced over there, fists clenched. 'Rein it in, Liddell.'

Struan looked over at him. 'Alright, gaffer?'

'Calm down, son.' Marshall grabbed him by the shirt sleeve and dragged him into the corridor beneath the stairs. 'What's going on?'

'Where?'

'Between you and DC Paton there. Looked like heated words to me.'

'Nothing's going on, gaffer.'

Marshall held his gaze and looked right through the mask of professionalism to see just another bully. 'I've had enough of you, Sergeant. I've no more time for your nonsense.'

'My *nonsense?*'

'Gashkori might put up with it. Taylor might, too, but I don't.'

If Marshall was in Struan's position, he might point out that Marshall wasn't actually on the team or in any position of authority. But no. Typical of all bullies everywhere when faced with a bigger bastard, Struan tried to schmooze and charm and wriggle out of any trouble.

'What exactly are you accusing me of, gaffer?'

'Bullying. And not for the first time, either.'

'Come on, gaffer. I'm not bullying her, I'm...' Struan's eyes darted around the murky corridor. 'I'm just trying to get a tune out of a broken instrument.'

Marshall waited until his gaze settled on him. There. 'Weirdly enough, DC Paton manages to get results when I ask her to work on something. DCI Gashkori is impressed by her work ethic, not to mention her results.'

'You mean for her taking credit for someone else's work.'

'*Sergeant.*'

'What?'

'You're in a position of leadership, that means you need to inspire people to work for you, not belittle them into—'

'Belittle?'

'Belittle. You're bullying her.'

'That what she's said?'

'No. She's tough. But it's what I've *seen* with my own eyes.' Marshall held his gaze until he was sure he wasn't going to get anymore backchat. There. 'Right now, I need you to do two things for me. First, you're going to act professionally in all your interactions with DC Paton.'

'I do that anyway.'

'*Sergeant...*'

'Okay, fine. I'll bend over for her and take it. What's the other thing?'

'There was a call between Holly and David Sylvester on Sunday. I want to know everything about it.'

Struan frowned. 'There wasn't.'

'That sounds very definite?'

'Gaffer, you might think I'm a dickhead, but you should know I'm a very thorough dickhead.' Struan tapped at his temple. 'I know the calls both of them made. And there's nothing on the log.'

'We know he called *Kayleigh*. I'm asking you if he called *Holly*.'

'Acting like I'm stupid or something... I know what you asked. And I'm telling you it either didn't happen or Sylvester's got another phone we don't know about.' Struan sniffled like he was at the start of a cold Marshall would rather not get. 'Are you asking me to do something here?'

'I am. I want you to go through every call Holly made and received. Standard phone calls made over the network. Anything on her landline, assuming she's still got one in this day and age. But focus on any calls made over apps like Whats-App, Messenger, Schoolbook. Find out if she contacted him.'

'Sure. Okay. But to do that we'd need her phone. And we don't have it.'

'No, but we can get her data traffic from the network, which will give us a lead on what apps she uses. Then you can request that from the service.'

Struan looked away, sighing like he knew precisely how much work that was going to entail. 'Right.'

'Sergeant, is this too much for you?'

'No. I'll get you your result, just please stop asking how the sausage is made.' Struan barged through the door back into the office space.

Marshall took a few seconds to recover from it. His ears were still burning, heart thudding.

Trouble with someone like Struan, it made him think of that quote. 'Never wrestle with pigs. You both get dirty and the pig likes it.'

Well, Struan was absolutely covered in it.

And Marshall hated confrontations like that. Didn't mean he wouldn't do them.

Maybe he'd been too hard on Struan, maybe he'd stepped over the line into a bit of bullying himself, but—

There it was. The backswing of the bollocking – think you'd overstepped the mark.

Struan was a total arsehole. End of story.

Marshall eased back through and saw Liana slipping into his old office. No sign of Jolene.

Struan was sitting next to Paton.

Marshall walked over, shooting Struan a raised eyebrow.

In the office, Liana was running a hand across her bump. She looked at Marshall. 'You want to talk about it?'

'Nope.' Marshall walked over to the whiteboard. Whatever Taylor had up there looked more like fantasy football than police work. He wiped it clear and uncapped the blue pen. 'Right. Where do we start... Okay.' He started scribbling. 'We know there was a call between Kayleigh and Sylvester. Now, we've learned about one between Holly and Sylvester. He'd been trying to contact her, then she wilted and answered it on Sunday.'

'According to Douglas Fairbairn.'

'Indeed.' He glanced at her. 'You know him. Should we be suspicious?'

'*Knew* him, Rob. Years ago. His mental health's gone massively downhill since then.'

'Do you believe him?'

She dragged her top teeth over her bottom lip. 'I do. Yes.'

'Okay. The problem is, we've got no record of this call ever being made. I've asked DS Liddell to focus on that. Could lead us to Sylvester, maybe.' Marshall went back to the whiteboard. 'But anyway. The next thing we know, Holly just so happened to turn up at the caravan exactly as Sylvester was abducting someone he attempted to murder.'

'You think this is dodgy?'

'It's bugged me for a while, to be honest. More than I maybe let on earlier.' Marshall shook his head but the doubt still clung to his brain. 'But that phone call could explain the coincidence of her being by that caravan.'

'You mean, she was there because he lured her there to witness it?'

'Precisely. Like you said to Andrea earlier, he wants to see torment in his victims. What could be worse than Holly knowing that if he'd been convicted, Kayleigh wouldn't have died?'

Liana nodded slowly. 'So why did Sylvester abduct Holly again? And why kill Jamie?'

Marshall shrugged. 'To torment her further?'

'I mean, yeah, but still... It's a bit woolly, isn't it?' Liana blew air up her face. 'Rob, I'm not sure this is helping any.'

'It is.'

'I mean *you*, Rob. It's not helping you any. I think you need to talk.'

'Nope. Not doing that. We're here to profile the case and help find her. So tell me if Sylvester still fits?'

'Of course he does.' Her eyes danced across his mad scribbles on the whiteboard. 'We know a few things about Sylvester. First, he's an opportunist and he's got no home base. Just switches rental accommodation constantly. That makes geographic profiling hard, but it means something if we can pin down his movements, know where he's been and when. And he's proven to be able to fit in anywhere.'

'You think so?'

'Don't you?'

'Well, not really. Most people seem to notice him. Like the women in the cafés. His eccentric behaviour sticks out a mile away.'

'Okay, but he's hiding in plain sight. And he's still living the same life. He's still staying in odd locations, still doing his jigsaws and just being weird. But not creepy weird.'

'That doesn't answer my question, though. Does he still fit?'

'Rob, do you think he doesn't?'

'This torment angle you're bringing up is making me start to doubt it. The first cases were all sharp shocks. Pushed off a cliff or in front of a train. Where's the torment in that? Strikes me that his main driver is asserting power and control over his victims.'

'Precisely. What could assert more power and control over someone than abducting them?'

'Maybe, but that's highly organised behaviour from someone who spends his days drinking pots of tea and solving the same jigsaw puzzles over and over again.'

'You don't think jigsaw puzzles are signs of organising? The pieces represent chaos. You bring order to that chaos by solving the puzzle. You remove all grey areas until you've got black and white. Pieces all in the right place. Or down the back of the sofa.'

'Don't buy it.'

'Besides, we've got statements from two of those old cases about how he'd visited the locations again after moving on.'

Marshall frowned. 'This is news to me.'

'What do you think I was doing when I was up all night?' Liana yawned into her fist. 'I ran the interview transcripts through my AI app. The technology is incredible these days, Rob. But yes, in both cases the visits were ostensibly to book next year's accommodation, but I think it was to witness the torment first hand – he spoke to the owners of the B&Bs a few months after they suffered the death of their child.'

Marshall jotted it down on the board. 'Okay, I can maybe see this, then.'

'You agree?'

'I don't disagree and that's as good as you'll get out of me today. I just want to make sure we're looking for the right guy.'

'Oh, I *know* we are.' Gashkori was leaning against the door jamb, rubbing at his nose. Marshall didn't know how long he'd been there. Didn't want to ask. 'You pair making any headway in finding him or Holly?'

Marshall ignored him, keeping his gaze on the whiteboard. 'We're working on it, sir.'

'Sure.' Gashkori shook his head. 'Trouble is, all this theoretical nonsense isn't helping us find them, though, is it?' A nervous twitch jerked him away from the door and into the office, where he started pacing.

Marshall had seen it in other SIOs – a cocktail of too much stress and too much caffeine. Shaken, not stirred.

Liana smiled at him. 'I'll head back to Gartcosh and dig into these other cases. There might be something in those.'

'You do that.' Gashkori watched her go, then shifted his focus to Marshall. 'Surprised to learn you were down here rather than doing what you agreed?'

'Came down to speak to Sylvester's brother. Bit of a waste of time, but you've got to go through the motions.'

'Leave no stone unturned.' Gashkori joined him by the whiteboard, his frantic eyes dancing across it. 'Take it you heard?'

'Aye.' Marshall couldn't avoid it any longer. 'I was with Andrea when she got the call.'

'Just heard myself. Brutal. Incident at HMP Glenochil. Took a couple of calls to find out it was Davie Elliot who was stabbed. Rushed to Kings Park hospital in Stirling.'

Marshall felt like he'd been sucker-punched in the gut. 'Have you got an update?'

'All I heard was it doesn't look good.' Gashkori ran a hand down his face. 'Prison stabbings seldom end well. The ferocity and desperation. Not to mention the fact it was probably paid for by someone, so the killer wanted to be absolutely sure they'd get their money. Or make sure their loved one would be off a hit list.'

'Fingers crossed he pulls through, sir.'

'Aye, even though he leaked a load of information to a very bad man, we still don't want this kind of shite happening, do we?' Gashkori looked at the whiteboard and let out a deep sigh. 'Okay, enough of this mumbo jumbo for now. I'm going to have DI Elliot out for the foreseeable, not that she should've been here after yesterday. So, I'm asking you to step in for a bit.'

'Feels like I've done that a lot recently.'

'Look, Rob, do you want it or not?'

'Of course I do.'

'Good. Your priority is finding Holly and Sylvester, preferably before he kills her.'

49

Stirling...

No good came from the city.

Or nobody good, that's for sure. Full of bastards.

Elliot had never met anyone from the place who she liked. Kind of like the worst bits of Glasgow in a city that looked a bit like Edinburgh.

Ach, who was she kidding? The place was fine, the people were fine, it was her who was the arsehole. And her fault this was happening.

She stormed along the corridor into the depths of A&E. Way busier than the Borders hospital she was used to, with a frenetic energy that nipped at her throat. She turned a corner.

Shunty was standing outside a door, tapping away on his phone. He looked up at her. 'Ma'am.'

Screaming and shouting came from a room nearby.

'What happened?'

Shunty kept his distance, like she was going to hit him. 'A specialised escort unit took Davie from court to a confidential prison where he was to await sentencing. He was placed in a protected area in the prison under an assumed name. Nobody knew his true identity.'

'Which prison?'

'Even I don't know. And there are three around here it could be. Another two in the Greater Glasgow area.'

'Who did it?'

'I can't say.'

'Was it himself?'

Shunty shook his head. 'A guy waiting on a murder rap got to him...'

'Who?'

'Ma'am...'

'Rakesh. You owe me. Tell me the truth. Now.'

'Someone called John Hughes.'

Elliot felt like she'd been stabbed. 'Was it Rancid John?'

'I don't know.' Shunty shrugged. 'Stabbed him in the showers after courtyard exercise this morning. Davie was rushed here, then I got the call. I've been trying to phone you, but... I'm sorry to say, he died a few minutes ago.'

'Wait.' She collapsed back against a painting hanging from the wall. '*What*?'

'I'm sorry, Andrea. I called and called. I left messages all over, trying to track you down.'

The news was a cricket bat to the stomach. Hard wooden pain against soft flesh. The anguish fizzed up her spine, then zapped at her brain.

Made her fucking *cry*.

She wiped the tears away. 'Fucking hell, Shunty, you lead with that!'

'You asked me what happ—'

'Were you with him when he died?'

'No.'

'Did you speak to him?'

'Just before.' Shunty frowned. 'I don't know the technical term, but he went into some kind of seizure. I'm so sorry.'

'Did he say anything?'

'Aye. He said to tell you he was sorry and that he loved his three kids. He knew he was dying.'

Elliot blew air up her face. The tears flowed thick and fast now.

'He also said... I'm not sure I've got it right, but... He was kind of muttering and stuff. I'm not sure. But it was something like you should spend more time at the caravan.'

'The *caravan*?'

'Do you have one?'

'His family do, aye.'

'Said he wishes he'd had more holidays as a family. Said you were happy at the caravan and that happiness has the most value for him.'

'He said that?'

'I'm paraphrasing as he was in a lot of pain and not wholly coherent, but essentially that.'

'He loved that place. We had some good times there.' Elliot wiped away the fresh tears. 'And we won't have them again.'

50

M arshall wheeled Taylor's whiteboard through into Elliot's office, hoping to avoid the owner's rage at wiping off his fantasy football nonsense. He took one long look at it – scanning each word and phrase and connecting line – and a sickening feeling built up in his guts.

All this work he'd done with Liana was just pissing about in the margins – they were no closer to finding Holly or Sylvester.

Maybe Gashkori was right – Marshall needed to prove he was a proper cop. All he'd shown was the complete opposite.

Could be it was time to accept he wasn't a real cop and never would be. Time to just bugger off and do something intellectual and clinical. Maybe even leave the police.

But giving up didn't suit him.

And they needed to find Holly.

Jolene walked in, clutching two coffees. 'Thought these might help?'

'I'm up to my earballs already.' Still, Marshall took the coffee from her and sipped it through the lid. And realised he'd used one of Pringle's many stock phrases. He toasted Jolene with the cup. 'But thank you.'

She wasn't looking, instead focusing on the nonsense filling the board. 'How's it looking?'

'Bad.' Marshall let out a slow breath. 'I need a plan and soon.'

'This isn't a plan?'

'Nope. This is just... Stuff. Hopefully Liana can turn it into something coherent and blow the bloody doors off.' Marshall sipped more bitter coffee and scanned through the work again. His gaze stopped on one box. 'How's Paton done with the telephony?'

'No idea. Struan has her doing some stuff with forensics.'

'I *told* him to focus on—'

'Relax. I did it myself.'

Marshall felt anything but relaxed. 'Have you found anything?'

She got out her notebook and flicked through the pages. 'A call was made from Sylvester's mobile to an unknown phone on Sunday afternoon at quarter past three.'

'Have you traced it?'

'Recipient was in Whitley Bay. Two cell sites in the town were hit.'

Marshall jotted it on the board. 'So, it matches up with Holly taking a call. But it's not her number?'

'Nope. A pay-as-you-go phone.' She snapped her notebook shut. 'I know what you're thinking. A burner. But she's not a drug dealer, guv, she's a victim of a horrific crime. Stands to reason she'd want some anonymity and protection.'

Marshall nodded along with it. 'Have you got the calls on that phone?'

'Two that day. The other was to Douglas Fairbairn.'

'So that checks out.' Marshall walked over and added the information. 'It does look like Sylvester lured Holly to Eyemouth to witness what happened to Kayleigh. Which was Liana's assessment.'

'Okay.' Jolene rested her coffee on the edge of the desk, precariously close to falling off. 'So Sylvester abducted Holly, repeating what happened twelve years ago. And now he's imprisoning her for some reason we don't know.'

'Liana thinks it's to mirror his coma.'

'Whatever that means.' She picked up her coffee and drank some more. 'Still remains that if we find him, we find her. Right?'

'Or we find her body.'

'Grim. So where do we start?'

'Liana's going through the list of locations from the missing period. Fairbairn thought Sylvester had kept on killing in the twelve-year gap, deaths we hadn't picked up. Hardeep's working on them, but I think there could be something in there. It seems like he's got a set of locations he repeatedly goes to. Cycling through them every year or two. If we can pin him to any of the deaths in that list, then the whole lot comes into play. Gives us potential locations he'd run to.'

'So you believe Fairbairn?'

Marshall shrugged. 'No reason not to. Liana knew him at uni. He might be insane, but he knows his stuff.'

'So, the first lot were all across northern England, right? And if these are him, Sylvester seems to have shifted to operating in Scotland.' Jolene dropped her coffee cup into the bin. 'I mean, it's not like he's gone to New Zealand or the Pacific Northwest of the US, is it? There's not a border between Scotland and England, so I don't see the point.'

'Moving his focus to Scotland means a different police force. In fact, these go back to before Police Scotland was formed.' Marshall got out his phone and found the list in his emails. 'Some were Dumfries and Galloway, while others were the Borders bit of Lothian and Borders, and the non-Glasgow bits of Strathclyde. Then the rest will be Police Scotland.'

'So he could hide under the chaos.' Jolene walked over to the pristine map of Scotland on the wall. 'Read them out, then?'

'Obviously we've got Kayleigh in St Abbs to add to this population. And the murder-abduction in Reston, but that seems to be a different type of case.'

Jolene started circling those on the map on the wall. 'And the rest?'

Brodick on Arran.

Troon in Ayrshire.

Rothesay on Bute.

North Berwick in East Lothian.

Lochranza on Arran.

Maryport in Cumbria.

Campbeltown down on Kintyre.

Wigtown in Dumfrieshire.

Crail in Fife.

Marshall walked over and examined the map. 'That's quite a geographical spread. But I don't see anything in it.'

Jolene was scanning it too. 'Andrea's going to be fuming about what we've done to her new map.' She winced. 'Okay. The thing with this stuff is he's not likely to return to them, right?'

'Not sure. Liana thinks he might return to witness the torment months later. And that's assuming he's ever been anywhere near these.'

Jolene pulled out some paperwork. 'On the plus side, we've got access to his accommodation in St Abbs and Jedburgh. Jim McIntyre's leading the investigation into that.'

'He found anything?'

'Nothing much.' Jolene squinted at the map, then scanned through a sheet of paper. 'The place in St Abbs... All we've got were some old jigsaw boxes in a bag marked to go to charity.' Her frown deepened. 'Oh, hello. Here.' She tapped her finger on the page. 'One of the jigsaws has a label on the back, like someone owned it?' She tapped on the map, pointing to the isle of Bute lurking at the top of the Firth of Clyde in that section between the Ayrshire coast and the protective tail of Kintyre stretching down the Irish Sea. 'Old Craig's Bunkhouse in Rothesay.' She frowned again. 'There's another jigsaw from there too.'

'How does that help us?'

'Don't you see? Rob, he's nicked jigsaws from there. Recently.' She tapped at the map. 'And Marianne Henderson was found in the harbour just before Christmas last year. He's been there recently. He might've bolted there.'

E lliot hated the family room in any hospital, but this took the biscuit. So sterile. Devoted to death and despair. The flowers on the coffee table were wilted and limp. The box of tissues was empty, but she just couldn't cry any more tears. 'Shunty, I'm sorry for being a dick and a bully to you.'

Shunty frowned at her. 'What do you mean?'

'Nothing. You're a good cop. Okay?'

'Are you sure about that?'

'I don't know.' Elliot smiled through the pain. 'Maybe we should just go back to me saying you're crap.'

'The first few calls I made... I was ringing to say I'm sorry for saying all those things in court. I couldn't lie, but... You really need to remember your passwords.'

'I'm trying to.' She reached her hand across and held his. 'Thank you for being with Davie when he... When he went.'

'It was the least I could do. I just hope I gave him some comfort.'

'He knew you, Shunty. You may not have been his favourite, but your presence will have given him greater comfort than a stranger would. He'd know you'd pedantically pass the message on to me. And I've taken great comfort from it.'

'Thank you, ma'am. Are you going to?'

'Going to what?'

'Go to the caravan?'

'Probably, aye. It's a bit cold just now, but over the summer... Aye. I'll take the kids there. We did have some braw times there.'

'Where is it?'

'Berwick.'

'In England?'

'Right. Just over the border. Got amazing views up and down the coast. I love where I live, but like that song says, all that's missing is the sea.'

'Sounds nice.'

'It is, Shunty. It is.'

Someone knocked on the door.

Elliot reacted without thinking. 'Come in.' Now she'd said the words, she didn't want anyone else in there. Didn't really want Shunty, but he was smart enough to know to shut up a lot of the time.

Bob Cook eased his way in, wincing like he had severe back pain. Marshall's dad. A big man, but age was devouring him – he was skinny everywhere except his plunging gut. Losing muscle at that age wasn't a good thing – all those falls and nothing to make you bounce. He stepped over to them. 'I'm so sorry for your loss, Andrea. That shouldn't have happened.'

She swallowed hard and gave him a curt nod.

'How are you bearing up?'

She managed to raise a shoulder in response.

Gashkori followed him in, but kept his distance, hands in his pockets.

Elliot sat back on the sofa. 'Just trying to process it all.'

'Totally get that.' Cook sat opposite her, next to Shunty. 'I blame myself for what's happened and I'm taking full responsibility. This was supposed to be sealed up tight like... like nuclear waste. Nobody knew where he was, except for me.'

Elliot frowned. 'You think Hislop did this?'

'I don't see anyone else, do you?'

'Why, though? And why now?'

'Maybe it's as simple as him wanting to make sure Davie stays silent. Could be he just wants his money back. Or maybe he hates having to stand up in court. Either way, he's got a super-strong motive, don't you think?'

'I just don't understand how.'

'Probably speaking out of turn here...' Cook swallowed hard. 'But it's patently obvious to me there's still a leak.'

'Not just Davie?'

'No. Either in that station or in the court system, someone's passed on his identity and location.' Cook stared into space. 'The name was supposed to be top secret, but I guess nothing's foolproof. I'm going to get to the bottom of it, even if it's the last thing I do.'

'Possibly. Could be anyone really. Doesn't have to be a cop.' Gashkori was shaking his head. 'Trouble is, there are a million ways you could get around those protocols. The easiest would be trailing the escort detail from court.'

'That's rubbish, though. Even if someone followed a big black van from the court to a prison, they'd lose them on the way. You'd have to split the tail several times, but they're experts at spotting them. As soon as they did, game over. Van goes elsewhere.'

'But if the van was headed in that direction, there was Glenochil, Stirling and Polmont, possibly Low Moss and Barlinnie, but they're unlikely. Someone in each of those prisons, they just need to match a photo with the new fish.'

Cook didn't have anything to say to that. He shrugged.

Elliot was glaring at him. 'You were supposed to protect him.'

'And he did.' Gashkori sat down next to Elliot. 'Someone like Gary Hislop will have people in all the prisons. Or he'll know people who do. And it just so happened this Rancid John lad was the one who got the nod to strike now rather than say, Wee Stevie Skelton in six months' time after Davie had been sentenced.'

Cook nodded along with the logic. 'Still, I'm going to interview this Rancid John until he squeaks.' He looked right at her with burning intensity. 'I truly am sorry for your loss.'

'I'm not.' Elliot sighed and it felt like the tension of the last year just melted away. 'I'm glad this whole thing has come to a head, to be honest with you. Not gonna lie, I was stuck in this loop of not being able to trust him but also feeling guilty because of what he'd done. I couldn't make a decision either way. I knew the right thing to do, but I felt like I couldn't do it. At least this way, I don't have to decide anymore. The decision is out of my hands. And I have closure.'

'I hope you can maintain that closure, Inspector.' Cook narrowed his eyes at Elliot. 'You know this Rancid John character?'

She shook her head. 'Just his reputation.'

'Right, right.' Cook clapped his thighs then got to his feet, but it took a couple of goes. 'I won't rest until we know the full story. Okay?'

She'd heard that so many times. Had even spoken it herself.

She fixed him with a hard stare. 'Are you confident you'll get Rancid John to give up Hislop?'

'No, but I'm as persistent as my laddie. And he's a tenacious bugger. I'll have this Rancid John lad singing by teatime. I just don't know which day of which month.' He frowned. 'Have you any idea why he's got that nickname?'

Gashkori nodded. 'He's called John Hughes. There's

another one from Liverpool with the same name, who gets called Honest John. Doing twenty for a series of armed robberies in West Lothian.'

'Still doesn't explain why he's Rancid John.'

'Oh, you'll see. Or rather, you'll smell. He doesn't wash unless he's held down.'

'Right.' Cook nodded at them, then left the room. He popped his head back in. 'Shunty, mind if I have a word?'

'I'll see you later, Andrea.' Shunty got up and followed Cook out into the corridor.

Leaving her with Gashkori.

He sat back in the chair. 'I'm backing you, Andi.'

'*Backing* me?'

'In case anyone says anything about you.'

'I wasn't aware that was a possibility, Ryan.'

'All the same. Nobody could understand what you've been through, but you're still standing. Still fighting the good fight. That takes a hell of a lot. Now, I'm going to suggest you go home and decompress from this. I'll drive you, if you need it?'

'No, but thank you. Think some time alone in my head will help me process things. But thank you, sir.'

'Don't mention it.' Gashkori looked over to the closed door. 'I'm going to sit in on the interview. Between the two of us, we'll get him to sing. Mark my words.'

52

The wee man with the clipboard kept waving at them, hurrying them on. Bright yellow jacket. Scowling.

The Clyde was a murky brown-green behind him, much like the thunderous sky overhead.

The wee man rolled his eyes at them, then beckoned the other car forward.

'Come on, come on.' Marshall's fingers twisted the key. The ignition finally kicked in and the car shot forward and rolled onto the ferry.

The wee man stuck out his hand to the car behind.

Marshall let out a deep breath. 'Last one on.'

Jolene laughed. 'Not sure I could handle another hour waiting here.'

'Is my company that bad?'

'No, but...' Jolene opened her door and got out onto the deck.

Marshall let his seatbelt go.

His phone chose just then to ring.

He checked the display:

Elliot calling...

Not a call he could bounce.

Jolene was looking around at him, so he held up his phone until she nodded, then he answered it. 'Hey, Andrea, how are you doing?'

'Take it you heard he died?'

'I'm so sorry.'

'Yeah, hearing that a lot.'

'Because people care for you, Andrea. Nobody wants you to be going through this.'

'Right, aye. Guess so.'

'How are you feeling?'

'Numb. Empty. Angry. Relieved. I feel pretty fucking broken by it, to be honest, Robbie. I was going to wait for his release, you know? I'd been hoping he'd get a short sentence because he shifted his plea. Then we could get back to our life. I mean, we always planned to enjoy a long retirement, but now? Now it's all fucked. Totally fucked.'

'Look, I know a thing or two about what it's like to lose someone that close to you. I'm here if you want to talk.'

'It's why I'm calling you. Everyone else... When they say "I'm sorry for your loss" it just makes me think, why? Why are they sorry? But you, Robbie, you've worn these shoes. You know what it's like. So aye, I *will* take you up on that offer.'

The ferry clunked and thrummed as it set off.

'Where the hell are you?'

'The ferry to Rothesay, would you believe?'

'What the hell are you doing there?'

'Going "doon the water" as they'd say in Glasgow.'

'I mean, what are you going to do on Bute?'

'Right. We've got a lead on Sylvester's recent movements. Might come to nothing, but I'm desperate just now, to be honest with you.'

'Aren't we all.'

And Marshall did feel desperate. Two stolen jigsaws felt like a bit of a stretch, but all the psychobabble he and Liana had got through was getting them no closer to finding him.

Being on a ferry heading across the Clyde was motion. Movement. Felt like he was *doing* something rather than staring at a sodding whiteboard and trying to conjure Sylvester's whereabouts from the ether.

'Listen, Robbie, I'm just about back in Lauder. I've got to pick up the kids and break the news to them, but I'll call you later. Okay?'

'Of course. Any time.'

'Thanks.' Click, and she was gone.

Marshall sat there for a few seconds, trying to process it. Sure, he'd worn those shoes but they were a different size and style.

His girlfriend had been an innocent victim, but Davie Elliot was guilty as hell, and indirectly responsible for the deaths of a few people.

It might've taken Marshall twenty years to get closure, but it wouldn't take Elliot anywhere near as long.

He got out of the car and followed Jolene's path up the narrow staircase to the café in the middle of the boat.

She was sitting at a table, dipping a spoon into a bowl of soup. 'Did you want anything?'

Marshall looked at the queue snaking around the display, then shook his head. 'I'm fine.' He sat down. 'Considering it's half three on a Wednesday, the ferry's rammed.'

'The guy at the till was saying the last two were cancelled while they fixed something.'

'Ah, that'll explain it. I thought it was loads of people coming back from the Asda in Wemyss Bay.'

'Hardly. There isn't one. Nearest big supermarket's a Tesco up in Port Glasgow. Or a Morrisons down in Largs.'

'Brutal. I mean, the Borders is the middle of nowhere, but you've got all the shops you need within half an hour's drive, pretty much wherever you live. Anything is an hour into Edinburgh. But having to get a ferry to go to Tesco?'

'Islanders are hardy folk, Rob. It's all about having three freezers in your garage so that monthly Tesco run lasts you the whole month. And growing your own or buying directly from the farm. And one thing the island has is farms.'

'Wouldn't catch me living here.' Marshall could actually go for a soup, now he saw hers. 'You seem to know a lot about the island?'

'Mum grew up in Rothesay. She lives on Mull now. Living in the Borders for fifteen years drove her mental. She needed the sea.'

'So you're from island stock?'

'I'm a half-breed. My dad's English. Grew up in Oxfordshire. Met Mum at Edinburgh uni. So...' She sat back and sighed. 'God, this soup tastes like coffee and hot chocolate.'

'Ouch.'

'I'm joking. It's really nice.'

Marshall couldn't decide on whether to brave something hot or go local and get an Irn Bru. 'Andrea called me.'

'Shit. How is she?'

'Not great. But also, you know Andrea.'

'Oh, aye.' Jolene stirred her steaming soup again. 'She should've kicked Davie to the kerb a year ago. Can't believe she was going to stand by him after what he did.'

'True love, eh?'

'I don't know if it's that, or...' Jolene went back to her soup. 'You want to go up on the deck and take in the journey?'

'Sounds like a plan. Maybe clear my head.' Marshall got to his feet. 'You know, I think I'll get myself some soup first.'

53

It didn't take a genius to figure out why they called him Rancid John. Like Andrea Elliot said, he stank. Absolutely reeked. A mix of tramp, rotten melon, sour coleslaw and dead badger. All with a massive dose of infection.

Bob Cook felt his eyes watering as he sat across from Davie Elliot's killer. 'Name's Bob Cook. I'm in charge of your case. This is DCI Ryan Gashkori, who's working on a related matter.'

Rancid John stared at him. The rest of him was a stinking mess, but his blue eyes were clear as the Aegean. He looked young, seventeen if a day, but he had the posture of someone who'd spent most of his time on the planet in trouble with the law, one way or another. The fact he was that young, living in the Central Belt and his reputation had spread down the Borders... Aye, that was a career criminal operating at the peak levels in the under-nineteens world championships. 'I killed him, if that's what you're after.'

Cook sat back, acting all casual. 'So. You're confessing?'

Rancid John nodded. 'I'm not a liar. Don't want a fucking lawyer, by the way. Keep asking me if I do. Lying bastards are worse than pigs like you pair.'

'Tell us how you killed him, then?'

'Stabbed him in the shower, aye?' Rancid John looked pleased with himself. 'Clean kill.'

'Doesn't smell like you were in the shower yourself.'

'Don't judge me because I don't subscribe to the beauty industry myths. I like my natural fragrance.'

'Eau du roadkill.'

The joke didn't land. 'Don't fucking mock me, dickhead.'

'I'm not mocking you, I'm celebrating your work. Like a surgeon, aren't you? Clean, precise. Got to admire a man's handiwo—'

'Shut the fuck up.'

'Two cuts and he was gone. Usually, you need about fifty, sixty, but your work needs to be applauded.'

'Take that as a compliment.'

'Where did you get the shiv?'

'Oh, look at you. Big boy knows prison slang!'

'You're not the first daft wee laddie I've interviewed. At some point there'll be a last one, but there's life in this old dog yet. You're sitting there, thinking you're the bee's knees, but the truth is you're just another wee ned off the conveyor belt in the factory that builds daft laddies. Don't kid yourself that you're anything special. But you'll start speaking to us if you want any leniency here. If you want any chance of avoiding the worst people in this place, the kind who will do much worse things to you than you did to Ian Carson.'

Not his choice of name, but it was supposed to give Davie some security. And had failed at the first test.

Rancid John swallowed hard. 'Heard that shite patter before.'

'Tell us. Where did you get the shiv?'

'Made it myself. Not difficult. I've got a toothbrush, but never have cause to use it.' Rancid John flashed his rotten teeth and gave a blast of cat-piss breath. 'Until now. I won't tell you how I sharpened it, but it clearly worked. Amazing how light you feel when the guards haul you away, isn't it?'

'So you're some kind of vigilante? Is that the deal?'

'No, I just don't like those pricks who think they're better than people like me.'

Gashkori cleared his throat. 'You're on a murder charge, right?'

Rancid looked over at him. 'So?'

'Had a look through the case file. Other part of Glasgow from the one I used to work. Says you killed a single mother and two children, didn't you?'

Rancid sniffed. 'So?'

'You don't think that makes you lesser than other people?'

'I'm better.'

'Better. Okay.'

'I'm the one clearing vermin off the streets. Not you lot. You just make things ten times worse.'

'Killing two kids is—'

'That bitch was just going to raise those kids to be two more versions of herself.'

'Those children were one and three years old.'

'Can see the writing on the wall, man.'

'They were your own children.'

'The big one was. The wee man... I had my doubts.'

Cook had dealt with people traffickers and loads of drug gangs. Men who'd shoved poor refugees onto boats, knowing they'd probably not make the crossing, or if they did, would be sent back to Albania or worse. But he hadn't met anyone so casually evil as Rancid John. His lack of hygiene was the best thing about him. 'She had a restraining order against you, right?'

'Nope.'

'Sure. Okay. We know she did.'

'That's all bullshit, though. Just cos some judge in a wig says something, I can't see my wean? How's that fair?'

'You previously hospitalised them. Why else do you think you're in here rather than on bail? Because you're a threat to your community.'

'People should be scared of me.'

Cook held his gaze for longer than he wanted. 'Who asked you to kill Mr Carson?'

'Nobody.'

'Okay, but you heard he was coming in, right?'

'Pal. You and I both know the score here. I'm going to serve a life sentence, so killing again isn't going to add anything to my tally. Now, all I'll tell you is me and Mr Carson had a beef on the outside.'

'Where did this beef happen?'

'On the internet.'

'The internet. Right.'

'Had a wee argument on Schoolbook. Marked his cards. Just so happens to be running around the exercise yard with me.'

'That's a big coincidence.'

'One of those things where the universe gives you what you want. I was just settling the score with the universe.'

'Didn't think you'd be a crystal-toting hippie.'

'Nobody does. But I believe in fate. Besides, I've got nothing to lose, so I'm pretty fucking proud of my work.'

'So who told you to—'

'That's my final answer, gents. Can I get back to my cell?'

Aye, Gary Hislop had played an absolute blinder here. Getting this arsehole to do his bidding. Someone he could trust to keep his mouth shut because he had nothing other than an attitude. And he wanted a vicious reputation to protect him through that sentence.

Cook got to his feet. 'Well, good luck with the rest of your many sentences. Sure you'll be out by the time you're my age. Give or take.'

'That's it?'

'I know when I'm wasting my time. You don't want to talk, so I'll just let you rot away. Smells like the putrefaction has already started.'

'The what?'

'I'd read out the dictionary definition but I doubt you'd understand. About ten days after something dies, it starts to decay. These wee micro-organisms feed on it and produce chemicals by the means of a foul smell. If I was you, I'd get yourself checked out. You might be dying.'

Instead of it having the desired effect, Rancid John just laughed. 'I'm not saying anything to anyone.'

Aye, maybe Bob Cook was losing his touch.

He took one last look, then followed Gashkori out into the corridor. Even out here, he could taste Rancid John's stench on the air.

Gashkori snorted. 'Waste of time.'

'I don't know. One to come back to in a few years once a wise old jailbird has had a word in his ear. And I know a few of them...'

'Not so sure on that score.'

'No. Guess not. One thing, Ryan, you can at least take comfort in the knowledge that you've finally met true evil.'

54

'Last on, but not last off.' Marshall put the car in gear and followed a silver Citroën off the ferry towards the town.

Rothesay spread out along the coast in both directions, a tiny section of civilisation on a wild island. A crescent of hills, covered in houses looking across the water to the Argyll hills and Loch Striven. Just breathtaking scenery – so much mystery and magic.

The traffic lights were currently green, so Marshall blasted through. 'You know what? I can actually see the appeal of living here.' He followed the street up past the Co-op. 'But I suspect that's the closest thing to a shop here.'

'There are other shops, but that's the supermarket.' Jolene was tapping away on her phone. 'You been here before?'

'Once. Mum brought me and Jen here when we were wee. I don't remember much about it, other than having a tantrum because I wanted to play in the arcades.' Must've been the one they were passing now – probably all those coin grabbers rather than fighting or shooting videogames.

She waved a hand to the right. 'Mum's family still have a

caravan up by Port Bannatyne, if you fancy a weekend with Kirsten?'

'Where's that?'

'Slightly posher town a few miles up that way. It's pretty much connected to Rothesay. On the way up to the other ferry.'

'There's another ferry?' Marshall took it slowly as they passed the castle, an old ruin right in the middle of the town, surrounded by a moat. 'Why didn't we go that way?'

'The safety warning is longer than the actual journey and they should just put a bridge up...'

Marshall laughed.

'And it's a hell of a long way round, way up past Stirling and across Loch Lomond and all that. Beautiful scenery, if you get the weather, but hellish if you don't.'

If you get the weather...

The unofficial motto of the Scottish tourist industry.

Marshall drove past the museum and the police station, then along a straight road heading out of town. A gentle climb up to higher ground, rather than the steep inclines he'd seen.

'Sure this the right way?'

'Aye, just on the left here.' Jolene frowned. 'Sorry, that's it on the right there.'

A Victorian farmhouse hid behind a thick hedge, incongruous with the surrounding architecture. Over the road, a corner shop was in a three-storey turn-of-the-century tenement block you'd find in Glasgow or Edinburgh. Opposite were some turn-of-the-millennium flats, in red brick and dark slate.

Marshall parked right outside the shop. 'You want to lead here?'

'Thought you'd never ask...' Jolene got out first.

Marshall followed her around the corner to the gate between the beech hedges. The gate squealed as she opened it, then walked up the path. He stopped by the sign, which would've been fancy in 1983, but just looked tattered now and the text was just about legible:

Old Craig's Bunkhouse

Didn't even have the 1 in the area code. And why you'd have needed to know the number way back before even the dream of a mobile phone was beyond him.

Jolene knocked on the door, one of those replacement double-glazing jobs that now looked in dire need of replacing itself.

The door opened and a young man stood there, dressed in a lumberjack shirt and beige shorts. A navy work belt, studded with hammers and screwdrivers hanging down. 'Can I help you?'

'Looking for the owner?'

'That'll be me, aye.' He thrust out a hand. 'Craig Craigie.' He smirked. 'My old boy was a bit of a joker. He was also Craig Craigie too. But I'll be buggered if I name any of my kids Craig.' He cleared his throat. 'Sorry, are you guys looking for a room, because we're shut for a couple of months while I do the place up.'

'DS Jolene Archer.' She held out her warrant card. 'Wondering if we could have a wee word?'

'Sure. Come in, come in.' Craigie ushered them into the house.

Marshall let Jolene go first, then walked along the plastic sheeting over the stripped floorboards, sanded but still unsealed. The place smelled of sawdust and glue. The living-room floor was covered in old bedsheets ready for painting. The skirting boards were all sanded smooth.

Craigie went into a brand-new kitchen, with navy blue units and worktop. Landscape photographs hung on the white walls: beaches and dunes and wild surf.

A giant extension led out to a dining area, with enough windows to make the place glow. 'Tea? Coffee?'

Jolene glanced at Marshall. 'We're fine, sir, but thank you.'

'Don't mind if I do, though?' Craigie didn't wait for a response. He stuck a mug under one of those taps that poured boiling water, then filled it and set it down on the counter, stirring in scoops of instant coffee – surely the wrong way round...

'What's this about, then?'

Marshall caught a whiff of the acrid granules. 'Sir, did you know a Marianne Henderson?'

Craigie stared hard at her for a few seconds. He tapped away on his phone then tossed it down. 'Excuse me?'

'Who did you just message?'

'Nobody.'

'Does the name Marianne Henderson mean anything to you? Maybe a guest here?'

Craigie shrugged.

'You are still operating as a B&B, right?'

'A guesthouse, as my wife would rather call it.' Craigie poured in some milk, avoiding eye contact. 'It's my old boy's place. He passed away five years ago. Used to work in Glasgow. Thought it'd be nice to move back over here, let my kid grow up somewhere with scenery. I tried running it as it was, but it's... It's been pretty miserable, I have to say. This isn't an easy business. Kind of a summer trade, don't really get much in the winter. Between us, I'm doing this place up to sell.'

'But you do get some trade in the winter, right?'

'Some, aye.'

Jolene showed him a photo on her phone. 'Do you recognise this man?'

'Oh aye, he stayed here. John Collins.'

Marshall frowned. He'd used an assumed name in Jedburgh, but not in St Abbs. 'John Collins?'

'That's the name he gave.' Craigie shrugged. 'Why are you asking, like?'

'Has he been here recently?'

'November and December, aye. Only punter staying here.'

'You know the precise dates?'

'Not off the top of my head. The ledger's in storage somewhere.'

'But he was definitely here?'

'Sure.' Craigie took a deep drink of coffee. 'Aye, he was definitely here at the end of November. St Andrew's Day. We had a big haggis meal, but nobody came, so he ate three quarters of two chieftain haggises. I mean... Thing is, I got him to leave in December.'

'Oh? What did he do?'

'Nothing. Needed to get on with the renovations. I mean, he was in the crappest room we've got, but he was the only person here and it got to the point where I needed to get this kitchen done but he just wanted to sit in here drinking pots and pots of tea, doing jigsaws all day.'

Marshall caught Jolene's flick of eyebrows – it certainly sounded like Sylvester.

Jolene jotted it down. 'Was that his first stay here?'

'No. Been here a few times. Going back to my old man's days, I think.'

Marshall looked at the dates again.

Marianne Henderson was found in the harbour by the ferry terminal just before Christmas last year.

Jolene looked up from her notebook. 'Reason we're asking, sir, is two of your jigsaws were found in a room in a guesthouse in St Abbs.'

'Where the hell is that?'

'In the Borders. Not far from Berwick.'

'With you now.' Craigie looked at them like they'd gone insane. 'Jigsaws? You're here because of some jigsaws?'

The doorbell chimed.

'Sorry, I need to get that.' Craigie charged off through the house without getting their approval.

Jolene was frowning at Marshall, but she didn't say anything.

Raised voices rattled through the house, but Marshall couldn't make out any words. Soon drowned out by footsteps.

Instead of Craigie, a uniformed cop entered the room. Tall woman, early forties. Looked like she knew a thing or two. She shook Marshall's hand. 'PC Alex Robertson.' Then Jolene's. 'Nice to meet you. Where are you guys from?'

'I'm based in Gartcosh.' Marshall showed his warrant card. 'DS Archer's based in Galashiels.'

Robertson nodded slowly. 'You're a long way from home.'

'We are. Reason we're here is we have a list of cases we believe might be previously unknown victims of a serial murderer.'

'You suspect Marianne Henderson might be one of them?'

'That's correct. Do you mind—'

'Marianne...' Robertson glared at them. 'You should've contacted me first.'

'Prefer to speak to people directly.'

'Well, you've upset Mr Craigie. He called me. Well, he texted me. And I came as soon as I got it. I'm investigating his daughter's death.'

'His daughter?'

Robertson raised an eyebrow. 'Marianne Henderson.'

'Not Craigie?'

'She's his stepdaughter. Still had his wife's ex-husband's name.' Robertson walked over to the kitchen window and looked out across the muddy lawn. 'She killed herself at Christmas. She was fifteen. Craig's thrown himself into the renovations but he hasn't been able to grieve. I mean, how can you after that?'

'How did she die?'

'You know she was found near the harbour, right? The wake from the ferry dragged her body in.'

'I meant how.' Jolene glanced at Marshall. 'Did she fall from a cliff?'

'A cliff?' Robertson laughed. 'There aren't any cliffs on Bute, save for Dunagoil way down south. No, we think it was a common-or-garden two packs of temazepam, then she took a header off the sea wall at high tide.'

'I'm sorry to hear that.'

'Well, it sadly happens with alarming frequency here.' She turned around and glowered at them. 'Don't you think it's a bit crass to come here asking a grieving father about *jigsaws*?'

'The suspect in our case left two in his room, both with stickers marking them as belonging to this place. Mr Craigie confirmed the suspect stayed here. It appears he stole them. But he's currently missing, so we wondered if it might lead to his whereabouts. He's a serial murderer and he's abducted a surviving victim of a previous attack.'

'Did he... They were part of Mr Craigie's mother's collection. So they had some sentimental value. He wondered where the jigsaws went.'

'Of course we'll return them once the case is over. But for now, they're evidence.'

'Craig said you're looking for this John Collins. Is that...?'

'His name is David Sylvester. John Collins is an alias.'

Robertson narrowed her eyes. 'I've been searching for him ever since.'

'Did you ever speak to him?'

'Once. My belief is this John Collins was abusing Craig's daughter. And she killed herself because of that.'

55

Having to sit in your living room and break the news to your kids that their dad's dead. That he was murdered in prison.

Elliot wouldn't wish that on anyone.

Not even on the vermin who'd killed her husband.

Rancid John. Gary Hislop. Take your pick – they'd both played their part.

She couldn't think of much worse, if anything.

Harry clung to Charlie, who was supporting his younger brother. Both of their faces soaked with tears.

Elliot's mother between them, hugging them so tightly.

Sam, though...

She was absolutely broken by it. Not that you could tell from her face, as straight as if she was going into Edinburgh on the train with her pals. But her eyes had gone. Shooting around the room, nervously searching for answers. Or for her father. She fixed her glare on Elliot. 'Can I speak with you, Mummy?'

She hadn't used that name in years. 'Sure. Of course. Whatever you want to talk about, it's—'

'I mean, alone.'

'Right.' Elliot smiled at her mum. 'Can you...?'

'Of course.' Mum wrapped them in a deep hug. 'Come here, lads.'

Elliot followed Sam out into the hallway, then through into the kitchen.

Sam perched on the stool at the breakfast bar. 'Is it okay to feel like it's not all bad?'

'Depends, Sam.' She let Elliot cuddle her from behind like she was the wee girl who called her Mummy again. 'It's always good to get stuff off your chest. Why don't you talk to me about how you feel?'

'Right. Thing is, despite him being a bit of a boomer bigot, I loved my dad. I mean, I thought the world of him. But he never accepted me, did he? Just thought I was a tomboy. He couldn't accept I might be an enby. Said I'd grow out of stuff.'

'He was starting to come around.'

'Was he? Because the last thing he said to me was how pleased he was that I'm a normal girl again. All I wanted from him was to be accepted for being myself.'

'And he did.'

'Really? Because it didn't feel like that.'

'He did, his last words were that he loved his *three* kids. Sometimes in death people find clarity. They call that grace. Look. Your dad was...' Talking about Davie in the past tense caught her in the throat. Her eyes stung with tears. 'Confused by it all. And a lot of the confusion wasn't just about him not accepting you or understanding it or whatever, it was about him feeling threatened by this world. He didn't understand a lot of it and it made him feel unsafe.'

'He was the one making me feel unsafe.'

'I know. And he regretted that. He just wanted to love you, but didn't know how to show you that. One thing you need to understand, Sam, is the world me and your dad grew up in is very different to the one you and your brothers know. We'd no idea what "heteronormative" meant until you mentioned it. You all get so much stuff off YouTube and TikTok and whatever. We didn't even have the internet in our houses growing up. It was very different for us. All three of you have had touchscreens and social networks and Google since you were in nappies.'

'Are you saying it's *our* fault?'

'No, that's not what I'm saying. Just that our world was very closed off when we were growing up. Nobody connected in the way you do. I mean, it's a double-edged sword, because everything is so tribal nowadays. But your father... Put it this way, he didn't know anyone who was even gay at his school, let alone trans or whatever.'

Sam rolled her eyes. 'What, so they only invented gays in 1997?'

'No, but it was hard for people to come out back then. You'd get into fights because of it. Severely bullied. Even killed. A lot of people hid their sexuality from people. The number of cases I saw where someone was blackmailed for it... Nowadays, it feels like there's more chance...' She caught herself. 'Look, gay kids are never even in the closet now, let alone keeping it a secret and pretending to be normal, whatever that means. And normal is a much wider thing.'

Sam swallowed hard, but didn't speak.

'But your father was starting to understand your world.'

'Was he? How?'

'By reading up on stuff. Watching videos. Trying to get his head around it. But he loved you. Loved all three of you, but especially you.'

Sam was staring at her with those big brown eyes. It seemed like the message was maybe going in. Maybe.

'Thing is, Sam, a colleague of mine was with your father when he... When he went. He told him to make sure we spent more time together as a family. Us four.'

'What the hell's that supposed to mean?'

'The only time your dad ever felt okay was when he was with you three. All of you. All five of us. He lived for his home life. Weekends. Holidays.'

'But did he die for it too?'

'What's that supposed to mean?'

'I want to know how it happened.'

Elliot blinked away more tears. 'Look, I don't know myself.'

'Shut up, Mum. You're a cop. You know everything.'

'I swear. I just got told he was dead. I haven't even seen his body.'

'Oh.' Sam shut her eyes and it seemed to hit her right then. 'I...' She reopened them and stared at Elliot. 'Please. How did it happen?'

'He was in prison and someone stabbed him.'

'Seriously?' Sam drummed her black-painted fingernails on the kitchen counter. 'Was this because of what happened in court yesterday?'

'I don't know.'

'But you think it might be?'

'Maybe. It's complicated. The whole thing's very, very messy, but...' Elliot sighed. 'Thing is, we might never know why it happened. And that's a tough thing to deal with.'

Sam nodded along with it. 'I miss him.'

'Me too, honeybee. Me too.' Elliot wiped the tears from her eyes. 'He wasn't exactly the wokest person in the world, but he had a massive heart and he loved you.'

Sam turned around and wrapped her mum in a massive cuddle. 'Please don't leave us.'

56

Marshall raced along the narrow road from the A7 down to Clovenfords. A spiderweb of stars dotted the sky – so dark here, it was like it was already midnight. And you could even see the Milky Way tonight.

He was so tired, though. Fuelled only by a can of Wakey-Wakey from the café on the ferry. He barely noticed the 20 sign at the top end of the village, so he hammered the brake then weaved through the bend, taking it easy on the steep path down to the roundabout. The road lined by modern houses, all the residents cosy and tucked up inside. Gameshows, Netflix, football.

He swung a left behind a bus that didn't pull in at the stop, then took the turning for the Clovenfords Hotel.

His car stopped before he got it in the space.

Bastard thing.

He was lucky it got all that way from the ferry in two goes – the only stop had been in Stow, where Jolene's husband met her at the crossroads.

Marshall got it to start, then nudge into the space, on the third attempt. Really needed to sell it. He got out into the cold air and let out a plume of breath. Might be April, but it was still bloody freezing. He raced up the steps into the hotel and he walked through to the bar side.

Jen and Kirsten were nattering away at the table in the window.

'Rob?'

Marshall spun around.

Bob Cook was at the bar, just as the barman put a pint onto his tray. 'Can I get you a drink, son?'

'Just a tonic water, thanks.'

'A tonic water?' Bob laughed, but his eyes betrayed him. He looked like he'd seen something dark. 'Are you pregnant?'

Marshall gritted his teeth through the dad joke. 'Just a tonic, aye.'

'No gin or vodka?'

'I'm driving.'

Bob laughed again, then winked. 'Aye, but who's going to catch you?'

'Just a tonic, thanks.' Marshall held his gaze and watched him order, just so he didn't stick a "cheeky" spirit in. 'You okay there?'

'Just... When you get to my age, you think you've seen it all. Then...'

'What happened?'

'That Rancid John lad. Swear, son, never met anyone like it.' Cook ran a hand down his face and the despair seemed to leave him. 'Go on, I'll bring these over.'

'If you're sure...' Marshall walked over to the table in the windows.

Jen's face looked like curdled milk. 'I mean, who puts *mushrooms* on a burger?'

'I would, but I don't hate them like you do.' Marshall sat down in the space between, giving them both a peck on the cheek. 'How are you both?'

Kirsten winced. 'We heard about Davie Elliot.'

'Right, aye. Horrible business.' Marshall sat back and let out a deep sigh. The news still hadn't sunk in. The guy he'd nodded at or chatted to every day for a year. The husband of a colleague. 'Andrea called me. She seemed okay, but... How do you deal with that?'

Jen took a sip of wine, emptying her glass. 'I mean, you kind of did?'

Marshall looked away from her. He caught Kirsten smacking Jen on the arm.

'Sorry, I didn't mean that.' Jen leaned forward, her thirsty eyes looking over to the bar. 'I don't exactly like Andrea, but nobody deserves what she's gone through in the last year.'

'This Elliot you're talking about?' Bob dumped the tray down and sat at the end of the table. 'Awful, awful business.' He started passing out their drinks, then stared at his son. Marshall had seen Cook a few times in the last year, but the overfamiliarity was beginning to cloy. He'd never be his 'old man' or even his father, but Cook seemed to think he was and everything was totally cool between them. 'This doesn't go any further, okay, but I spoke to the laddie who did it.' He took a big gulp out of his pint and gasped. 'That's better.' He spun it around on the beermat. 'Some people you speak to in prison, you have some sympathy with them. Takes a lot to kill someone, believe you me, but you meet enough someones and you understand why it might be possible to do it. You get an inkling of what they've been through, the path that's led them to that act. But him... Nasty wee rat boy from Bo'ness. Not a shred of humanity in there. He won't be getting out of jail anytime soon. Or ever, if I get my way.'

He took a sip from his drink and it hit him – he was bursting for a pee. 'Sorry, I need to go to the toilet. Drove all the way back from the Bute ferry in one go, pretty much.'

'*Bute?*' Bob was scowling at him. 'What the hell were you doing there?'

'Long story.'

'Is it, aye? Well, you go ahead and drain the lizard. We'll be waiting when you get back.'

Marshall walked towards the gents, smiling at the barman as he passed.

Someone bumped into Marshall and almost sent him flying.

'Steady!' Marshall rounded on him.

Toby the sound man was propping up the bar, struggling to stay upright. 'You!' He jabbed a finger at Marshall. 'You! Cop! Come here!'

Marshall didn't want to refuse him. 'I'm going to the toilet. Back in a sec.'

'Aye, aye, bullshit. You lying sack of shit. They took my laptop!'

'And you'll get it back soon, sir.'

'Bullshit. Fucking Holly. Fucking prick. You found her yet?'

'Not yet, sir.'

'Typical. She got my mate killed, didn't she?'

'Okay, Toby.' The big barman wrapped an arm around him. 'Think you need to get to your bed, eh? Maybe a coffee or a glass of water.'

'Coffee? At this time?' Toby looked at him, then seemed to snap into focus. 'Alrighty.'

Marshall passed him a business card. 'Give me a call if you don't get your laptop back by Monday.'

'Aye, lying cop bastard.'

'Time for your bed, son.' Marshall walked off, pleased someone on the investigation was actually doing their job. Whether they'd get anything from the laptop was anyone's guess. He went into the gents and barely made it to the urinal in time.

Toby had cracked. The stress of losing a friend and a year's work had broken him.

What was it about true crime that warped minds?

Was it the fact you needed a warped mind in the first place to think you knew better than the professionals?

Marshall finished up and started washing his hands. He shut his eyes and saw the M8 from Glasgow to Edinburgh again – he'd driven it so frequently in the last year that he could describe every twist and curve in either direction.

When to switch lane to avoid a crunching pothole.

When to stick to the slow lane to speed up.

When to pull in to avoi—

'You asleep there?' Gashkori was frowning at him.

'No, sir, I'm just knackered.' Marshall yawned into his fist.

'What the hell are you doing here?'

'You say that like your sister hasn't already told you.'

'She did, aye.' Marshall still wasn't sure about it. His sister really needed to change her taste in men. 'But while I've got you, we found a guesthouse in Rothesay where Sylvester was staying last year.'

'Oh? Wait – have you got him?'

'If I did, I wouldn't be telling you in the toilets at a hotel in the Borders.'

'Right. But he was staying there? Wait, on Bute?'

'Aye. One of those cases from the missing period checked out. A probable murder just before last Christmas.'

'Right. Excellent.' Gashkori caught Marshall's yawn. 'This profiling work. What's your take on it?'

'I've got my doubts, sir.'

'Go on?'

'I've been pretty vocal to add qualifiers to any agreements I've given. After all, nobody likes the guy who at the end says, "I always knew it but never said", so I wanted to be clear.'

'Of course. But what specifically?'

'I think there are gaps in matching the profile to Sylvester. For starters, the fact he didn't want the attention of the kills when we caught him. The way he's kept running. Those literally don't match.'

'Do we have a problem?'

'The problem here is groupthink. Liana is the smartest in the country, so everyone wants to think what she thinks.'

'They?'

'She Who Cannot Be Named. You. Anyone.'

'Right. But not you. And, of course, you're smarter?'

'Not saying that, but I have different expertise. And different biases.'

'Sure you do.' Gashkori stepped past him and went into the cubicle and shut the door.

Great.

Marshall left the gents and walked back through to their table. 'Guess you're out of the closet now, Jennifer.'

She looked around at him with a vicious scowl. 'Eh?'

'Your boyfriend's in the gents.'

Bob laughed. 'Ooooh, do we finally get to meet him?'

'You know him, Bob.' Jen was blushing. 'Ryan.'

'*Gashkori?*'

'Aye. Got a problem with that?'

'Well, well. Good work on keeping it a secret from the experts. Me and your brother had no idea, did we?'

'No.' Marshall reached over for Kirsten's hand. She clutched it tightly.

'Forgot to say, Rob...' Jen tipped some more wine into her glass. 'That rumour about Owusu being dead? Another friend in BGH said it's true.'

'How did they hear that?'

'Mutual friend.'

'What happened?'

'Carjacking gone very wrong. Kid was killed too.'

Marshall felt a stabbing in his gut. 'Thanks for checking that out.'

Gashkori sat down next to Cook, placing a pint of Guinness in front of himself. 'That about Dr Owusu?'

'Aye.'

'Heard about that.' Gashkori stuck his nose into the foam and glugged his beer. 'Word is one of Hislop's people knew where she was in South Africa and decided to bump her off.'

'Christ. Why? Because of Jim?'

'That's the logic. But I had a meeting with him a few weeks ago about—' Gashkori looked away and cleared his throat. 'Something. And he seemed pretty bad. Like crackers. I had a word with the boss about whether he should even be at work. She said she'd think about it.'

'Well, she's thought about it now. He's in a home.'

Gashkori frowned. 'An old folks' home?'

'It's a mixed residency place. Balfour Rattray's brother's in there, for instance.' Marshall looked at Bob. 'Same one as Grumpy.'

'My dad's nowhere near as senile as Pringle, that's for sure.' Bob stared into his mostly empty glass. 'Impressive work at his age.'

Jen scowled at him. 'Or tragic?'

'Oh, aye. Very tragic. Very tragic indeed.'

Gashkori took a long drink from his pint. 'On the drive here, I spoke to Andrea Elliot. Asking to still work... Begging me to... I mean...'

Kirsten scowled at him. 'You can't be serious?'

'Deadly. I'll keep a close eye on her.'

'You're not going to let her, are you?'

'No. I mean, when she comes back. In like a month. But it'll inevitably be sooner than she should be back.'

'Wise.' Bob finished his pint. 'But she's a tough cookie, that one.'

Gashkori shrugged. 'All the same, she's just lost her husband. She needs to grieve.'

'Totally.' Jen sank a bit more wine. 'Rob, I thought you'd bring Thea along. Right?'

Gashkori frowned. 'What are you talking about?'

'Rob had the temerity to tell me how to raise Thea.'

Marshall regretted agreeing to Thea's request. And coming to this meal. 'That's not true. All I did was pass on a message of concern from her.'

Kirsten frowned. 'What's she concerned about?'

'How Jen doesn't want her to come home.'

'That's bullshit and you know it.' Jen shook her head. 'She feels I don't want her there, which couldn't be further from the truth. I didn't know you were meeting her so frequently, brother dearest.'

'I mean, you would know if you ever let her come home.'

'Bugger off, Rob.' Jen tipped more wine into her glass. 'Nobody cares about my side of this, do they? Thea's all I had in my life for so long. Her arsehole father had me barefoot and pregnant in the kitchen when I wasn't working. I mean, not literally, but you know what I mean. Went through hell with him and my job is a nightmare. I've been a mum for eighteen years now, first and foremost. That's enough. And now she's flown the nest, damn right I'm letting my hair down.'

Kirsten folded her arms. 'You don't ever *stop* being a mum.'

'No, I get that, but... Don't I deserve some time just being me?'

'Sure, but telling her to not come home? Isn't that a bit cold?'

'Until you have kids with my idiot brother, I'll not listen to your advice on how to raise her.'

Kirsten sat back, shaking her head. 'O-kay.'

Marshall raised his hands. 'Jen, I just want to make sure she's okay.'

'And what about me?'

'I know *you'll* be okay.'

'Right.' She looked over at Cook. 'Thing is, Mum let me and Rob stray too far off the lead, so I never learnt what's right and what's wrong.'

'You blaming that on me?'

'Why's everything have to be about fault and blame? I'm just trying to raise my daughter, that's all.'

'I've raised a daughter and it wasn't easy.' Bob shook his head. 'But if you push them away, they have a habit of staying away.'

Jen turned to face the waiter, ready with his notepad and pen. 'Hi, can I have the fish and chips, please. And another bottle of the house white? Thanks.'

57

Marshall powered up the road towards Stow, on that little section where you could finally blast past any slow traffic – wouldn't get another shot until Fountainhall, a fair few miles up the road.

Kirsten was in the passenger seat, yawning hard. 'It was nice to spend time with your family again.'

'Was it?'

'Well, not all of them, no.'

'Felt like a disaster. I saw how you reacted to Jen overstepping the mark.'

'Your sister's got a bloody mouth on her, but she was a pal long before she was a sister-out-law. Thing with her is she doesn't mean anything by it, but it hurts.'

'You haven't discussed it with her?'

'*Her*? God no. You heard her stuck in the middle of that gossip about Belu. It'd be all over both our workplaces by the time you got this thing to start.'

Marshall laughed as he overtook a van with not quite enough space until the bend. He pulled back in just in time, but got a toot on the horn from the van. 'Still, she shouldn't have said that. It must've hurt.'

'I've got pretty thick skin.'

'Have you?'

'Some of the time.' She smiled at Marshall. 'Rob, I'm just glad your dad was there to defuse the situation. He seems like a good guy. Wise old owl. Wily old fox.'

'Aye, well, I would've appreciated some of that wisdom growing up. Maybe me and Jen wouldn't have ended up quite so fucked up.'

'I'm worried about her. I don't think her and Gashkori are a good pairing.'

'Why?'

'Well. A few things really, but the main one is he seems like a nice guy.'

'And my sister only deserves a bastard?'

'No. But that's how he *seems*. He's charm personified. But when he wants something... That's when you see the real Ryan Gashkori. He's an absolute nightmare at work. Just makes a nuisance of himself until people give in. People like me. So he's always trying to jump the queue. He was as bad back in his drug squad days.'

'And why's that make them a bad match?'

'He's a selfish prick and, despite her rant tonight, she's actually pretty selfless. You don't become a nurse unless you are. But something's not right. He's toxic, don't you think?'

'Only see that in the professional side. What do you mean?'

'Well. The way he's gone from staying in your old room above the garage to shagging her in the main house.'

'I can see your point.'

'Do you agree with it?'

'Maybe.'

'What's up?'

'Just something Thea told me the other night. She found some cocaine in the kitchen last time she was home.'

'Seriously?'

'Sounds like it.'

'You think it's why Jen doesn't want her home?'

'Maybe.'

'Has Jen taken drugs in the past?'

'As a student, aye.'

'What are you going to do?'

'My boss is seeing my sister. Twisting my melon a bit, but there's not much I can do, really. If I tell him about it, who knows what he might do.'

'He's not your boss, though?'

'No, but I've been asked to step in for Elliot after what happened to Davie.'

'When did that happen?'

'This afternoon. Was going to tell you, but the day got away from me.'

'So you'll be straddling being a cop again and working with Liana.'

'I'll be glad to get away from her, to be honest.'

'I'm not too sure what I think of you two working together again. She's digging a big hole for herself. Not making many friends. Not getting any results.'

'I've just tried to park her up at Gartcosh so she can't cause any more havoc.'

'Was it her fault you were in Bute?'

'Partly. She didn't unearth it, but it's her piece of work. I was the one who connected the dots.'

'See, you make a great team...'

'Come on, enough of that passive-aggressive stuff. It doesn't suit you.'

'I wasn't being—'

'You were. And I keep having to tell you, I'm not interested in her. Or anyone. I love you, Kirsten.'

That shut her up.

They drove through Stow in silence, past the oversized church and the bookshop at the crossroads, then weaving through the older part of the village, and out the far side.

'Bute was nice, though. We should go for a weekend there.'

'No fucking way.'

'What have I done? Because I'm having to work with Liana?'

'You need to stop being so paranoid, Rob. No, I just spent way too much time there as a kid.'

'Well, you could show me it as an adult?'

'Let me think about it.' She nibbled at her fingernail then caught herself. 'Are you remembering I've got a hospital appointment tomorrow?'

'I am. Do you still not want me to come along?'

'I can fight my own battles, but thank you for offering.'

DAY 4

THURSDAY

58

Gashkori's hand shook as he sipped his coffee. To Marshall, it looked as though he'd kept on drinking with Jen and Bob Cook until the wee sma' hours. Thick stubble over his face, with the empty gaze and deep voice of a man with bitter regrets about how hard he'd hit it the night before. 'Rob, you want to give your update now?'

'Sure.' Marshall joined him in the middle of the room and looked out at the huddled mass of officers facing them. 'First, we've confirmed the first of potentially many additional crimes in the period between Holly's incident in Whitley Bay twelve years ago and the attack on Kayleigh on Monday morning. Marianne Henderson's body was found in Rothesay harbour just before Christmas last year. We also know David Sylvester had been staying there prior to that.'

Gashkori nodded through the chatter. 'But did he kill her?'

Marshall shook his head. 'She appears to have taken her own life, sir.'

'Appears to have?'

'I've only seen the summary version of the post-mortem, sir, which revealed high levels of benzodiazepine in her liver. Cause of death was drowning.'

'Okay, so why don't you track down the full version?'

'I have requested it.'

'Excellent. Was that treated as a murder?'

'Nope. Local uniform constable was working on it. Didn't think it was a straight suicide.'

'Okay, well, I think we need to focus on—'

The security reader chimed and the door clattered open. Elliot waltzed through, hands in pockets. An absolute state – hair sticking up at the back and sides. As she approached, Marshall could see her makeup was way too heavy, smeared on rather than applied. Her blouse was misbuttoned, trouser flies undone. She pulled up a seat and sat at the edge of the crowd, with tears in her eyes.

A flutter of whispers passed through the room.

Marshall gave Gashkori a flash of his eyebrows then walked over to her. 'Can I get you a coffee?'

Elliot looked up at him through clown-style eyeshadow. 'I'm fine.'

Marshall crouched next to her. 'Come on, you're not fine. Let's have a chat.'

She looked at him for a few long seconds, then nodded. 'Okay.' Her voice was a tiny fragment of sound. She got up and slowly walked over to the door.

Marshall shielded her from watching eyes, but it seemed like their colleagues for once had the good grace to avert their gaze and focus on Gashkori. He led her back through into the quiet of the reception area. 'You want to get something here or—'

She wrapped him in a deep hug. 'Robbie, I don't know what the fuck to do.'

Marshall let her cling on as long as she needed to. But she

wasn't letting go anytime soon. 'Shouldn't you be at home with your kids?'

'I know. But I don't know if I can. Mum and Dad are with them, but... Grieving's hard work, Rob. It's really shit.'

'I know that first hand.'

'Right. You know.' She broke off and glanced over at the empty security desk. 'Thing is, I've already grieved for our marriage. After what he did... Now, I'm just grieving for the kids' other parent now. At some point, I'll grieve for him. He was my best friend.'

Marshall nodded.

'Last night, when I told the kids, I thought I was being strong. That I could stay strong. How I was there for them and their needs. Sam... She...' Elliot wiped tears away with both thumbs, smearing eyeshadow across her cheeks. 'I had this big, long chat with Sam about how Davie didn't accept her. Then I cuddled the boys like they were babies again. And I stupidly thought that was it. All done. No more grief. But I didn't sleep a wink. Just kept... *thinking*.' She spat out the word. 'That's *our* house, Robbie. Both of us chose it, chose the furniture. Christ, both boys were conceived there!'

Marshall held her gaze. Grief was an absolute bastard and warped your mind. 'People say that time heals all wounds, but it doesn't. You don't just stop feeling the pain. You just learn to forget. That's all. But grief still hits you when you least expect it. And it still stings just as badly as the first time you heard. When your life changes.'

'I spent the night trying to process how I feel, but now... Robbie, I just need to be a cop for a bit.'

'I'm not sure—'

The door opened again and Gashkori walked through, eyebrows raised. 'Andrea, with all due respect, this isn't the place for you. I need you to kindly bugger off home.'

'Right.' She sucked in a deep breath. 'Don't you want me to hand over to Marshall?'

'Come on, Andrea. We all know you haven't really got much to hand over. You two have been passing the baton back and forth over the last few days.'

She shifted her focus between them. 'Sorry, you're right. I shouldn't have come in.'

'No, you did what you felt you needed to. It's good to see you. Means I can do this.' Gashkori wrapped her in a sterile hug. 'I know how hard it is, Andrea, but you're a tough cow and you're going to get through this.'

She broke off and stared at the floor. 'Will I, though?'

'You will. Of course you will.'

She nodded at that, then looked at them in turn. 'I'll be in touch.'

'No. That's my job, Andi.' Gashkori smiled. 'I'll call you tomorrow, okay? Today, you need to focus on your kids and yourself. Please.'

'I want to stay here. Focus on work.'

'Andi, come on.'

'I'm useless at home. I can't just sit around. I want to be here, working, solving this bloody case.'

'Andi, no. We've had this chat. You can't be here.'

'You've got so much work to do. And you're under so much pressure, Ryan.'

'Aye, that's for me to bear, not you.' Gashkori pointed at the door. 'Go home. Spend time with your kids. Maybe go through Davie's effects, if it'll help.'

Elliot scowled at him. 'Have you found anything that could point to the source of that final leak?'

'Final leak?'

'How they knew where Davie was.'

'There's not a leakers' club, you know? From what I heard last night, it was a personal beef. Davie was just in the wrong place at the wrong time. You're a good cop but a great mother. Do what you do best. Be there for your kids. And that's an order.'

'Okay, sir.' Elliot took a deep breath, then walked out of the station into the dark morning.

Gashkori rubbed at his nose. 'Well, that was a bit weird.'

'People do unexpected things when they're grieving.'

'Ain't that the truth. Thing with Andrea is she's got a massive chip on her shoulder, has had for years. That all comes from somewhere and something like this is going to force it out.' Gashkori pointed at the door. 'Can you head back in? Bursting for a pee.'

'Too much post-session water, eh?'

'Had one pint last night, Rob.' Gashkori narrowed his eyes. 'But if you must know, I was up half the night arguing with your sister.'

'About what?'

'That stuff with Thea. I'm on the same page as you, Rob. Jen should encourage her to come back. It's not right.'

'You know, Thea said she'd found something she thought might be cocaine in Jen's house.'

Gashkori raised his eyebrows. 'Seriously?'

'Seriously. In the kitchen.'

'Jen doing coke? How could that be true?' Gashkori was shaking his head. 'Thing with our relationship is it's not what you think. I'm still in that flat most nights because our shifts don't exactly tally together. And your sister... If she's doing that in the house...'

'Don't say anything to her about it.'

'I won't.' Gashkori tapped his nose. 'Secret's safe with me.' He laughed. 'Who am I kidding? I need to get her to stop.' He walked off to the gents toilet, scowling. 'Bloody hell...'

Aye, Marshall shouldn't have said anything there. Stupid twat – he should've talked to Jen about it.

Jen was going to kill him.

He pushed back through into the briefing.

'—taskforce of people searching for Sylvester and Holly.' Taylor was at the front, hands in pockets, eyes narrowed at Marshall. 'Naturally, it has thus far drawn a blank. We received a few rogue sightings down near Sunderland and Middlesbrough.'

Marshall joined him at the front. 'Why were they rogue?'

'Well, because they're not Sylvester. The local police services have confirmed two people matching their description were tourists visiting places in the area.' Taylor cast his gaze around. 'Though you're a pretty desperate tourist if you're visiting Sunderland.'

Not many laughed, just Struan really, but he more than made up for his colleagues.

'I want to stress again how hard our task is. David Sylvester is a guy who's spent the last ten years or so completely off the radar. He's got very good at hiding. So we need to keep up the discipline and maintain it. We *will* find him, one way or another. Nobody's that good. And when we do find him, we find her.'

Despite the big talk, Marshall didn't hear anything approaching a plan, but he wasn't going to say so in front of the team.

Taylor looked around the room. 'Paton. How are you doing with those video files from Toby Horsfall?'

'Eh, they're with forensics.'

'Trevor.' Taylor drilled his gaze into the lead CSI. 'How are we doing with them?'

'Haven't got the people to work on it.'

'Can you find them?'

'Got a request to get some skulls from Gartcosh, but you need to approve it.'

'I will look into that, of course.' Taylor was blushing. 'Anyway. Those DNA traces from the caravan and Holly's house. I asked you to fast-track them on Tuesday. How are they going now?'

'We're doing all we can, Cal.' Trev shrugged. 'There are a lot of traces to get through, so it's going to take its own sweet time to process.'

'I don't need to stress the urge—'

'Yeah, yeah, I get it. But there are only so many hours and so many trained specialists. Besides DNA isn't going to find your abductor, is it?'

'Just do what you can.' Taylor gave a fierce smile, then cast his gaze around the room. 'We're contending with both an attempted murder scene at Eyemouth and a murder one at Reston, we need to dig deep, okay? We've drawn blanks so far, but I'm hoping DI Marshall can point us in the right direction. Rob?'

'No pressure, eh?' Marshall cleared his throat. 'We're reworking the criminal profile from the original cases, but I think we all know it's David Sylvester. Now, as I was saying earlier, we have a potential set of cases in the west of Scotland, plus one in north-west England, which could cover his activities during the twelve-year period. The only one we've successfully validated so far is in Rothesay on Bute, where he stayed under an assumed name. He appears to have stayed there more than once, so I want to fast-track this analysis. If, say, just a quarter of these cases are valid, then we might find somewhere he's staying at again.'

Gashkori had reappeared, but stayed at the back, tapping away on his phone.

'But to make any progress, we'll need additional resources. Hardeep who works for me is building up a picture, but it's slow going and his skills are better used in refining the profile. Yesterday's result took six hours for DS Archer and me, so if I could get another two pairs of officers, we can speed things up and maybe find out where he's staying?'

'Sure.' Gashkori smiled. 'Cal, give the man some skulls?'

Taylor didn't seem too impressed. 'Okay. I can give you McIntyre and Watson to start with.'

'Another two would make a huge difference.'

'Aye, I know.' Taylor jotted it down. 'Just let me check the resource allocation and I'll get back to you.'

Gashkori checked his phone. 'Ah, I'd better take this. Can you close things off, Cal?'

'Sure.' Taylor stared up at the ceiling, struggling to focus on anyone. 'On a personal note, one of our colleagues lost a loved one yesterday. You've probably all heard, but DI Andrea Elliot's husband was murdered. Davie Elliot. Most of you knew him, but...'

Marshall felt a jab in his back and turned around.

Gashkori beckoned him away from the throng, leading him into his office. 'Rob, can you get over to BGH? Kayleigh's just woken up.'

59

Marshall rushed through Borders General Hospital towards the intensive therapy unit, located on the far side of A&E, as though that department were the gatekeepers to prevent people like him getting in there.

And the chief gatekeeper was standing in position, ready to stop him.

Jen, hands on hips, face like a skelped bum. 'Wondered if Ryan would send you.' Her scowl deepened as she dragged him over to a small room at the side. 'Doesn't even have the balls to show up himself, does he?'

'Jen, I'm just here to get on with my job, okay?'

'Right. Aye. Sure.' Her bottom lip trembled. 'You went over the line last night, Rob. *Waaaaay* over the line.'

'About what?'

'What do you think? The stuff about Thea.' She frowned. 'Hang on. Is there something else?'

'No.'

She looked at him like she didn't believe him. Which was a look he'd seen so many times. 'This whole thing is none of your business.'

Marshall didn't want to get into that kind of semantic nonsense. 'Jen, I get it. You're free now and you want to enjoy your freedom with your new boyf—'

'Don't for one second think that I don't love Thea, Rob. She's my girl. Always will be.'

'Okay, but if you make her feel shit because you don't want to see her? And if I'm the only one she can talk to about that?'

She collapsed back against the wall. 'Nobody understands what it's like...'

'Mum might.'

'Jesus. That's a bit of a low blow.'

'But a fair one.' Marshall backed off. Trouble with having a twin was neither of them knew when to back off. They'd spent their whole lives tormenting each other. 'Look, Jen, I saw how much booze you put away last night. Kirsten had a glass or two, while you had the best part of two bottles. And that's just while we were there.'

'So you're counting my units now?'

'You work in healthcare. That's more than you should have in a week.'

'I've seen you getting smashed, Rob.'

'Not saying you haven't, but it's a pretty rare occurrence these days.' And this was another blind avenue. 'Look, it's important for you to live your life but please make sure Thea's still part of it, okay? I'm not sure she's having that great a time in Glasgow.'

Concern twisted Jen's forehead. 'Has she said something?'

'No, but... Being on your own in a strange city... It's unsettling. I'm just asking you to be there for her. You're her mum.'

'I am there for her. She messages me all the time!'

'Messages aren't parenting. Let her come home. Otherwise, she'll come back but she'll stay with her dad and—'

'That arsehole...' She tried to leave the room.

Marshall blocked her exit. 'But I do have something to ask you.'

'You can just ask, you know?'

Marshall felt the rage burning in the pit of his stomach. 'Have you ever taken cocaine?'

Her mouth hung open. Marshall couldn't tell if it was from the shock of the allegation or of getting caught. 'Are you serious?'

Marshall nodded. 'Deadly.'

'Where's this come from? Thea?'

'No.'

'Aye, sure. You're a terrible liar.' She shook her head. 'Look, I'll give you the honest truth because you're you. You're right, I drink a lot more than I should, but I'd *never* do coke.'

'When you were a student, you used to—'

'That was then, Rob. Party drugs like ecstasy and speed. But never anything stronger. And I've seen cokeheads in here and— No! Just no fucking way!'

'Okay.' Marshall stepped back. He didn't know whether she was telling the truth or lying to his face. Sometimes the lady protested too much. Trouble with addicts was the addiction became the only thing in their lives. Denying the truth came with the territory. 'I believe you. I'm just worried about Thea, that's all.'

'If you must know, I did extend an invite for any of the next four weekends. All of them if she wanted.'

'That's good.'

'Not really. She's not coming home. Little madam is at a party this weekend, even though she should be studying for her end-of-year exams. And you're right – one of the reasons I don't want her here is so she doesn't see her father.'

'Why's that a problem?'

'Because Paul is Mr Party, isn't he? And Paul being Paul, he encourages her to party when she's back. Because he's shagging someone not much older than his own daughter, he drags Thea along to these things. So if there's someone bringing coke into my house, it's not me. So it must be her or him.'

'That doesn't necessarily follow.'

'Paul might be her dad, but he's no father. You know how much of a dickhead he is, right?'

'Always have. But you don't let him in, so how could—'

'Shut up!'

'Okay! Okay!' Marshall raised his hands. 'I'm sorry I've upset you. It's just... I'm worried about you. I'm worried about Thea.'

'Right. Sure. Of course you are.'

But he had that feeling, like he needed to make it up to her somehow. 'How about we go out for the day this weekend?'

'You honestly want to spend time with a coke fiend?'

Marshall smiled at her, but the ache of worry still lurked in his guts. 'Look, I haven't spent enough time with you since I moved out. Maybe we could go for a walk up a hill?'

'With Ryan's knees?'

'I meant, just you and me.'

'Oh, right. Okay. Good.' And yet again, Marshall had managed to dig a different hole. And one he'd struggle to get out of. 'Anyway. I'm here to see Kayleigh.'

'Right.' Jen rubbed at her forehead. 'Her parents are here. Flew in from somewhere in Australia. Arrived yesterday after, like, three flights from hell. They want to speak to her now she's woken up, but I've held them back so you can get in there first. They're just about to kick off and complain. So, please can you be quick?'

'I'm here to be thorough.'

'Right. Of course you are.' Jen led him along the corridor, past a big mural of the Borders Railway that filled a wall. 'You know something? I feel quite shocked that Thea could think I'd take drugs.'

'She's just worried, Jen.'

'That or she's deflecting blame onto me. Here.' She opened a door and stepped back. 'Try to keep her calm, please.'

'I'll try.' Marshall entered the room.

Kayleigh lay on the bed, eyes closed. Her face was a mess, all cut up and bruised. The fresh surgery scars were only about half of it. Her eyes flickered – she was clearly on some extremely strong drugs.

But she was awake.

She was breathing.

'Hi.'

And she was talking.

'Hi, Kayleigh. My name's Rob. I'm a police officer.' Marshall kept his distance from the bed. 'How are you doing there?'

'Like I've died and gone to heaven.' She coughed, then examined his face closely. 'You're not much of an angel, though, are you?'

He smiled. 'More of a devil.'

That got a laugh, but it looked like it cost her. 'Has someone told my parents?'

'They're here. Just need to ask you a few questions, then you can see them.'

'Oh. Okay.'

'We're searching for your attacker, Kayleigh. If you could tell me what you remember about the incident, it might help. Is that okay?'

'I didn't see much. Heard someone in the bedroom. Dark. Tried to get up. Knife to my throat. I can't remember much about it. Except they stabbed me. Dragged me across the grass and threw me. Threw me off the cliff.'

'Did you see his face? Or his—'

'*He*?' Kayleigh scowled at him. 'It wasn't a man. It was a woman.'

'What?' Marshall felt a punch in his guts. An arm around

his own throat, a knife against his skin. Hard to breathe. He fumbled his phone, then picked it up, his heart pounding. He sifted through the photos of David Sylvester until he found one of Holly. He held it out to Kayleigh, but he couldn't speak.

'That's her.'

60

Marshall burst into Gashkori's office and grabbed the nearest free chair, at the head of the table.

The room stank of marker pens, stale cigarette smoke and the cloying sweetness of brown sauce. Gashkori, Taylor, Struan and Jolene sat around a conference box in the middle.

'You're saying we've got it the wrong way round?' Liana's disembodied voice came from the box, a mishmash of a triangle and a circle that some tech company must've thought looked like a prop from a sci-fi film. 'That Holly has been the one killing?'

'That's what we're saying, aye.' Gashkori rolled his eyes and mouthed, 'Keep up.' He gestured at Marshall. 'Rob?'

'I've just got back from the hospital and Kayleigh confirmed it was Holly who attacked her.'

'Interesting.' Liana clicked her tongue. 'But, Ryan, what you said isn't necessarily true.'

Gashkori sighed. 'How do you mean? Rob just said he—'

'No, that's not what I mean. I'm just thinking out loud and I'm sorry I've pushed your buttons...'

Gashkori gave the conference box a dark look. 'Go on?'

'Okay. So, we now know Holly's the one who attacked Kayleigh. That doesn't mean we don't know that Sylvester wasn't the killer of all the others.'

Gashkori sat back in his chair with a creak. 'So why would she attempt to kill Kayleigh, then?'

Liana paused. 'I need to do some thinking on that score.'

'But you've said all along that Sylvester fits the data?'

'He does. He did. He still does.'

Marshall grunted.

Gashkori looked over at him. 'Rob, you've got something to say?'

'I've always had doubts, but the data matched him. Most profiles... there's an element of fuzziness going on. We build the profile based on data from the victims and the locations and the natures of the crimes. That helps us dig into why someone would be so motivated to commit the act. And then we match the suspects against that.'

'And what's your point, caller?'

'Often, we're not working with perfect data. Far from it. And the result is the profiles are, say, three-quarters correct.'

Gashkori laughed. 'Okay, so something as trivial as the killer's gender is in that slight margin of error?'

Liana gasped. 'Well, quite.'

Marshall shut his eyes. 'I think there's still a lot of stuff in there that can help—'

'But this has all been a waste of time, hasn't it?' Gashkori looked around the room for support. 'I mean, if you've got their sex wrong, what else have you screwed up?'

'No.' Liana's voice was a bark from the conference box. 'I've been over that profile so many times. Like Rob said, there's still a hell of a lot of stuff in there that works.'

Gashkori shrugged. 'Like what?'

'Well.' Liana paused. 'The motivations are still the same. And... Um...'

Marshall took over. 'She's actually right. The profile is still mostly there. Sure, the killer's gender was wrong. But that doesn't mean the application of the profile when applied to David Sylvester was incorrect.'

'Sounds like defensive mumbo jumbo to me, Rob.' Gashkori rasped a hand across the stubble on his head. 'And I hate people being defensive. Right now, I need to know where they are. Has she taken him? Has he taken her? That's it.'

'We don't know, sir.'

'Great.' Gashkori laughed, shaking his head. 'Just marvellous.'

'Sir, I've been thinking about this on the way over from the hospital.' Marshall held his gaze. 'David Sylvester moved around a lot. Stayed in downmarket B&Bs. Befriended people, who subsequently died. It's still probable he killed all those people. But it's also possible he stopped with Holly. Some realisation over what he was doing to people, how close he came to losing his freedom. But what we didn't know is how much that profile applies to Holly. She could've followed him and watched him making friends in villages and towns. Then when he moved on, *she* struck, not him. In that scenario, he's innocent, but she's guilty. And she framed him. After all, she's known him since she was fifteen.'

'I'm not sure, Rob.' Sounded like Liana was hammering a pen off her desk. 'We don't have anything other than Kayleigh's word that Holly did it.'

'But we don't have anything other than *Holly's* word that David Sylvester attacked her.'

Gashkori sighed. 'Okay, you brainboxes. What do you propose?'

Marshall sat back and folded his arms. 'Well, the big thing we need to address is who's been killing them. If it's him, we've got a lot of information. But if it's her, we've got gaps. To do that, we need to figure out how it all started. Who killed first. And if, like I said, she's been following him, why? Was there a connection between them?'

Gashkori seemed to brighten, finally. 'Can you dig into that?'

Marshall nodded. 'I'll take lead on it, but it's Liana's skillset more than mine.'

'Excellent.' Gashkori cracked his knuckles. 'Okay, so let's divvy up the work here. Marshall, you're taking lead in the thinky. Pull together any connections between Holly and Kayleigh, and between Holly and Sylvester. Find out why she'd want to kill Kayleigh. Why she'd want to kill him.'

'Sure.'

Struan frowned. 'So you think Holly killed her boyfriend? That cameraman guy?'

Marshall caught a glimpse of Jamie lying on the living room floor. Pointing to the door. Saying 'Holly'. 'Shit, he wasn't saying she'd gone. He was saying she'd done this.'

Gashkori stared hard at him. 'So Holly killed him?'

'It appears that way. Was Sylvester even there?'

Taylor shrugged. 'The useless sods in forensics haven't finished processing it.'

Gashkori pointed at him. 'Cal, I want you to lead on the search for Sylvester and Holly. Unearth everything in both of their lives. Find them.'

'On it.' Taylor got to his feet and left the room. Then popped his head back. 'Struan, when you're ready....'

'Sure.' Struan got up and followed him out.

Marshall leaned over to the phone. 'Liana, I'll call you in a minute.' He ended the call. 'Jolene, can you get her on the phone in Andrea's office?'

'Sure thing.'

Marshall got up, but didn't leave Gashkori on his own. 'We'll get to the bottom of this, sir.'

'You better, because this is an absolute disaster, Rob. An absolute clown show. How the hell did you not know it was a lassie?'

'Because the killer exhibits typical male characteristics.'

Gashkori laughed. 'Doesn't sound very woke.'

'It's neither woke nor unwoke, sir. It's based on the science, which is based on data. Female killers tend to use more covert MOs, like the classic of poisoning.'

'Hang on.' Gashkori narrowed his eyes. 'Sounds like more arse covering to me.'

'These crimes aren't that different from poisoning, are they? Sneaking up on someone to push them off a cliff isn't that different from a bit of arsenic in the mushroom soup, is it? I mean, it's the total opposite of shooting someone or sticking a knife in their guts. The difference between the aggression of a typical male crime versus the cold-bloodedness of a typical female one. These murders were on the precipice of the two. It's a highly violent act, but it's also covert in nature too.'

Gashkori blew air up his face. 'So how did you fuck it up so badly?'

'You want the truth? It all goes back to Jacob Goldberg, I'm afraid. He had a proclivity for blending suspects into profiles. He liked to get results to boost his standing and get more funding. Sometimes that meant using the suspect to lead the profiling, which is how you end up with this mess, where the suspect is potentially a victim and one of the victims is a suspect.'

'See why I don't trust profilers?'

'If this was Liana or me doing this from scratch, we wouldn't have made the same mistake.'

'But you've led us down a garden path to the wrong bloody shed!'

'Sir, when you pick up something so old in pressurised

circumstances like these, it means we don't know when we're building on shaky foundations.'

'So this is my fault now?'

'No. That's not what I'm saying at all. It's our fault and I'll take full responsibility for it. But you've got to let me fix the mistakes, okay?'

'Mark my words, when this is over, those words will haunt you.'

'Sounds like a threat.'

'Sounds like it, doesn't it?' Gashkori clapped Marshall on the arm. 'Now, why don't you go and be a good little criminal profiler and help me find her, aye?'

Marshall wanted to stay and fight him, but that wasn't going to get anyone anywhere. 'Okay.' He left the room and walked past the bustling desks towards Elliot's office. Weird being in here rather than in his old one next door.

Liana was standing at the whiteboard, absently cupping her belly in her hands.

Marshall frowned at her. 'Thought you were at Gartcosh?'

'Started driving as soon as you called me. I dialled in on my car on the way down.'

'Didn't sound like you were driving?'

'Phones filter out the sounds nowadays, Rob.' She was scribbling things on the board, then turned around to Marshall. 'Saw you deep in discussion with Ryan.'

'Breaking news: he's not a fan of profiling.'

'I don't blame him. At times like this, nor am I.'

Jolene came in and sat at the meeting table. Not bearing coffee cups this time, just a frosty look on her face.

'You okay there?'

'Why wouldn't I be?' She threw a hand towards Liana and the whiteboard. 'Ryan told me I'm stuck with you two doing this guff when I should be out there finding them.'

'Why's that a problem?'

'Because I'm just not good at this stuff. It melts my brain.'

'No, you're exactly what we need.'

'How?'

Marshall pointed at them in turn. 'You and Liana are at opposite ends of the spectrum. You're all about action, she's all about observation. We need both.'

'I'm just going to ask you stupid questions.'

'No such thing. If we can't answer why, then we've got a big problem.'

'Then I'll slow you down.'

'Since Monday, we've both been going too fast on this. We need careful consideration.'

'Sounds like bollocks to me, Rob.'

'We need to work together, okay? Think about what we gained in Rothesay yesterday.'

'Aye, absolutely hee haw. Sylvester didn't kill her. Holly didn't either. She killed herself.'

'Maybe he did. And maybe Holly had been there too. That's where you come in. Once we're done here, can you get on the phone with PC Robertson and see what you can find about Holly staying on the island?'

'Fine.' Jolene scribbled it down, but didn't move from her seat. 'Ryan was right, you know? Your stupid profile didn't exactly help. It was wrong.'

'I agree.' Liana took the chair next to her. 'But the reason it was wrong is the likely perpetrator presented herself as a victim. It's a data issue.'

'Fourteen people have died, minimum, and it's a *data issue*? These are people's lives!'

'I know. And if you treat it any other way, you'll go insane. And if you're insane, you won't be any use to anyone on this case.'

Jolene sat there shaking her head.

'Okay.' Marshall collapsed into a chair, deliberately rattling his forearms off the table to create enough racket to distract them. 'Let's focus on what we have to add to the profile. Kayleigh is nineteen. An Australian on a gap year in the UK. Living in coastal Berwickshire. She fits the profile of the victims so far, near the top end of the age range. And we've got Marianne Henderson in Rothesay. Fifteen, so at the lower end of the range. Apparent suicide.'

Liana walked back to the whiteboard, cradling her belly. 'So, we need to update the profile with both of them, whilst removing Holly as the final victim in phase one. I'll do that.'

'Jolene, can you get someone to dig into connections between Holly and Kayleigh. Telephone calls, emails. Any meetings. Go around the cafés too.'

'Sure. I'll get Jim McIntyre on that.'

'And get Paul Watson to work with Hardeep on the other potential victims. We just need the data at this point, so focus on getting all of the files sent through, aye?'

'Will do.'

'We should speak to Doug Fairbairn again.' Liana circled his name from amongst Marshall's messy scribblings. 'He's the source of that information. If we get what he knows, it could be helpful.'

'Unlikely, but can you do that?'

'Sure.'

Jolene looked up from her notebook. 'Don't mention about Holly being the attacker, yeah?'

Liana rolled her eyes. 'Do you think I'm stupid?' She tapped her pen, seeming like she was going to throw it at Jolene. 'Before I can rework the profile, we need to go through the gaps.'

Jolene looked up. 'Such as?'

'Well, the biggest one is the trigger for killing. With Sylvester it was this incident in Greece. What could Holly possibly have?'

Liana jotted something down, then sighed. 'It wasn't just the Greek incident. His whole upbringing was traumatic. Chaotic. But he had stability from his grandparents.'

'His brother confirmed that.' Marshall nodded. 'But that's the one bit of the profile I actually agree with. Shame Holly's parents are both dead, otherwise we—'

Jolene frowned. 'Eh?'

'They're both dead.' Marshall focused on Jolene. 'She told me on Monday.'

Jolene laughed. 'That's bullshit. They're still alive.'

61

Jolene found a parking spot just off the main road into Whitley Bay, or what Marshall remembered it as. 'You been here before?'

'A few times, aye.' Marshall let his seatbelt go and took in the long sweep of the North Sea. The open green hid the sandy beach that stretched back north towards Berwick and Eyemouth. The knackered old amusements were still trading, like the one in Rothesay. The Spanish-style town hall. At least, he assumed it was the town hall. A giant white stucco building, at odds with the Victorian brick townhouses across the road.

One of which housed Holly's parents.

Marshall swallowed hard. 'Should've checked that they're still alive, shouldn't I?'

'Just as well your pal did.' Jolene winked at him, then opened her door but didn't get out, just let the cool morning air in. 'So this is where she said she was taken from?'

'Right. Down on the seafront.' Marshall pointed back the way, to the car parks on the links. 'David Sylvester was staying in a guesthouse a few streets over, near to his gran's house. Not long after she died. Got chatting to her in a café. Spoke to him over a few weeks. She went missing, turned up in Eyemouth. She blamed him and we believed her. And I sat in on the interviews. *I* believed her.'

She opened the door fully and got out. 'Don't blame yourself.'

Marshall followed her, but found it very hard not to. It'd started raining and he had to believe that was for him. Always seemed to either piss down here or you'd just freeze your nuts off. The address was up a back lane that seemed to lead somewhere important, but Marshall couldn't tell where.

The backs of posh-looking houses lined one side of the lane, with bulbous bay windows filling most of the gardens. Some five-a-side pitches sat opposite, hidden by thick bushes.

Jolene opened a gate four in and walked up the path. A chest-height wooden fence surrounded a small garden. She knocked on the door and looked around. Bay windows on both sides, but the blinds were drawn.

The door opened to a crack and a pale eye peered out. 'Hello?'

'DS Jolene Archer.' She held out her warrant card. 'Looking for Alan Fenwick.'

'Mr Fenwick's not well.'

Jolene widened her smile. 'We need to speak to him urgently.'

'I see.' The door shut.

Marshall saw movement through the blinds. 'Well, you were right.'

'I hate being right about the wrong things.'

The door opened again. A thin woman stood there, wearing a nurse's uniform. Not official NHS garb, but that of an agency carer. 'Mr Fenwick is very unwell, I'm afraid. If you're coming in, I need you to mask up.' She held two out for them. 'If he catches Covid, that's the end.'

'Totally understand.' Marshall took one and snapped it on

with something like nostalgia for the pandemic. Nostalgia, as Jacob Goldberg used to say, literally translating from the original Greek as *pain of loss*. A triggering memory of an awful time. 'Is he okay?'

'Better you see for yourself, like.' She led them into the front room. 'I'm Rosie, by the way.'

Alan Fenwick lay on a bed in the middle of the parquet floor, his eyes trained on a wall-mounted TV showing Sky Sports News.

Holly's lie about him dying wasn't that far from the truth – he had the shrunken face of a late-stage cancer patient. Oxygen piped into his nostrils from a tank. The room smelled like death.

Fenwick looked over at them, his eyes moving slowly. Each blink took a few seconds. 'Going to be a tough summer for the Mags, like. This FFP nonsense is killing the game as much as VAR.'

Jolene smiled at him. 'You a Newcastle fan?'

'Man and boy, for me sins. You?'

'Husband is, aye.'

'Do you understand this FFP, lass?'

'It's now called "Profitability and Sustainability", but yeah. I do. Or thought I did. I know they were trying to change it again.'

'I'd ask you to explain it to us, but I don't think I've got enough time left alive.' Fenwick laughed, a deep rattle that seemed to shake his bones. 'Cancer, in case you're both wondering. Started in me lungs, spread to me lymph nodes. Once it's in there, it's game over, man.'

Rosie smiled at him, but there was no warmth in her eyes. 'He refuses to go into a hospice.'

'I want to die in me own home. I've worked hard all me life to pay for it.' Another laugh, sounding like he'd coughed up a lung. 'I want to haunt the fucking place!'

Jolene laughed along with him.

'So why are the police here?'

'We need to ask you about Holly.'

'Right.' His eyes went back to the telly. 'What about her?'

'When did you last see her?'

'Not in fucking years. Since around the time she started saying to people I was fucking dead, like.'

Jolene glanced over at Marshall. 'Why did she do that?'

'Why did that girl do anything? To get attention. To manipulate people. She poisoned me wife against us, like. Belinda's living in Málaga now, isn't she? Still, I managed to keep this place so it's all a win, isn't it?'

'Did she talk much about David Sylvester?'

'Him?' Alan spat on the floor, making Rosie groan. 'That arsehole ruined me daughter's life. She wasn't the same after all of that.'

'Were you here when it happened?'

'Wish I was. I would've knocked his fucking block off, I tell you.'

'Where were you?'

'In fucking Málaga. Had a place over there. The wife's got it now, like.'

'We understand he took Holly to the family caravan.'

'Aye. When she told us what happened... I just wanted to burn it.'

Jolene frowned at Marshall. 'You didn't?'

'Nah. Haven't got the courage.'

Marshall felt his skin tingle. Another lie and one he'd stupidly believed.

'I'm not daft. Thing was worth a packet, lass.'

'You know who owns it now?'

'Aye, me! Haven't been there in years, mind. Just rent it out to people. Get a decent income from it, like.'

62

Marshall powered up the hill towards the caravan park, with Eyemouth spreading out around them. His phone buzzed with a text from Thea:

> You spoke to mum about what I said? WTAF? Thought it was a secret???

Ah, shite.

He definitely shouldn't have said anything to her about that.

And now wasn't the time to deal with any of it.

Still, he needed to sort this out.

> Let's talk this evening, okay? I'm worried about your mum

He put his phone away and focused on the here and now.

Jolene pulled into the car park area.

The area was filled with cops. Plainclothes, uniform and the black-clad ninjas of Edinburgh's Methods of Entry team.

'Subtle...' Marshall waited for Jolene to pull up then got out. Somehow the sun had decided to appear and, considering it was only April and had been freezing just an hour ago, it burnt his neck.

Gashkori was in the middle, sitting on a picnic bench, fawning over the lead ninja's assault rifle. He clocked Marshall's approach, cleared his throat and stood up tall. 'Rob. Finally.'

The ninja extended his hand. 'Inspector Sergio Bertorelli.'

'DI Rob Marshall.' He shook the hand, just about matching Bertorelli's iron grip. 'How's it looking?'

Bertorelli looked across to the caravans. 'Fine. Pretty standard, like.'

'I'm worried this is going to be a stand-off.'

'Are you.' Bertorelli gave him a withering look. 'I'm not. Contain and negotiate is a waltz for us. High probability of success. And if it goes south, you didn't kill 'em. We did.'

Marshall's worst fear. 'Have you been around the neighbours?'

'Not our job.'

'Our lot have, aye.' Gashkori scratched at his neck. His eyes were more feral than a colony of wildcats. 'Neighbours have seen someone going in there today so we think she's in there.'

'How sure?'

'They weren't sure, Rob. It was early.'

'Okay. So we don't *know*. Do we have anything to say either of them are here?'

'Her car was spotted yesterday. It's missing now, though. Struan's searching for it. Probably dumped it and walked back.'

'Definitely hers?'

'Curtain twitcher took a photo.' Gashkori held up his phone. 'Anyway, it's at the opposite end from Kayleigh's caravan, but it might explain how they knew each other.' He shook his head. 'Have to say, this is melting my head a bit.'

'You and me both.' Marshall sucked in a deep breath. 'How do you want to play this?'

'Well.' Gashkori gestured at the ninja. 'Cranberry and his team are going to raid the thing.'

'Cranberry?'

Bertorelli rolled his eyes. 'It's not like I shagged a turkey...'

Gashkori clapped his arm. 'He had cystitis. Drank some cranberry juice.'

Bertorelli shrugged. 'Sure you know the drill with cops and shitty nicknames?'

'Seen worse names. Like Dr Donkey.'

'You?'

Marshall nodded.

'*Maaaaan.*' Bertorelli pointed over at a caravan, smirking. 'Curtains drawn so we can't see inside, but the windows are open at the top on both sides. Couple of smoke grenades and some flashbangs. Time it with a frontal entrance. Won't know what's hit them.'

'That's a bit extreme. I was thinking—'

'Of talking? Right. Sure. Thing is, we called her mobile with a view to talking her out, right? Didn't answer. Phone's off now.'

Marshall stared at Gashkori. 'I want in on this.'

Bertorelli looked him up and down. 'You firearms trained?'

'No, but I've known both suspect and victim for twelve years.'

'We could do with that knowledge in a pinch, alright.' Bertorelli looked at Gashkori. 'Your call, Ry?'

'Risk assessment is they're not armed with a gun, just a knife.'

'A knife we can handle. It's like a game of rock-paper-assault rifle.' Bertorelli looked at Marshall and laughed. 'Having someone familiar with the players in there can be massively helpful. Split-second decisions are much easier with a decision maker on-site. We do need a negotiator, though. Are you trained in that, Rob?'

'Yup.'

Bertorelli narrowed his eyes. 'Is that "yup" as in "I have", or "yup" as in "I'm lying to get a bit of excitement in my sad life"?'

'Three week-long blocks at Hendon over six months. Operational deployment in six active situations over three years in the Met.'

'Fine, you're go, then.' Gashkori picked up a stab-proof. 'Oh, and make sure you wear this, aye?' He tossed it to Marshall.

Marshall caught it and strapped it on. A little tight, but he'd manage. He hoped he wasn't going in there because Gashkori wanted him out of the way permanently.

Bertorelli tossed his rifle to a mate, then got out his handgun. 'Right. Kebab, Dawn Chorus, John. You're with me.' He got three nods from his big lumps. All armed with rifles dangling from their shoulders, with pistols holstered next to their stab-proof vests. 'Rob, you stay outside until we clear it, okay?' He put on a helmet and tossed one over to Marshall. 'Get this on you, sunshine.'

Marshall put it on but it was a little too small for his massive head, so something hard pressed against his skull. And he felt naked without their body armour. 'Take it you'll be using an Enforcer to gain entry?'

'The Big Red Key will be no use here. Caravan doors open in the way.'

'Ah.'

'Just makes it easier to kick in.' Bertorelli pulled down the visor like he was going to do a spot of welding. 'Okay, lads. On three, okay?' He ran low past the caravans, his gear rattling and jangling.

Marshall followed, with the trio coming up behind him. His breath came in short bursts and his heart thudded as they closed on the caravan. The last one in the park, right at the northern tip, with cracking views across the sea.

He wanted to throw up.

Bertorelli stopped at the bottom of the steps, then waited

for his mates to get into position. Three nods, then he vaulted up to the top step and put a hand on the door handle. Raised a thumb to indicate it was unlocked.

Marshall joined him.

Bertorelli counted out one on his thumb, added two on his forefinger, then spread out the middle.

Kebab pulled the pin from his grenade, nodded at Dawn Chorus, then at John. All three lobbed their munitions in the windows at the same time as Bertorelli opened the door.

A violent crack of lightning and a vicious flash.

Smoke poured out.

'Go, go, go!'

Marshall stepped aside as Bertorelli burst into the caravan.

The other three entered and crashes and thuds came from inside.

'Bedroom, clear!'

'Bathroom, clear!'

'Living area, clear!'

'Marshall, in you come.'

He followed them inside. Hard to see anything through the mucky visor and the smoke. He stood in the living room, swinging around, trying to focus as the air cleared a bit.

Bertorelli was in the kitchen area, scanning things quickly but thoroughly. He pointed into the corner. 'There you go.'

Marshall walked over to the sofa and the smoke cleared.

Through the haze, he saw a body lying there.

63

Marshall sat on the bench, running his hand through his hair. Hard to shake free from the adrenalin surge from the raid. Or the shock of the discovery. Or the comedown afterwards. Like a blood sugar collapse after eating three Easter eggs.

He looked at Gashkori, shared a brief flash of confusion and rage, but neither said anything.

Marshall saw Holly's father on his death bed, laughing and joking about the fortunes of his football team.

He should phone him.

Someone should break the news to him.

'Has anyone briefed her dad?'

'Local cops have given the death message, aye.' Gashkori rubbed at his nose. 'Trying to get hold of the mother in Spain is proving a bit trickier.'

'Rob Marshall.' Dr Leye Onatade stood there, holding out his hand. 'I'm the new Dr Owusu.'

Marshall shook the hand. 'It's been a while, mate.'

Leye laughed. 'That means you're the new Andrea Elliot?'

'The old one's still kicking around.' Marshall winced, glancing at Gashkori. 'Do you know Belu?'

'I knew her. Haven't heard from her in a while, though.'

'Trying to get in touch with her, Leye, so if you could...'

'Will keep an ear to the ground, my friend.'

Gashkori frowned at them. 'Take it you two know each other?'

'Very well deduced, detective.' Leye smiled.

'We worked together in London. Solved a few murders, didn't we?'

Marshall nodded. 'Not as many as I'd like.' He shielded his eyes from the sun. 'Didn't know you were up here?'

'Fancied a change of pace.' Leye shrugged. 'London's a big place. Too big. Sometimes you want somewhere more sedate. With fewer murders. And a lot fewer Nigerians. Nice being the only one for a change!' His laugh was infectious. 'Anyway, I've got a body to inspect, my friend, so I'll see you later. We should catch up sometime.'

'I'm up for that.' Marshall watched him go. 'I didn't know he was here.'

'He's a good guy. People talk highly of him.' Gashkori let out a deep breath. 'Anyway, I've got a big mess to sort out, so I'll catch you later.' He walked off.

Leaving Marshall alone with his thoughts. He needed to spark himself into action here.

Sort something out.

Focus.

Deliver.

But he just wanted to sit there.

A car pulled up and Kirsten got out. She walked over and wrapped him in a cuddle. 'You okay?'

Marshall let his breath go slowly. 'Ask me later, because right now I've no idea.'

'Heard you went in with the Methods of Entry team?'

'Not like that. Just waited for them to assess. But I haven't done that kind of thing for a long time.' Marshall looked her up and down. 'What brings you here?'

'I had the dubious pleasure of having She Who Cannot Be Named call me in to accelerate things.'

'Trev not going fast enough for her?'

'As if anyone could. Forensics is one of those things you can just throw bodies at and get results quicker. She's sending a few of your chums down from Gartcosh.'

'Makes sense, I suppose. Though I don't think it'll help in tracking down—'

'Better go.' She pecked his cheek and walked off towards the caravan.

'Talking about being out of the closet.' Gashkori was sucking on an ice lolly, which seemed to be his idea of sorting things out. 'You make a really cute couple.'

'I'm not in the mood.'

'Right. Sorry.' Gashkori perched on the bench next to him and slurped at his lolly. 'How are you feeling, soldier?'

'Still processing how I feel about it. It's a surprise for sure, but...'

'I get that.' *Sluuuurp.* 'Still, it's nice to get some clarity on the whole thing.'

'I don't think we do, do we?'

'I think so. This morning, we thought Sylvester had abducted Holly when he killed Jamie. But now... We think *she's* taken *him.*'

Marshall stared into space. 'I went into that caravan expecting a shootout or a hostage situation, with Sylvester pointing a gun at her, screaming insanity at us. And we found her body. Not at the bottom of a cliff or scraped across train tracks, but stabbed on a sofa. It's possible she took him. But it's just as possible that Sylvester did. And probably more likely.'

Slurp. 'If that's the case, why didn't he kill her in Reston?'

'I don't follow?'

'Well, Sylvester broke into their home. Stabbed Jamie. Abducted Holly. If he's just going to kill her, why go to all the bother of bringing her to this caravan? Why not leave her with Jamie?'

Marshall hadn't thought of it like that. 'He wanted something from her.'

'You and Liana were talking about him tormenting victims? Does that still apply?'

'Assuming they're even his victims... If there's a sadist here, it's Holly. But maybe he wants her to suffer for all she's done. I mean, he told me he's been hounded by the police for twelve years. His words. So maybe he feels he's owed some kind of retribution from her.'

'Aye, maybe.' Gashkori slid a big segment of his lolly down the length of the stick. 'Here's trouble.'

'Lads.' Leye dropped his bag at his feet. 'I need to get back to base, but I've carried out my initial assessment. Stabbed through the abdomen. Transected the descending aorta and she bled out within seconds. Thing with training in Nigeria and working in London is that, sadly, you see a lot of knife crime. So you could say I'm an expert.'

'What kind of a knife are we talking?'

'Much bigger than the one used to killed Jamie up in Reston. I'd say it's one of these anti-zombie monsters you see a lot in London. You know the sort. Almost machetes.'

Marshall nodded. 'I know the sort. I was seconded to a case in East London a few years ago when a journalist was killed with one. Some kid on a bike. Where did he get one from around here, though?'

Gashkori looked up at him. 'Jamie.'

'Eh?'

'Jamie the cameraman. He had one of those knives. The

sound guy, Toby, he told Elliot and Jolene that Jamie threatened someone with one.'

'So Sylvester killed him and took the knife, then killed her with it?'

'It appears that way.'

'Holly turned Sylvester into a double murderer.'

Marshall tried to process it. Like Gashkori said, Sylvester had broken into the house, killed Jamie, abducted Holly, only to take her to a caravan to stab her.

Leye twisted his lips, creased his forehead. 'But... I spoke to Kirsten, is it? She said the blood spray is straight, which would imply it's a surprise attack, unlike at Reston.'

Gashkori frowned. 'You mean she didn't turn around?'

'Exactly. If you stab someone when they don't expect it and you catch an artery, then most of the time they turn and the blood sprays in an arc. If they see the attack coming, the blood sprays but it's straight. One thing to note is the spray has been cut off, stopped, blocked, so I'd suggest your attacker would've been covered by Holly's blood. And I mean coated in it.'

'Have you found any blood-soaked clothing?'

'Not my department, but as far as I'm aware no clothing has been recovered from the property.'

'Are there any signs of torture?'

Leye stared off back in the direction of the caravan. 'Cuts up her arms, on her thighs, at her throat. Nothing that would cause her to bleed like that. And she was restrained, given the marks on her arms. If you ask me, I'd say he was torturing her. He just got what he wanted out of her and killed her. Cold-blooded, man.' He frowned. 'But... First, there's flesh under her finger-nails, so it'd appear they got into some kind of fight, where she attacked him. And there's a second blood spray.'

'You think she might've wounded him?'

'It's possible. It's possible both are hers. But it's also possible

that's his. Until we see the attacker or we get blood types, we
don't know.'

'Okay.' Gashkori finished his ice lolly with a final slurp. 'Let
me know when you can run the post-mortem?'

'I'd already scheduled to do Jamie this afternoon, so I'll run
them both and focus on Holly first.'

'Thanks. I'll send someone to attend.'

Marshall avoided Gashkori's gaze.

'Catch you later, lads.' Leye trundled over to his Bentley and
got in.

Gashkori stuffed his lolly stick in the wrapper and pocketed
it. 'So, does this change anything?'

'Sounds like he's possibly wounded. Or covered in blood.'

'Why would he be torturing her, though?'

Marshall shrugged. 'If you'd been accused of a string of
murders you didn't commit, wouldn't you want to know that
she'd done them? And how? And why?'

'Good point.' Gashkori stared into space. 'We really need to
find him.' He got his lolly stick back out and licked at his
fingers. 'Need to get rid of this. I'll speak to Cal, see if he's
getting anywhere. It's possible Sylvester's not got far. Then
again, he could be halfway to Cumbria by now. Make yourself
useful, would you?'

'I'll try...' Marshall watched him go, then got out his phone
and checked for messages. A couple of missed calls from Liana
and a text. He opened it:

> Rob,
>
> Been thinking through the discovery. Got a few
> mins to run it through?
>
> L x

He hit dial and put the phone to his ear.

'Gaffer?'

Marshall swung around and clocked Struan's approach, heading right for him – for once, Marshall was the gaffer in question. He ended the call before she answered. 'What's up, sergeant?'

'Seen Gashkori?'

Marshall motioned in the direction he'd gone in. 'He was going to speak to DI Taylor. Why?'

'Right. Right. It's just, uniform have found Holly's car.'

64

Marshall was out of the car before Struan stopped, his feet hitting the tarmac hard. He pushed into a run, racing towards Holly's Toyota.

Empty, the driver door hanging open. Surrounded by four uniformed officers. Beyond it, a squad Focus and a Land Rover both idled.

The local sergeant was pointing into the car. 'Blood all over the seats, sir.'

Marshall peered into the car. Didn't look like a lot of blood, more like second-hand stuff from the attack.

Meaning Sylvester probably wasn't injured.

Struan joined them. 'Think that's from when he took her from Reston?'

'Maybe.' Marshall crouched down and inspected it closer. 'Hard to tell.' He looked around the immediate area.

The main road led down to the village and the harbour, while the fields were inland. A path led north along the line of the cliffs towards the lighthouse.

Marshall looked at the uniform sergeant. 'You got anyone down in the village?'

'Two lassies going door to door. The place is pretty small – if there's a looney running around bleeding everywhere, locals would've called it in.'

'Remember – we don't know if this is his blood or not.' Marshall tried to run through the options.

Sylvester had pulled in on the outskirts. Like the sergeant said, it was unlikely he'd gone into the village.

If he was bleeding from an attack... Hard to figure out where he'd go. A hospital would ask questions he wouldn't want to answer. And he wasn't medically trained himself.

The fields looked clear, but they didn't know when the car had been left. Could've been hours ago, giving him time to get clear.

Leaving the path up to St Abb's Head, but that would be a similar story to the village – plenty of people hiking up there, with plenty of views. A man dripping blood everywhere would draw attention. Even a man smeared in someone else's would.

Surely someone would call it in.

The other option was someone picked him up. Probably not a taxi, unless a lot of money was involved. They didn't know of Sylvester having any friends in the area, but that wasn't the same thing as him not having any.

Marshall had the sick feeling deep in his guts that Sylvester had got away once again. 'Struan, can you contact DI Taylor and update him, please?'

'Sure thing, gaffer.' He walked off, fiddling with his mobile.

The sergeant's radio crackled. 'Control to Jeffries. Over.'

'This is Jeffries, receiving. Safe to talk. Over.' The sergeant stepped away, back towards the Land Rover.

Marshall inspected the car again. No sign of the knife – one of those anti-zombie ones, according to Leye. He looked up to ask Struan, but he was over by the car, talking on his phone.

Marshall snapped on a pair of gloves and opened the boot.

Empty, save for a small bag. He spilled the contents onto the fabric.

Toothbrush, toothpaste. Two pairs of Y-fronts. Two pairs of balled-up socks. A 5,000-piece jigsaw.

Sylvester's stuff, alright.

So where the hell was he?

He'd run off without his go bag. Meaning it was likely the blood was his.

Desperate, bleeding, worried the cops would catch him.

Where would he go?

'Guv?' Sergeant Jeffries was back. 'You Marshall?'

'That's me, aye.' Marshall started putting Sylvester's gear into an evidence bag. 'What's up?'

'Just that... That call.' Jeffries pointed up the path. 'Control have a report from a dog walker at St Abb's Head. Spotted a man covered in blood heading towards the cliffs.'

65

Jeffries was behind the wheel, powering his old Land Rover around the bend, then following the road up the hill. To the right, the loch glistened in the afternoon sun. The rocky crags towered over them, the hillside a mix of fallen boulders and gorse. 'Aye, I know every blade of grass up here. Based in this place for seventeen years.'

Marshall clutched the handle and scanned the road up ahead. 'That's reassuring.'

Two men with dogs walked towards them.

Jeffries slowed, winding his window down. 'You okay there, lads?'

They looked at each other like they'd been doing something they shouldn't. The taller of the two nodded. 'Fine, aye?'

'Haven't seen anything unusual?'

They shook their heads.

'Okay, thanks.' Jeffries drove on, his window grinding as it went back up. 'Maybe this is bollocks.'

'Aye, let's see.'

Jeffries followed the road around the bend, then straight on towards the cliffs.

People walked along the paths worn through the grassy area below the road.

A man came running along with two dogs, waving and pointing back along the way.

'Oh, here we go.' Jeffries sped up along the final stretch, then pulled into the car park overlooking the sea.

Marshall got out into the stiff breeze. The sun was still hot, burning at his face. He swung around a full circle but couldn't see any sign of Sylvester.

A man ran towards them. 'Guys, there's someone over there!' He pointed towards the lighthouse, set down below them.

'Get to safety! There are officers in the other car park!' Marshall set off over the rough ground towards the cliff edge.

The gate was hanging open.

Sylvester was shaking the door to the old lighthouse, now turned into high-end holiday cottages. His white T-shirt was covered in blood. The giant knife in his hand flashed in the light. He turned and spotted Marshall walking down the steps towards him. Eyes bulging, Sylvester shot off away from Marshall and vaulted the white wall surrounding the lighthouse.

'Shite!' Marshall followed him across the grass at the side. Took him two goes to get over the wall. Once he was over, he couldn't see Sylvester.

He traced the line of the cliffs, up and down, then stopped dead.

Sylvester stood at the edge, staring down.

Marshall scrambled across the grassy bank, then took it slowly as he closed on Sylvester. 'David.'

Sylvester turned around slowly. He was holding his knife against his stomach. 'Stop.'

Marshall complied with that, raising his hands. They were

overlooking a rocky natural harbour hundreds of feet below them. 'It's okay.'

'What is? What they did to me? What you've done to me? You've made my life hell! For twelve years! And you're still doing it!'

'Is that why you killed them?'

Sylvester shook his head. 'You wouldn't understand.'

'Come on, David, drop the knife. Come with me to the police station and talk to me.'

'I'd rather talk here.'

'Fine.' Marshall took a step closer. 'Where do you want to start?'

'Holly called me on Sunday.'

'Is that what happened?'

Sylvester nodded. 'I thought it was Kayleigh.'

'How?'

'She'd stolen Kayleigh's phone. I liked her. She was a nice person. But she's dead.'

'She's alive, David.'

'What?'

'I spoke to her this morning. She survived the fall.'

'My God.' Sylvester held up the knife, thick with blood and torn flesh. 'My God.'

'What did Holly say to you?'

'She told me to meet her at her caravan at nine o'clock on Monday morning. If I didn't go, she'd kill Kayleigh. If I reported it to the police, she'd kill her. And it didn't matter in the end, did it? She'd killed her before I got there. I found her body in the caravan.'

That didn't stack up. 'David, I told you, she survived the fall.'

'I know. But I panicked. I ran off to get help. But I realised you'd just frame me. Just like Holly tried to. But I had to check if Kayleigh was still alive. When I went back, the body was gone. And Holly was there. She saw me. Shouted after me. She must've thrown Kayleigh from the cliff. I...'

'Did you speak to Holly again?'

'In person. I knew where she lived now. I wanted to know what happened to Kayleigh. Why she did that. Why she did any of it. She wanted to speak. So I went to her home in Reston. I just wanted to speak to her and make her go to the police. Clear my name.'

'You broke in, didn't you?'

'She was there. She was going to run away.'

'Did you kill Jamie?'

'The cameraman? He attacked me.' Sylvester held up his knife. 'I got him with this. He stopped attacking me.'

'Why didn't you kill Holly?'

'She begged me not to. Said she could stop it. Clear me. She'd made my life a misery over the years. Sent me messages. I'm a friendly man. But... she had all these videos of me, talking to... girls. Said I'd been touching them inappropriately.'

'And had you?'

'No! I'm just... I want to be their friend.'

'Like Marianne in Rothesay?'

'See? You think I had something to do with that, don't you? Nobody believes white, middle-aged men. We're the modern-day pariahs. I'm fucked. Totally fucked.'

'David, what happened in Rothesay?'

'Marianne was a troubled girl. But Holly got in her ear, encouraged her to kill herself. Holly did it for the sport, because she could, and you lot fell for it.'

Marshall's own phone rang.

Pringle calling...

Of all the times...

He bounced the call and put it away.

Sylvester was watching Marshall like a cat would a small bird. 'It was Holly who was the serial killer. It's always been her. She killed people. Then she framed me. Made me take the blame. Leaving all these girls dead, but I didn't know.'

'And that's why you murdered her.'

'No.'

'Come on, David. Let's just—'

'Weird thing is, I knew her when she was small. Fifteen, I think. She spoke to me one day. Very friendly. And I'm a friendly person.'

'This was in Whitley Bay, wasn't it?'

'Right. I didn't know, but she'd killed someone. Pushed her onto the train line. Someone in her class at school. Charlotte. I knew her. Nice girl. And she got away with it because she threatened me. Thought I'd be a great patsy, so she followed me wherever I went. She used to message me and I was stupid enough to respond. She knew where I was. Was able to find the girls I spoke to. Killed some of them. But her problem was that you were closing in. Public requests for information. She'd lose her patsy or she'd get caught herself. Then she did it once more, but to herself. And made it look like I'd taken her. And the police were all set to arrest me, but the only evidence you had was her statement. Some of the evidence pointed to me, but not all of it. Enough to give the police a prime suspect. Me. But not enough to convict.'

'We didn't prosecute you because the evidence wasn't strong enough. If you'd said it was her, we'd have—'

'I was guilty in the court of public opinion. Never charged, but everyone knew I did it, even though it was Holly. So I went to Arran, where nobody had really heard about the story. She followed me there. And she kept on killing, but I didn't know.'

'How did you find out?'

'She told me to confess. But I'd done nothing wrong!'

'So you didn't abuse Marianne or Myleene?'

'No! I talked to them, that's all.'

'Have you got any evidence of your innocence or her guilt?'

Sylvester reached into his pocket.

Marshall was ready to dive to either side.

Sylvester tossed a smartphone over. 'There's a video recording of her confessing to the crimes. The code is 0000, because it's all been for nothing.'

Marshall was still wearing the gloves from St Abbs. He unlocked the phone, then sifted through the photos app and found a video recorded that morning. He tapped play, but kept one eye on Sylvester.

The inside of the caravan, dark outside but the lights on full. Holly sitting on the dining chair, tied to the arms, staring into the lens.

'My name is Holly Fenwick and this is a full confession of my crimes. I won't list the names, because you've heard them all before. But all of those girls I said David Sylvester killed... It was me. All of them. Every single one. And there are more, but I think you've got that list too. Marianne Henderson was the last one. Rothesay at Christmas time. I persuaded her to kill herself. Gave her the sleeping pills to do it. Temazepam I had for my anxiety. Stockpiled them. I was with her, holding her hand as she died, then I pushed her into the sea. Like so many of the others. And then Kayleigh Rothbury... I tried to frame David Sylvester for her death.'

Marshall watched the subtle movement, her fingers working away at the tape tying her arms down.

In the real world, Sylvester was staring at his knife blade.

Off-screen, Sylvester mumbled something Marshall didn't hear. Maybe the lab techs could clean it up.

'Why did I kill Kayleigh? Because Douglas Fairbairn

believed me about you, David. He thought I was telling the truth and he came to me with this list of people he thought you'd killed, David. But it was all me. And I knew it was only a matter of time before he went to the police. Who knows what they'd find? Like twelve years ago, I needed to get them to charge you. To prosecute you. And this time I needed it to stick. I needed you to be prosecuted for it all. Or to be dead but there was no doubt it was you. Then I'd finally be clear.'

Sylvester appeared on the screen, next to her. He mumbled something else.

'Of course I will.' Holly stared at him. Then she tore away the tape and barged towards him.

The knife spilled out of his hands.

Sylvester wrestled her to the floor but she caught him in the face with an elbow and got up.

Sylvester lunged at her.

She caught his arm with the knife.

Blood sprayed everywhere.

Sylvester screamed. 'You bitch!' He punched her hand and the knife spilled to the floor. He punched her in the throat and she tumbled back onto the sofa.

Sylvester bent over then stabbed her in the chest.

The blood sprayed all over him. All over the floor.

Sylvester stood there, watching her die. 'What have I done?'

The video finished.

Marshall looked over at Sylvester. 'Thank you.'

'You see what happened there? Not just the bit with me stabbing Holly and killing her. What she said. Why she did all of this.'

'This shows us everything. You clearly acted in self-defence, David. Drop the knife and come with me now. We can get this all sorted out and you'll be home for tea. Maybe do the jigsaw in the boot?'

'It was an accident.' Sylvester pressed the same big knife

against his chest, right over the heart. 'Remember that when I kill myself. It's you and her who did it.'

'David, stop—'

Sylvester plunged the knife into his heart, then tumbled off the cliff edge.

66

M arshall sat on the boot of the Land Rover, sipping sugary tea. Everything felt tight. *Everything.* His legs were like overhead power lines. His head was a big lump of candyfloss.

'Rob.'

He looked up and saw Gashkori. 'Sir.'

Gashkori sat next to him. 'We've fished him out of the water.'

Marshall swallowed. 'Okay. Cool.'

'Leye's having a look. Freaky natural harbour down there. Local lad said it's called Pettico Wick Bay. Be interesting to know more about that. Whether there was a village here or something.' Gashkori looked over at him. 'You're not okay, are you?'

'Nope. Wish I'd stopped him. Such a stupid death.'

'Some people can't do prison, Rob. You know that. Davie Elliot for one.'

'True.'

'Pretty fucked up, though. He just stabbed himself?'

'Right through the heart. Then he... tumbled into the water.

Thought I'd persuaded him it was okay. Thing is, he showed me that video. A decent defence lawyer could get him off. Or with a minimal sentence. I tried to persuade him it was going to be okay, but... He just stabbed himself.'

'He said Holly had been framing him for years? What over?'

'Photos and videos of him with young girls. Maybe he was an abuser. Maybe he just didn't know what to do around people. Who knows?'

'I suspect you'll get to the bottom of it.'

'More like a job for Liana.'

'Right, sure.'

She walked over, all tucked into a thick coat. 'Hey, are you okay?'

'I'm not, but I will be.'

She gave him a curt hug. 'It's been good working together, but let's not do this again.'

'Sure. Let me know when junior drops and if you want to go mountain biking.'

'Will do.' She nodded at Gashkori. 'See you around, Ryan.'

'Thanks for all your work on this.'

She shrugged. 'Didn't exactly achieve much, did I?'

'We all did. Catch you later.' Gashkori sipped his own cup of tea and watched her teeter off towards her car. 'Listen, Rob, I wanted to thank you for stepping into the breach here. I know we don't see eye to eye but I appreciate the work you've put in.'

'Thank you, sir. It's been... Well. I don't think any of us have enjoyed it, have we?' Marshall thought of Craig Craigie in Rothesay, working away on his refurbishment, while his step-daughter rotted in a grave. 'But there are a lot of families who have answers now.'

'Thing is...' Gashkori clicked his teeth together. 'It's a real shame we have no room on the team down here because I could use you.'

'Right. Unlike a year ago?'

'I've started to appreciate what you've got going for you.'

'Okay. Well, I didn't expect anything. Back to Gartcosh I go. With a bucket and a spade and hand grenade, hi ho.'

Gashkori laughed. 'You do important work there. It suits you.'

'Sure.'

'Oh, man.' Leye dropped his bag at his feet. 'Where are you lads getting that tea from?'

'That sergeant...' Gashkori clicked his fingers. 'Jeffries? One of his lads has a tea urn in the boot of his car.'

'Ah, excellent. It's freezing now, man. I could do with something to warm me up.'

'Ain't it just.' Gashkori finished his cup and set it down between himself and Marshall. 'You get a look at Sylvester?'

'Yeah, there wasn't much left, to be honest with you. Probably wasn't quite dead by the time he hit the water, but that fall killed him and turned him into pâté. Shattered four vertebrae, burst his abdomen and his heart.'

Gashkori exhaled slowly. 'Brutal.'

'I won't have time to process his post-mortem until Saturday morning.' Leye looked at Marshall. 'You mentioned Belu Owusu earlier?'

'Right?'

'I thought you'd like to know. I heard from a colleague of ours that she was officially reported missing in South Africa.'

Marshall narrowed his eyes. 'Does that mean she's dead?'

'I'd say there's a good chance.'

'Come on, Leye, I'll show you where the tea is.' Gashkori walked off. 'See you around, Rob.'

'Aye, sure.' Marshall finished sipping his tea and looked around at the cops doing their busy work.

Belu was officially missing...

Jesus.

And he'd bounced a call from Pringle.

He got out his phone and listened to the voicemail.

'Rob, hi. It's Jim.' D:Ream were playing in the background, almost drowning out his voice. 'Listen, I know it's early doors here, but I. Fucking. Love it here. I want to stay. Can I? I love it. And you've been so good to me. Can I be a royal pain in the—' He whistled. '—and ask you to bring some more of my stuff? I got a list made up of what I want. You can bin the rest or keep it, I don't care! I'd do it myself but we've got karaoke this evening! Cheers!'

67

E lliot sat on her bed and let out a deep groan.

Their bed.

Her bed.

Their bed.

Her bed.

All of the boxes of stuff from the wardrobe and the garage were pressed against the wall, just a little patch of carpet visible on this side of their bedroom.

Her bedroom.

It had taken her a while to figure out what was hers and what was Davie's, but here she was, finally doing what she'd avoided doing for a year. Her plan had been to stick his stuff into a storage unit for when he got out.

But then things changed, didn't they?

Now her future was a bit clearer, she just wanted rid of it all.

No, she *needed* rid of it.

She'd taken out the few keepsakes which would enrich her life or remind the kids of their dad. She had a pile of stuff that needed to be recycled.

The rest she'd burn.

The fire and smoke would cleanse and put everything right.

Aye, what a load of shite.

Three boxes down and she'd found nothing worth saving, some to burn and too much to recycle. Not what she'd expected, but it'd do. It'd have to do.

The doorbell rang.

Sodding hell.

She pushed up to standing and her knees ached. Getting to that age where simple movements could cause mild injury, serious enough to annoy for days at a time.

She padded through to the landing in her monster feet slippers.

Sam's door was shut, so she listened and heard the deep voice of Tam talking with her daughter. Elliot nudged it open and the sound of Billie Eilish meandered out into the hallway. 'Keep that door open, young lady.'

Not that Elliot was one to talk – she'd been up to all sorts with her boyfriend when she was young.

She rattled down the stairs and picked up the post she hadn't heard being delivered. Shite, shite and a bill. She opened the door.

Jolene stood there, holding up a bottle of nice red wine. *Very* nice red wine. 'Hey.'

'You read my mind.' Elliot stepped aside. 'Come on in.'

Jolene shrugged off her coat as she stepped into the house. Might've been baking earlier, but it was a cool night now. She hung it up like she lived there. 'How are you?'

'Not great.' Elliot took the bottle and led her through to the kitchen. 'Davie's folks are looking after the boys tonight. It's like they think it's the last time I'll let them see them.'

'What about Sam?'

'Upstairs with that useless sod of a boyfriend.'

'How's she doing?'

'Better today, actually.'

'And you?'

'Much, much worse today.'

Jolene gave her a kind smile. 'I saw you at the briefing this morning...'

'Fucking stupid, that. Giving Gashkori ammunition. Knowing my luck, I'll get a nickname.'

'I mean, us cops can be dickheads, but you've just lost your husband. I doubt even Gashkori and Taylor would be *that* dark.'

'I think Ryan wants rid of me. He'll use that against me.'

'Well, I *know* Ryan wants you to be okay. We all do.'

'Right. Sure.' Elliot uncorked the wine and poured out a small amount into a giant glass. 'You want one?'

'Got the car.'

'Just a wee snifter?'

'Oh, go on.'

Elliot poured out barely more than a splash. In that size of glass it looked positively sarcastic. 'Thanks for calling me earlier. I appreciate you keeping me in the loop.'

'Don't mention it. Just thought you'd like to know.'

'So Dr Donkey didn't save the day after all?'

'No. If you ask me, he's a bit shaken up by it. Sylvester stabbed himself in the heart right in front of him.'

'Sounds hellish.' Elliot sniffed in some of the wine. *Glorious!* 'I know I grind his gears a lot, but Robbie's a good guy. I kind of miss having him on the team. Is he sticking around?'

'He's going back to Gartcosh.'

'Shame. Robbie can do the police work once he gets his head out of the clouds. Or his arse.' Elliot sipped at her wine. Absolutely gorgeous. 'Thank you for this.'

'My pleasure.' Jolene clinked her glass then took a deep sniff, but didn't drink any. That wine-tasting course hadn't just upgraded her tastes from Blue Nun, but had turned into a full-blown wine snob. 'How are you feeling about Davie?'

'Fucking shite, to be honest. So conflicted. Got so many different emotions running through my head, you know? I'm glad it's over. But I miss my best friend. Present company excepted. I'm angry at what he did. Angry he's going to fuck up my kids even worse than they otherwise would be.'

'Yeah...' She stared deep into her glass. 'It's a lot to take in.'

'A hell of a lot.' Elliot finished her glass already and tipped more in. 'This is incredible. Where did you get it?'

'The place in Melrose on the corner. Special offer on it.'

'Right. Need to get some more myself.' Elliot sipped it. 'Did I tell you bloody Shunty was with Davie at the end? Met him at the hospital yesterday. They didn't save him, but... I can't get his last words out of my head. David said something like, he wishes he'd had more holidays as a family. Said we were happy once and that happiness had value for him.'

'What the hell does that mean?'

'No idea.' Elliot shrugged. 'And it's pissing me off, to be honest. I mean, is he trying to make me feel guilty? We haven't had a holiday since before the pandemic and, even then, it was to bloody Harry Potter World down in Englandshire. Last real holiday was... maybe a couple of years before that when we went to Disneyland in Paris. Things were tight. Always were, but... They're about to get a lot tighter.'

'Did Davie have life insurance?'

'Aye. Weird thing is, it'll be double since he was murdered in there. But still, it's not going to amount to a whole heap of beans, since he was a tight bastard who thought he'd live forever. I'd much rather have him than the money. Despite all these weird thoughts rattling around in my head, you know? But I think he died with a lot of regrets. The stupid prick had been taking bungs for years from Hislop. I hope he regretted it. Nothing could make up for it. *Nothing.*'

'You really think Hislop paid for it?'

'I don't doubt it for a second. Practically told me he did. But

I also know we won't be able to pin it on him. Heard Bob Cook took a swing at Rancid John. Got a confession out of him, but it's meaningless. Didn't name Hislop.'

'Hislop's still under surveillance, though.'

'I know. But he's too smart for us. Too smart by half.' She finished her second glass and an idea hit her square in the eyes.

Christ – for a detective, she could be thick as pigshit sometimes.

68

Marshall glanced over at Kirsten. 'Thanks for coming with me.'

The headlights caught her face. She was bored and maybe a little bit irritated. 'Don't mention it.'

Marshall took the turning he'd had etched into his brain.

And it hit him – why she was being so cold.

'Sorry. I forgot to ask. How was your appointment?'

'Thought you'd never get round to it...'

'I mean, it's not really an excuse, but having someone kill themselves in front of you...'

'Aye, you're forgiven. This time.' She reached over and rested her hand on his thigh. 'I had my scan.' She sucked in a deep breath. 'Basically, I've got endometriosis.'

Marshall looked over at her. 'I've heard of that. But don't really know it means.'

'Consultant said it explains why I'm not pregnant. I mean, it's not *impossible*, but it can be very hard. As we're finding. I've got like a twenty-five percent chance of getting pregnant. And staying that way for the full term is even harder.'

Marshall gave her hand a squeeze. 'What did they say?'

'The way she explained it... the tissue you usually get in your uterus starts growing outside it. In my case, it's in my ovaries and fallopian tubes, possibly in my bladder and intestines but they haven't tested those yet.'

'That doesn't sound good.'

'It's not. There's an op I can get done, but... in my case it's unlikely to make any difference.'

'Do you think you should?'

'I want to try anything, Rob. IVF's pretty much our only option.'

'Okay.' Marshall nodded. 'We should do it.'

'You're sure?'

'Of course I'm sure.'

'You don't want to think about it?'

'Any thinking was done a long time ago. But an operation... I don't want to risk losing you.'

'It's not one of those ops.'

'Okay. Cool.'

She looked over at him with wide eyes. 'So you're sure?'

'A hundred percent.' Marshall pulled into Pringle's drive. The house was pitch black. The security light didn't even come on. 'Thank you for doing this. It means a lot.'

'You've got so much on your shoulders, Rob. I shouldn't have said me not getting pregnant was down to you and your stress levels. It's all my fault.'

'It's not your fault. At all. Please don't talk about fault. This is just the path we have to go down, okay? We're still young-ish and healthy enough. It's totally fine whatever happens.'

'Are you sure?'

'I said I'm sure.'

She reached over and kissed him, then sat back and gestured over at the house. 'How much stuff are you taking?'

'A few bags of clothes. I'll bring him back here in a few weeks and get the rest, once he's figured out what he needs.

Problem is, I half expect him to change his mind at least twice in that time.'

'Yeah…'

'And this gives me a chance to turn everything off so he can't retrospectively burn the place down.' Marshall opened the door and got out into the freezing night.

The lights flashed on in the house and D:Ream droned out into the night: 'Things! Can only get better!'

'Stay here, okay?' Marshall started jogging over to the house. 'Oh, shite.'

'Is Jim here?'

'I don't know. Someone is.' Marshall got his keys out, but the door wasn't even locked – it was hanging open. He stepped inside and grabbed the baseball bat from behind the console table. 'Hello?'

The music was deafening.

He paced through the hallway, scanning into the living room. Nobody there.

A flash of movement in the kitchen.

'Hello?'

A woman was in there, prodding her phone screen with her finger.

Marshall tightened his grip on the baseball bat. 'Hi, can I help you?'

She looked around at Marshall with wide eyes.

Belu Owusu.

Very, very much alive. Sarah was in front of her, covering her ears with her hands. 'Rob?'

'What are you doing here? I thought you were—'

'I can't hear you! I can't get this music to stop!'

Marshall walked over to the counter and pressed the play button on the top of the speaker.

The whole house fell back into silence again, leaving just the ringing in Marshall's ear.

'Right. Thank you.' Owusu crouched down. 'Sarah, can you occupy yourself elsewhere?' She watched Sarah go, then fixed Marshall with a stare. 'Rob. You look like you've seen a ghost. What's up?'

Marshall let out a sigh of relief. 'Belu...'

'Rob, you're scaring me. Are you okay?'

'It's just... There's a rumour going around that you've been... that you were killed.'

'Rob.' She laughed. 'I'm still alive, nobody's killed me.'

'I can see that. But... You don't have a car?'

'It's parked in the garage.' She rested her fists on her hips. 'Who's been spreading rumours about me?'

'People at the hospital.'

'Those racist arseholes...'

'It all comes from a position of concern.'

'Sure. Of course it does. Let me tell you, okay, South Africa's nowhere near as bad as it used to be. And I've heard all of these rumours about me. Thing is, there's some truth in it, you know? I had some people following me, but I stopped them. These *rooinek* arseholes were from the Scottish Borders. They aren't anything compared with what I'm used to in SA.'

'What did you do to them?'

'Nothing.'

'But someone did?'

'I know people, Rob. Those idiots were sent back here with their tails between their legs. I'm not claiming their legs were working, though... But nobody comes after me or my daughter.'

'What are you doing back here?'

'Looking for Jim. Do you know where he is?'

'I don't know if you've been listening to my voicemails, Belu, but I assume—'

'Sorry, I lost my old phone and they won't switch over the number because I live in South Africa now.' She got out her mobile, as if that would suddenly make Marshall's voicemails appear. 'What were you saying?'

'Basically, Jim's been struggling. Badly. A lot more than normal. He almost burnt down the house the other night.'

'Shit.'

'Twice. Left the iron on and...' Marshall pointed at the oven and saw the door was still hanging open. The pizza was still in the sink. 'He left a pizza in the oven while he was upstairs.'

'This is the dementia?'

'Right. Thing is, it's not looking good for him. You know his boss?'

'DCS Miranda Potter, right?'

'Right. Everyone calls her She Who Cannot Be Named. But she's put him on leave.'

'So where is he?'

'He's in temporary respite care in Gattonside.'

'That's miles from here.'

'I know. It's a good facility. My granddad's in there. I know the staff. He'll be looked after until I can make a long-term decision.'

'Rob. This is...' She puffed out her cheeks. 'This isn't my decision to make. I haven't been involved with Jim for years. Never really was. And I've moved on. Me and Sarah. I've got a nice place in South Africa. A good job at a good hospital. Sure, there's still a lot of murders in SA, but it's getting better. Sarah's in a good school, she's got friends and a good future.'

'That's a bit cold.'

'So is Scotland at this time of year.'

'So why are you here?'

'Because that's the sort of bullshit I keep telling myself. That what he's going through is nothing to do with me. But he's my daughter's dad, Rob. I'm here because I want him back in my daughter's life. And... I don't think it's fair that you're making the decisions alone. Is it true that he's not a cop anymore?'

'That's right.'

'Does he really need to be put in a home?'

'I don't see another option.'

'Okay... So... I want him to move to South Africa with us. Live with us until he can't handle it anymore. Or I can't.'

This was a lot.

A hell of a lot.

Marshall had gone from thinking she was dead to... to having her take someone he'd been forced into caring for halfway around the world.

'Are you sure about this?'

'I feel so fucking guilty about what you've had to put up with, Rob. I just couldn't handle it and I ran away.'

'Still, there's a big difference between that and having to be the carer for someone in Jim's position.'

'Rob. It's fine. Listen, you were going to have to put this house up for sale to help pay for his care, right? That can pay for a carer back home. But this is your home, isn't it? You'd have to stop living here.'

'It's fine. I don't have any right to live here. But Jim deserves dignity and the best care. Not saying he won't get that in Gattonside, but it'll be good for him to see his daughter. And you.'

'Are you sure?'

Marshall nodded. 'I'm not just being selfish here. This is a weight off my shoulders, but... I think it's what's best for him.'

69

The caravan park was eerily dark. At this time of year, Elliot would've expected a few lights on, but it was just her, her car and Davie's old torch. Fancy thing he'd got in an Amazon sale. Brighter than the noon sun in Africa but as complicated as a nineties video recorder. She walked up the steps and pointed the torch in the windows, narrowing the beam and scanning around the place.

Nope, nobody in there.

She slid the key in the lock and was relieved Davie's folks hadn't changed the locks or anything so petty. She stepped inside and shivered, rubbing her feet on the Dunpender Sonas doormat – Davie's old man's favourite whisky. Baltic, like someone had left the freezer wide open. She rubbed her hands together trying to get some sensation back.

'*He wishes he'd had more holidays as a family. Said you were happy at the caravan and that happiness has the most value for him.*'

Davie's dying message, relayed via the medium of Shunty.

And Shunty was such an exacting bastard that he'd remembered it verbatim.

Davie had been sending her a message about the money and where to find it.

The filthy blood money he'd received from Hislop.

He was telling her to come here.

But why? Where had he left it?

The place was as stuffed as Davie's parents' conservatory. Knickknacks and trinkets everywhere. Shelves full of porcelain frogs. A big telly with the red dot of standby – bloody thing would be left like that for weeks, so she turned it off at the wall. Bookcases stuffed with books, a few times over – could be anywhere in there. The drinks cabinet full of gin and bottles of whisky in presentation cases.

Davie liked his wine, but he loved his whisky. Same with his old man.

Nice bottles, too. Glenfiddich. Ardbeg. Dunpender. Macallan. Bushmills. Borders Distillery.

A lump in her throat.

Dunpender was the one up in East Lothian. They'd visited there before the kids were born and went to the tasting room. She'd bought that bottle for him as a date anniversary present, back when she was a stupid romantic.

Sonas? Didn't they make posh speakers for wankers like Pringle?

Elliot googled it. Turned out it meant 'happiness' in both Scottish and Irish Gaelic.

That doormat.

Hmmmm...

She eased the bottle out of the box and set it down. A few healthy measures taken out of it, but not bad for almost twenty years. Nothing attached to it. No clues written on it.

Just a bottle of whisky.

She shone the torch into the presentation case.

Something glinted at the bottom.

She grabbed a long wooden spoon from the pot by the

cooker, stuck the long end in and scraped away at it. Tape ripped and she tipped it up.

A key dropped out onto the floor.

Christ...

Elliot grabbed it and checked it. Inscribed with D+A on one side. She walked over to the door and lifted up the mat.

Jesus.

He'd built a safe into the floor of the caravan.

Her hands started shaking as she slid the key into the lock, then twisted it.

It unlocked.

She took a deep breath, then opened it.

The thing was stuffed with cash. Thousands of notes. Tens, twenties and fifties. She flicked through it. At least a hundred grand.

Davie had said something like two hundred grand.

This was a massive problem.

She should turn it in, shouldn't she? Use it as evidence against Hislop.

But would anyone believe her? Would they be able to prove a link between Davie and Teflon Hislop?

Could keep it. Use a little at a time to look after their kids. Pay off their mortgage. The life insurance gave her cover – people would expect her to pay off the house with that and be a bit flush for a year or so. She just had to be sleekit about it.

Aye. It was a no-brainer.

70

J en was in the kitchen, digging a spoon deep into a tub of ice cream. Her ice cream.

'Hey, there.' Gashkori kissed her on the top of the head. 'Hell of a day.' He sat opposite her and waited for a reaction. Something. Anything. He didn't get it. 'Can I have a spoonful?'

She finally looked up at him with fire in her eyes. 'No.'

'O-kay. Just a little taste?'

She gave him that look, then went back to her ice cream.

'You okay there, sweetheart?'

She sighed into her ice cream tub. 'Ryan...'

He felt a trickle of sweat run down his spine. 'What's up?'

'No easy way to say this...' She looked at him again, this time with ice. 'I'm breaking up with you.'

Gashkori felt like he'd been kicked in the balls. 'What? Why?'

'I want you out of here by Sunday.'

'Sunday? What? How the hell am I going to find anywhere by then? My place in Glasgow's on a two-year lease!'

'All about you...' She dumped her spoon in the tub then thumped it onto the table. 'Sure you could get a room in a hotel or something while you sort it out.'

'Jen. What the hell is this about?'

'The coke.'

'What coke?'

She took a deep breath. 'Ryan. I've had a bloody awful day. First, my brother tells me he's heard from my daughter that she found some coke in here. So now I'm a cokehead in his eyes.'

'What, that's bullshit, isn't it?'

'Yes. I'm not a cokehead. But you are.'

'Come on... What the hell are you talking about? I'm a senior detective!'

'Second thing, Ryan, was I actually spoke to Thea about it. Once I got her past the disgust at her uncle talking to me about it, she explained. When I was taking my glass over to the bin, she found a little bit by the toaster.'

'But that'll be like flour or sugar, surely?'

'Didn't taste like that to her.'

He laughed. 'So Thea's an expert on coke now? Is she taking it through in Glasgow?'

'*Ryan.* When I found a wee bag of white powder in your laundry, you told me you didn't do that shite anymore.'

'And I meant that. It's past tense. Christ, we talked and talked about it.'

'So why don't I believe you?'

'I don't know. Babe. I told you the truth. That was from an undercover thing. Years ago. In an old jacket. I haven't touched the stuff in like forever.'

'You know something? I could choose to believe you. But it's the shadow of a doubt that's breaking me. You're making me choose between trusting Thea and trusting you. And I just don't think I can trust you, Ryan.'

'Seriously?'

'Have you taken coke here?'

'No!'

'Okay...' She picked up the ice cream, tossed the spoon in the sink, then wedged the tub back into the freezer. She pulled out a bag of frozen mushrooms and hurled it at him. 'So what the fuck is that in there?'

Gashkori caught it and some sliced mushrooms sprayed all over the table.

'Tell me that's not cocaine inside. Go ahead and lie to my face!'

Gashkori didn't have anything to say to that, just took the pouches from the bag and eased them into his jacket pocket. 'So, that's it?'

'Ryan, I'm not going to grass to your boss. I just want you gone. I do love you. But I hope you get help for this. I really do.'

'I'll go back to my therapist.' Gashkori walked over to the bin and dropped the bags in. 'I'll go cold turkey. I did it before.'

'Clearly didn't work, did it?'

'It'll be different this time.'

'It won't change until you sort out your head. And I don't want you to stay here tonight. Go over the road and see if they've got a room.'

'Jen! Come on!'

'I can't live like this. My ex-husband used coke. And I don't want that in my life.'

'It's not *in* your life. I swear!'

'Ryan. I don't trust you. We've only been seeing each other for, what, four months? It's easier to break it off now, rather than let this blossom into something bigger that'll be much more painful to get out of.'

'This isn't right. Please, Jen. I will change!'

'I'm serious.' She pointed at the door. 'Go! Now!'

Gashkori knew when to fight and when to run. 'I need to get some stuff. Clothes, phone charger, laptop.'

'All in a bag by the door.'

'Fine.' He got up and put his jacket back on. 'Please, can we talk about this tomorrow?'

'I want you out now. I can't trust a thing that you say or do. For all I know there are drugs planted around the house and you'll have the place raided, so I'm going to be up all night, searching.'

'Come on... I wouldn't do anything like that. I know you hate mushrooms, so... I thought it—'

'Go. Now. Please.'

'Fine.' Gashkori walked off, shaking his head as he pushed out into the cold.

Fuck's sake.

He could get in the car and drive away, maybe find a hotel closer to the station. Just a B&B for a few nights.

What she said about him planting gear there. How could she think that?

The Clovenfords Hotel would do fine. Wouldn't be too far from Jen in case she reconsidered.

He got in his car and turned it on, then crunched back up the drive, rounded the corner onto the main road and pulled into the hotel car park. A trivially short journey, but she'd feel better if his car was away.

Place was so busy he had to park in the overspill by the glass recycling bins. He didn't know why until he walked down to the entrance and saw the sign:

Pub quiz tonight!

He walked in and it was mid-question.

'—played for Zimbabwe and Liverpool?'

Gashkori walked up to the bar and caught the attention of the owner.

He got a nice warm smile. 'What can I get you, Ry?'

'Well, a pint of the black stuff and,' he leaned in close, 'a room for the night.'

'Oh?'

'Long story, mate.'

'She kicked you out?'

'Something like that. Got anything?'

'Aye. Quite busy tonight, but we've got a choice of two. Both look out the back, though. How long for?'

'A week?'

'Nice one. You can shift rooms tomorrow, if you fancy.'

'Sounds good.'

'If you join me at the other door, I'll sort you out.' He tipped on the Guinness tap and started pouring. 'Let me pour this first. Sounds like you need it. Be settled by the time we've got you fixed.'

'Cheers, man. I appreciate it.' Gashkori smiled at him, then walked through towards the entrance to the hotel side.

He spotted the two men sitting in the plush sofas and stopped dead.

Callum Hume looked up at him, eyebrow raised. 'You got a minute there, champ?'

'Aye, sure.'

His pal scuttled off, leaving Gashkori a warm sofa right next to Hume.

Hume sat forward and took a drink of red wine. 'Fancy seeing you here.'

'Aye. Listen, I got your text. Was just going to drop in and see how you were getting on, but something came up.'

'All good, I hope?'

'Like you care.'

Hume put a hand over his heart. 'Of course I care!'

'She's kicked me out.'

'Oh. That's shitty.'

'It's my own doing.'

'Us boys, eh? Who'd stand us!' Hume took another sip of wine. 'Decent plonk in here, have to say.' He leaned in close. 'Heard about that case you've been dealing with. A lassie pushed off a cliff, eh? Must be a bit of a relief to do that and get away from investigating our mutual friend for doing sweet Fanny Adams.'

'We both know our friend didn't do *nothing*. And he's been pretty busy recently, hasn't he?'

'Did your man Cook get anything out of Rancid John?'

'Believe me, Cook isn't my man. And he got nothing out of him.'

'Sure of that?'

'Very. I was sitting next to him when he interviewed him. He might be a stinky bastard, but Rancid John took it like a man.'

'Oh, that's good to hear.' Hume picked up his wine glass but didn't drink any. 'Still, that deserves a wee celebration, eh?' He slipped something into Gashkori's coat pocket. 'There's you go, son. Something a bit less liquid for your enjoyment. That's from our mutual friend.'

Gashkori touched the plastic bag but knew not to take it out in public. 'You'll have to thank him for me.'

'Will do. He's very grateful for the help.'

The owner walked past with a pint of Guinness, then stopped and frowned. 'Come and get me when you're ready.' He handed out the glass.

Gashkori took the pint and smiled at him. 'Will do.' He waited until the owner had disappeared. 'You need to tell our friend that I've stopped.'

'Have you now? The powder or the co-operation?'

'Both.'

'And you think you can just walk away, eh?'

'Don't just think it, Callum. I'm doing it. I need to clean up my act.'

'Thing is, some men take money. People like Davie Elliot. Others enjoy certain substances, like yourselves. Others... let's say it takes less tangible things to persuade them to help us out. Any which way you cut it, it's payment for information. And you and I both know the information you've provided directly led to a man's death.'

'Our friend didn't waste any time taking action, did he?'

'I always believe the sooner you get the bin to the kerb, the less your house will stink.'

Gashkori tried to process it. 'That doesn't make any sense.'

'This isn't the first time, Ryan. It's not just what Davie Elliot gave us. Plenty have popped their clogs as a result of information you've put our way over the years.'

'I've got to stop this. The information and...' Gashkori sipped his pint and got foam all over his top lip. 'And the drugs. It's out of control.'

Hume rested his glass on the table again. 'Okay. Off you fuck.'

'That's it?'

'We always knew this day would come, Ryan. Sometimes it doesn't, but most of the time it does. So our mutual friend and I discuss things in advance. How we want to play this situation. Most of the time, we decide that we've got enough from them. Let them go.' Hume picked up his glass again. 'Then at an opportune moment we kill the pricks.' He slammed the glass down. 'But you... Ryan, today's your lucky day. Might want to buy a lottery ticket or seven. A ton of scratch cards.'

'You're letting me go?'

'You've been a good servant.'

'It's not going to be that simple. I might be exposed.'

'Why?'

'Because I told you the prison Davie was in.'

'So?'

'I shouldn't have known.'

'Why's that a problem?'

'I called a friend, who confirmed that only Bob Cook knew where he was.'

'Then he'll get fingered, not you.'

'That's not how it works. He's leading an investigation into these leaks. I've never seen anything like. Whether I keep helping you or not, whether you kill me or not, this might all connect to our mutual friend.'

'We've discussed this, you and I. You said you'd make sure our relationship doesn't come out.'

'It's not all under my control.' Gashkori sank a chunk of the pint and the buzz hit him hard. 'I've been very, very careful. But I'm not perfect. Nobody is.'

'Let's just hope it comes to nothing, then.'

'We're fucked, Callum.'

'No, we're not. And they won't pin it on you. You've got plausible deniability.'

'How? I gave you the plate of the escort van. I told you and you got Davie killed the next again day. If you'd waited...'

'We needed to hit then. Davie would've leaked. Or spoken up. He's got a family. Thing with family men like him is they're vulnerable to us. But that also makes them vulnerable to people like Bob Cook. They feel guilty. They want to put things right. But you need to think this through, Ryan.'

'That's us square, Callum. I'm out.'

'Our mutual friend will be the judge of that.'

'One last thing, then we're clear. Okay?'

Hume looked around at him. 'I haven't asked for anything.'

'This is the other way round. I'm giving you something. Then that's it.'

'Go on?'

'I told you before that a deal was afoot for Davie. When he

changed his plea, they were going to make him serve three years, then he'd be out. Cook is determined to get to you and our mutual friend. I mean, it's pretty fucking obvious who arranged for Rancid John to kill him.'

'Proving that's a different matter entirely.'

'Never bet against a man like Bob Cook.'

AFTERWORD

Thank you for reading this far into the book!

It's been a little break since the last one, but I managed to clear the decks with the final Fenchurch novel, so now Rob is my only active character, at least for this year. I've got plans for another two novels in the series, tentatively sometime in August and 30th November for *His Path of Darkness* and *This World of Sorrow*. I had this *not* on a pre-order, which actually helped my mental health – it's ready when it's ready. And it's only six months since the last one, so it lets a few extra people catch up with the whole series.

I liked writing about another part of the Borders, very different to the inland hilly area I usually feature – it hopefully gives you some idea of how big the area the team covers is; there's also a huge chunk to the west around Peebles, Broughton and Westlinton, which I will think about for the next two novels.

A few notes on the book:

The surf schools at Coldingham Bay are fictional; there is a real one called St Vedas, which is very good, I understand.

Breda's Bakes and Keith's Bread in Eyemouth don't exist, but are named after two good friends of mine. But the fish and chip shop, with ice cream parlour (sadly I can't dabble anymore as it triggers my AF), are both excellent.

Two great people gave me the name of the new pathologist – Leye Adenle and Ayo Onatade. Check out their work!

Huge thanks, as ever, to James Mackay for all the editing during the conception and execution of the book – enjoy your retirement! And this book wouldn't exist without the keen eyes of John Rickards, for copy editing, and Julia Gibbs, for proof reading. And a huge thank you to Angus King for his excellent work narrating the audiobook editions – you should check them out; his performance brings a whole new dimension to the books.

And Rob and co will be back in August – watch *this* space: https://geni.us/EJMiFS

Sign up to my newsletter for FREE and get access to exclusive content and keep up to date with all of my releases on a monthly basis.

Thanks again!

Ed James

Scottish Borders, February 2024

MARSHALL WILL RETURN IN

His Path of Darkness
Autumn 2024

ABOUT THE AUTHOR

Ed James is a Scottish author who writes crime fiction novels across multiple series and in multiple locations.

His latest series is set in the Scottish Borders, where Ed now lives, starring **DI Rob Marshall** – a criminal profiler turned detective, investigating serial murders in a beautiful landscape.

Set four hundred miles south on the gritty streets of East London, his bestselling **DI Fenchurch** series features a cop with little to lose and a kidnapped daughter to find..

His **Police Scotland** books are fronted by multiple detectives based in Edinburgh, including **Scott Cullen**, a young Edinburgh Detective investigating crimes from the bottom rung of the career ladder he's desperate to climb, and **Craig Hunter**, a detective shoved back into uniform who struggles to overcome his PTSD from his time in the army.

Putting Dundee on the tartan noir map, the **DS Vicky Dodds** books feature a driven female detective struggling to combine her complex home life with a heavy caseload.

Formerly an IT project manager, Ed filled his weekly commute to London by writing on planes, trains and automobiles. He now writes full-time and lives in the Scottish Borders with a menagerie of rescued animals.

Connect with Ed online:

Amazon Author page

Website

ED JAMES READERS CLUB

Available now for members of my Readers Club is FALSE START, a prequel ebook to my first new series in six years.

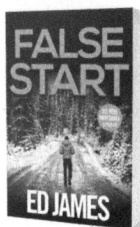

Sign up for FREE and get access to exclusive content and keep up-to-speed with all of my releases on a monthly basis.
https://geni.us/EJM1FS

ND - #0150 - 070425 - C0 - 216/138/25 - PB - 9781916583313 - Matt Lamination